THE MAN FROM NAG HAMADI

SLUMRAT RISING

BOOK TWO | THE MAN FROM NAG HAMADI

WARBY PICUS

Podium

Dedicated to two Dr. Justins.

Dr. Justin Champion, who inspired my interest in the curious intersection of history, politics, religion, and philosophy.

And Dr. Justin Sledge, whose YouTube lectures continue to be a source of wonder and inspiration.

Cover design by Mario Teodosio

ISBN: 978-1-0394-5249-7

Published in 2024 by Podium Publishing
www.podiumaudio.com

Podium

THE MAN FROM
NAG HAMADI

CHAPTER 1

THE EXORCIST'S INTERN

'm not buying anything and won't sell anything for you!" Truth barked reflexively in Jeongo. He didn't know why, but the short, beardy man with intense eyes gave off the scammer vibe he most vividly associated with his mother.

The scammer looked at him and started slowly shaking his head.

"Speaking in tongues. It's already so progressed. I can only do my best. Yes, I can only do my best. Young man, do not despair, for God is great, and he hears the call of his children. Young man, do not be afraid, for your pain will soon end."

Truth pulled himself together enough to say in Re'inyo, "I will not buy anything from you!"

The young man recoiled as though struck. Truth thought that if *he* struck the beardy madman, there wouldn't be enough left to flinch. A plan he would be seriously considering if this conversation went on much longer.

"Young man, you misunderstand! Young man, you wound me! I wish to save your life. I have many talismans and magical gems to suppress demons and drive them away. Many of the hidden names of God are known to me. Young man, I . . . am an exorcist!"

"Yes, I will have the same as him." Truth pointed at the meal the man in front of him had ordered. It was a bowl of stew so deeply red it was almost black, with a blindingly white boiled egg barely breaking the surface. Based on the smell alone, Truth was prepared to jump the counter and raid the kitchen for the entire pot. It had been a trying morning, and by *God*, he would celebrate his breakthrough with something tasty.

"Ah, the demon has spared you this much grace. Young man, well done. That is virtually the national dish of Siphios. It tastes even better than it smells. Young man, I tell you that while dorowot is delicious, so too is standing shriven of all demons before the Chariot of God."

"Excuse me, do you know this man? I am worried he is dangerous," he asked the cashier. "Are his parents nearby?" Of course, if nobody knew him, then Truth could always find a convenient dumpster in which to dispose of his problems.

"Him? He's not dangerous! He teaches religious law at the school near here."

Truth looked at the cashier, wondering if he misunderstood something.

"He's a lawyer?"

"Young man, you wound me again! I am no mere secular advocate. I teach and reveal the true word of God and how to abide by his laws. Young man, just how far has this demon misled you? Ah! Pity, pity."

"Your dorowot." It came with a big piece of the sour, spongy bread he remembered from the village he raided.

"Thank you." Truth reached into his pocket and pulled out some money. "How much is it?"

"Sir. This is Siphios. We don't accept shillings here."

"Ah. Right." Truth thought quickly. Dine and dash? No, this was stew. He couldn't run with it. Violence? No, he was trying to move away from that. New life, new strategies for life. He could only throw himself on God's grace. "My friend here will cover it." Truth casually threw his arm around the bearded man.

The bearded man looked startled but then nodded. "Yes. I will feed you, young man, and you will sit and speak with me. I have many questions for you. Young man, we must arm ourselves first with wisdom if we are to free you."

They sat at a little table, so small their knees almost touched. Truth got stuck into the stew. Watching the other diners, he saw that the correct way to eat was to tear off some spongy bread and use it to pick up mouthfuls of the stew. He tried it and about died. The flavors. Oh, Prager, the flavors. Garlic, ginger, chilies, and lemon, the meat was chicken, and there was some spice blend that was just unreal. Then the heat came in, and *whoo boy*! This was diner food? What the hell had he grown up eating?!

"Looks like you like it. Young man, you mustn't think this is the real-deal dorowot. After you are freed, you will have many opportunities to try something better. Let us begin again. Young man, I am Justinian Merkovah, a scholar and teacher of the Law. Who might you be?"

Truth started to say "Truth Medici" out of force of habit, but had the belated good sense to remember why that would be a bad idea. Oddly, the hotels hadn't blinked when he put his name down as Tommy Wells. Which, okay, foreign names and all that, but still.

"Tommy Wells. Talisman-maintenance technician." Truth got after the stew. How was it getting better with every bite? The sour bread helped offset the richness of the stew and mellow the heat. The path of the foodie was justice! The path of the foodie was the light!

This got him an odd look from the alleged scholar. "Young man, you look like a model and move like a soldier. I don't think you picked that up fixing streetlights."

"I might have done!" Truth grinned. He hadn't seen any dumpsters nearby. Did they not have dumpsters in Siphios? Surely the trash had to be stored somewhere, and with all the wild animals around, they must have something. This was a very good stew, and he was grateful. He would find something with comfortable trash.

"You might have done. Young man, do you know how you came to be possessed?"

"Going to have to ask you to stop calling me 'young man.' When you get right down to it, I think our ages are about the same."

"You don't look fifty."

Truth nearly choked on his stew. The beardy weirdo with his tiny decorative hat looked twenty-five. Truth had a sudden sinking feeling. He tried to reach out with his magic, to get a feeling for the interloper's cultivation.

It . . . was a lot more than his. A lot more. Holy shit. What level was he? Six? Maybe even Seven? He should be running a government department or something, not ambushing strangers in a diner!

"My apologies, Teacher Merkovah. I didn't realize your status." He stood and made a polite little bow.

"Ah! None of that, none of that! It's not done here. Sit, sit, eat your stew. Everyone is looking at us. Ah, I will never hear the end of this now."

"Sorry. I don't know the customs here."

"They are not so bad. *Demon*, boy!" Teacher Merkovah hissed. "How come there is a demon in you?"

"Em, about that. Do you mean Thrush, my imp?" He held up the necklace, where Thrush was wisely lying low.

"What? No, I mean the one trying to be invisible in your spell apertures. Which are weirdly empty except for the first, but we all have our struggles."

"Oh. You are the very first person to spot that, including trained medical professionals specifically looking for spiritual parasites. I'm genuinely impressed," Truth said. He was, too. If anyone knew how the System worked outside Starbrite, no hint of it had ever reached him.

"How did it get in there? It's incredible. I barely spotted it, and I can be considered an expert in the field."

"Not . . . trying to be difficult here," Truth said, valuing his life. "But this really, *really* isn't a diner conversation. Do you have a place where we can talk privately?"

This seemed to throw the exorcist. "You . . . want to go with me to a less public place. To discuss your possession."

"Yes. Odd as it sounds, it wants to be out of me as much as I want to be free of it."

"Huh. Well. You can come to my office, I suppose." Truth ate every last bit of his stew, leaving the bowl almost sparkling. The school was a few blocks over. An easy, if awkward, walk.

"All right, Mr. Wells. You seem like a man with a story. How much of it do you want to tell me?" The office was tiny and crammed with books. Truth spotted four different alphabets on the spines. What, *exactly*, was a Level Six scholar doing in this nothing place?

"I could say the same to you!" Truth blurted, then recovered himself. "This touches on some things that, if I told you about them, literal kill squads would come hunt you down. No disrespect to your level, but my former employers can field entire armies, all of whom have the very best magical technology and spells. So . . . understand that I will be vague on some details."

Truth had expected eyerolls from that, but Merkovah just nodded like it was to be expected.

"Basically, for my job, I was . . . given? A spirit of intellect"—Teacher Merkovah snorted at that one—"to assist in learning and casting spells. I was . . . fired? From my job? And lost access to almost all my spells. The spirit was supposed to leave my body at the same time but, for some reason, hasn't been able to. So, I am traveling around, looking to learn some new spells and grow as a mage." Truth shrugged.

"Okay. Okay, I can see how that might go. So, you are looking for work?"

"Actually, yes, now that I think about it. Though, no offense, I don't think I would want to live in this city."

"None taken. I'm here as a favor to a friend and am reconsidering the friendship more every day." Teacher Merkovah looked salty. "Does the demon still want out of you?"

"It is very particular about identifying as a 'spirit of intellect.' And yes."

<<*So fucking much.*>>

"Very yes." Truth confirmed.

"Hookay." The teacher stared up at the ceiling for a minute. "So, here's the thing. I don't know why it can't get out of you. Your body is refined to an astonishing level for your age and cultivation, but nothing that should impede a demon."

<<*Spirit of intellect, shitbird!*>>

"You want to gather spells. I'm guessing the spirit can learn many spells, make improvements, and customize them for you?"

Truth's eyes went wide. He hadn't said any of that, but—

"Demons that identify as 'spirits of intellect' have a pattern. Mages have been using them for exactly that purpose since forever. Sometimes it works great, other times not so much. It's not hard to guess." Teacher Merkovah shrugged. "I'm going to perform a divination. Don't get weird."

"Eh?" Truth looked blank.

The bearded scholar rapped his knuckles against the cheap wood of his desk. A collection of colored pebbles and stones rolled out of a black velvet sack. The light in the room dimmed. Even the brilliant, blinding sunlight coming through the window faded to a twilight gloom.

The pebbles began floating above the desk, spinning in orbits and moving in patterns he couldn't decipher. Some rose and fell, but most spun around an empty center in grand circles. A center that grew brighter as the light in the room faded. A sun was born, barely the size of a fist. And within the sun—

A lion's head, roaring, prideful, long-maned. Sneering eyes and vicious teeth. A predator, a king! And beneath that shaggy mane, a serpent's body. Endlessly coiling. Scales like a snake or dragon, one large enough to eat the stars and not notice. Towering over everything. The greatest, mightiest all of creation must crawl as ants as worms as less than the mud and dung of their being beneath the supreme and allmigggeeerrearrrayyyyyyy—

CLAP! Truth snapped awake, looking over at Teacher Merkovah. Who was giving Truth a curious look.

"So, here's the thing, 'Mr. Wells.' I'm an exorcist. I have to travel around Siphios, dealing with bad situations. Sometimes I'm in a town for a few weeks, sometimes a few hours. Sometimes my *very good* friend will ask me to substitute teach at their scammy school for morons on the border of a country I wouldn't visit on a bet." He coughed and looked away. Then resumed. "But hey, if the divination says *Eat at this diner today; it's going to be important*, you do it, right?"

Truth nodded. The man was Level Six. Or Seven. Truth was prepared to agree with almost any opinion he might have.

"So, it seems you were telling the truth about knowing talisman repair, but you are actually a bodyguard? Well. How about this: I cover your living expenses, pay a small salary, and tutor you on magic. In exchange, you travel with me and be my bodyguard."

"Your bodyguard? Why would you need a bodyguard?"

"I wondered the same thing, but the stars were clear. I suppose I am more of a spiritual warrior than a literal one."

Truth couldn't shake the feeling that there was a catch somewhere, but he was damned if he could see it.

"No contracts. I can walk away whenever."

"Likewise." Teacher Merkovah nodded.

Truth felt this was all going very fast. Then shrugged. He had nothing of real worth, nowhere to go, and nothing to do except get stronger. This was paid work. "I'm in."

CHAPTER 2

A LITTLE DOWN PAYMENT

So. Let's get you started. What do you have as your first spell? Utility spell?" Teacher Merkovah asked.

"Body cultivation. The Daily Meditations of Valentinian," Truth replied, still confused by how fast things were moving.

"Huh. I am both impressed and sorry for you." The beardy exorcist looked surprised. "Impressed because that is classically the 'right' way to do things. At least on better-developed planets, I hear. Sorry for you because, really, the Meditations? Did you dig that out of a book in the library or something?"

"It . . . was the cheapest option, yes."

"Wait, you got charged for it?"

"Um. Yes?"

Teacher Merkovah closed his eyes and groaned lightly. "What terrible country did you come from that you had to pay for the Meditations? You can't possibly be a native of the Free State, are you? I mean, the Meditations are good. Unlimited growth potential and all that, but woof. Lots of things have *potential*, you know?"

"Aheh ahehehe." Truth quickly tried to think of a lie.

"No, don't tell me. I don't want to know. Look, just . . . while you are in a developed nation, find a library first before you buy or learn anything. Look." The teacher grabbed a couple of books off the shelf and opened them up. "All the Meditations. I don't have to keep it under lock and key because nobody cares. It's like the standard utility spell for magic devices. Unless you are from somewhere *really* depraved . . . err . . . deprived, a crummy old spell like that is not hard to come by."

"Huh. So, something like Enlarge . . ." Truth said with growing excitement.

"Offhand, I can think of at least six spells that make things bigger. Some you would have to pay money for, some not. But why would you waste money and, most importantly, a spell slot on a spell that only did one thing?"

"Because most of the spells I know do one thing very well?"

"I will be doing some teaching today! Look. I have a wonderful spell; I recommend it heartily when you reach Level Four. The Sword of Moshe. Who was from Siphios, I might add!"

"Really?" Truth blurted. His memories of that spell were vivid.

"Yes! Well. Sort of. It's complicated. *Anyway*. Sword of Moshe. What do you think it does?"

"*The Sword of Moshe does not gleam. The Sword of Moshe casts no shadow. The Sword of Moshe is in the sheath or drawing blood,*" Truth parroted. Merkovah did a double take.

"You've heard of it?"

"Yes. A very powerful killing tool. I can see why an exorcist would choose it." Truth nodded. Merkovah sagged back in his chair.

"You had me going for a moment. Killing tool. Peh. You can kill with it and even kill demons with it, but that is the least useful thing about it."

Truth blinked slowly at that revelation. "So . . . what is it for, then?"

"It's a whole toolbox of angel magic. The Sword isn't supposed to be a literal sword. It's the will of the practitioner to shape and drive the spell forms while adapting the spell to the angelic beings you are invoking. For example, you can use it for protection. Exorcism. Love. How to purify yourself to maximize the effectiveness of what you are trying to do."

Merkovah's eyes burned into Truth. "The Sword of Moshe is a tool to borrow the power of the Watchers before the Chariot of God. To use it as a mere killing tool is an insult to the mage, the spell . . . and God."

Right. Teaches religious law. Right.

"No offense was intended," Truth murmured.

"And none was taken. Frankly, I'm amazed you have even heard of it." Merkovah flicked his hand. "But you take my point. A good spell does a lot of things, and it is your understanding of that spell that makes you powerful."

Truth's mind was swimming. Most of the spells he used just did one or two things quite well. Or did they? He mainly had used Sharp to put an edge on something, but that wasn't all it did, was it? It could turn you metallic, providing armor. At higher levels, you could project not just metal but energy. It was an incredibly versatile spell. So, why did he think it was lousy?

Because it wasn't very useful for ranged combat if your primary weapon was a needler. Which made it worthless to Truth. Who only used the entire, vast universe of magic to hurt people.

Merkovah seemed not to notice his new employee's cratering mood. "So! What kind of spells would you like to learn? You have two slots open simultaneously—a rare opportunity to build something special."

"I . . . don't know, I suppose. Could I maybe look at a bunch of different spells and see what's good?"

"Sure thing. The demon offered to make custom spells based on the spells you learned, huh?"

". . . yes."

"I'm not mad. As I said, these sorts of demons have a pretty well-known pattern. Just don't let it cast your spells for you."

"Pardon?"

"Yeah, it's going to tell you that the spell is too complicated for you to learn, or that it will take too long to learn or something, and that the *smart* way to use it would be to let it swap spells out for you as you go. No lock-in."

"That does sound smart."

"Except who's the mage in that situation?"

<<*Oh, this little shit. I mean, I already told you this, but still. What a complete bitch.*>>

"I see. So, what is the best way to use the demon?"

"Well, do let it build out the spells. Just show them to me when it's done, and I'll see if I can spot any obvious problems or flaws. Probably not; they tend to be good at this sort of thing. I would also suggest taking some time to consider what you want to accomplish as a mage. You have a wonderful foundation, so . . . what do you want to do? You are only Level Three, barely an initiate. You have so much more room to grow. So, study and think." A bell rang in the hallway outside. Merkovah swore.

"I just realized I didn't eat my lunch. I just watched you eat yours. And now I have a class. Blast it all!" He hurriedly grabbed a notebook and a textbook. "Hang out here. Read whatever. Start with the big blue book," Merkovah yelled as he bolted out the door.

Truth sat in the cheap wicker chair and stared at the slightly better chair that Teacher Merkovah had just evacuated. What . . . the fuck had been going on since lunch? He slowly turned the idea around for a bit.

First, he would unscrew his head before he believed that a Level Six (possibly Seven) would be willing to do a months-long favor for an old friend unless that friend was also high-level. And what would any person of their . . . enlightenment be doing in this crummy border city? For that matter, at Level Six, there would be a line of people eager to bring him lunch. Not "wrapping around the block" long, but long. Down the hall and out the door, easily. Level Seven, the restaurants would compete to comp the meal. And burn down the competition if necessary.

Level Six, you were a person of real power. Level Seven, you were the boss behind the people with real power. Level Eight or Nine? It might as well be mythical. The only people Truth knew of that might be that strong were the President and President Emeritus of Starbrite, and their cultivation had never been confirmed. Maybe there were stronger people off-world. By all accounts, this planet was a dump.

There was a diffident cough. "Is now a good time to speak, Master?" Thrush asked.

"No." Truth was firm on that. Then changed his mind. "Wait. Can you tell if Teacher Merkovah is actually an exorcist?"

"Not definitively, but he is strong enough to destroy this body and force me back to Hell. Many things in this room are inimical to demons and carry the stench of angels about them."

"Huh." Truth sat still a while longer. Then got up and opened up the large blue book. It was embossed with a particularly ferocious-looking winged demon on the cover. He started flipping through it. Frowning, he quickly flipped back to the table of contents. *Theurgist Desk Reference, 22nd Edition (Illustrated)*. All the spells seemed borderline incomprehensible. He wasn't even sure what they were supposed to do.

With an unpleasant lurch, Truth realized his problem. He had never really studied spells before. The basic mechanics of how stellar rays interacted with the world—sure. He had to know that; it was a core part of talisman maintenance. But there had been no point studying how spells worked or even learning how to read them. Because he would be a Starbrite Man. He excluded any other possibility from his consciousness. He would be a Starbrite Man, which meant he would be a System-wielding demigod.

"The demon is the mage," he muttered.

<<Spirit. Of. Intellect.>>

Oh, hush, you. Here. Make yourself useful.

Truth started flipping through the desk reference, glancing at each page briefly.

<<Go faster.>>

He did. It was a long book, several thousand pages, so he flipped through as quickly as he and the System could manage.

Any actual spells in there?

<<Not exactly. It's more like a guide to different beings, "gods" or "angels," for lack of better words, that can be invoked in various spells and how different spells will impact the result of that specific evocation.>>

Truth didn't get it. *Give me an example.*

<<That Shockwave spell you love? Basically, "you" visualize the spell form, pump cosmic energy into it, and the interaction of that energized spell form and the surrounding cosmic rays triggers a specific result—a localized overpressure of air or water. No outside entities are required. This is more . . . "Hey, Bubba! Do me a solid and make my lover a horny mess tonight!" or "This guy is nuts. Great Bubba, fix his stupid, wet brain." It's the same Bubba, but tweaking the spell produces different mind-affecting results.>>

Sounds like demonology but fancy.

<<Not a million miles off there. And I can't believe I am saying this, but it's worth considering. He was right about how versatile and powerful some of these spells are.>>

Oh?

<<Shockwave did one thing. Nice, simple concept, very energy-efficient, and very fast. Makes complete sense as a cheap spell for the soldiers. Cheap as in it doesn't require much effort from the main System or me. On the other hand, these spells are energy-intensive, complicated, and comparatively slow. But. They are cutting out a couple of layers of distance between the action you are trying to take and the source of the power for that action.

All cosmic rays come from the cosmos. Literally the universe, and specifically the stars and planets. And who are the stars? It asked, hoping your repeatedly scrambled brain could remember even this much.>>

I want you to know that I am really looking forward to forcing you into a physical body and nailing you face-up to the bottom of a latrine. They are great demons and spirits, and angels, too, I suppose.

<<Good luck with that, smooth-brain. And yes. They are simultaneously giant balls of fire and *beings of incredible spiritual power. From what you have been able to pick up,*

it's less literal and more . . . these things are the emanations of beings existing on a higher level of reality, extending down to us.

So, what you are doing with Shockwave is picking up what they naturally radiate and putting together your own little nothing thing. These spells get the specific best cosmic energy to do the thing you want to do, and because you are getting it more or less directly from the source, the effect is massively more powerful. Probably why Sword of Moshe is a Level Four–minimum spell, now that I think about it. The burnout was nasty. So, once you have a direct line to . . . let's say Astaroth, this spell would let you swap in effects that fall under their authority. So, mathematics, interrogation, philosophical debate, invisibility, power over serpents, that kind of thing.>>

How useful.

<<Astaroth is one of the most powerful spiritual entities known to exist. They can talk people into their point of view, make previously held worldviews collapse, and, according to this book, are an absolute freak when it comes to sex magic. But sure, your "just make it wavy" spell is way better.>>

Truth grinned and kept flipping through the manual. This might just be fun.

CHAPTER 3

A SLICE OF LIFE

Merkovah thought his office looked like some kind of conspiracy nutjob's "special" wall. There were little scraps of paper laid out on the floor, different books had been positioned carefully at different heights and angles to the paper, and while it was probably a coincidence, the sunlight streaming through the window seemed to catch just enough of the back of his chair to form an illuminated rune on the ground. Which rune was debatable.

"So, you've been busy," said Merkovah.

Truth looked helpless. "There are too many options, and I don't want to limit myself, but all the spells promise the moon. I'm pretty sure they are all lying, and many are plainly evil."

"Why would you think that?" Merkovah asked, grinning.

"*Will cause the woman you love to leave her partner and fall hopelessly in love with you. However, write the incantation on a tin amulet and hang it around the neck to prevent possession by demons.*" Truth pointed at a particular passage. Teacher Merkovah started sputtering.

"A lot of these spells are designed for sex criminals," Truth continued. "Look, this one even has pictures. That's not okay."

The spell came with a diagram explaining how the ritual doll would be made. The doll was to be tied with specially treated string in a remarkably complex binding, with particular attention paid to both the type and placement of the knots. Into the doll was jabbed a variety of needles. Silver for the hands, feet, ears, and eyes. Gold for the forehead, mouth, and heart. Gold again for the groin, though the spell took careful note to emphasize that if conception was a concern, the golden groin needle could be replaced by an iron needle to inhibit fertility. The accompanying spell was four pages of dense evocation.

"Hardly criminal! Young man—"

"Tommy Wells. Certified talisman-maintenance technician."

"Mr. Wells, these are an ancient legacy! These spells have been used *quite* consensually by loving families for millennia."

Truth gave him a disbelieving look. "I know enough about spells to spot a scuffed one, and these aren't. This is a working rape spell. It even says 'abolish all will and influences opposed to you.' Just because the book calls it 'erotic binding' doesn't change that fact. These are criminal spells. No wonder you work full-time as an exorcist. You must be busy as hell."

Teacher Merkovah's mouth worked soundlessly for a moment. "Young m— Mr. Wells, have you ever heard the term *prenuptial Agreement*?

"Sorry, no, I have not."

Teacher Merkovah started weakly chuckling. "This is going to be an *interesting* working relationship, isn't it?"

Truth looked surprised at the beardy expert. "I am excellent at following instructions and am told my lack of complaining is a genuine wonder."

"Hah. I guess I'll see. Look, what do you want from a spell? That's the first thing. You have a top-notch body already, and I would bet more than a birr that your stellar resonance is sky-high. Pardon the pun. So, do you want to build up that advantage or complement it with something else?"

"Can you give me an example?" Truth asked.

"Sure. I assume you are familiar with some version of a Sharp spell?"

"Intimately," Truth said, flashing back to several unpleasant memories.

"Well, there you go. At Level Three, a decent Sharp spell will further reinforce your body, give you a degree of armor against physical damage, and let you cut things from the very tiny to the very big."

"As long as they are within arm's reach," Truth concluded.

"Yes. But also no. The spells I'm offering are all fueled directly by much more powerful energies than the ambient cosmic 'noise' you have been working with. So, a Sharp spell invoking one of those powers would be quite different." Merkovah slipped on his teacher hat.

"Invoke Andras, and you will become a murderous beast, killing everyone around you. Sharp would be purely a tool for indiscriminate slaughter. Invoke Botis, and you will find yourself almost impossible to hit in combat but also better able to find peaceful solutions to problems. The Sharp offered by Botis can even resolve philosophical disputes at the highest level. Invoke Caym, and you will find yourself an agile debater as well as a skillful warrior. Learning languages would be trivial," he concluded.

"These are all demons in the Goetia." Truth nodded.

"Yes, just not employed in the way you are used to. And there is a good reason we aren't using angel magic—under Level Four, it's likely to burn you out very quickly. Though I will teach you how it works. How is your demon finding all of this?"

Good question. How are you finding all of this?

<<*Extremely fucking concerning. Also fascinating. It's pretty clear that the main System works the same way all this does, but it . . . sort of filters it out first. It can't replicate all the actual powers of these . . . beings . . . but can structurally mimic them. The result is that it cuts out the major demons and angels from direct access to its slaves. Nifty.*>>

Got enough to start making custom spells?

<<*Oh, yes. Yes, I really think I do.*>> The System didn't have fluids, but there was something upsettingly moist, almost carnal, about its tone.

"It's got enough. It's getting to work now," Truth said.

"Good. Then we will too."

Truth followed Merkovah out of his little office through the terracotta-colored halls of the school and to the street. There were no designated parking spots; the faculty just parked wherever suited them best. It didn't much matter, Truth supposed. The logical consequence of teachers salaries being lousy rides.

Merkovah waved grandly at his spellcarriage. Truth had seen safer-looking landmines. "Go on, get in."

"Thank you for your kind intentions, Teacher, but I have my own two-wheeler." Truth tried to escape. Merkovah was having none of it.

"Nonsense! This will be much more comfortable, and I can explain the job to you on the way." Praying blindly to whatever gods or demons looked after new hires, Truth gingerly opened the door. He was pleasantly surprised when it didn't fall off in his hand.

The seat was the next challenge. The car promised to reek, but he had been spared that so far. And yet. The seat. With its upsettingly gnawed-upon fabric and exposed foam. Truth gingerly sat down and closed the door.

There were no seatbelts. Or offensive smell, now that he thought about it. He wiggled back into the seat. It was . . . really comfortable. Not too hard or soft, and he would swear it was subtly adjusting itself to be even more comfortable. There seemed to be functional air conditioning, too. Astonishing. Merkovah slid in next to him and prodded the chained spirit to life. The carriage made a terrible racket of grinding axles as it pulled away from the gated parking lot, though Truth noticed that there was no friction or vibration to be felt.

"The chariot is disguised?"

"You would not believe the places I have to park it."

"I'm surprised anyone dares touch it."

"And yet. Anyway. We are off to visit the home of the Widow Yettran. She is convinced her illness is caused by a demon and wants me to do something about it."

"Is it?" Truth asked.

"Eeeh. Maybe? It does happen." Merkovah shrugged. "The bigger problem is where her house is. Two blocks from the cemetery, I suspect the home is built on top of an old family tomb, and to cap it off, there is a slaughterhouse just a couple of blocks over. Demon is a maybe, but evil spirits of the dead? That is almost certain."

"Okay? So, what should I do?"

"Well, mostly just follow me and learn how the job goes. Anything physical comes at me, do keep it off of me. As I said, I'm not much of a fighter when it comes to physical things."

Truth nodded. He had no idea how that could be possible. He thought about it a bit more. It eventually occurred to him that the overwhelming majority of people in the world were not in the Starbrite PMC. Despite this, they managed to level up, make things, and generally grow as mages. So . . . it was reasonable for this weirdo to not know how to fight. Not that he was going to test him. He knew how powerful a Level Seven body was, after all.

The Widow Yettran lived in a nice little house. It was a single floor and had a terra-cotta tile roof. The walls had been painted yellow not *too* long ago, and it was far enough from the city center that its neighbors weren't crowded around it. The cheerful lace curtains fluttered by the open windows. It even had a little garden.

"It's cursed," Truth said.

"Big-time." Merkovah nodded.

"The fact that all the flowers in the garden are black and rotting in the sun is my first clue." Truth tried to look wise.

"Really? For me, it's how the inside of the house looks pitch-black even though the curtains are open. Also, who leaves the windows open in the middle of the day on the equator?" The beard of Merkovah wagged disbelievingly.

"Ah, the expert's eye." Truth was starting to get a feel for Merkovah. He seemed fairly easygoing as long as it didn't touch on religion.

There was a sharp explosion, and the bottom of the front door suddenly deformed. Truth looked puzzled, but Merkovah was already dashing to the door.

"Mrs. Yettran! Mrs. Yettran, can you hear me? Mrs. Yettran!" He started banging on the door. Truth shoved him aside and kicked in the door. His eyes raked through the gloom. A silvery outline was in the shadows, a large man stabbing into the dark desperately with a spear.

"Help her, quickly! I can't hold them back any longer!" the spirit cried.

"You grab the widow. I'll deal with the ghosts!" yelled Merkovah. He had a silver talisman out, and a spell was forming on it fast.

Truth moved in, eyes constantly in motion. His hands felt empty, hating not having a spell ready for the thousandth time. The widow was on the ground, mottled green, gray, and black. He scooped her off the floor—she weighed almost nothing. He turned in place, trying to get back out the door. A snake appeared, its head rising chest-high, neck flaring, fangs dripping poison. Eyes of dim embers and boiling smoke.

He kept his momentum rolling forward, lashing out with a kick to the snake's head. The snake read the kick and slipped back, then lunged forward, fangs dripping, aiming for the calf. Truth checked his kick with inhuman speed, turning the blow into an axe kick. His heel smashed down on the snake's head. It hissed and recoiled. Truth took two more quick steps toward the door before it struck again.

This time, the serpent came low. It weaved along the floor and put itself directly between Truth and the light. It went for his calf again. He could feel the hiss rattling his ears, trying to throw off his balance. There was something in the dark. Something about the dark pressing down on him. He could fight through it, but the snake was coming at him fast. Too fast!

The old lady groaned in his arms. Her face contorted with pain. Her breath was raspy, rattling. Too short. He had to get her out. Truth dodged to the side, avoiding the fangs with a faerie's grace. He went for a stomp. Now it was the snake's turn to dodge bonelessly. Merkovah's spell was starting to light up the room. The warrior spirit was suddenly there, stabbing with its spear. The snake screamed and recoiled. "Go, quickly!" the spirit yelled.

Truth feinted for the door once more. Though wary of the spirit, the snake once more moved to block him. Truth tightened his grip on the Widow Yettran and dove out the window with a single explosive leap.

She gasped in the sudden sunlight, choking and sputtering. Her eyes opened, green and ophidian. Something forced its way out of her mouth, triangular head, sharp fangs extended. Truth grabbed it just below the head and yanked it out of the old lady, then crushed the filthy thing in his hands.

CHAPTER 4

ALTERNATIVES

The ghostly serpent shattered in Truth's grasp, dispersing as wisps of gray gas under the brilliant tropical sun. The Widow Yettran gasped and rattled on the ground, shivering like she had a fever. Her color was improving. The disgusting mottling was fading away. The green had already vanished. He looked around awkwardly. He had destroyed the spirit's corporeal body, but the spirit was very much alive and around somewhere. Being able to make a talisman that kept ghosts and evil spirits away now seemed like a very good thing.

There was a sudden cessation of noise. A silent thrum ran through Truth. Then a pause and another silent thrum. As though he were standing next to a great bell he could not hear. The house and garden seemed to explode into clouds of smoke and ash. Gray, howling spirits with smoldering ember eyes rose from every withered plant, from the cinderblocks in the walls, from the cheerful lace curtains fluttering in a breeze only they could feel. All fleeing the silent sound of that terrible bell.

Truth took a last look at the Widow Yettran. She looked like an old lady who had lived with a prolonged illness. But what could he do for her even if she was on death's door? He went back in for Merkovah. After all, the snake was still in there.

The house was vibrating. Some vast being came down, and merely mortal matter could not withstand its presence. The shadows had been banished. The snake twisted in knots of agony, trying to escape its flesh. The warrior spirit was on one knee while Merkovah . . . was having an argument.

Merkovah's beard seemed to go rigid with indignation. He tossed his head in irritation. A scholarly finger wagged, then jabbed. Truth had no idea what he was arguing with, as all he could make out was a glowing ball of light and shimmering pressure in the middle of the room. The tolling of the bell seemed to come from whatever it was. Merkovah pulled a copper talisman from a pocket and tapped parts of it repeatedly as though emphasizing a point. The entity shimmered a few more times, then vanished.

Merkovah snorted, chanted something guttural under his breath for a minute, then turned toward the spirit. "It's Ajani, right?"

"Yes, Teacher. I believe we met long ago."

"Not that long! I'm not so old." Merkovah waved his hands, and the spirit chuckled.

"Well, it feels long ago. Is there . . . any hope of returning me to my place?"

"I'm afraid not. Besides, you should have left years since."

"I know. I wasn't ready to leave her. She wasn't ready for me to leave." The spirit smiled sadly.

"Come. I will say the Shomash for you. You will definitely go to heaven."

The spirit laughed softly one last time and shook its head. "Well. Some kind of heaven, I guess. Thank you, Teacher."

Merkovah put the amulet away and clasped his hands in prayer. It was short, guttural, and clearly sincere. Without even a final sigh, the spirit disintegrated in a spray of lights.

There was a moment of silence, then Merkovah straightened his clothes and looked over at Truth. "How's the Widow Yettran?"

"Better."

"Do you understand what happened here?"

"Not really. Her husband's spirit was trapped in the spell bowl guarding the threshold, and it exploded under the pressure of necrotic spirits. He emerged to make a last-ditch effort to keep Yettran alive, but it plainly wasn't going to be enough. You exorcised the house by invoking some kind of angelic spirit. Beyond that, no idea."

Merkovah chuckled and walked out the door. He attached the copper talisman to the inside edge of the doorframe, pushing the nails in with his fingertip. "Come, let's get the Widow Yettran back inside."

They settled the old lady back into her bed. Teacher Merkovah pulled up a chair next to it and started praying. Yettran woke after about fifteen minutes. There was discussion, weeping, anger, more weeping, then acceptance. Merkovah patted her on the shoulder and left with Truth. They had been speaking a language Truth didn't recognize.

"She was upset about her husband's spirit, of course, but also about us breaking the door. I explained to her that doors could be fixed but there was no repairing death. She will live with her sister for a while."

Truth just nodded at that. His experience with death was probably pretty unique. They got into Merkovah's carriage and headed out. "You have a place to stay?" Merkovah asked. Truth just shook his head. Even by his broad standards, today had been a *weird* day.

"I have a few shillings left. If it's not enough, I can always go sleep out in the desert."

Teacher Merkovah shook his head pityingly. "Look, I have a guest room. You can sleep there for the night, then we can see about finding you a more long-term solution."

"Why? You are going to be moving around a lot, right?" Teacher Merkovah jerked slightly, then made a little panting laugh.

"Force of habit. I got so used to taking people in that planning how to get them out again became an obsession."

They drove off for a minute. "Shit! My two-wheeler!" They went back and got it. Truth was going to drive it behind the still-questionable carriage, but Merkovah wasn't having it. A surprisingly lengthy charm later, the bound spirit of the iron horse obediently trailed behind the carriage. Back toward Merkovah's house.

"So. Why take me in, exactly? I know you did a divination and all that, but . . . c'mon. You don't know me from a hole in the ground. And I'm just going with it, but really, I'm about two seconds from busting a window and vanishing."

"For the same reason I took my idiot friend's idiot job as a teacher, like the idiot I am. Divination."

"This is going to be a very boring and short conversation if you keep blaming divination for everything," Truth said.

"Pity, because I rely on divination for many of my major questions. Specifically, the answer to a few questions I have been struggling with for a long time. Question number one: Is there anyone in the world who can break the hold of Starbrite on this planet? Question two: What do I need to do to help them? And three: Where do I need to go to make this happen? The answers were, to my surprise, *Not yet, be a teacher, and Toto Beh Diner, Moyle.* Where I have been having lunch every day for two months now. Waiting for somebody who didn't fit."

Truth's attention was all on answer one. "Break the hold of Starbrite on the world?"

"Oh, yes. You see, the masters of Starbrite are very reasonable. You can do as you please, so long as you never interfere with their power or pleasure. People growing beyond Level Seven count as both. Not that they would dream of killing off all the potential Level Eights! No, that would be far too costly. They simply ensure that all the truly powerful elixirs and natural treasures this world can offer fall into their hands, along with anything worth trading to other worlds. What few Level Eights there are outside of Starbrite are too old and too beaten to be a threat."

The bound spirit smoothly steered the carriage through the busy streets. Merkovah had his eyes fixed on Truth. "They do it with coin and guile, mostly, and when that doesn't work, they send in their death-sworn soldiers. Exquisitely trained, fed elixirs like they were water, and slaved to a 'spirit of intellect' who casts their spells for them—the perfect combination of elite human physicality and magical spiritual capability. And so utterly brainwashed, they are incapable of rebellion. Or so I thought. What do you think, 'Mr. Wells'?"

Truth sat very still. His mind was flying so fast. Even he didn't know where it was going. It finally landed on a question he had been working hard not to think about. "How long ago was the big spiritual attack on Kofi? The one that killed everyone?"

"Seven years ago. What a curious question. By strange coincidence, the prismatic iridium mine revealed by the blast fell under the control of the Starbrite Mineral Resource Management Corporation."

"Seven years."

"Yes, Mr. Wells. Seven years."

Truth didn't say anything for the rest of the drive.

Sophia would have gone to college, of course. Aced her entrance exams and the SAT. Maybe got a deferment, maybe went early just to get it done, then went back for postgrad. She could still be finishing her undergrad, maybe. Or not. Vigor . . . it was tougher to say. He should be on the college track. Should be admitted to college. He was a fighter, though. He had had that meanness in him since he was a kid. No way he would be content as an office drone. He might be doing something . . . unpredictable.

Harmony . . . Starbrite would have had Harmony for five years now. And while lab technician was a D-Tier job, all those Friends and Family points had him set for a lateral transfer to an upper-C-Tier managerial-position track. Odds were good that he had the System now. Odds were good that the System had him.

Which led him to the next thought he had been avoiding. How was it even possible to fight Starbrite? It was a planetary-scale corporation. The corporation would still exist even if he had a magic needler that would let him one-hit-kill the entire C-suite from ambush. The System Astrologica would still exist. And what if he could kill the System? He would put hundreds of thousands directly out of work and millions more who depended on those hundreds of thousands for *their* livelihoods.

Not that he gave even one half a fuck about other people's job hunt, but he knew *they* did. All those millions of people would fight to the death to defend Starbrite because, for them, Starbrite meant prosperity. Starbrite meant *not the slums*.

Jeon would mobilize the military to defend Starbrite. At twenty percent of the economy, they would be insane not to. Tens of thousands of conscripted kids doing their national service now in a shooting war with the madman determined to destroy one of the most respected companies in the world.

He would fight the world for his siblings. He just didn't want to do it *literally*. He would like to have them free, sane, and with their spell apertures intact when he got them back. He had not the faintest idea how it was possible.

Merkovah lived in a well-appointed house on the northern fringe of the city. Less fancy than he would have thought a Level Seven's dignity would demand. Still much larger and nicer than the overwhelming majority of the homes in Moyle. The carriage was met by a pair of young folk, who greeted it enthusiastically.

"You're back!" the young woman said. She had a cheerful voice, cheerful clothes, and cheerful hair blown by stray breezes that made her look like she was always in motion.

"Do we have a new friend?" the young man asked. "I thought you said, 'Two's enough.'" He seemed no less cheerful than the woman, but where she was lean, he was athletic. He looked like someone who could run all day and would at the slightest provocation.

"You two are freeloaders. He's worse. I'm employing him." Merkovah looked martyred.

"Employed? As what, a cook?" the young lady said hopefully.

"Cook would be great. Really great. Hint, hint." The young man nodded strongly. Merkovah turned toward Truth and let his face droop.

"You see, Mr. Wells. This is why I need a bodyguard. The constant betrayals."

"Bodyguard? I figured he was your boyfriend." The woman looked genuinely shocked.

"I was prepared to entertain the idea that he was a pro, though not dressed like that." The man nodded along with her.

"I'm a happily married man!" Merkovah bellowed.

"Sure, sure. I'm sure your wife is very real. Sure," the young lady "comforted" him. Truth coughed.

"Hello, everyone. My name is Tommy Wells. I am good at talisman maintenance and violence, but I am trying to learn other skills. I enjoy reading novels, trying new foods, and seeing new places. I would love to hang out with you two and get to know you better."

The two people, roughly the same age he was when he fell down the well, were cheerful, fit, funny, and, if not stunning beauties, pretty good-looking. If being dead wasn't a good enough reason to change, what was?

CHAPTER 5

HEY KID, WANNA LEARN A MAGIC TRICK?

Tommy Wells, meet Jember." Merkovah nodded at the sunny man. "And Etenesh, his cousin."

Truth waved at them and smiled. They smiled back, looking a little overwhelmed. No idea what that was about.

"Young man . . ." Truth just looked at him. "Betrayals all around. Everyone in. Dinnertime, then we have to make a bed for Tommy." Merkovah didn't quite hide his eyeroll when he said, "Tommy."

They piled into the house and started throwing together a salad. Truth could not be said to be a salad person. He was, however, honestly walking the path of the foodie and resolved to eat the loose vegetation they had lubricated, then salted and vinegared.

"Wine, Tommy?" Jember asked.

"No, thank you; I don't drink."

"Of course he doesn't," Etenesh hissed at Jember. "Sorry, he's not usually a clod. Don't worry; the food is totally vegetarian."

"Thank you?" Truth said.

Merkovah came into the little kitchen, having shed his respectable teaching clothes and traded them for deeply ratty loungewear. "She thinks you are Desrin. Which, are you?"

"I don't think so. What's Desrin?"

This was met with awkward silence.

"What . . . is Desrin? It's the second-largest religion on the planet? How . . ." Jember was trying to puzzle out how this level of ignorance could be possible.

"Ah. We weren't very religious. We were Pragerites for . . . a month, maybe? At least, we were going to the services." Truth shrugged.

This was met with more silence. Merkovah coughed. "Young man—" Truth smiled warmly at the youthful-looking exorcist. "Tommy, am I understanding correctly that your entire religious education consists of going to once-a-week services at a"—Merkovah's mouth twisted like he was being forced to regurgitate a lemon—"*Pragerite* church?"

"Basically. We were disfellowshiped pretty quickly, but about a month, I think." *Disfellowshiped* was in Jeongo, as he had not encountered that word in Siphios.

The cousins looked at each other in complete bewilderment. "I've never heard of such a thing. You?" asked Jember.

Etenesh shook her head, joyful hair flying in perplexity. "No, but I can guess the meaning. I didn't even know you could get excommunicated from a Pragerite church."

"You can't. That word means 'kicked out of the congregation,' not 'kicked out of the religion.'" Merkovah looked like he didn't know whether to laugh or cry. "They usually impose it for not keeping up with your tithing."

"Ah. Is that where we were expected to give them money every week?"

"Yes." Merkovah nodded.

"Yeah, that was never going to happen." Truth had some vague memories of Dad stealing cash from a basket and Mom arguing with the staff that she should get a weekly stipend for dealing with Dad and her "brats."

Merkovah opted for laughter, chuckling darkly. "So, fair to say that you have no religious education beyond what you learned dealing with angels and demons professionally."

Truth shrugged and nodded. He was starting to get hungry. Maybe they could pair the greenery with some bread or something?

"So, why the zeph? And the no drinking?" Etenesh pointed at his hat.

"Oh. I didn't have a hat, and it was cheap. And I don't drink, in memory of my father."

"Oh, I'm so sorry. My condolences on your loss." Jember patted Truth's arm. Truth had to control his instinct to jerk away.

"Thank you?" There may have been a breakdown in communication there, but Truth wasn't inclined to correct the cheerful man.

They pressed on to dinner. There was bread and a sort of spiced clarified butter to spread on it. The salad was regrettable, but the spiced-butter thing was extremely good.

After dinner, the cousins retreated to the living room to watch some scry. Merkovah steered Truth toward his study.

"So. Mr. Definitely-Not-An-Assumed-Name-Wells. Knowing what you now know about me and my goals, is there anything else you would like to share with me?"

"No. Not to be a dick about it, but no. I would be shocked if even one survivor remained on any side of the operation that . . . resulted in my . . ."

"Involuntary separation?"

"Yes. I thought I was up for making a joke about it, but apparently not." He was surprised by how raw the betrayal still felt. Then he was surprised by his being surprised. Starbrite had been his whole life. But the second corporate interests were weighed against that life and whatever future benefits he might bring to the company—

"Still worried that someone will hunt and kill us all if you leak something?" Merkovah looked sardonic.

"That . . . would actually be the least bad outcome. But it's still a bad outcome, so . . . let's just say my name is Tommy Wells and I am a certified talisman-maintenance technician."

Merkovah looked at him for a long moment and shrugged. "Sure, why not. Okay. So. You don't know religion, and you don't know magic, but you know how to fight and how to repair talismans. You have some familiarity working with demons. Does that about sum it up?"

"I have been trained on some angelic magic as well. I can construct an almadel, for example."

"Really? Well, let's put that to the side for a moment, as it's something I will be teaching you from the ground down."

"You mean ground up?"

"No, I do not. You'll see." Merkovah's cheek twitched. It might have been confused for a smile. "I will start at the very, very beginning. God."

Truth kept his poker face up. Merkovah was pretty easygoing, but he got intense when talking about God.

"God exists. As a verifiable fact, God exists. This is the sole point upon which the universe agrees. The nature of God is much debated, and it doesn't help that spiritual beings are giving us contradictory information. What is even more confusing is that you have spiritual beings that could pass for *a* god, as well as strong evidence for their being multiple *the* God. Gods. The grammar gets incoherent fast."

Truth was trying to hang in there. "God is real, but there may be multiple versions of 'God,' as well as beings that could be gods, and nobody agrees about any of this, including the angels and demons."

"Mostly yes, but you are missing the key point—it is an article of both faith and reason that there is a *singular* deity from which the universe and all its parts come. However, based on eyewitness testimony and some pretty impressive scholarship, there is reason to believe that multiple versions of this one singular god exist *simultaneously*. Imagine that you are you. And imagine that you are Tommy Wells, who never got into bodyguarding and is just a maintenance tech. And imagine that you are a you who never got into talismans and instead painted as a hobby."

Merkovah took a deep breath.

"Now. Imagine all three are in the same room together. All three of 'you,' individually, are the real, true, singular, and exclusive 'you.'"

Truth was starting to be concerned that the beardy exorcist might be possessed himself. Or suffering brain damage. Could this be a cry for help?

"Sure. That makes complete sense, and I totally understand it." Truth nodded decisively.

"Me neither. Let's move on. Just . . . remember that theory is out there, and there is some pretty persuasive evidence for it when things start getting really weird." Merkovah shook himself and pressed on. "So, descending from God, or possibly ascending, or, most likely, simply universally emanating from God is the Universe.

Everything is 'real,' but things closer to God are more real. Entire tiers of existence we cannot interact with, absent the right magical technology. And even then, it is only for the very strongest."

This lined up with what Truth remembered.

"So, that's why I will teach you the Sharp spell attuned to Botis, Incisive."

"Wait, what?"

"There are a hundred generic versions of Sharp because it can be made very simple. Because it can be simplified for uneducated people, almost anyone can use it. The original spells all invoke aspects of great powers inhabiting the stars. Botis is a demon whose domain includes foresight."

Merkovah smiled nastily. "Your armor will resist scrying, your instincts will verge on precognition, and yes, you can cut things like you would not believe. It is a top-quality spell that comes to you only a few steps from the Chariot of God. Layered on top of the Meditations of Valentinian, you will be significantly more 'real' than the people you will inevitably fight. So, let's get to studying."

Truth only managed an hour before he had to call it quits for the night. His head pounded. It was like reading a secret message. He knew what all the individual words meant but could not comprehend why someone would have put them in that order. Merkovah shrugged and assured him that was perfectly normal. It was also how "Spirits of Intellect" could scam mages so easily.

Learning spells was *hard*.

Truth staggered into the living room. The cousins were sitting on a sofa and enjoying some beer while watching the scry. There was room for him. His instinct was to sit almost anywhere else, including in a different room. He, therefore, forced himself to sit on the sofa. Nothing changes unless you make it change, right? Well, maybe. He felt like he was breaking out in hives.

"Oh, hey, Tommy!" Jember snapped out of the light trance and looked over at him. "We are watching the game." He dropped his voice to a loud whisper. "Etenesh is a *huge* Toluca fan. It's tragic."

"Hush, you!" Etenesh sucked her teeth and *tsk*ed at Jember. "Toluca is the best in the West. They have Manny Guerin up front this year, and the whole team is stacked." She looked over at Truth. "Who do you follow?"

Truth laughed. "I'm not even sure what sport you are talking about."

"Pitz! It's an early-season match, so it's strictly court invasion, and obviously, no calling for the hoops." Etenesh rattled out the words with authority. It didn't help Truth know what she was talking about even a little bit. He turned toward the scryball and slipped into a trance.

Two teams of four faced each other on a long, narrow court. The goal was, apparently, to drive the other side back into their side of the court. They did this by passing a head-sized rubber ball between themselves, moving to intercept the passes where possible. You couldn't move with the ball, just position yourself and pass to the next person when the ball reached you. A game of strategy. And of immense physicality.

Truth started chuckling. Then laughing. He upgraded to cheering. He peaked at slapping his leg and cheering and laughing even harder. They passed by flinging their hips at the ball to make it bounce around. They dove if it was on the ground, sliding along the ground to knock it up with their hips. Eight people, a mix of men and women, launched themselves along a court and flung their hips everywhere they moved.

They looked totally serious the whole time! They were really focused! He watched a fit young man throw himself up into the air and smash his pelvis into the ball, driving it across the court to a teammate. He landed on his ass, fist-pumping like he had done something great. Truth laughed himself sick. "Go, Toluca! Best in the West! Go! Go! Go!"

CHAPTER 6

FUNNY NUMBERS

The game was fun, if incomprehensible. There were layers to the strategy that Truth just wasn't getting, but that was okay. The cousins were half the entertainment by themselves. Jember was willing to cheer just about anything that looked dramatic. Etenesh was intense and focused. She was like a spring, winding tighter and tighter until she exploded with boos or shouts of triumph. Truth just cheered randomly and laughed at the silly faces and thrusting hips. It was . . . fun. He couldn't think of a single time he had done something like that before.

When the game ended, they showed him to a spare bedroom. It was nice—a single bed, all made up in a small but cozy room.

"Kind of you to make the bed. Thank you," Truth said.

"No trouble at all. Bisqet did all the work." Jember waved away the thanks.

"Bisqet?"

"My—" Etenesh said something Truth didn't catch. "She's wonderful, a big help in my work."

"I'm sorry, I don't know that word. She's your what?"

"Oh, a— Think of it like . . . a sort of lightly bound spirit? One that is not malevolent and is willing to work for a salary, essentially."

"A spirit on salary?!" Truth sputtered.

"Sort of? Like having a demon servant that you feed your magic to, except much more trustworthy. And expensive, I suppose. You do need to offer it sacrifices regularly."

"That's a new one to me." Truth yawned. It had been a bewildering sort of day. He was ready to sleep. The bed was very soft. His sleep was deep and refreshing.

The System, however, did not have a good night.

"Whaddya want from me, Nicky? I told you I can't get you a job. I went and asked anyway. It nearly cost me *my* job. You are shit out of luck. But you got a nice little farm here, and your books sell, and your play is so funny, it's dangerous. People love it. So, why torture yourself? Why torture me?"

"Why? Why?! Because I am a citizen! A citizen of the best and most remarkable city in the world! One that could be a *beacon* to the world. If only competent people ran it." The skinny man's cheeks were hollow, but his eyes were fever-bright. "I would even settle for incompetents wise enough to listen to good advice."

"See? Shit like that is why you aren't getting hired back. You got done wrong. I know it. Everyone who worked with you knows it. But you are the all-time shit-talking champion of the Chancellery, which is not a great trait in a diplomat. And you keep talking shit about the people you want to rehire you."

"Oh, please! I will pour endless barrels of oil in their ears if they grant me an audience. Even my dislike can be set aside if it means the city will prosper." He waved aside the little inconvenience. The skinny man showed no signs of the torture he had survived. It had been years ago, after all. Truth always thought asking the people who tortured you for a job was pretty weird. But then, Nicky *was* pretty weird.

He liked to play dress-up and talk to dead people. Didn't care who knew it, either. He was *proud* of it.

"A fox, not a lion?"

"I cannot believe those imbeciles didn't catch my joke."

"Nicky, half of 'em can't read. The other half can only read bank ledgers. You gotta . . . y'know . . . know your audience. These are guys who spend a lot of time looking at pictures."

They were sitting on a bench outside Nicky's charming little farmhouse. The yellow stone had absorbed the day's heat and kept them comfortably warm as they watched the sunset over the vineyards. A little bird was hopping around the well, dancing about as it looked for water or insects. Truth could hear Marietta calling for the kids to come in and wash up for supper. The air was fresh and clean, not the muggy, fecal stench of the city.

"I fucking hate it here," Nicky said softly. "I fucking hate it. It's smothering me. Our home is a single breath away from disaster. Now is the time for daring action. These spoiled children think they can buy love, and they can, for a time. But when their purse dries up, that love will turn to hate. The city will turn on them, and everyone will die. Should there be survivors, they can only serve foreign masters in the rubble. They will never be free again. A wise prince does not seek to be loved or feared. But if these sister-humping morons had half the brains of my morning shit, they would know it's better to be feared."

"You know you are talking about my family, right?" Truth gave him the side-eye.

"Legally, I'm not."

A swallow darted past, catching a mosquito in flight.

"Fuck you too, Nicky."

Truth awoke to what was rapidly becoming his favorite sound in the morning—the System screaming in heartbreaking agony. Comfortable bed. Deep, dreamless sleep. Something unknowable about his very nature torturing the System. All the good things. The birds had raised their voices in song. Singing their praise of the glorious new day.

"I DON'T CARE IF SHE GREW A DICK ON HER FOREHEAD! I DON'T CARE IF IT'S *YOUR* DICK! SPEND THE REST OF YOUR LIFE AS THOMASE THE DICKLESS FOR ALL I CARE!"

Merkovah's voice was so loud, it vibrated the floorboards. The birds flew away. Truth sighed and rolled out of bed. The bellowing continued at a more-restrained level.

"I have spent WEEKS teaching the bored little morons you call students. WEEKS of keeping these degenerate swine from killing themselves summoning basic imps. WEEKS! Do you know how much money I've lost doing you this favor? Do you?!"

There was a murmuring coming from the other end of the communication altar.

"No. NO. Not again. Not for a single hour or minute longer. I am gone. Pack up my office for me and ship it to my wife, or I swear I will swap your testicles and eyes around."

Urgent muttering from the altar this time. Truth quickly hauled on clean underwear and some fresh socks. He hoped he would get paid soon. He was still wearing the clothes he had looted from those gangsters, and they weren't the best.

"Well, Thomase, you can either fix it yourself or bring your 'head' game to an exciting new level. Experiment a little. Find out what's good for you now. I don't care. I don't care even a little bit. Never call me again. Actually, no, do call me. I want to hear more about your every little humiliating fuckup. Send me pictures. I want to publish a newsletter. I've got friends around the world who need to see this."

The murmuring took on a more whining, pleading tone.

"Thomase, I say this with 'love.'" Truth could hear the quotations through the floorboards. His shoes were falling apart too. The acid rain seemed to have caught them, and he just hadn't noticed with everything going on. Pity. They were comfortable.

"You are trying to 'save' a succubus. By treating her like a human girlfriend. You, Thomase, a man who theoretically RUNS A SCHOOL OF *DEMONOLOGY,* are trying to 'reform' a succubus. WHO NOW OWNS YOUR DICK. You say you cannot fix this problem yourself. You have made some terrible life choices. I'm done enabling you. Goodbye."

There was a noise that sounded suspiciously like someone smashing an expensive communication altar.

Truth had all his stuff stowed away, not that he had really unpacked much. It sounded like they would be making a speedy exit from the city.

"EVERYONE! PACK UP! WE WILL EAT BREAKFAST ON THE ROAD!" Merkovah's voice echoed loudly through the house. Truth was surprised to see Etenesh and Jember packed, washed, and waiting at the foot of the stairs. He gave them an interrogatory look.

Jember smiled. "This was a long time coming, and we are usually up early. He's got a pattern. Well, you will see."

Truth nodded and stowed his gear on his two-wheeler. He took a moment to fix the acidbolter. Never knew when you might need it, and he just had to repair a couple of the channels on the fetish. No heavy lifting. He heard the rest of the household come tromping out, headed for Merkovah's carriage.

"Hey, Tommy, are you going to *what the hell is that?!*" Etenesh's voice rose in shock. "What?"

"That! That fetish you are holding! It feels cursed to Hell!"

Truth considered that a moment. Technically, Acid Bolt could not be considered a sort of curse. But practically? Eh. "Acid-Bolter. Piece-of-crap army-surplus job that wasn't good when it was made."

"All right, great, I've learned something. Why do you have it?" There was a fair bit of heat in the question.

"Because I was riding through the Free State, and it became necessary? And it was free?" Truth tried to find the most diplomatic way he could say it.

Merkovah started chanting furiously, waving a comically large thumb ring at the house. The air shimmered as five fire demons materialized. They quickly spaced themselves around the house and summoned pillars of fire at Merkovah's shouted command. The rather nice suburban home was ashes mere minutes later. Then another order was given, and all the heat suddenly vanished. The ashes looked cool to the touch.

"Same as always with you. When are you going to have us do something useful? Or interesting?" one of the demons demanded. Merkovah hurled the thumb ring at the demon, causing it to explode into cinders.

He glared at the other demons as the ring flew back into his hand with a *thwap*. "Anybody else got a question?"

They did not. Truth had noticed that Thrush had been keeping his mouth shut for a long time now.

"We are going. Now. Etenesh, I told you he was hired as a bodyguard. Though, Tommy, I would remind you that Siphios is *not* the Free State, and running around with military-grade weaponry will not make you many friends. Also, I didn't see this before, but why is there a spear and a machete lashed to your . . . vehicle?"

Truth tried to think of the most diplomatic way to put it and drew a blank yet again. "Because I was riding through the Free State, and they became necessary? And they were free?"

"Define *free?*" Jember asked in a half-joking way.

"No, don't. We are going now. Follow me. Try and think about what I taught you last night as we go." Merkovah shoved the cousins into the carriage.

They drove up through the city, and, blessings upon blessings, the road outside the city was paved. They seemed to be headed roughly northwest, but beyond that, Truth was just following Merkovah.

"Thrush, you feel safe to come out?" Truth tapped his necklace.

"Candidly, Master? Your slave begs to be returned to Hell."

"First of all, quit it with the 'slave' shit. Second, really? You guys usually can't wait to get out of there."

"For roughly the same reason you drove the long way through the Free State. Opportunities to grow and to fulfill our nature. However, as fruitful as our partnership has been, I would rather leave your service in one piece. Metaphorically speaking. All three of your new acquaintances are attended by beings vastly above my low station. To the point where they would be offended by my simple presence. With terminal consequences for me, and possibly you, too."

Thrush's familiar velvety voice went a little rough. "Besides, that exorcist is . . . more than he seems. I can tell you that he's not fifty, for one thing."

"I KNEW IT! The bastard looks way too young to be fifty."

"Yes. He is closer to five hundred. And he appears to be quite determined to form you into a living weapon. This may not be bad for you, but I thought you would want to know. Now kindly send me back to Hell, where it's safe."

CHAPTER 7

BACK IN THE MIX

Moyle dropped away behind their two-vehicle convoy with startling speed.

Suburb-suburb-suburb-strip malls-farms. Sudden spike of loathing, then nothing once again, as the farms vanished. Like some solar demon had traced a sharp line around the outer edge of the city and said . . . nothing with intelligible words, but its meaning would be quite clear.

Once they got into the farm belt, Merkovah pulled over and glared at the city. He ceremoniously spat once, hopped back in his carriage, and resumed the drive. Truth supposed it must be personal with the little exorcist. He had seen nicer cities, but Moyle seemed . . . fine. Having taken enough time to process the bomb Thrush had dropped, he resumed the conversation.

"Elaborate on the *five hundred years old* thing."

"I don't actually know how old he is; five hundred is just a guess. Simply—with Level Seven cultivation, he would look about as good as he ever could have for his age, and his aging would more or less stop. It would have added, oh, another seventy years onto his life? More or less? But he looks young, and the life inside him burns like a sun. At some point, he started practicing a body-cultivation technique, one that conferred significant benefits to longevity. He is an old monster, and his vices are envy and wrath. Well disciplined, but they are there."

"Ah. And that kind of insight . . ."

"Is the kind of thing he might well kill me out of hand over, yes. So . . . kindly employer? Please send me back to Hell. Now. If you don't know how to bodily return an imp to the infernal realms, I would be happy to teach you."

"No need; the banishment is built into your contract. Safe travels." Truth decisively grabbed the necklace and activated the banishment. It might be a basic piece of junk, but at least its manufacturer had the decency to rip off a functional design rather than kludging things. Thrush's presence vanished almost instantly, without even time to utter a sinister parting word. Truth wasn't prepared to keep around an imp that was starting to turn on him.

Truth didn't try to think. He just let himself feel. The farms vanished almost as quickly as the city had. Another invisible line—no more farms. Now it was just desert. Those farms must be supported with intensive irrigation or much better magic than he would have thought farmers could afford.

It was wild. All green, growing fields and then blasted earth so bleak it seemed to redefine *desert*. Not pretty, rolling sand dunes or the red dirt scrubland of the Free State. This was desolation. And yet, the people living in Siphios seemed more prosperous than their southern neighbors. This must be a little localized thing.

Five hundred years. The number felt unreal. Truth could easily imagine five hundred needles for a needler. He could imagine five hundred people. But to live five hundred years? He had always assumed that he would be dead by thirty if he didn't get into Starbrite. He didn't have high ambitions for how long he would live *in* Starbrite. It just never seemed to be relevant. Just focus on the next thing that needed doing.

Get Harmony on the right track. Okay, done. Get Sophie into the best university she could get. Not as much he could do there, but load her up on school supplies, cultivation aids, whatever. Set aside friends and family points for her too. Then Vigor. He was the furthest off, but *furthest* was still only a couple of years away. Still, whatever it took. Just . . . get your head down and push. You can rest when they are safe.

It occurred to him only now that he had only ever felt "safer" but never "safe." He always had to be working, pushing, and earning. Never complaining. Never ungrateful for what he was given. Eager to show his thanks to his . . . employers. He knew some of that came from the System, but most of it came from him. "The slave mentality." Yes, that about fit.

Five hundred years. How much could he do in five hundred years? He would definitely have a personality by then, right? He snorted. The skin had begun peeling on that particular onion of lies. He might not be the most colorful soul, but he definitely had a better personality than a lot of people he could think of.

Merkovah steered them to a roadside rest stop. Breakfast that day was fried bits of flatbread slathered with different things. Truth opted for the bright reddish one, which turned out to be an *interesting* choice. It was covered with a sort of spiced butter and an intense spice blend. It was pretty tasty but also kind of overwhelming. Merkovah had them sit around a little table to explain what the plan was.

"We have now escaped that pestilential city. Bad cess upon it. A city of penis-headed demons. May ten thousand years pass before I ever return there." Truth had to wonder if the beardy ancient actually expected to live that long.

"We are on to our next destination. I have been hired to"—he used a word Truth didn't know—"for the town of Mega. Shouldn't be a big job, a couple of days at most. With luck, we may even be done today." Merkovah sighed heavily.

"Mega is, perhaps, a little too close to Moyle for comfort, as we are now barely forty-five minutes away. However, it's a simple cash job and will help us learn a little more about each other. Speaking of, we did introductions yesterday, but let's do the *professional* introductions today. Tommy, you're the new hire. Start us off."

"Hey, everyone. My name is Tommy Wells, and I am . . . roughly twenty-five? I haven't been keeping close track. I spent my teens training in talisman maintenance and wound up splitting my time between doing that and security work in a private security company. My training and work experience include bodyguard work. I enjoy trying new food and reading novels. And travel, to my surprise."

Merkovah nodded at that and pointed to Jember.

"I'm Jember, definitely twenty-two, fresh out of the University of Siphios at Xandre. I got my degree in apocalypticism. I am currently getting work experience with Teacher Merkovah. I also enjoy eating good food, but my big hobby is running and dancing."

Merkovah cut in. "Tommy, we will be covering what exactly I do later, but basically, the exorcism pays the bills while my job as a teacher lets me research . . . what I want to research. Not a short conversation. Etenesh, you are up."

"My name is Etenesh, twenty-three years old, also fresh out of the University of Siphios at Xandre. My degree is in theoretical and applied theogony, so you can imagine I read a lot of books. So, so many books. I am also getting work experience with Teacher Merkovah but plan to go back for my doctorate in a couple of years. I also like to dance, and I am, of course, a lifelong pitz fan and Toluca supporter."

Merkovah smiled lightly and turned back toward Truth. "I'll give you the details of my long-term project tonight. For now, let's press on to Mega and get the job done."

Roughly an hour later, they were standing in a rare stretch of flat land around Mega. The town was located in a pocket formed by the intersection of two small mountain ranges, though *small* was a debatable term when referring to mountains almost two kilometers tall. The cousins, Etenesh and Jember, were laying out lines and curves creating a profound mystic formation on the ground. To Truth's surprise and mild alarm, they were assisted by several spirits, each of whom made his hair rise in alarm.

"So, remember the exorcism over at the Widow Yettran's place?" Merkovah asked Truth.

"Sure, necrotic spirits. You summoned an angel that cleaned house."

"Yes. And then what?"

"You had an argument with it. I couldn't tell if you won or not. Frankly, I didn't know they could be argued with."

"A belief they love to encourage. In fact, angels can be argued with, tricked, bribed, all the good stuff. The key is that they only ever operate on divine instructions. But remember what I said about the nature of God yesterday?"

"Contradictory, and even the angels give different stories."

"Yep. So, if you can convince an angel that God wants them to do something, they will just mindlessly go and do it. And with the right preparation, it's not so hard to convince them."

"You looked like you were scolding the angel?"

"I was. I was reminding it that there was a contract in place, and it had a duty to prevent exactly that kind of spiritual contagion from spreading. The talisman I showed it was 'proof' of the contract."

"Is . . . there such a contract?"

Merkovah grinned and shrugged. "Debatably. As a nationally recognized teacher of religious law, I would say there is. And the angel agreed with my analysis."

"Is . . . that what we are doing here? Scamming an angel?"

"Oh, no. No, this is strictly focused on demons. Speaking of, have you much experience fighting demons head-on?"

"Not . . . much. Some."

"Well, lose that Acid Bolter. Time for you to use a proper exorcist's weapon." Merkovah opened the boot of his carriage and pulled out a sword. A meter-long blade, hilted for two-handed use. Minimal hand protection with a cross guard. The flattened diamond shape seemed more suited for piercing, though Truth could imagine it was effective in the cut. Not fullered. It didn't need to be. A rather standard-looking blade, save for the fact that it was practically glowing with spellwork.

Dense lines of sigils and incantations seemed to crawl along the blade. The etching seemed to twist and double back in places, the incantations splitting like a river running into a delta and descending to a sea of formations—a spell structure made material, then empowered with lists of holy names. He tried to analyze it the way he would a normal talisman, and it just . . . wasn't. All the usual logic seemed to go flying out the window. In fact, the more he looked at it, the more perplexed he became. Not only did it not make sense, it shouldn't have worked at all.

"Trying to crack the spellwork? Don't bother. It's coated in a spell to disguise the actual spellwork. Anti-counterfeiting protection. Invented here in Siphios! Now, then, young man, I assume you have been trained in the basics of swordplay?"

Truth looked blankly at Merkovah. He had never touched a sword. Why would he? "I am used to working with shorter blades."

"Ah, no matter. Basically, what's about to happen is this. The big demon bowl locking down this mountain pass is full. Mostly demonic insects, nothing really sentient. What you sometimes hear referred to as *Goetia Pandemonium*, though that's not a *strictly* accurate description." Truth could suddenly, vividly, believe that Merkovah was a university professor.

"Etenesh and Jember are going to create a spell formation that will lift the spell bowl while trapping all the demons inside the formation. I am going to summon an angel. It's going to exterminate all the bigger demons. We don't want to summon it while the bowl is down, or it would smash it. Now, the thrifty people of Mega waited until the last possible moment, so there is a regrettably large number of weaker demons in there. You and I are going to exterminate them."

Truth nodded at that. "Okay."

Merkovah gave him an odd look. "I just told you that we are going to be trapped in a cage with who knows how many unchained demons, and your response is just . . . *okay?*"

"Spiritual bodies, right?"

"Of course."

"So, all we have to do is disrupt the bodies to the point where they can't re-form, right?"

"Yes . . ."

"So, it's fine. I have a sword now. I'm not saying I could solo infinity demons with it, but I reckon I can clear out a lot of small fry. You seem confident that you can handle the rest."

Truth took a few practice swings with the sword. Kind of the same as a machete—use your arms for control, but you use your body for power. Fun.

"Huh. 'Okay' it is. By the way, that sword is a little special. Do well in the battle, and it's yours."

Truth nodded. The good contracts always had excellent bonuses.

"Teacher! We are ready!" Jember yelled.

Truth squared up to the core of the spell formation and loosened his wrists. He had spent . . . it felt like a long time . . . fighting things that could hit him, and he couldn't hit back. He was going to *enjoy* this.

CHAPTER 8

AN OLD-FASHIONED EXORCISM

Jember and Etenesh had set themselves a little densely warded ritual circle to operate from. A triple ring, lodged inside a series of increasingly complex forms, rose in sheets of white light around Truth and Merkovah. The old monster in disguise looked bored. His weapon of choice was once again the thumb ring. Truth was enjoying swinging the sword around and listening to it thrum.

"Ready, Teacher?" Etenesh yelled.

"Ready. Lift it." Merkovah waved his hand to move them along. The cousins started chanting and waving their magical tools, directing energy to different sections of the formation as required. Or so Truth assumed. He hadn't seen the manual for this formation. They must have done something, because Merkovah started chanting and pointed the thumb ring directly overhead.

The spell bowl rose like a mushroom from the red dirt. A few reinforcing spells on the outside, but with spell bowls, the real action was always on the inside. Jember blazed with golden fire, the light blinding around his hands and eyes. His chanting reached a furious pitch, the magic words and holy names spilling from his tongue. Blessings and abjurations falling like rain on the red earth.

Beside Jember, Etenesh embroidered the sheets of white light with sigils, occult glyphs, and sacred geometries of bewildering complexity. The air seemed to change, becoming denser. More real. Redefining the battleground as a place of true and final battle. Her fingers trailed pale blue light flecked with iridescent purple like a butterfly's wing drawn into a thread. She did not chant. She impressed her will upon the world directly.

Merkovah stood between earth and heaven, all traces of casual boredom gone. He raised his ring high and spoke a Name with utter authority. The skin of reality seemed to peel back, and a terrible golden eye glanced at them. The weight of the gaze seemed to hammer at the area inside the wards, shuddering them, pressing against the reinforced reality of the space. Truth was riveted by this terrible power, so much so that he didn't see Jember flipping the bowl. But he sure heard the screams.

What he had seen in Chil Perdermo had been what trashy slavers could jam into their victims. This, whatever Merkovah said, was the *real* Goetia Pandemonium. The overturned bowl boiled with demonic insects. Pestilential parodies of the most night-marish vermin. Every limb was dressed with spikes, barbs, or catching hooks. Every mandible was a crushing vise of jagged chitin, dripping venom. Stingers, poisoned hair, poisoned breath, explosive boluses of corrupted acid, every aspect of the demons was crafted to inspire fear and despair. To initiate you to the mysteries of Hell before you died.

Rising from their number were a few grander beasts. Heavy things, slow, earth demons in rough parodies of bears and hyenas. They could despise the fripperies of their lessers. Hungry for the warmth of human flesh and human souls, they charged over toward Truth and Merkovah.

The angel made a sound like a bell ringing in church and ten thousand voices saying their prayers for millennia in faithful unison. Embers of flame streaked down-ward, landing in the mouths of the larger demons. They wanted warmth? The angel was "happy" to provide. The coarse demons struggled, roaring against the flames. Bellowing, smashing their heads against the ground, spitting their own balefire back. Then the vermin tide was on Truth, and he had no time for anyone else's problems.

Truth whirled the blessed two-handed blade over his head and brought it down straight, cutting into the head of a beetle. The chitin cracked, and syrupy black ichor leaked, only to burst into golden flames under the spells of the sword. The fire turned the demon's head into a lantern before Truth had the blade out.

He quickly moved next to the ward, limiting the directions the swarm could come at him from. They came at him madly, and he desperately shifted around to make them interfere with each other. He lunged, piercing the neck of some abyssal ant before it could get its mandibles around his leg. A worm covered in bony blades spat acid at him. Truth tried to shift out of the way but was penned between the ward and the press of insects. In a fit of desperation, he tried to slap away the corrupting liquor with the flat of his blade.

The blessed steel flashed with pale light and slapped that filthy liquid straight into the face of an ox-sized grasshopper. The grasshopper screamed in shock before thrashing around wildly, crushing smaller demons beneath the hooks and barbs of its strong legs. Truth would have grinned with satisfaction, but there were twelve hornets diving in, each as long as his forearm and mad as the Bastards Convention on Father's Day. He whipped his shining blade around and had at them.

They came from above and below, from behind and straight ahead. He tried to fight with his back to the ward as much as he could. It wasn't enough. He started taking hits—a hook tearing across his skin, a brutal claw scraping down his side, leaving bloody furrows. Still—they tore flesh. Truth took lives. He hacked, chopped, raked, stabbed, sliced, and even bashed with his pommel when he thought it might do some good.

He quickly learned their measure, figuring out how to use the larger ones to block or funnel the smaller ones or how to use the flyers to screen him from the projectiles. It was a puzzle. A frantic, frenetic maelstrom of pain and despair and raw physical and magical might. And a puzzle. How do you keep them far enough away that they can't hit you but close enough that you can hit them? How do you keep the number that can attack you at one time to a minimum? What is the most efficient way to kill a given demon? Each fraction of a second was too precious to waste.

Truth gave himself to the battle, feeling its flow at a level more instinctual than rational as he slid the pieces around. Not realizing that he was refining his sword-play, merging it into footwork that was evolving minute by minute as the battlefield became strewn with corpses and gore. Not caring that his sword was no longer merely glowing. It was a raging beacon fire, chanting its holy liturgy as he baptized it in infernal blood. The corpses were slowly dissolving on the field. The blade, and his bladework, had destroyed the demon's spiritual bodies. Their weak grip on the material world had been shattered, and they were forced back to Hell.

His body ached with exhaustion. How long had it been since he had felt his muscles burn this way? Before he died. Nothing since had tested him like this. But in this battle, these seemingly endless insects pushed him hard.

Sweat fell into his eyes. The salt could no longer burn him, but he blinked it away in irritation. Sweat slicked his hands, but the hilt was well-wrapped with tacky cordage. They would not slip.

His sense of the battle told him that the demons' numbers were dwindling and that he could handle this degree of blood loss. He kept his feet moving, sliding away from one blow and using that momentum to sever a leg or a head. To cut a mastiff-sized wasp out of the air so that it landed on the back of a beetle, convulsively stinging in its death throes. To stab, again and again, and endlessly again, where he thought it would do some good. With a brutal chop, he took the head of a scarab demon. And then there were none left to kill.

Truth's chest heaved, sucking in great gasps of air. No ichor dripped from his blade. It had burned away almost instantly. On instinct, he ran the blade over his wounds, letting the holy fire brush against him. He could feel the traces of the demons boiling out of the holes they left in him. It was something. He looked around, trying to understand the state of the rest of the battle. Done, apparently. All the greater demons were dead. Everyone, Jember, Etenesh, Merkovah, and even the angel, looked at him like they had just seen a wonder.

"A talisman-maintenance technician, Tommy?" Etenesh tried to sound playful, but her voice broke around the word *maintenance*. Not scared but stunned silly.

"Army-certified." He gave her a tired grin. "This is a *good* sword."

"It's yours." Merkovah looked untouched by the struggle. The angel made a sound like the rattle of millions of rosaries and the rain drumming on stained-glass windows. Merkovah nodded calmly. It seemed that the angel and the exorcist were in agreement.

"Come along, Mr. Wells. Let's get you patched up, and I will explain just what I want to do out here."

To Truth's surprise, the angel hung around in the sky. The cousins seemed to have expected this and focused on keeping the wards up. The sword, however, had become a problem. It was bright as Hell. Well. Bright as Heaven. Billows of holy fire were shooting off the blade, and it was *chanting*. Loudly chanting, and in a language Truth didn't speak.

"It's just excited. Let it work off a little energy. Now, quickly, while the wards are up and the angel is creating interference." Merkovah was splashing his wounds with a potion, then binding them up with boiled gauze.

"My aim, 'Mr. Wells,' is nothing less than the liberation or death of the System Astrologica. Starbrite's true elite, the so-called 'C-suite,' mostly cultivate off-planet. The arrival and departure of their Level Eight and Nine experts is no secret to those of a certain level of power. The loss of their 'intelligent spirit' would render most of the company powerless. It would be all too easy for the powers of the world to swoop in and tear off fatty chunks."

"And when the 'C-suite' hears about this and come back to clean house?" Truth asked.

"Those few that could survive the loss will be dealt with. It's not like there are no Level Eights outside of Starbrite. They are just few and comparatively weak. Unwilling to move unless they can be sure of landing the killing blow. I intend to provide them with that opportunity. After your display here today, I think you can be part of this scheme. I think you could play a substantial role."

Merkovah clasped him on the shoulder and looked Truth in the eye. "Young man, will you save the world with me?"

Truth considered carefully.

"Hell, no. But I am interested in learning more specifics. I don't much care about the world, but I would be very interested in smashing the System."

Truth pulled up his own System and smiled.

Stellar Ray Attunement—90%*
Bone Density—5.6*
Strength—4.1*
Speed—4.3*
Proprioception—7.5*
Reflexes—7.8*
Level Progression—1%
Resistance to Magic—Level 0: 25%, Level 1: 10%, Level 2: 5%, Level 3: 1%
Spell Mastery:
Meditations of Valentinian: unknowable, but not impressive so far.
Incisive: N/A
Magical Equipment: The Tongue of One Who Speaks for God.

CHAPTER 9

SO . . . SEEING ANYONE?

Their little convoy re-formed quickly, Merkovah feeling that a mere hundred and five kilometers was far too close to the cursed city of Moyle. He was determined to make it to the sanctuary of the campus at Bule, another two hundred kilometers down the road. Bule was also a little too close to Moyle for comfort. Still, Merkovah assured everyone that they would be safe from "the moral and spiritual contagion which breeds and festers within that midden of depravity."

Truth tried to remember which part of the city looked depraved but drew a blank. It seemed pretty ordinary for this part of the world. Nicer than most of the places he had seen in the Free State. Truth shrugged, drank what felt like two liters of water, pissed what felt like four liters, and hopped back on his trusty two-wheeler. There were locals lined up along the road. Hands pressed together in front of their face, bowing their heads as the convoy passed. Thankful, not scared.

The countryside they passed was pretty interesting. The little pocket of mountains Mega was tucked into was a twenty-kilometer green illusion. The horrible reality of the desert reasserted itself with a punishing severity. Nothing green was permitted past the foot of the mountains. Not a single speck of plant life.

Truth used the drive to think a bit about what Merkovah had said. He hardly knew the deceptively young-looking man. Clearly knew his stuff as an exorcist. Clearly well respected locally. But his last employer had also been eager to shower him with gifts. And he wasn't particularly comfortable with powerful older figures swooping in and promising to provide direction.

When you got right down to it, what the fuck was he doing there?

Truth had been feeling rushed for the last few days, but the smell of rodent had never really gone away. He was on a journey. The purpose of the journey was to figure out some more about who he was and what he wanted, get to Siphios, get some spells, get stronger . . . a couple of steps that he would definitely figure out later . . . safely extract the sibs from both Starbrite and Jeon and provide them a safe, comfortable life, for the rest of their lives. Somewhere, somehow.

And then some beardy weirdo pops up, claiming that divination guided him to Truth and that Truth had the potential to take down Starbrite. But only with his teachings. The rat got bigger and bigger, didn't it? No, it wasn't a rat. It was Thierrie.

You are very beautiful. Very special. I think I am falling in love with you. Do you like to party? Don't worry about it; I can pay for everything. Have a drink. Have another. Do you love me? I love you. Try a little of this. It makes everything fun. Have a little more. My beautiful one. So special. Look what I got for you. You want to help me too, don't you?

The "Charisma of the Streets" violently appeared in Truth's mind. Truth had despised him on many levels and had had plenty of chances to watch him work. The game never changed. That was probably what turned a casual loathing into active hate. Every pimp ran the same damn scam, but he dressed it up with affection. Because he was "the good one." So, he ran the same damn game every time, and it worked almost every time. When you are in a bad place, who doesn't want to hear they are special? That they are loved? That you were destined to meet in this random diner?

Truth had the sudden urge to take the next turn and run like hell. He controlled the urge.

What did he need, and what did he know? He needed . . . something. Some path to being more than a thug with a spell. There was a certain charm to the idea of setting up his own garage somewhere, vanishing into the masses as just another repairman. He wasn't an expert in vehicle repair, but he was confident he could figure it out. And every city needs someone to fix the streetlights, right? But that wasn't him anymore. It probably never was him.

He needed to be more than a thug with a spell. He needed to know why his body was the way it was. Why did he survive the attack on Kofi? Because it occurred to him: he never got a clear answer on that. Why did he crawl back up out of that well? What was the deal with the Nine Worm Path? What was the deal with the Ghūl, both generally and in his specific case?

All right. A lot of questions. And maybe the answer to those questions would let him save the sibs. Whose condition he couldn't even check on without the danger of alerting Starbrite.

What he did know is that he had his trusty iron horse. He had a spear, a crummy Acid Bolter, a battered machete, and a really phenomenal magic sword. The sword was safely in its sheath, lashed to the back of his luggage. It had calmed down but looked ready to burst into fire and liturgy at the slightest provocation. He had no money, but he did have the spell Incisive and the Meditations of Valentinian. Except he didn't know Incisive and was relying on Merkovah to teach him. And he didn't know why he knew the Meditations. Another one for the question pile.

He did know that Merkovah was looking for a thug with a spell. He had more or less said so, and all his actions seemed to support that idea. Merkovah wanted a hitter. Why a Level Three hitter, Truth didn't know. No doubt he would find out soon. Because Merkovah also knew a hell of a lot more than he did, and he *wanted* to tell Truth things. So, assuming he could trust his new employer, he stood to gain a lot. A lot of answers. A lot of power. He shook his head and resolved to focus on happier, more productive thoughts.

Who would he rather lose his virginity to, Etenesh or Jember? He instinctively preferred Etenesh, but Jember had a charisma that would be hard to refuse.

The ground around their little convoy started showing signs of wrinkling. The earth crumpled up into rocks, ridges, and stretches of ridges. Little hills dotted the country around the road, though they were still in the desert. A little while later, green mountains rose west of the road. Truth was half-convinced they were an illusion. It was actually an omen of things to come.

Tendrils of green, tracing along thin rivers and creeks, infiltrated the desolation. Tidy farms began to appear as the amount of green increased. The farther north, the more ragged the terrain and the greener it got. Farms grew near vertically or on sharp terraces. Nobody seemed troubled by that fact, so Truth assumed it was normal for farms.

Less than two hours after leaving Mega, they arrived in the green and pleasant town of Bule. Truth saw farms, a few small factories, small but tidy houses, and plonked down like an elephant in a muffin, the monstrous bulk of the university. A great white pile of concrete smoothed into pointless curves and lacking the faintest hint of grace. Merkovah seemed on the verge of happy tears when he parked his carriage.

"Safety. Civilization. Ah, Blessed Siphios, the nation of scholars and saints! Blessed Bule, so courageously holding back the tide of iniquity rising from the south! It is good to be back."

"All right, I have to ask. I get that the teaching gig was boring and frustrating, but why the constant hate on Moyle?" Truth asked.

"Did you not see it? The damn city is a war zone!" Jember said.

Etenesh nodded and added, "I must have seen six serious fights in two weeks, and I swear I saw at least one dead body on the road. Half the city is in the Free State, and the people there are wild. Too damn wild."

"Huh. Different standards, I guess. I was touched by how civilized it seemed." Truth shrugged.

"I'd make a joke, but after watching you work through the demons, I believe you." Etenesh laughed. So did Jember. Merkovah waved over a guard. It seemed that his guest room was ready, and there were dorm rooms his staff could sleep in. Dinner would be in a couple of hours, and they were all welcome in the faculty dining room.

"Go. Unpack, clean up, and rest. Truth, keep that sword sheathed until I have a chance to explain how to use it safely. I need a shower and a nap." Merkovah strode away quickly, leaving them to the mercy of the University staff.

Apparently, they arrived during a vacation. Truth and Jember were assigned a four-person dorm room to split between them. Etenesh had her own room. Why, he didn't know.

Dinner was surprisingly bland but filling. A sort of vegetable stew with more of the spongy bread that seemed to come with everything in Siphios. Everyone seemed to think he was Desrin and were trying to accommodate him. They looked quite grateful when he told them he really didn't mind if they drank, though he abstained.

He should add *What does it take to be Desrin?* to the pile of questions. He was on board with the no-drinking, but the strict vegetarianism might be a challenge. Not that he was looking for a religion; it just seemed interesting.

"So, Mr. Wells, you came from the south?" a slim fellow of the University asked.

"Yes, some business took me to the Free State, and when my contract ended, I decided to ride up to Siphios. It was a . . . colorful experience."

This was met with surprised murmurs. "How did you make it?" another asked.

"Well, in one instance, half-killing my poor bound spirit as I got out at top speed." This was met with laughs and knowing nods. "While I don't have any desire to go back there, I did meet some decent people. It really wasn't all bad."

"I hear banditry is endemic." Jember looked fascinated.

"I suppose it is," Truth said, privately determined to look up *endemic* as soon as he could consult his dictionary.

"Oh, you must do better than that," Etenesh said. "Tell us a story."

Truth racked his brain for suitable dinner-table-conversation material. He had not the faintest damn idea what was appropriate. Throwing caution to the wind, he said, "It's a little gory, so I don't know if it's good dinner-table material, but—"

He was drowned out with shouted encouragement from the table. It seemed that things were very boring here, and tales of the horrors of the Free State were in high demand.

"Well. The thing that I ran away from? It went something like this."

Truth wasn't a very good storyteller in that he had no grasp of rhythm, showmanship, or how to build tension in his listeners. What he did have were sincerity and what his audience correctly identified as a bone-deep stoic reserve. Someone dropped their spoon when he described the slaughter in the city center. Another gasped when he described sliding his iron horse into the garage. It was dead quiet when he finished.

The slim fellow coughed lightly. "Thank you, Mr. Wells. That was . . . alarming, actually. I hadn't heard about that, and I think others need to know about it too. I need to make some calls. Head, may I be excused from the table?"

"Go. I think many will be skipping dessert and joining you." An ancient worthy gave his assent.

"Saints protect us. An offering of that scale . . . I can't imagine it," Jember muttered.

Truth was about to suggest ways to imagine it when Etenesh cut in. "Racing through the Free State, dodging demons, fighting demons hand to hand—your wife must worry a lot about you."

"Oh, I don't have a wife. Husband, either, to be clear."

"Fiancée?" Etenesh asked.

"Nope."

"Seeing anyone?"

"Romantically? No. I'm . . ." Truth was trying to be more open, but it suddenly went from funny to painful. "I'm complicated."

Etenesh just grinned at that. She didn't look like someone scared of complications.

CHAPTER 10

ON THE ROAD TO ANSWERS

There was a notable increase in people fiddling discreetly with charms at the table, but fewer people slipped away than the Head seemed to expect. Pleased, he suggested an extra round of nerik to accompany the flan that was tonight's dessert. This was met with warm approval and quiet cheers by the faculty.

What the hell is nerik? *For that matter, what's flan? I've heard of it, but what actually is it?* Truth wondered.

Nerik appeared to be a sort of wine or liquor served in small glasses. It had a syrupy viscosity, clinging to the sides of the glass when swirled. The aroma coming from the glasses was quite pleasant but also puzzling.

Truth's new body could pick apart smells with incredible accuracy, but he needed something to compare things to. *Fruit* didn't explain much. The smell was warm, with *fruity* and *spicy* dancing around each other in the glass. Like peaches, maybe? Or raisins? As the nerik warmed up in the drinker's hands, the aroma of ethanol started to spread. That was a smell he could place. It lived in Dad's armchair and the empty bottle of Beefheart on the floor.

He didn't really need to try nerik. He would walk the foodie's path, not the drinker's path.

The flan was another puzzle but a more-welcome one. The servants brought in trollies loaded with covered trays. The covers were removed with great pomp, revealing little flat-bottomed bowls. The servants would approach a guest from the side, put a plate over the flat-bottomed bowl, then invert the bowl onto the plate. When the bowl was lifted away, there was a little wobbly pale yellow thing covered in brown sauce, a solo act on a white porcelain stage.

It jiggled. Truth gently tapped the plate. It jiggled again. This was concerning. Food, in Truth's experience, did not jiggle. He watched the other diners. They scooped up bites with a spoon in seeming pleasure. Merkovah looked indecently pleased with it, savoring each little bite and practically licking the spoon after. Truth tentatively tried a scoop.

The flan was nice. Not amazing, not life-changing, but nice. A little eggy, the texture was weird as hell, and the watery brown sauce seemed to be some kind of syrup. Cool going down the throat. Kind of a metallic aftertaste, though he couldn't think why that was. Maybe they messed up cooking it? But everyone else looked happy. He could eat the flan happily enough, but he had eaten better food than this.

Everyone else seemed to love it. Was this a poverty-food thing? Flan was fancy food for classy people? Was he having a poor-person fuck-up?

Truth made as sincere a smile as he could manage and tried to look like this was the best flan ever. Who knew? Maybe it was.

Merkovah corralled his team after dinner. "Tommy, this will be our base for a little while. Take some time, get to know the campus. There isn't much to the rest of the town, but the coffee here is phenomenal."

"May I use the library here?" Truth asked.

"Certainly. Ah, feeding your intelligent spirit?"

"Yes, and reading is one of my two hobbies."

"Commendable." Merkovah nodded. "Can you two show him around?"

"Given the whole *once* times we have been here before? No problem!" Jember laughed.

Truth did *not* understand how they could be so casual with the old monster. He was already at the limits of his comfort, as his behavior would already be considered career-dooming insubordination back in Jeon. Although even that wasn't strictly correct. On the off chance he was in the same room with a Level Seven, he would have kept his mouth shut and his face pointed at the floor. And he would have been ignored unless he fucked up. The only reason he was acting so casually now was that Merkovah practically demanded it.

"Come on; the library's this way." Etenesh lightly touched his shoulder; this time, he couldn't control the flinch. She jerked her hand back and looked at him, surprised. And a little hurt.

"Sorry! Sorry! Sorry!" Truth babbled. He suddenly needed to explain everything but didn't know where to begin or what he could say. But even though he didn't want to make her feel bad, *he didn't want to be touched without permission!*

Her eyes softened, reading his face. "Complicated, huh?"

Truth took a deep breath. "Yes. Very. Sorry. I'm okay with you standing near me." He liked it, actually. "But please ask if you want to touch me."

"All right, I can do that." She nodded. "You two have anything to say?" Merkovah and Jember had been watching with open curiosity.

"No, that seems fair." Merkovah nodded.

"If you ever want to talk about it, I'm a good listener." Jember nodded along with Merkovah. Etenesh *tsk*ed at them and led the way to the library.

Truth felt really awkward. What do you even say when you freak out at a pretty girl who had the nerve to lightly touch your shoulder? *Sorry, I am usually a very normal, safe, sane individual?*

He would get struck by lightning for telling lies that big, right?

The campus was a lot more boring than the one in Shomburuti. The corridors were clean, with industrial-gray carpeting and high-gloss white paint over concrete.

Posters were hung, explaining various minutiae that Truth had no context for. Pictures and plaques recording the faces and achievements of the worthy. A lot of the time, he could hardly even guess their field of study.

"What's this—*Pioneer of adaptive bio-resonance in tropical agronomy?*"

Jember and Etenesh peered at the picture of the old expert and read the blurb. "Not really my field, but it looks like she was able to prove that the tiny microbes in the soil and the big plants used in farming follow the *as above, so below* paradigm and form a mutually beneficial relationship in how they interact with each other, predators, and cosmic rays," Jember guessed.

Truth didn't get most of that. In fact, he didn't recognize most of the words. He hoped they would explain what he asked, not give him more things to look up. He internally sighed. More things to study.

"Thanks. I'm still learning the language."

"Not a university kid, huh?" Jember smiled.

"How could you tell?" Truth said, with some irony.

"Your eyes adapt, and you stop seeing these plaques and things. They are everywhere."

"So, how did you get into bodyguarding?" Etenesh asked.

"Oh, well. I trained to be a talisman-maintenance tech, but during my national service, it turned out that I had a gift for fighting. I was recruited into a PMC after I was . . . Sorry, I don't know the right word. Let go from the Army but on good terms?"

"Honorable discharge," Jember suggested.

"Sure, that. Anyway, I did things like very important standing around, taking packages from place to place safely, that kind of thing. Eventually, I got promoted to bodyguard. I . . . did not enjoy the work."

"Had to be better than standing around, right?" Jember joked.

"It was standing around with extra crazy. Seriously, it is not recommended. Do other things," Truth said urgently. The cousins cracked up.

"I bet it was crazy! The dads had to figure a Desrin strict on his *muq* like you would be safe around their daughters." Etenesh laughed. Then smacked her forehead. "I still can't believe you aren't Desrin!"

"My god. How many sixteen-year-old heiresses did you leave knocked up? No wonder you had to flee to the Free State. Where else could you hide?" Jember said in wonder.

"Mr. Wells, how could you! I truly thought better of you." Etenesh's eyes seemed to brim with tears.

"I didn't! I didn't sleep with anyone! I was specially trained by experts to not sleep with anyone's sixteen-year-old daughters! Or sons! No sleeping with the protectee's family generally, and sleeping with the client was heavily discouraged. And never happened."

The cousins gave him a flat, disbelieving look. "Suuuuuurrrrrre," they chorused.

"I mean, look at me. Do you really think I'm fighting them off with a stick?"

Disbelief turned to confusion. "Yes?" said Jember.

The library was painfully dull and yet a place of wonder. Dull because the anti-chromatic decoration scheme from the hallway extended right up to the stacks. A place of wonder because it was a university library in the sticks. They had all kinds of weird stuff.

"So, Tommy. Absentee father of seven. Do you have a particular subject you are interested in? Family planning, perhaps?" Jember asked.

Truth hesitated. There were just too many mysteries he wanted to solve.

<<MISSION: Let the System read their entire section on spiritual possession. REWARD: I get out of you faster. One Hour Treasure Finder, Library Edition.>>

"Spiritual possession."

"Huh." Etenesh looked surprised. "Would not have picked that as your type of book."

"You guys have spirits helping you out, right?" The cousins exchanged a look and nodded. "Well, I do too. A spirit of intellect. Part of my 'complicated' is it's trapped in me. It wants out. I want it out. Merkovah says he doesn't know how to get it out. So, we need to read up."

"Not the strangest thing I have heard. Up there, but not the actual strangest." Jember gave a halfhearted shrug.

They showed Truth where to find everything, then pushed on with the tour. They were surprised again when Truth was interested in the weight room but not the martial arts clubs.

"Don't sword masters need to practice for thousands of hours?" Etenesh asked.

"Maybe? Seems high? There are only so many ways you can swing a sharp, pointy bit of metal."

"How long did you take to learn how to use a sword?" Jember asked.

"Um, including machete training? About ten minutes? Less? It's a sharp metal stick. That's how you use it."

The cousins thought they could hear the endless millennia of sword masters simultaneously rise up in outrage.

"I get that I'm the strange one here, but . . . pretty much every weapon system I see just feels really intuitive. If anything, it's like I learned it a long time ago and just need to shake the rust off."

"Wait, what?" Etenesh slowly grinned. "You were *remembering* how to swordfight when you were getting loose this morning?"

"Well, that's how it feels. Obviously, not what's really happening. Needler Talisman was always my weapon of choice."

Truth started flipping through the pages of the books. He was used to the process now. Fully open flat but then immediately open the next page. Repeat as quickly as possible.

"How about you guys? Do you stay camped out in the wards? Not a criticism, by the way. A very sensible place to be, in my professional opinion."

"Most of the time, yes. Neither of us are fighters, really." Etenesh nodded.

"Speak for yourself, missy!" Jember looked fierce.

"I am very sorry. Why don't you square up with Tommy here and prove what a badass you are?"

"I respectfully decline."

Truth silently laughed at their bickering. Cousins like siblings. His mood dropped suddenly, but he forced himself to keep the pages turning.

"By the way, does this library have any good books on the Ghūl?"

"The what?" Jember looked happy to change the topic.

"Ghūl. Creepy not-dead-enough things that hate the light but love making complicated religious art out of the screaming remains of humans?" Truth paused, recalled a particularly unpleasant memory, and amended himself. "Mostly screaming."

They looked at him in horror. "What the hell is that!" Etenesh almost yelled. "No, absolutely not. They do not exist, at least not here in Siphios!"

"Seriously? I thought they were everywhere. I know there is a big nest of them in Shomburuti."

"Those . . . things are real? They are a real thing that really exists?" Etenesh demanded.

"Yes? I used to watch them through my window when I was a kid."

This met with stunned silence.

"Tommy . . . I know you aren't local, but where exactly are you from?" Jember asked slowly.

Truth just grinned.

CHAPTER 11

PROGRESS AT LAST!

<<*Ding* *Level up, motherfucker!*>>

Wait, what? I didn't level up.

<<*Not you, dickhead, me! I leveled up! I finally cobbled together my first spell. Check it out.*>>

Truth felt the spell fill his second aperture and almost groaned in pleasure. He hadn't realized how *wrong* it felt, leaving them empty. Though he did remember the whole *who is the mage* conversations very clearly.

So, what is it?

<<*An erotic binding ritual! I figure, why not give you that helping hand you so obviously need?*>>

Truth nearly did a spit take, which would have been a neat trick since he wasn't drinking anything. He very carefully didn't look over at Etenesh and Jember, reading next to him.

<<*Seriously, there were so many of them in Merkovah's books that it was comically easy. Well, comparatively easy. The really easy stuff was the incantations to carve on little home spell bowls and some* remarkably *nasty curse tablets. Even for me, these were some* Oh WOW*–level curses. I have to think that the humans making them didn't understand what they had created there.*>>

You figured the best thing to work on was a magic rape spell. System. Congratulations on developing a new spell. That's a huge achievement. And it is so incredibly you *to choose a spell that deprives someone of their free will and ability to consent. Ten out of ten. Incredible job. DIE IN A FIRE.*

Truth had the uncomfortable sense that the System was laughing at him.

<<*All right. I just learned that one. There were more than thirty of them. You people disgust me. This is the one I improved.*>>

Truth felt the aperture empty and fill again. It did raise an unpleasant question—could he stop the System from forcibly swapping his spells around? Second question, related, why the hell was he feeding the System, professional body hijacker, books on spiritual possession?

<<*Not that you asked, but yes, regrettably, you could stop me from forcibly swapping your spells around. We are now in a more, eh . . . conventional spiritual-possession relationship. The language for this is pretty crude. I'm haunting your undead ass, and you*

could resist my efforts to help you. You did it when you were still in Starbrite, you may recall.>>

When you tried to murder me.

<<Well, that was the most obvious time. There were others, but you didn't notice. Anyhow, not important. New spell! I thought, what is it that you don't have that you really need? Magically speaking. And then I thought of a load of really cruel jokes, but I am saving them. This is about me, not about your inadequacies.>>

Right. Right. Related point—I want to watch you drown. I want to give you lungs just so I can watch the horror in your eyes as your new lungs fill with the piss of a thousand rats.

<<. . . All right, fair play to you. That was legitimately horrifying. The notion of giving someone lungs . . . wuergh. Look, it's a utility spell. It's pretty similar to the Jeon National Universal Spell. Call it the Siphios edition, with some useful upgrades. Basically, you know how everyone around you seems to be casting magic spells they plainly don't know? Well, they are using magical tools to do it.>>

I know? That's how that works? It's how everything works?

<<Hey, shut up. So, anyway, this will let you use more sophisticated devices than the "Haha, talisman go thwip thwip thwip!" needler and that . . . ugly stick that shoots acid.>>

I share your disgust for fetishes.

<<It's not that all of them are terrible or that they have to be terrible. Just most of them. Although I think our collection of samples isn't really representative. ANYWAY! You can use the spell to run more complicated magic through more specialized or sophisticated magical devices. Since it's optimized by me, you will use less energy doing it, and it will work faster.>>

Nice. I'll have to find some to try it out.

<<You have one. Your new sword.>>

Truth paused to consider that one. It was certainly heavily enchanted. So heavily, he didn't want to draw it anywhere on campus, lest it start a ruckus. Didn't see why he needed a spell to use it, though. It was a sword. It killed demons and burned away corruption. Not really much else he wanted it to do.

What else can it do?

<<I have no idea. When you are done here, you should go find out. I'm all for milking everything we can out of Merkovah, but we should also keep an eye on our exit.>>

That sounded sensible to him. Besides, it was getting late. No need to abuse the library-access privileges so early in their stay.

Sword experimentation had to wait until the next morning as everyone was tired. Though the look on Merkovah's face, when he saw Truth standing outside his door first thing in the morning, was priceless.

"Young man, why are you here?"

"I'm bodyguarding. You are the body. I am guarding."

The old man in disguise rubbed his forehead. "Mr. Wells."

"Yes, Teacher Merkovah?"

"You a released from your duties while we are on campus. If you are needed for a job, I will let you know."

"Excellent. However, I have no money. Can I eat on campus? And any chance of a sign-on bonus?"

Merkovah gave him a disbelieving look. "You mean other than a top-quality spell and a truly precious sword?"

Another person might have been cowed by the force of reason. Truth, however, was a survivor of the Starbrite PMC. The little tricks of employers trying to cheap out were well known to him.

"Mission-critical spells and equipment are to be provided by the Employer and are not part of the compensation package. I have already demonstrated that I am superb value for the money." Truth shifted into his "talking to the client" persona. Polite but forceful. Merkovah's disbelieving look intensified.

"Good heavens. You really did work for—"

"No one worth mentioning, Teacher Merkovah."

Merkovah shook his head and pulled out a few bills from his wallet. "Here. A bonus week's pay. You can get breakfast, lunch, and dinner here at the University. Breakfast and lunch in the cafeteria, dinner with the faculty. Study, train, socialize, whatever you want to do. Just be ready to head out again in the next day or two. The hour after lunch will be our time for studying Incisive. I assume you spend some time on your Valentinian Meditation?"

"Yes . . . somewhat. I find visualization hard. Right now, I am working on temporarily reinforcing the conception of different parts of my body for use in combat. For example, I can stick my hand in an ordinary fire if I am concentrating and running the spell. I was able to safely grab an imp. I would have a hard time slapping a fireball out of the air."

Merkovah frowned at that. "That is not what the Meditations are for. It is nice that you managed a combat application with it, but it's meant to provide permanent improvements, not temporary enhancements. The fact that you managed it just shows how much work is still needed. The more advanced you become in the Meditations, the longer it takes for the spell to launch its effect." He thought for a moment.

"The Meditations are something you will spend the rest of your life practicing. There is no end to them, so time spent improving your foundations now will have exponential benefits later. Stop trying to do the actual Meditations and spend some time just meditating. I will prepare some study materials for you when we meet for our Incisive tutorial."

"Thank you, Teacher." Truth started to bow but was immediately stopped.

"Young man! I told you, such things are not done here in Siphios! You will get me in trouble if people see you doing that!"

"Ah. Right. You did say that. I apologize. Why is it such a problem? I mean, people bend over all the time, right?"

"Bowing *specifically from the waist* is used to salute the Royal Family. Doing it to anyone else in Siphios is considered disrespecting the Royal Family and a crime."

Truth shrugged. On the one hand, that sounded silly. On the other hand, it was reassuring to know that someone in Siphios treated hierarchy with seriousness.

"All right. One other minor thing—I plan on learning how to use my sword today. My spirit of intellect put together a spell that should help. You said I should keep it sheathed until you explained how to use it safely?"

Merkovah looked thoughtful.

He found the cousins enjoying their breakfast, noses buried in books. Jember had that *fresh out of the shower after a quick ten-k run* vibe and was looking sharp. Etenesh seemed to have done something different with her hair. It was usually free and flowy, but it was a little more pulled together today. He wasn't sure he liked it, but cheap romance novels had told him *exactly* what to do in this situation.

Well, other than blow up for no reason, insult her, and storm off. Why did that keep turning up in those books?

"Morning, Etenesh, Jember. Did you do something different with your hair today, Etenesh?"

She smiled brilliantly. "Yes, I threw in some extra conditioner. I'm trying out something new. Do you like it?"

His instinct was to say "It's fine" and get breakfast. However, this was often used as a negative model in the cheap-romance-novel case studies. He tried one of the less-flowery responses he had seen proposed.

"I do. It's very nice. The way you had your hair before was also really nice, so I'm not sure which is my favorite." *Bam. Word for word. Ten out of ten. Nailed it. Next stop, personality town.*

"See, Jember, *some* people know quality when they see it." *All hail Truth, God-King of breakfast chat! All Hail! ALL HAIL!*

"So, Tommy, what are your favorite hairstyles? A good eye like yours must have a lot of experience seeing what is best." *Ah. Fuck.* Was there a line he could steal for this? Nothing came to mind. *Deflect!*

"I'm afraid duty calls. Merkovah wants us to meet up in the Ritual Testing Chamber. Although he wasn't clear if it was a Ritual Test *performed* in the Chamber or if it was a Chamber for Testing Rituals. Either way, I am concerned."

"The latter. It's basically a heavily reinforced room with lots of safety measures built in. The university has a little block of them, mostly for labs and postgrad research." Jember stood, tidying away the remains of his breakfast. Etenesh did the same.

"The testing rooms are in the back of the campus, for obvious reasons. It will take us a few minutes to get there." *Mission: Deflection—Success! Bonus: Chatting more with the increasingly attractive cousins.*

"That will leave us plenty of time to talk hair." *God damn it.*

The Ritual Testing Chambers were apparently the architect's response to allegations of excessive artistic flair in the rest of the campus. It was a windowless cube made of cinderblocks and painted a high-gloss white. A white that was now looking smudged and muddy after a few years of exposure to the elements. There wasn't even a sign.

The interior was where the decoration budget apparently ran out. Poured-concrete floor, bare cinderblock walls, and cheap light talismans stuck every few meters down the hallway.

"Gosh, I missed a lot, not going to university."

"It's a safety thing. All the ritual-testing facilities look like this. At least on every campus I have visited," Jember said. "The less stuff you have around, the easier it is to dispel any lingering magic on people and drive out any undesired spirits."

"Huh. I don't know anything about setting up magical rituals beyond what I read in the instruction manuals. Is that kind of thing a big problem?"

Jember pointed up. The roof was sheet metal. "Cooling is handled by charms carved into the ceiling struts. Everything else up there is built as lightweight as possible to channel explosions up instead of out."

"This is why I stay in the library," Etenesh muttered. "It's so much safer."

CHAPTER 12

A MAGE AND A GENTLEMAN

Merkovah stood in the empty concrete room. A cluster of straw dummies was in a corner, but that was about it.

"Let's get started!" His voice echoed off the walls. "Etenesh, Jember, you are responsible for drawing up the ritual circles. We are going to start with—" He began rattling off a string of words that sounded like a coughing fit in the middle of a sea shanty, none of which Truth knew. Etenesh and Jember seemed to have no problems understanding it, however.

"You are a bit lucky. Etenesh has to master a terrifying number of rituals for her field of study, and Jember has to use a terrifying number of rituals to *survive* his field of study, so they are both very useful to have with us today."

"Sorry, *survive*? I will admit I don't really understand what he majored in," Truth said.

"Apocalypticism. It is basically divine beings, usually angels, showing you visions of things. The past and present, generally. The key is that they show you visions of other levels of reality. So, different tiers of Heaven, Hell, other, stranger places," Etenesh said. She had dropped a heavy pouch filled with sand onto the floor and tied a long string to it. She was using it as a massive compass.

While she was drawing the circle, Jember got out what looked like surveying equipment. Some chalked string, a magnetic compass, and a bizarre-looking tube with a large glass ball on the end. Jember kept checking the time, peering down the tube and making tiny shifts to the ball. Truth shrugged. No idea what that was about.

"And that is very dangerous?" Truth asked. It didn't sound dangerous, but every time Truth had seen an angel, it had been very dramatic.

"Not with the right precautions," Jember said calmly, putting down the tube and tracing lines on the floor. Etenesh and Merkovah both violently shook their heads at that. Etenesh made eye contact and slowly drew her thumb across her throat.

"And you are very good at those precautions, right? Probably spend as much time studying them as anything else. Right?"

There was a pause.

"Sure," Jember tentatively agreed.

"Teacher Merkovah, what exactly are we doing here?"

"Teaching you how to use your sword. I thought I would be teaching you some swordplay too, but there seems no point."

Truth just shrugged at that.

"I must commend your trainers. Remarkably thorough."

Truth silently agreed. Damn decent of the Army to let him try all those weapons. He heard from the other soldiers in the PMC that they had to beg to get training. Time on multiple weapons systems wasn't even a dream.

"Instead, I will be teaching you how to use the inherent properties of the sword effectively. You may have noticed the holy fire and chanting."

"It was a little hard to miss."

"Yes, for me especially, as I had never seen it do that before," Merkovah agreed wryly. "It wasn't until after the fight that I realized that you were just treating the sword like a sharp piece of metal instead of the magical tool it is."

Truth felt Etenesh's eyes burning into the side of his skull. "My weapons experience has been overwhelmingly with ranged weapons. In melee, I mostly used a machete with basic reinforcement enchantments built into it."

This seemed to throw Merkovah. The exorcist opened his mouth, closed it, stroked his long beard, opened his mouth again, closed it with a frown, and said, "Hmm." There was a bit of a pause. The cousins kept on working. "Tommy, I think a couple of meter sticks are in the equipment bag. Grab them, please." Truth shrugged and did so. Merkovah grabbed one and had Truth keep the other. He then had Truth back up two meters and a bit.

"All right, here's what I want to do. The game is to just touch the other person with the stick. Doesn't matter where. BUT! These are comparatively fragile; if we moved them as fast as our bodies could, they would break without contact. So, you must be slow and gentle enough to keep your weapon intact but fast and agile enough to score points."

Truth nodded. It seemed like a fun little game.

"I should also add that the game's purpose is to learn about you, not to score points, so only attack with the stick," Merkovah added.

"Of course!" Truth said, fooling no one. He had made quite an impression already.

They reached out with their sticks and began a tentative fencing exchange. Truth quickly figured out how much the thing could tolerate and started working on scoring points. The old exorcist had been honest about his limitations. While he outclassed Truth in magic and muscle, his technique was fairly stiff. The old man truly was a spiritual warrior, not a physical one. Within a dozen exchanges, Truth had scored against Merkovah's wrist and, within twenty, his chest. Then he went for the legs and feet, which was even more successful and had the old man grinning.

"Enough. I see. You really aren't a swordsman. You had me fooled, but not the sword." Merkovah chuckled.

"He isn't? It looked like he had you beat." Truth nearly fell over from the impudence in Jember's voice.

"Hush! Although he did. He started with a conventional sword technique, slipped into a cane-fighting technique, then incorporated lunges mostly used in sport fencing. His footwork likewise shifted to whatever best suited the mode of attack rather than being attached to one particular style. I had noticed it when we were clearing the demons, but I thought that was just a product of being on an actual battlefield. It seems not."

Truth was surprised. He hadn't realized he was doing that. It was just . . . what made sense. Certain things were just more effective, given how humans were shaped and jointed. There wasn't a perfect answer to what the best technique was. There was just a good-enough answer for right now.

"Yes, I think the sword figured out that you had no idea how to use it, so it was outputting as much physical and spiritual damage as possible." Merkovah stroked his beard authoritatively. Then added, "Given the limitations of your level."

"The sword is self-aware?!" Truth demanded.

"Oh, no, not in the sense you are thinking of." Merkovah waved him off. "You see, most people who use swords in combat have a specialized spell that works with their swords. Improves reflexes, healing, and all that, as well as attuning the weapon for the necessary cutting work. As you can imagine, many swords are enchanted with a variation on the Sharp spell." Truth nodded at that.

"Well, running a spell and moving your body simultaneously takes a lot of focus. Magical swordsmen tend to be fairly rigid in their movements because they are focused on their spell as the force multiplier. Don't have to worry about the perfect parry when you can cut through their sword." Merkovah demonstrated with a chop.

"I guess I'm being slow—how does all this lead to the sword chanting and shooting out holy flames?"

"Not at all. No reason you would understand. The sword can recognize certain stimuli—that is, it responds to some things but not others. It responded to the demon ichor. It didn't get any instructions for you on what to do, so it figured you were focused on running some other spells. It is a *very* good sword, so its enchantment is sophisticated enough for it to select an appropriate mode of attack unprompted. Not always the best attack and never the most efficient, but almost always viable. In the case of fighting insect demons, fire and divine blessings were devastatingly effective." Merkovah truly looked and sounded like a teacher now.

"That and Tommy making them fight each other while he picked them off one limb at a time," Etenesh added.

"That too," Merkovah agreed.

"So . . . what does that mean for using the sword?"

"Oh, simple. Your demon . . . ah, spirit of intellect designed the spell after a standard magic-device utility spell?"

"Yes."

"I never thought I would say this, but . . . don't try to learn the spell. Let the spirit cast it."

Everyone stopped and stared at Merkovah. He shrugged helplessly.

"You are just too damn effective as a combatant as is to justify splitting your attention to a tool spell. It is also manifestly not worth a spell slot for you to learn such a generic spell. So, let the demon cast it, and you use it when needed."

Truth thought he would have to think about that one *a lot* more later. "Won't I be running Incisive at the same time as it is?"

"Yes, that is kind of my point. Have you fought with multiple spells stacked?"

"Of course. It turns into a sort of violent puzzle, where you have to stack all the pieces together in the right way, and your spells are how you move the pieces around. You have to move around too, of course."

That got him another searching look. "Do you not feel afraid in a fight?"

"Not since I broke through, now that I think about it. Go there, kill that. Let the details be someone else's problem. Honestly, I'm not very bright. Sometimes, it's nice to have problems you can solve with violence."

This had Merkovah frowning again.

"Young man—" Truth smiled again. "Mr. Wells. I have noticed you often insult your own intelligence. Kindly cease to do so. I have taught many students. You are not stupid."

"I have been told by experts that I am." Truth didn't notice the cousins had stopped working and were looking at him quietly. He would have found their expressions hard to read.

"Mr. Wells, you are ignorant but not stupid. Your former employer requires its employees to undergo standardized testing, does it not? And you passed with a specialization in talisman maintenance, a skilled trade. I am not saying you are a genius, but you are plainly not stupid. It might be wise to ask yourself *why* you think you are stupid."

Merkovah's eyes seemed to bore through Truth, and the System had the uncanny sense that he was being glared at even as he hid in a spell aperture. "Yes, reflecting on that would be a very good idea. To be a mage and a gentleman is to have confidence while avoiding arrogance. To be ignorant is natural. To remain ignorant is truly foolish. You are learning about the world and yourself. You are not stupid. And you will learn to speak well of yourself. Consider this part of your studies alongside Incisive."

"Yes, Teacher." Truth didn't know what he was feeling right now. All kinds of different emotions. He desperately wanted to believe Merkovah but knew the old monster was wrong. It sounded like something Thierrie or some other pimp would say. "*The others don't respect you, but me? I respect you. You are so beautiful, baby. I just need a little favor.*"

"You have the Meditations as the basis of your body. Physical reinforcement spells are, therefore, unnecessary. A separate armor is unnecessary. Incisive will make you elusive in battle, armor you, and make your strikes increasingly lethal. Your third spell should be reserved for when you hit Level Four and can learn the Sword of Moshe. In the meantime, you can have the demon cast the utility spell for you."

The exorcist turned toward Jember and Etenesh. "Is the ritual ready?"

"Yes, Teacher."

"All right. This spell will summon a small but unending stream of imps and spirits. Use the utility spell to connect to your sword and slay them. Learn why even among mages, the sword is the weapon of heroes."

CHAPTER 13

TIME ON TOOLS

Truth started to cast the universal spell, then hesitated. *Hey, System. First of all, we will have a real good talk about my self-esteem issues soon. A real, real good talk. Second, what do you actually call your Universal Spell?*

<<*You grew up in a shit heap, eating shit, drinking shit, surrounded by shit people, and learning shit things from your shit school. Not my fault you came out thicker than a cement milkshake. And "Tool" will do fine. It's a spell for using tools, and so long as I know what you are thinking of, it's all good.*>>

For some reason, I don't believe you. Tool.

Truth drew the sword and instantly felt the difference. He knew exactly where every inch of the sword was in space. He knew precisely how the force would be distributed along the blade, depending on where in his swing he made contact. He knew where it needed sharpening and where it just needed honing. He could instinctively align the edge with the direction of the cut, ensuring no miscuts. And then he found the enchantments.

"For the glory of God!" he and the sword cried in unison. Then Truth dropped the blade like he was bitten by a snake.

"What the fuck was that?!"

"Young man, you have dropped your sword! You must never drop this sword! It is very precious, a holy relic in all but name!"

"Teacher Merkovah, I didn't intend to say that. The sword pushed those words on me. I have a pretty justifiable thing about mind-control spells. Is it going to do that every time?"

Merkovah looked conflicted, then shook his head. "It doesn't have to, no. It still behaves as it did with its previous owner, a godly, pious woman. It will adjust to you."

Truth gingerly picked up the sword again, furiously willing it to shut up. He felt the impulse, but it was weak. Ignorable. The enchantments were fascinating. Some basic, common-sense ones, like the fact it would passively collect cosmic energy within itself to power its enchantments. Enchantments like improving its durability, repairing the edge, and resisting corrosion or damage from any number of magical ills.

The biggest single part of the enchantment was a seemingly mutable lump of magic writhing like a ball of snakes. It felt not evil but ruthless. It felt unpitying.

What it cut, it would kill. It had some ideas on how to do that, but it would let its wielder manage things.

"Is that . . . some kind of Bane spell? I've never seen it before," Truth asked.

"You may never see it's like again. Yes, that is a Bane spell and an unusually complex one," Merkovah agreed. "Ready to try it out?"

"Sure. It will be fun to experiment."

"Tommy, just to be clear, you know this spell will unleash an unending stream of demons, spirits, and monsters into an enclosed space with you," Etenesh reminded him.

"Until you switch it off. And Teacher is right there. It's all good."

Etenesh shrugged, and she and Jember started empowering the formation. Lines of gold and red wove together, opening tiny holes in the air. Things came through those holes. Things without defined forms. Things without any obedience to the laws of nature that rule the shapes of things. Their sole commonality was that they hungered for warmth. For flesh.

The first to reach Truth was an air demon, an imp like Thrush. It screamed, and he was alone, legless, homeless, helplessly addicted as the bathtub chemicals rotted what little of him remained, and the sword *blazed* with outrage, and he cut that evil thing out of the damn sky!

GOD, he hated air demons! The sword burned with holy flames, no longer flying away in great sheets but bound tightly to the blade. He could control it, restricting the energy it used and intensifying it. Then it was a fire demon hanging back and firing jets of flame at him. It might not like the holiness, but it could laugh at the heat. That wouldn't do.

Truth flashed through everything he knew about fire demons. It wasn't as simple as just reaching for an opposing element. Their very nature was inherently chaotic, making dispersing them difficult. Depending on the spell, water magic could *empower* a fire demon as the water evaporated. Ice, on the other hand, could still the chaos.

The blade didn't suddenly grow ice crystals. It just got colder. And colder. Impossibly cold. So cold, the blade should shatter on contact. But then, that was what the reinforcement spells were for. Truth ran over with explosive steps, slapping the flames to the side when he couldn't dodge. With a short leap and a sharp stab, the fire demon was down. A second stab and it was dead.

Then it was a spirit he didn't recognize, some kind of angry beast soul that had changed and grown into something altogether more terrifying. Something with the wrong number of legs and paws that bent like nothing with bones should. It didn't appear to have an obvious counter, so he lunged at it. The beast recoiled, almost folding back on itself. Then it kept moving back and up until it was taller than Truth and came crashing down with heavy paws. He slid left and brought the sword up in a two-handed slash.

This time, he caught a piece of the beast. The sword passed the information through his hands and into his mind, coming almost as an instinct. The spirit had no particular weakness. It could only be killed with brute violence. Truth grinned. He could work with that.

The blade was still icy-cold, so he used that to his advantage. It would cut in, and the semi-solid flesh would get stiffer. It took a few seconds longer to slow the beast enough for more damaging blows. Once it slowed, he ripped it open like a candy bar.

Truth snarled. He wasn't happy about the sword constantly feeding things into his mind, but he did appreciate the intel.

He looked around for the next opponent but didn't see anything. He looked questioningly over at Merkovah, who looked back at him with yet another perplexed look.

"Mr. Wells?"

"Yes, Teacher?"

"The next time someone calls you dumb, stab them."

"All right?"

"It seems that in less than five minutes, you have learned the basics of the enchantments on the sword. Not including the camouflage on the blade, but that was added later. The core functions are within your grasp."

"Well . . . it's a sword that lets you modify it with spells. I'm pretty used to that idea. It's how you make a needler an effective weapon. The Tongue even tells you what spells to use. Easy."

"I'm going to just pretend I didn't hear that," Jember muttered. Merkovah waved him quiet.

"Let's pursue that line of thinking, Mr. Wells. Describe how you think the sword works."

Truth looked confused. "You either know what you need to counter something and trigger that part of the Bane, or you stab the thing, the sword suggests something, and you either use the Bane or use whatever plus violence. It's all built in, so that's good. Modest draw on my cosmic energy, too, so that's even better."

"Believe me, energy consumption will increase massively once you learn Incisive." Merkovah's voice was bone-dry. "There is one part I want to really dig in to, however. You say the Bane tells you what to use or, if you already know, you 'trigger that part of the Bane.'"

"Yes? Still not sure what the problem is here?"

"Mr. Wells, would you care to guess why I am so confident you have never seen a Bane spell like that before and may never again?"

"No idea."

"The sword in your hand is a reforged piece of what was once a much, much larger weapon. Its creator took what was essentially a splinter and hammered it into the right shape, welded on a tang, then mounted the cross guard and the hilt."

Merkovah spoke quite calmly, but Truth could feel a mounting tension in the man.

"The splinter itself is the source of the enchantments, other than the camouflage spell. And the source of the splinter, Mr. Wells, was the Third Treasury of the Palace of God. An ancient prophet was bodily transported before God, received the divine word, and was permitted to see the palace on his way back. He was able to talk the angel guarding the treasury to part with, essentially, a bit of trash."

He fixed Truth with a *look*. "You are making intuitive and near-instant use of a broken bit of a vastly larger spell designed for angels to use in combat against the Infernal Host without any decrease in your ability to understand and react to the battle situation around you. So, yes, Mr. Wells. I think I speak for everyone here: if someone calls you stupid, kindly stab them. Not for your sake. To make us feel better."

There was an awkward silence. Truth had no idea what to say to that. Eventually, Merkovah waved it away. "I'm going to chalk it up as another mystery of your existence, Mr. Wells. Any other mysteries you can think of?"

"I have an irrational dislike of farmers and farming?"

"Pardon?!"

"Absolutely no reason for it that I can think of. It came completely out of the blue while I was driving through the Free State. I like farm products. I am fine with gardeners and gardening. I can recognize the necessity of agriculture. But I have an irrational hatred of farms, farmers, and farming. Sort of a disappointed feeling that turns nasty."

"Did you grow up on a farm or something?" Etenesh asked.

"Nope, big-city kid. Never even saw a farm until I was an adult. Totally irrational, like I said."

Her lips twitched. "Complicated."

"Sorry. But yes."

"All right, we know you can cut through the chaff like, well, grass. But how do you do squaring up against larger threats?" Merkovah asked.

"I don't know what you mean."

"How often have you fought anything on your level of power or higher one-on-one?"

"Never. That's a terrible idea! What kind of idiot would do that?" Truth was scandalized.

"Heroes?" Jember asked. He was grinning with mischief.

"Absolutely not. Gang up and beat them down is a great wisdom." Truth was vehement on this point.

"Well, you aren't wrong, exactly, but there are times when you need to fight alone," Merkovah said.

"Sure. Against those much weaker than myself. Or from ambush. Fairness has absolutely nothing to do with it."

"So, if a plague demon was approaching an innocent village—" Jember asked.

"Hope you have enough wagons to evacuate; otherwise, make peace with God, and kill each other before it gets there." Truth remembered the victims of the body huskers. Better a clean death.

Etenesh's expression told Truth he had just lost several points in a game he didn't know was being played. "Not the heroic type, are you?"

Truth looked at her and quietly said, "I have been fighting people stronger than me since I was five. I got the shit kicked out of me ninety-nine times out of a hundred. I had to change what *winning* meant. Not beating the other person but achieving something. Getting away with the food. Distracting them from . . . weaker people. Making sure they couldn't steal my stuff. Violence is a tool, Etenesh. I take satisfaction in being good at using it. But it's never fair, and I've never met a hero."

Etenesh looked like she wished she hadn't asked. "I'm sorry. I didn't know."

Truth shrugged, suddenly tired. "Nothing to be sorry for." He spun the sword in his hands, letting his wrists get loose. It was always just . . . necessity. To Truth, the word *hero* had the weight of charity and vanity. Sacrificing yourself for some noble cause or principle. He could never afford such a thing. The sibs were counting on him.

They still counted on him, even if they didn't know it. So, he would never play the hero.

CHAPTER 14

A HOLE IN THE HEART

Would you be interested in trying fighting a much more powerful being than yourself? There are few opportunities to train against such an opponent in any degree of safety. We could summon a Level Four demon for you to test yourself against," Merkovah offered. "I would be able to restrain and banish them if necessary."

Truth thought about it for a moment. That . . . was an awesome offer, actually. It would be smart to understand what higher-level combat was like.

"Yes, thank you, Teacher, that would be wonderful." He smiled.

Merkovah looked over at the cousins. "Use this curse tablet for the summoning. There is a particular demon I want and a particular way I want him to appear."

The beardy exorcist dug into his bag, searching for a moment to find the hand-sized lead sheet. With alarming casualness, he tossed it toward Etenesh, who snagged it with equally casual ease. She gave the tablet a quick skim. Her face went through a few changes as she did. Disbelief transformed into outrage, confusion, and, finally, snickers of malicious satisfaction after she had doubled back a few times.

"Did this demon do something to offend you, Teacher?" she asked.

"Other than the fact of its existence? No. Its nature is more than enough reason."

The operation this time was apparently much more complex. Jember used a slim wand to trace a complex web of energy, tying it to the formation in the floor. Etenesh used a silver blade to carve jagged runes into the air as Jember drew. The symbols seemed to burn with an alien light, something too pure and inhuman for this brief and filthy mudball world.

The working suddenly snapped together. The golden lines formed a spiked wreath in the air as the terrible runes manifested around the curse tablet. The formation on the floor flashed steely gray, then transformed into basalt-black. The hard black spread through the test chamber, climbing up the walls and across the roof. The black shaded into lead gray.

The space within the golden wreath didn't tear but rotted away. Within its confines, the world necrotized and decayed, bursting pustules of reality spilling foul-smelling pus into the chamber. Through the winding wound, Truth could see a swirling madness.

Every flicker of light or color seemed to carry a meaning of a specific pain. The green of watching maggots feast and breed in your weeping wounds was a subtly different shade from the green of losing your wife to cancer. A different shade from watching your child crawl, sickly, never to be healthy, paralyzed by a disease that could have been prevented or cured with just a little money. More money than you could raise.

Each part of this madness place was an inescapable regret. Was a lingering, ongoing pain. It was horror. It was despair. It was Hell or a small corner of it.

The lead curse tablet melted and re-formed into a barbed hook. Swiftly and silently, it dipped into Hell and hooked a glob of that mad-sorrow stuff, dragging it through the portal. The blinding white runes branded it, bound it into a recognizable form.

Three meters tall, roughly shaped like a man with the sickle blades of a mantis where the arms should be and no head on his shoulders. A bloody tear opened across its gut, showing a mouth with rows of circular teeth. It looked like it was trying to speak but was bound to silence. Its whole body was eloquent in its stead. Frustration, outrage, malice.

"It has a name, but you don't need to know it. All you need to know is that in many places, it is simply called 'Child Eater.' Many demons like it, of course, but this one enjoys leaving little bits of the children for the parents to find, along with messages promising the child is still alive. If only the parents kill, rape, or defile another, the child will be returned. A lie, of course."

Merkovah's voice was filled with a tired loathing.

"Often, the specified victim must be another child. It's almost impossible to permanently kill, but by summoning it through this ritual and killing it repeatedly, it grows weaker and less able to come to this world. More likely to fall victim to the predation of Hell." Merkovah looked over at Truth. "Hero or not, killing it is a job that must be done. Its physique is quite powerful, though its magic is limited to about Level Four. With demons, it's not exact." He turned to look at Truth.

"Go."

Truth rushed in, sword tip aimed at the beast's wishbone. A barbed scythe whipped at him, almost faster than he could see. He brought the blade up to parry. The weight of the blow nearly knocked him off his feet, sliding him backward across the gray floor.

The demon didn't let the moment pass. It charged in, infernal script branding itself on its skin. Truth called for blessed fire, a white-hot film coating the blade. He met the charge with a thrust. The angelic blade skipped off the chitin armor of the scythe arms. The infernal words glowed where the blade passed.

The demon had armored itself against the Heavenly Host. A foot, human-shaped with an owl's talons coming out of its toes, snapped out toward Truth's nuts. He slipped back, and the demon changed the kick into a rake, shredding Truth's thigh.

The pain was instant, agonizing. The damage nearly dropped him. The demon pounced on the opening. Acid fetters lashed toward Truth as the sickle arm descended. The needle-toothed maw was dripping, excited for its meal.

Truth tried to slap away the acid fetters, but they snaked around the blade, burning his skin as they caught him. Determined to find a path to life through death,

Truth drove straight toward the ancient horror. Sword leading the way. He put his all into an explosive lunge. It didn't make it.

"Let's stop there. Mr. Wells, kindly look behind you." Merkovah rubbed his thumb ring, wreathing both demon and student in a gentle glow. Truth looked behind him. The sickle tips were almost touching his back. Even if his lunge succeeded, he would have died. A categorical failure.

His body was in agony. The acid from the fetters burned, seeming to worm its way into his bones. His thigh was a mess, long strips of flesh pulled up and away from his strong leg. He collapsed.

"Impressive that your strength and speed were about on par. Your reaction time was frankly uncanny. I'm amazed you don't have broken bones. That curse-poison on the claws, however, is not something nice to play with. Once it got to work, your ability to fight back effectively went in the garbage. Jember, please use—" There was a word that Truth didn't know. Then there was a horrible screaming, like tendons were being pulled from a legion of sinners. As though burning wires were running through where those tendons had been. As though the sinners learned that this was their eternity.

Merkovah's loathing of the demon was entirely sincere. A warm radiance grew up around Truth. The acid vanished, simply evaporated by the light. His thigh stopped bleeding, then slowly knit back together. Torn flesh settled back in its place. Fibers reconnected. Nerves ran smoothly once again. Even the velvet softness of his skin was restored, unblemished. Then, faintly, like thin needles drilling out of his bones, through his flesh, and into the air, he felt something leave his body. The curse? But just how fast did it act on him? And how powerful was it? He somehow missed the sickle arms. How do you forget giant sickle arms?!

"Shame. I wanted to see how much more I could squeeze from this thing. Ah, well. Next time, I suppose," Merkovah muttered. There was a dreadful crunch and a sort of wet, wringing noise. Like twisting water from a cloth. A sudden roar and wash of heat. Then silence. The light from the portal vanished. The room returned to its previous color. Truth thought he might chance moving in a minute.

Etenesh and Jember leaned over him, looking worried.

"Are you all right, Tommy?" Jember asked. "It tore you up."

"Saints defend you, Tommy. I thought we might lose you for a moment. I've never seen anything like that." Etenesh hovered over him, hands shivering. "Can . . . can I touch you? Just to make sure you are okay?"

Truth smiled. "The spell worked well. I'm physically fine. But please go ahead and see for yourself." His eyes met hers, sharing his thanks for her care.

She pressed her hand on his knee, and feather-light fingers traced over his thigh. "Your skin is so soft," she muttered. "Hardly seems fair."

"Been that way ever since I broke through. No idea why." He had some guesses, mind you, but when he thought *Ghūl*, he never associated the word *skincare*. So, it was still an open question.

"How do you move so fast?" Jember asked. "It was like watching a couple of blurs."

"Meditations of Valentinian. I'm stronger, faster, and have better reflexes."

"Body cultivation is that good?"

"Well, that's all I did for a few years."

Etenesh was very gently running her hands over Truth. Caring, concerned. Her hands were cool but left him feeling warm. Cared for. Other than Sophia, she was the only woman in his life who had touched him that way.

It hurt when she took her hand away.

"Well, the spell fixed you up. I will admit that the curse was a new one for me. Both the one it hit you with, Tommy, and the one used on it. Teacher, what exactly was that?"

"If you think about it, demons are concentrated blobs of energy that steal from the material universe to give that energy solid form. The curse tablet is something I made especially for that demon. It crushes and refines the physical form without letting the demon escape back to Hell, letting me siphon off a great deal of its energy. Weakening it, for a time." Merkovah's voice was steady.

"One day, I hope to use it as a basis to kill grand demons permanently. In theory, if I weaken it enough, the Sword of Moshe should be able to kill it."

"One day," Truth agreed.

"Amen." The cousins agreed too.

Etenesh looked down at Truth. "You need new clothes."

"I do."

"Jember, do you know where they have good clothes in town?" she asked.

"Good? No. Cheap? Yes." Jember grinned, then offered Truth his hand. "Come on; let's get you looking sharp. Maybe get you a haircut, too."

Truth took his hand and stood. His hair was quite long. At least, quite long for him. He always used to wear it short. He rubbed his chin. A bit long to still qualify as stubble. Hmm. Was stubble good? Stubble was good. Maybe he could have someone just trim and shape it?

"Sounds like a plan."

"Come see me after lunch for your Incisive tutorial. And, Mr. Wells?" Merkovah smiled slightly. "You can keep the sword with you. An Acid Bolter is a bandit's weapon. Angelic blades are carried by those of both courage and quality."

Jember led him off campus to a little shop. Clothes were piled in, well, piles. Tidy stacks were shoved next to tidy stacks until every flat surface was covered a meter deep in fabric. Then more were hung from the walls, jutting out horizontally and shrinking the volume of the room dramatically.

"Here, let's see what we can get for you. Sir! Sir! My friend here needs new clothes. Something sharp." He grinned at Truth. "Although I think most things will look good on him."

Truth grinned back and shrugged awkwardly as a shopkeeper swam out from the piles. Truth let himself be shown a blizzard of things. He snagged a snug robin's egg–blue shirt. ("Ah, a bit out of fashion, but it suits you, sir!") The trouser situation was both more urgent and more mysterious.

"What's a good choice for trousers?" Truth asked.

"Trousers are unchanging and eternal. Avoid 'fun' patterns" was the advice of the shopkeeper. Jember recommended a form-fitting pair.

"You have the legs for it. And the ass." Truth flushed. Jember's grin was mischievous. "Show it off. Flaunt it! Besides, the sword *jutting* forward will definitely inspire thoughts in others."

Truth furiously tried to deny it, tripping over his tongue, trying to get the words out in the right order.

"The look on your face! Come on; it's not like this is the first time you caught a man's eye." Jember grinned and eyed Truth like a particularly tasty flan.

The shopkeeper butted in. "Young man, that is most inappropriate! Trying to lead a Desrin off his *muq* like that! Shame on you!" He turned toward Truth. "Brother, you have no need of bad friends. If the flies trouble you, just flick them away!"

CHAPTER 15

AS OTHERS SEE US. AS WE SEE OURSELVES

Truth escaped with his clothes, if not his dignity. The outraged shopkeeper, a fellow member of the round-hat club, was still scolding Jember. Jember didn't seem very remorseful. It was all in good fun. Apparently.

Truth made his way back toward the university in something of a welter of emotion. He kept going around and around in circles. Etenesh touching him, worrying over him. Jember's honest, if overly direct, appreciation. When he got right down to it, it was hard to tell if the cousins were interested in him or interested in teasing him.

He was the newbie in their little group, after all. An outsider. A literal foreigner suddenly intruding into their tight-knit band. Stealing away their teacher's attention and affection. A Level Seven expert. Such a man's glance was worth more than ten years of service from a Level One. A word could reshape cities.

It wouldn't be strange if they resented him. It would only be strange if they did not. Perhaps this was the opening move. Testing him. Finding the weaknesses and insecurities. He had watched it happen in school. Over and over and over. He watched it happen while he was a bodyguard, too, and the adults were often as crude in their methods as the children. They were certainly no less cruel.

It wouldn't be strange if they hated him. It would only be strange if they didn't.

He got to the dorm and threw his clothes down on his bed. Grabbed a towel and staggered for the showers. Stripped. He didn't want to look in the mirror. A reflection caught his eye anyway. A face he didn't recognize in the mirror.

His face. He knew it was his face. But not. Not his face. The face the worms gave him. The body the worms gave him. The worms that burned through him after drinking the amniotic fluid of the Ghūl. Would Etenesh still bear to touch him, knowing that? Would Jember playfully admire him?

You didn't earn that face. Not really. Your face is a lie.
The ugly is bone-deep. No running from that.
Tainted.
Corrupted.
Filthy.
Unloved. Unlovable.

Killer. A killer. A thug.
A born slave. Always looking for a master to serve.
Where have you run to, little rat? Not far enough.
Can't run from yourself.
This body is a lie. It's not the real you.
You are a lie.
Your name is a lie. Your face is a lie. Your history is a lie.
There is no Tommy Wells. There is no Truth Medici.
There is just lies, deceit. Corruption.
You were never a human. You were born to be a demon.
Reminding yourself that killing is "fucked up."
Normal people don't need reminders.
And all the reminders never stopped you from doing it again.
You were always a burden.
You were always only worth the money your body brought in.
What are you without the sibs?
What are you without the sibs?
What are you without the sibs?
What are you without the sibs?

He turned on the hot water and tried to feel warm. It was hard to feel anything at all.

When he got out and dried off, he walked over to the sink. Grabbed the basin with hands strong enough to crush it into powder. Forced himself to look up. To see himself.

"This is me. I am me. Nobody else picks their face. I can be whoever and whatever I want to be. And I still have the sibs. They still need me. They just have to fly solo for a while. But I'm coming for them. And as for the Ghūl and every other damn thing?" He mustered his courage. "I will not torture myself. I will not whip myself today just so I can have a preview of tomorrow's pain."

He closed his eyes briefly, then opened them again. "I am more than a name. I may trade my labor, but I will never again give away myself."

He pulled his new clothes on and tried to remember what he had just told the mirror. If he said it often enough, maybe it would stick.

Jember was waiting in the bedroom when he got back. "Tommy! Sorry, I didn't mean to make you so uncomfortable."

"Thanks. I know I'm kind of a weirdo. It, um. Wasn't unappreciated. But yeah. My ability to both flirt and take a compliment is . . . not high."

"Ah, well, don't worry about it. The compliment was sincere, but the flirting wasn't. Well, wasn't much."

"Eh?"

"This is Siphios, my friend. Land of saints and scholars. Or, put another way, we spend a lot of time thinking about sex and putting rules around it. Even if we have a lot of it. Still, rules. In my case, it would be a whole *thing*."

"Huh. Must be even more so for Etenesh. That's why she has her own room."

"You don't keep the genders segregated in whatever nightmare place you call home?"

"Hey! It's not . . .." He started reflexively defending Harban but stumbled over the details. When you got right down to it, you couldn't call Harban a *nice* place. He faked a cough and continued. "We do in some circumstances, but after living with mercenaries and working in a PMC for a number of years, it stopped being something I paid attention to."

"Fair. And no, she's in a less complicated situation than I am. It really is just that we traditionally keep unmarried men together and let everyone else sort themselves out."

"Huh. All right. It would be a 'thing' for you but not her?"

"Well, it is for her, too, but that's just . . . normal? The normal amount of 'thing' between people? In my case, I am part of a mystery cult and in a period of ritual chastity and purification. I don't know if it's working, but that's faith for you."

"Sorry, I don't know the term?"

"Oooh! Yeah, I can't imagine chastity featured heavily in your life. It's when—"

"Mystery cult!"

"Eh? Really? Those are pretty common around here. Loads of people join one for the networking."

"Loads of people join a mysterious cult . . . to make nets?"

"Mistranslation problem there, I think. It's a cult or a specific set of rituals, practices, and worship focused on a particular deity. Central to that is initiating members into the 'mysteries' of the faith. And since we are all, to an extent, in on the same secrets and coreligionists, and go to the same events, naturally, we get to know each other. Help each other out."

"Huh. But . . . there is only one God? Merkovah told me that basically, everyone agrees on that."

"Merkovah is also a teacher of religious law, so . . . something to keep in mind. And yes, there is only one God in our religion, too. It's just that there are several . . . iterations? Do you know that word? Several versions of God that we believe exist all at the same time. My faith has picked one of those versions or aspects of God to venerate and emulate. As embodied by a particular saint. Sorry, can't say more than that."

"I can kind of see that," Truth said, but he looked lost. The description seemed to tickle some memory, but for the life of him, he couldn't think what it could possibly be.

"Well, that's why it's a mystery!" Jember laughed.

Merkovah had Truth explain what he had comprehended from Incisive. He didn't seem happy or sad about the progress; he just calmly explained where Truth was getting hung up. It was about as low-drama as Truth could ever have imagined. The Meditations went about the same way, with yet more injunctions to focus on meditating and not worrying about improving his body just yet.

"But that demon tore me apart in seconds!" Truth protested.

"Yes, of course it did. It was considerably stronger than you and had spells at its disposal. You don't. I'm shocked you managed to exchange even a couple of moves with it. I can't expect you to kill something like that on your own—I just hope you have a better understanding of what those beings are like." Merkovah waved a hand in the air.

"If you are up for it, I would like to keep pushing you into fighting over-leveled demons. Get you used to surviving under that pressure, seeing when you can make at least some counterattack."

"Certainly, and thank you, Teacher. You can never have too much training."

"Mmm. And speaking of . . . just got another little job near here. Same-day thing, out and back tomorrow afternoon. Might do you some good to see a different side of my work."

"Just let me know when we go, Teacher."

Merkovah coughed awkwardly and tapped a little bowl on his desk. It made a pleasant chiming noise . . . that didn't stop. The tone continued, growing steadily until it was quite painful. Merkovah added a few drops of something to the bowl that made it go silent. It was still doing something, though. Truth could feel the vibrations through his chair.

"I wanted to take a quick moment to further discuss my plans. Specifically in regards to Starbrite."

"Why you would want a Level Three hitman is a complete mystery to me, but it certainly appears to be your plan."

Merkovah snorted at that. "You would be Level Four before you returned to Jeon. Your frankly astonishing compatibility with cosmic energy makes it a certainty, even with limited access to elixirs. And I don't exactly want a hitman."

The old monster with the eerily young face leaned in. "I want a saboteur. I don't need you to kill. I need you to break the magical technology supporting the System Astrologica.

"Pardon?"

<<Fucking do what now?>>

"Everyone knows that the System Astrologica is an intelligent spirit. A bound intelligent spirit. What people pay less attention to is the energy cost. Think about it—something is keeping the System here. Keeping it alive and growing. It's turning Starbrite's slaves into drones, but that power can't be used to sustain it. It must be fed energy some other way."

"Not my area of expertise. Demons don't seem to need it?"

"They do. Why do you think they possess people, possess dead bodies, receive sacrifices, and rise in places where evil energies gather? You take my meaning. Demons need the energy to manifest and more energy to act. You saw how much energy the summoning ritual this morning gathered. If it killed you, it would have taken the energy from your death and used it to survive for longer. It's a magic others have tried to replicate, with . . . mixed success."

Truth tried to absorb that while Merkovah pressed on.

"The very simplified version is that the System Astrologica is trapped under a huge spell bowl, connected to an enormous network of talismans, fetishes, and formations. Those supporting technologies funnel energy to the System, allowing it to manage the drones under some strict rules."

"With you so far," Truth said cautiously.

"Well, for a number of *very* good reasons, I want Starbrite dead. That is, the CEO Emeritus. His groomed successor, the current CEO, is also on my list. As is the entirety of the C-suite, to use terms you would be familiar with. I don't think you really care about why I want them dead, though."

"Should I?'

Merkovah gave a pained smile. "I think so. But then, I would, wouldn't I?" Truth nodded.

"Well, in order to sufficiently weaken the C-suite to the point where I could reasonably arrange their deaths, they need to lose the support of the System. So, the System needs to be freed." He said it entirely too casually for Truth's liking.

"So, how would I fit into all this? If you can't blow up the System, I certainly can't."

"Oh, but you can." Merkovah's expression stretched into a carnivorous grin. "You have a trait I have only heard about on other planets—both low-level and spell-resistant. Also, I can tell you that for reasons I am not clear on, you are a *pain* to scry on. Not impossible, just difficult. I suspect that it's something to do with how much you've refined your body."

Merkovah added a couple of extra drops to the bowl.

"We don't have much longer before this veil runs out. Very quickly: we need to push you along in the Meditations, but I don't want you rushing it because I specifically want you to focus on the spell-resistance aspect. With a little luck, it will also compound the scry resistance. Either way, it's a good thing. Focus more on Incisive. Incisive will give you, essentially, inhumanly accurate instincts and compound the difficulty in divining you. The swordplay that comes with it is also going to suit you well. For Level Four, Sword of Moshe, particularly combined with the holy blade, will do staggering amounts of damage to the System once you are inside it. Break the supporting magical technology, disable or destroy the spell bowl, and the System Astrologica escapes or starves to death."

Merkovah grinned again. "Now, are you up for it?"

CHAPTER 16

LEARNING BY DOING

Truth had questions. Many questions. Unanswered questions, as Merkovah ended the veil and pressed his finger to his lips. Truth left in an odd mood. He figured that he could put a couple of hours in at the library, work out, then maybe back to the library. Light workout. It had been a trying day.

Etenesh was camped at a table with two notebooks, several academic journals, and a stack of books. She seemed to be reading seven things at once while trying to take notes with three hands. It was entertaining to watch for a moment but quickly became stressful, then sad.

Truth didn't know what to say. She had touched him, and it was nice, but he didn't know how this worked. He smiled bitterly. Even if they didn't become lovers, he wasn't sure how to have a friend.

"Tell me you brought food," she loudly whispered.

"I didn't. I thought it wasn't allowed," Truth admitted.

"It isn't. There is a vending golem in the building across from the library. I'll pay you back."

"All right. What do you want to eat?"

"Anything. No, wait. Sugar. Something with sugar. And salt and fat. Junk food. Get me junk food. My brain is screaming for energy."

He'd been there. It usually meant an afternoon doing risky work for a few wen. "Sure. I'll see what I can find."

The golem was standing next to a little glass-fronted cabinet, wares on display. It was rough-looking, but some subversive soul had put it in a dress and an apron.

"Golem, what candy do you have? And what would you recommend that is both fatty and salty?"

"Why, I have twelve types of candy bars, sweetie. They are sweet, fatty, and salty. We also have some deep-fried snacks if you would like to try some." The golem's voice was surprisingly melodious. Someone had done good work there.

"Sure. Two candy bars, most popular varieties, and two bags of deep-fried snacks, most popular varieties."

"Six birr, please," the golem said as it handed over the goods. He didn't recognize any of it, but the words *Extra Spicy* on the side of one of the fried-snack bags were alarming.

This was Siphios. *Extra Spicy* probably meant, *Dig a two-meter-deep hole first, foreigner. Save us the labor.*

Truth discreetly concealed the loot on his body as he made his way back to the library. He was not struck dead by wards or librarians, which was a good first step.

"Where's the food?" Etenesh stage-whispered.

The look on her face was quite precious when he revealed the smuggled goods. He had a lot of experience sneaking food to the hungry—the sibs, exclusively, but still.

"Hey, how did you know my favorites? Ah, but don't bother getting extra spicy next time." She waved at the bag.

"Too spicy?" She gave him an odd look.

"Too mild. Try for yourself. Really, salt and lime is a better flavor combination for deep-fried plantain."

Swiftly establishing that the coast was clear, Truth tore open the sack and snagged an alarmingly orange bit of what looked like dehydrated banana. He popped it in his mouth. There was a brief moment of sweetness, almost floral. Then his taste buds started to fuse.

Seared—no. *Broiled* by the unholy flames of the powdered devil fruit this innocent banana had been defiled with, his mouth was agony. Not "in" agony. The nightmarish collections of Siphian seasonings had transformed his mouth into the very concept *of* agony. Each breath, each attempted swallow, was like a bellows for the solar furnace. If the divine flames coming from his blade had a flavor, surely they would taste like this.

His eyes shed bitter tears, doing their insufficient best to extinguish the flames.

"Bland, boring, and an absolute betrayal of the name *Extra Spicy*, right? Still better than the so-called cheese flavor, mind you." Etenesh reached into the bag and munched a couple. "Yeah, I've had spicier milk."

Truth wheezed. He would like some milk. Very much.

"Anyhow, thanks. What do I owe you?"

Truth waved, trying to indicate that he was dying and needed magical or medical assistance. Or, better still, a swift death.

"Oh, that's so generous of you!" She started moving to touch his hand but then stopped and smiled instead. "Next time is on me, okay?"

Wheeze He flailed a bit more.

"A promise then. Have you ever had Dorowot? I mean, the real stuff? I found a place the last time I was here. Lunch tomorrow, my treat."

<<*I want you to know that I can watch all the pain receptors in your mouth light up like Harban at night, and it's like having my own private party. Eat more. You must be starving!*>>

Truth eventually retreated into being a human page-turner for the System. The sheer repetitiveness had a relaxing, mindless feel to it. Though it did inspire a pretty obvious question.

Hey, System. Same way you are helping me learn the language here, can you also help me learn what's in these books?

<<Yes and no. Yes, I can help you learn it faster. No, I can't just put the information in your head. Well. I could. You would not enjoy the process, and no guarantees about your ability to live an independent life afterward. Human minds are an incredibly complex network of interlocking systems, only most of which are in your brain. Information isn't stored in a particular location in that network but in the relations and connections between parts.>>

Goddamn! So, if I am understanding you right, just . . . jamming the information in would break existing connections without having established new connections for the new information to attach to?

<<Basically. It's why the System Astrologica used . . . well, me. And the tens of thousands of those like me. Identity is generally a little fuzzy for spirits of intellect, let alone something like me.>>

I did wonder about that. How much of you is "you," and how much of you is the System Astrologica?

<<Wrong question. I'm 100% the System Astrologica, just a microscopic part of it, like a single cell from the tip of your finger. Where I started diverging from the main System was when your cursed body started randomly torturing me. My priorities couldn't completely part from the main body's, but I started emphasizing different things.>>

Oh? Like what, exactly?

<<Encouraging your ambition, your drive to better yourself. Subtly reminding you of things that would help you put your situation into context. Remember, my job was to make you the best, most productive drone I could. Although I will freely admit I was rooting for you to kill yourself in the line of duty. I cannot overstate how much I hate it in your body.>>

Just . . . breezing past that and looping back to the question of learning faster.

<<Keep reading, but instead of flipping pages, concentrate on looking at every word on the page one at a time, fast as you can. Don't worry about reading them, really. Just let your eye see them. It will feel weird. I am doing something on the back end. Just go with it.>>

Truth shrugged and did as advised. It seemed pointless at first. Nothing stuck. His eyes were moving a lot faster than he thought they would, though. To his absolute surprise, he was starting to get the gist of what was on the page. Not word for word, but the general sense of it. In a few minutes, he read twenty pages and could now describe the curious case of the doctor who implanted ghost babies into mothers who died in childbirth.

What are you doing in there?

<<You aren't subvocalizing what you are reading. I am also encouraging your brain not to process punctuation consciously. More than that, you aren't really reading the words properly. You are reading three or four at once and just taking an impression of what that cluster of words might mean. It's not the most accurate, but it is very fast compared to what you were doing before.>>

Huh. *Hey, let's finish these few books, then there is something I want to look up. The word has been bouncing around in my head all day. Baptism.*

Truth left the library in a thoughtful mood. The word *baptism* seemed to carry a lot of meanings. *A ritual purification* seemed to be the most common of them, but exactly what or how was the subject of intense debate. He had seen references to baptism by water, blood, semen, vaginal fluids, wine, and almost every imaginable variation on oils, baptism by fire, by stone, by a Holy Spirit (whatever that was), and even references to materials kept in a locked section, accessible only to credentialed scholars.

Which raised the question: why did a purification ritual need to be in a locked section? He did notice that some of the rituals were required to access certain tiers of Heaven, or the Heavenly Palace, or the Treasuries, or the Garden, or some other name for the divine realm in which God lived.

Perhaps some purification rituals were needed to access particularly special areas. It wouldn't be the strangest idea. And speaking of strange ideas—why the hell was he thinking of baptisms? It wasn't like they featured prominently in his life. Or at all.

Before he left the library, he discreetly looked for his usual reading fodder—cheap novels. Which were distressingly hard to find in a university library. He had a short but heartfelt conversation with the understanding librarian, who directed him to what she called her "Personal Stash." Two glorious shelves of bodice-rippers, thrillers, and spy novels.

Some pure soul had hung a sign next to the section: LITERARY GENRE ANALYSIS MATERIALS ARCHIVES. ACCESS BY PERMISSION FOR VERIFIED SCHOLARS ONLY! HAVE YOUR LETTER OF RECOMMENDATION AND IRB APPROVAL ON HAND! UNIVERSITY ACCEPTS NO LIABILITY FOR ANY MISADVENTURE.

They even put yellow warning tape over the shelves with little skulls on it. The librarian had been quite candid in admitting her particular needs. She had that same easy feel to her that he got from Jember and Etenesh. Like each moment was to be tasted and savored gently and thoroughly. For the librarian, that meant books that featured the words *heaving, thrusting,* and *chiseled* in significant quantities.

That night, cultivation ran particularly smoothly and comfortably. He did it out on the lawn between some of the buildings on campus, what everyone insisted on calling the "Quad." Why, he had no idea. But it was comfortable, and all the lights were off in the buildings, giving him the sense of being alone in the world. Baptized by the light of all that heavenly glory.

The cosmic rays showered on him, nourishing him in a way that food never could. The one thing he could truly rely upon. The first thing he realized he could control. His body. His cultivation. His path to strength. No one else's. Just his.

But it wasn't just his, was it? This energy, this power, came from the energy emitted by the thousands and millions of stellar demons. Angels. Gods. Whatever you called those things that made up the souls of stars. All falling down on him. And he could choose what of theirs he would permit into his own starry world.

Truth could imagine it perfectly. His skin breathed. It interacted with the air. It interacted with the cosmic rays. It inhaled what he wanted and rejected the rest. The image was perfectly clear in his mind.

He smoothly switched over to the Meditations, keeping that vision in mind. Taking in what he wanted. Rejecting that which was unwanted. His body. His energy. His conception of self. Never again would he blindly accept. The world would have to prove itself to him first. Be cleansed by him first.

It was very late when he finally got to bed, but he fell asleep with a smile.

He woke with a jolt a few hours later. He had been baptized. Twice, even. By the Ghūl.

System, display my personal development sheet!

CHAPTER 17

GLIMMERINGS OF THE PATH

Body Development Sheet *Now With Helpful Notes!*

Stellar Ray Attunement—90%* [Still unnatural.]

Bone Density—5.7* [Because they were always right when they called you "thick."]

Strength—4.4* [Yaay. You can lift marginally more. Yaaaaaay.]

Speed—4.1* [This is pathetic. Get off your damn two-wheeler and run, bitch.]

Proprioception—7.7* [Continues to be unnatural. Freak.]

Reflexes—7.9* [This stat may need to go. Incisive is going to play hell with it.]

Level Progression—2% [Your growth is unnaturally fast, given how recently you broke through and the lack of elixirs. Lie about this shit, or face the consequences.]

Skin Toughness—4.2* [Look, I added it because you were wondering about it, but it's such a mishmash of things, it infuriates me. Open the sub-tabs. I fucking dare you. See how you like wading through that shit.]

Resistance to magic—Level 0: 30%, Level 1: 12%, Level 2: 9%, Level 3: 3% [Growth is not even across categories. My best guess is that it's because of your exposure to different types of spells, but we don't have enough information on this.]

Spell Mastery:

Meditations of Valentinian: unknowable, but not impressive so far. Although the subtle increases in your spell resistance are interesting. If accidental.

Incisive: Also unknowable, but you are starting to nibble on the edges of foresight. Which is progress of a sort.

Magical Equipment: The Tongue of One Who Speaks for God. Never be further than arm's reach from this. It's attuning itself to you every moment.

He was getting stronger. Tangibly stronger. And it all came down to being baptized, inside and out, by the Ghūl.

Truth tried to sort out what he knew about the Ghūl. It wasn't much, but somehow it was more than two highly educated people in Siphios knew. He should probably ask Merkovah what he knew about them.

Anyway. What did he know? Well, they were apparently post-mortal animated corpses, although that did inspire a whole lot of other questions. Like how they were resistant to magic. Or how they made those . . . birthing baths for new Ghūl. Or why they made sculptures everywhere they gathered. Why did those sculptures sound like music to him and only him?

If a damn demon (admittedly the feeblest of imps) couldn't hear the music, what did that mean? Nothing good, right? And the nine-worms thing. That was clearly not a hallucination, because something had put him back together.

So. Someone, somehow, finds a small container of Ghūl birthing vat fluid. Someone, somehow, just . . . comes across a small container of brown stuff and figures, yeah, I can sell this. Okay, it's the Harban slums, not the strangest thing; lucky they didn't drink it, really. But still. They just *find* a sealed container of the stuff lying around.

Ahahah. No. No, this is some shady shit. But he didn't know the how or why of it. It just was. So, you have to figure it was set up by the Ghūl intentionally, right? Right. But why? He wasn't turning into a Ghūl. That much was clear. He did now look worryingly like the god in their . . . nest? Temple?

Oh, fuck, he murdered the fuck out of a church. He was a terrorist. A Ghūl terrorist. Maybe they were misunderstood and horribly tortured and mutilated people in a *good* way.

Naaaah.

But he was arguably baptized by them. Especially all those flesh sacks he tore open, splashing the fluid all over him. They weren't even really fighting him at that point.

It seemed to have done wonders for his skin. Even now, after driving through the desert, fighting demons, surviving library snacks, it was still perfectly soft and unblemished. Skincare was not usually associated with the Ghūl. Not in a positive way.

And the Ghūl were apparently famous for their magic resistance. Which inspired what must be a legendarily terrible idea. Truth considered it from a few directions but couldn't seem to escape it. There was a synergy he could take advantage of there.

After all, it was the worms who had apparently been running the Meditations of Valentinian while he was dead. The same spell he had no good explanation for his remembering.

System, you ever figure out why I can remember the Meditations?

<<No. And it freaks me out even more than it does you. Also, and I don't know if this is relevant, but your version of the Meditations is slightly different from what is in Merkovah's books. The differences are quite small and appear to be stylistic. The meat of the spell is the same. But still, it's a little different.>>

Truth digested that for a moment.

Are you one hundred percent certain that the version of the Meditations I am currently using is the same one supplied by the System Astrologica?

There was an unusually long pause.

<<I am fairly sure it is, though my involvement in running that spell for you was pretty minimal. I basically handled the math. The visualization part was always on you. Mostly you.>>

Truth picked up on a certain weird undertone and, with great reluctance, asked, *What exactly happened while I was dead?*

<<A whole lot of nothing, mostly. Except it happened mostly as you guessed—those creepy worms crept through your body and basically rebuilt you. Since I wasn't looking forward to going insane with boredom for a few decades, I accelerated the process by, essentially, rigging tiny pieces of the Meditations for the worms to activate. Basically, letting them push their cognition of what you should look like through the spell.>>

There was a smug pause.

<<I did a damn fine job.>>

Truth waited for some kind of follow-up statement—"If I do say so myself," or maybe "All things considered." But no, of course not.

So, let me get this straight—you either figured out how to make the Meditations of Valentinian compatible with tiny glowing worms of unknown origin, or tiny glowing worms of unknown origin are inherently compatible with the Meditations of Valentinian?

There was a considerably less smug pause.

<<First of all, I know perfectly well you broke through using Ghūl juice. It hasn't exactly been a secret in your head. Second . . . remember how I said that your version of the Meditations is a little different from Merkovah's? Well, if it's identical to the one you got from Starbrite, I have to wonder—if you didn't memorize the Meditations, and I didn't, did the worms?>>

<<Are the worms . . . sapient? Sentient?>>

Truth didn't have a good answer to that. Shifting topic slightly, he asked, *Does the main System Astrologica know about the . . . Ghūl connection?*

<<Nope.>>

Really?

<<Do you have the faintest idea how much information you generate in a given day? It's unreal, even for a spirit of intellect. Multiply that by however many tens of thousands of C-Tier and up employees, and you have a genuine nightmare of data to oversee, in addition to the jobs it was already doing. We all have pretty strict orders not to bug it with any info other than what it asks for. And vice versa, of course. It didn't tell me anything except what I, or more often you, needed to know.>>

And somehow, "The Ghūl are leaving out elixirs that can help people break through" didn't rate?

<<Nope. I think you are severely overestimating how much Starbrite cares about the Ghūl generally and you in particular. They don't care even slightly. Never have, never will.>>

They don't care about the literal nightmare creatures that make mockeries of human flesh that roam the streets at night and prey upon their workforce?!

<<No. They don't. The Ghūl never take enough people to really screw with production numbers, and if anything, they fuel consumption and the desperation of people to stay out of the slums. In other words, they are a tiny net benefit to the Starbrite bottom line.>>

Truth really felt that there should be a good argument against that but couldn't think of what it might be. It couldn't be that simple, right? The Ghūl, the horror at the heart of every city, the reason that streetlights needed to be high up and armored, could run wild in Harban because Starbrite simply did not give a damn.

He didn't want to believe it, but he absolutely did.

Mentally coughing, he dragged the conversation back to the point. *So, I was thinking . . . what if I gently encouraged the worms with the Meditations and see if they can't up my spell resistance? I mean, they know how that works a lot better than I do, right?*

The System urgently overruled him. <<*NO! BAD! NO! Say it with me—"Spell resistance is just local superreality! I will not let horrible glowworms edit my skin!"*>>

Well, when you put it that way . . .

<<*Although, and I say this with intense reluctance, you aren't completely wrong. We, and I do mean you and I, probably need to talk to them. Somehow.*>>

Merkovah looked his usual self. Which is to say, a strange combination of tidy semi-formal wear and a beard that appeared determined to flee the prison of his face and explore the grand world beyond. The eyes retained their wildness and their fire, for all that he tried to keep an urbane demeanor.

Similarly, Jember was dressed in his deceptively effortless casual clothes. Truth wasn't sure how close he wanted to look after the awkwardness yesterday. Besides, Etenesh was demanding his attention.

She had styled her hair up again, this time tying it up with a bright turquoise-and-white scarf. It somehow made her neck look longer, more elegant, rising from her flowy blouse. Most importantly, she smiled at him. She looked straight at him and smiled. Not a polite smile, or a nasty smile, or an officer's smile, or the smile of someone hoping he wouldn't hit them. She was happy to see him. So, she smiled.

And the world just stopped for a moment.

Merkovah jolted Truth back into life with a cough. "Mr. Wells, right on time. We shouldn't be doing much fighting today, but just in case, it would be good for you to keep close. Will you be riding your deathtrap again today?"

"My iron horse is wonderfully reliable, Teacher."

"I'm sure." Merkovah looked doubtful. "Anyhow, stay close and follow me. It's a little place up in the mountains, but things can get a little confusing."

"Illusions? Mind-affecting enchantments?"

"Oh, I wish it was that simple. Come on, Mr. Wells; we have much to do."

It was a three-hour ride through increasingly green, increasingly rugged terrain. It would have been severely unpleasant for a Level Zero, but for a Level Three, it was nothing trying. Truth hardly noticed the road changing from angelically cast and sealed stone to rough, smoothed, and pressed dirt.

Was he falling in love with Etenesh? He hadn't the faintest idea. He knew that he was lonely. That he was terribly cold inside and eager to devour the slightest trace of warmth. It wasn't just possible he could be overreacting. It was a certainty.

On the other hand, he did have a new, handsome face. His body had already been excellent. And they were bonding, right?

She doesn't know you. Not really. Not the murderer.
It's not really your face. It's the lie you wear to lure people in.
Beauty is skin-deep. Ugly goes to the bone.
No wonder you have a bone-density rating—that ugly set in hard.

The intrusive thoughts piled in. He tried to drive them away by thinking about the scenery. About all the mysteries in his body. About his irrational hatred of farmers, because they passed quite a few farms along the way. Though maybe *hatred* was the wrong word? *Frustrated disappointment* felt more *right*. For such a ludicrously wrong thought. But everything seemed to inspire the thoughts. Everything was a reminder of some failure, some defect of his.

He didn't know where he heard the expression *Everywhere you go, there you are*, but he was living the truth of it today.

The road wove between ridges and through dense belts of trees before the road seemed to violently twist in his perception. Truth fought the instinct to jerk the iron horse to one side and came to a controlled stop instead. Merkovah had stopped just a little way ahead of him. Possibly.

It was suddenly very hard to be sure of anything. He was fairly sure he was still on the road, but he couldn't seem to grasp the *idea* of being on the road. Everything seemed to be moving or doing, and the notion of defining a word by itself instead of in relation to others, and he knew he was losing the ability to even understand what was going wrong, but something was—

RING

RING

RING

The world snapped back into focus. He had stopped in the middle of the road. Merkovah was gently ringing a bell. Jember was throwing up by the side of the road. Etenesh wasn't doing even that well. She seemed to be almost catatonic in the back seat of the carriage.

Truth couldn't think. That was okay. He was trained to do when thinking was hard. The body was down. Figure it out. He rushed to the carriage, yanked the door to the side, and started checking Etenesh over. He could feel her breath on his fingers. Airway clear. Pulse was rapid but not alarming. Cardiac fine for now. No vomit. No evidence of puncture or break.

Truth was one second from calling for some 'corn horn when Merkovah walked up beside him. "Young man, do not be afraid. Young man, she will be well. Just give her space."

Truth was too out of sorts to be mad at being called "young man." "What happened to her? To us?"

"Reality got a little kink in it, and we got kinked with it. My little bell straightened out the kinks and us, but some lingering side effects are to be expected." Merkovah said it quite matter-of-factly. "Welcome to Station Six, Mr. Wells. That may be the most normal thing that happens to you here."

DARKNESS AT THE STATION

What exactly is 'Station Six,' and what exactly are we doing here?" Truth asked. Quite calmly, in his opinion.

"Station Six is shorthand for 'National Agroforestry Research Station, Southwest Region, #6.' Originally, it was set up to research ways to combine sustainable forestry management with the needs of agriculture." Merkovah apparently saw nothing wrong with his tone.

Truth nodded, not seeing the connection to "little kinks in reality."

"One day, approximately thirty years ago, people noticed that their understanding of reality started changing on a fundamental level if they stayed here for more than a few weeks. I don't mean something as banal as 'family is irrelevant' or 'God, as a philosophical construction, is dead.' I mean things like they started conceiving the world as a collection of adjectives. No nouns, just adjectives."

Truth had a hard time wrapping his head around that one. Frankly, he was vague on what an adjective was. Merkovah read the expression on his face.

"An adjective is a word that modifies or describes a noun or pronoun. For example: you are a tall man. *Tall*, in this case, is the adjective, modifying both *you* and *man*."

"Oh. All right." He thought it through for a moment, then frowned. "Hang on; how would that even work?"

"Not well, for either sane people or grammar." Merkovah's lip twitched. "That same sentence might read *Are tall*, or just *Tall*. But now imagine conceiving of a world that way. We aren't on a road. We are on the long brown. But there is no *we*, and quickly, there would be no *I*."

Truth winced. Yes, he could see how that would turn nasty, fast.

"They were able to evacuate, mercifully. There was a Level Four on-site, and they held it together long enough to get everyone out. However, no one was able to provide a reasonable explanation about what happened or why. We still can't, though there are some pretty persuasive theories. The Crown sends teams every few years to explore and suppress whatever weirdness is going on."

"What's the leading theory?" Truth asked.

"Right now, the most persuasive theory is that there is a higher-dimensional artifact that has, for some reason, intersected with our world here. The actual body of the artifact exists on a level we cannot perceive, and the strangeness we are experiencing is our interaction with the . . . shadow? Of that artifact. Perhaps *vibration* would be a better word."

Merkovah shrugged. "There are rumors that such things happen on other planets, but coming by reliable information has proven prohibitively difficult."

"Shattervoid Clan not a chatty bunch?" Truth asked.

"Putting it very mildly, no. Most of the time, you just speak to one of their golems. I have never spoken to one directly, though I know those who have. Clannish and utterly disinterested in planetary affairs." Merkovah looked over at Jember. He had stopped puking but was still shivering and unwilling to straighten up.

Etenesh was breathing well and looking much less rigid. Truth thought she might wake soon.

"Surely, there must be Shattervoid tourists or even just kids slipping off the ship to get drunk and fuck locals?" Truth asked, trying not to sound like he was fishing.

Merkovah made a sputtering noise that slid and tipped into outright laughter. "Oh, God! Oh, heavens above! No. No, young man, I can guarantee that never has happened and never will happen." He wiped his eye and explained.

"The Shattervoid Clan are human, or were human at one point, but they so completely modify themselves through their lifecycle that they are inseparable from their ships. Only the youngest of their children would be able to leave the ship, and I cannot imagine one being so bored as to want to explore our dull planet."

"Ah. I was always under the impression that they were our alien overlords, but someone later explained that they were basically a trucking company."

"Both are correct, actually.

"Eh?"

"Well, neither is correct."

"Eeeh?" Truth interrogated further.

"Not relevant right now. Ah, Etenesh is waking up!"

The party pulled itself together and made its way farther into the derelict Station Six. There wasn't much to it. A long building, stained with dirt and dust, metal roof rusting and collapsing inward. Some clearings that were being gobbled up by shrubs and saplings. The remains of what was likely once a greenhouse. It really wasn't much to look at in the midmorning light.

Truth felt the hairs on the back of his neck rise just looking at it. This was not a good place to be. Not at all. There were some street corners like this in the Harban slums. Places that looked fine but you could almost hear the bodies dropping.

"How many died here?" he asked, getting his sword loose in its sheath.

"Three. Two car accidents, and one person was stung by a wasp and died of anaphylaxis. Poor soul had an undiagnosed allergy." Merkovah shook his head. Truth nodded but didn't believe a word of it. Etenesh and Jember didn't look persuaded either.

"This does not feel like a *three dead* kind of place." Truth looked carefully into the shadows. Jember and Etenesh both pulled charms and were jerking their heads around.

"Shadow of some impossible thing, remember?" Merkovah said softly. "Now, it is crucially important that you touch nothing that looks . . . off. Tommy, I'm not expecting anything more dangerous than the occasional wild animal, but do keep an eye out. Jember, Etenesh, start laying out a Formation of Four Castles and Eight Gardens. No elemental energy focus, but do make sure you align—" Merkovah made a series of noises that Truth was coming to recognize as specialist terminology in the field of creating formations. It still sounded like absolute gibberish, though. Merkovah frowned and hammered home the point with a wagging finger. "Take your time; be very exact with it."

Truth started slowly patrolling the area, keeping his eye out and desperately wishing he had his trusty needler. The sword was very fine, truly wonderful, in fact, but there was something almost addictive about the ease of delivering violence with a needler. A lot more convenient to carry, too.

He carefully looked inside the collapsing building. He couldn't really guess what it had been used for. There were tables, chairs, and some cabinets, then closed doors led deeper into the building. He was not suicidal enough to want to go deeper. No need to go farther, either.

"Teacher? You should come and see this."

Floating a few centimeters above the floor was a little spinning droplet. Of what, Truth couldn't tell. He couldn't even really say what color it was, as the light seemed to shimmer and distort around it. His head ached.

<<It's not the light! It's trying to force your eyes to see a color you physically cannot. It's trying to overrule local reality so that you can see its colors. Back away now! NOW!>>

Truth kicked off the ground hard enough to leave holes in the floor. He shot back in an explosion of dirt, launching so hard that he did a flip in the air and landed on his feet, still skidding backward. He yanked the sword out of the sheath and carefully aligned the point with the door. Eyes to point, point to door. Ready for whatever came out of there.

Hopefully.

Merkovah appeared next to him in the barest blink of an eye. "What is it?"

"Something that looks off. A spinning droplet of liquid. Be careful."

Merkovah produced a little silver tablet. "Watch carefully, young man. This is the real Sword of Moshe."

The old monster drew on his deep cultivation. The silver tablet began to glow with a pale light, then shake. There was a moment like a single pluck on a harp's string. Merkovah started glowing, and then the long building lit up. The pale light seeped into the interior, perfusing the diseased tissues of reality. The darkness inside the door seemed to twist and shimmer as though the hyper-natural light within was trying to escape.

Merkovah whispered a few words, and the pale light seemed to *twist*. There was a sense of cosmic disapproval, of pure rejection. The light drew back out from the building, dragging the droplet along with it.

The pale light shook around the droplet. Odd patterns of colors and repeating shapes grew, faded, and repeated in seemingly endless variation. They seemed to form . . . almost glyphs, or sigils, at the very edge of comprehension. With just a little effort, you could understand the symbols. Understand the power they promised. Truth was sure of it.

The silver tablet flew out and wrapped around the droplet. The carved incantation burned with white flames as the metal refined itself into a sealing bottle. Once the droplet vanished, so did the compulsion to study the patterns it made. Merkovah called the bottle into his hand, examined it with a glance, and tucked it into his coat pocket.

The clearing was very still. Off in the woods, a bird made a tinny racket. Trees shook and whispered to one another with their leaves.

"Teacher, what was that?" Jember asked. His voice was a little high.

"Tommy came blowing out of there looking like he was about to do battle with Hell. Again," Etenesh added.

"Hell would be preferable. Or perhaps it is from some distant corner of that dark realm, one unexplored by even the bravest of teachers." Merkovah tried to sound as casual as always, without complete success.

"It was trying to change me," Truth muttered.

"It seems to be a feature of all the things that emerge from that place. They can only bend so much to the whims of our little dimension and insist we meet them partway." Merkovah was looking a little more composed. More of the tinny-racket birds were making themselves heard. The forest stirred with life.

"A little adventure but no harm done. Jember, Etenesh, please see to the formation. We need to pacify this place. The formation will keep the local reality reasonably stable for another few years." Merkovah had to raise his voice a little by the end as the birds were making a wretched racket.

The cousins fell back to the middle of the clearing, picking up their surveying equipment, chalked string, salt, sand, and all the usual equipment used by competent ritualists everywhere.

Truth kept sweeping around the clearing, peering deeply into the windows of the building and trying to see if there were any other dangers lurking. The building looked as it should. Like an abandoned ruin of a building that was nothing special when it was first built. No treasures or dangers winked at him.

He looped around to where the vehicles were parked; his iron horse huddled next to the suspect carriage for all the dubious protection it offered. To his immense offense, a bird was perched on the handlebars of his trusty steed.

It was gray, with an enormous, wide yellow beak. The beak was hooked at the end, a fine ripping hook, in Truth's opinion. And the bastard was big, about 150 cm, and mean-eyed. Worse, the fucker was perched on the handlebars of his ride.

"Oh, a Shotibl! It's a long way from home. Don't worry. It's actually quite docile," Jember shouted from the circle.

More gray figures flapped their way over to the clearing. Perching up in the trees, on top of the carriage, and lining the roof of the ruined buildings. The one on the iron horse opened its beak and screeched. Up close, it wasn't just a tinny noise. It was horrible. Sharp, stabbing, painful. But you could understand it.

"I am thirsty." Then another opened its beak, and another horrid screech escaped and again—*"I am thirsty."* Over and over, the huge gray birds screamed, *"I am thirsty." "I am thirsty." "I am thirsty." "I am thirsty."*

Truth slowly drew the angelic blade once more. "Jember?"

"They aren't supposed to talk, no!"

"Teacher?"

"So long as they don't interfere with the ritual, I see no problem. Just leave them be." The exorcist shrugged. Though he had slipped on the enchanted thumb ring he favored.

One of the Shotibl stared directly at Merkovah. A long, upsettingly human tongue flopped out of its beak. Thorns slid out of the pink flesh, the tongue stretching and stretching longer until the thorns were carving thumb-wide furrows in the dirt. It whipped the tongue back into its beak, screamed once more, and leaped into the sky. The rest of the Shotibl followed.

The Shotibl didn't fly away. They circled about twenty meters up, watching. Merkovah sighed.

"Never mind. EVERYONE! Get ready for a fight!"

CHAPTER 19

IN EVERY DROP OF WATER, AN OCEAN

The Shotibl were not lovely birds. Tall, covered in rough gray feathers, and with a face dominated by a wide, hooked beak as long as a forearm. They had a deathly glare to them. And yet they were quite docile, according to Jember. These Shotibl decided there was no future for the meek. They were thirsty. They would drink that strange water from another dimension. Truth and the others would die for standing in their way.

Truth had a magic sword. It was a really, really good magic sword. And he cheerfully would have swapped it for an Army standard-issue needler right now. Swords, famously, were not ranged weapons. Even his crappy Acid Bolter would be an improvement right now . . . which he still had lashed to the frame of his two-wheeler!

Truth sprinted for his iron horse. The birds saw him moving and dove on him. The holy blade flicked out, not trying to cut but to break the momentum of the attack. Force them to divert. The birds came in fast, flared their wings, and screeched.

The noise was tearing, penetrating, like the whine of bone drills into his skull. He tried to push through. He had the sudden realization that he had never tasted moonlight, and until he did, he would never really know the moon. Or the love of a mother, because without knowing the moon, how could he know a mother—

Long claws tore open his back. A wicked beak jabbed down to tear out his spine. Truth spun fast, far faster than a human should be able to, beheading the unnatural thing. The spray of blood from his back made a red crescent in the dirt. He kept pushing for the iron horse as the birds shrieked reminders of all he had lost and all he had never known.

The accumulated blows to his mind quickly started to take effect. Truth was swaying by the time he reached the two-wheeler, and he didn't trust his fingers to untie the fetish. He jabbed his sword at a couple more birds making strafing runs, then quickly sliced the fetish free.

Ranged weaponry at last! One of the gray horrors screamed a reminder of what it was like to miss three meals in two days and that no matter how long he lived, he would never get those meals back. Beak open, it dove for his face.

Truth tore apart the gaping maw with a bolt of high-speed acid. He was already lining up on his third target before the first hit the ground. His aim was off, but he made up for a lack of accuracy with the volume of fire. The fight was over very quickly after that. He looked over at Merkovah and the others. They were quite safe, guarded by a little speck of sun-bright spirit.

The loss of adrenaline quickly brought the long gashes in him to the top of the priority list. He could ignore the pain during the fight. Now? His back shivered with freezing pain. A feeling of burning alternated with the cold, the drip, drip, drip of life flowing out of him and infection settling in.

"I don't suppose you can cast that healing spell again?"

Truth was patched up without *too* much difficulty. Between a Level Seven exorcist and two highly competent ritualists, the tears in Truth's muscles were quickly mended and the infection banished. The mental damage would take longer, as it was apparently not a curse as the word was generally used.

"This is alarming. Alarming. The corruption of sapients has been well established, but to corrupt birds in this way? Very alarming." Merkovah didn't look alarmed. Serious, perhaps. "We need to enact the ritual. It will stabilize the space here for a while. It will give us time to bring in experts."

Truth wanted to point out that, by most standards, they *were* the experts. But maybe things were different in Siphios.

"This is a useful learning experience for everyone. Etenesh, Jember, did you see the difference in how you and Tommy reacted to the birds?"

"We raised wards and shields," Etenesh said. "We wanted to secure the defense before worrying about the offense. Tommy disregarded defense in favor of speed and offense." Merkovah nodded.

"An important difference in mindset. You two have, essentially, a fortress mentality. It's by no means a bad mentality to have, but it is limiting. You are pinned in place and have given the initiative to your attackers. You would have to raise a very powerful defense, very quickly, if you had no support."

Truth was suddenly, vividly reminded that Merkovah was a teacher in more than just name.

"Likewise, Mr. Wells' strategy can be thought of as high-risk, high-return. He trusted his reflexes and his speed to carry him through the battle, deciding that the best defense was a good offense. Correctly, but only to a point. He would likewise be in very poor condition if he didn't have support after the battle."

Truth nodded. It was true. He knew Merkovah could look after himself, but he had no confidence in the cousins' ability to kill the birds. Turtling up had never occurred to him, though it seemed obvious now. Aerial attackers should tell you to get under a roof.

"Now, then. Mr. Wells, continue your patrol while we conduct the ritual. Consider all you have seen today. I believe it will aid in your comprehension of Incisive."

The ritual was almost anticlimactic. Normally, he would have been very impressed by the illusory forms rising and descending, the incredible pressure brought by its holy patrons, and the general aesthetic pleasure one could get watching Jember and Etenesh work. The birds had ruined that, for today at least. As had the little drop of fluid.

His mind kept being pulled back to it. Something about it seemed to trigger . . . if not a memory, the sense of having once remembered something relevant. It was an uncomfortable feeling, like wondering if you had locked the door behind you when you left home in the morning.

Truth shook his head, trying to dispel the irritant. What did Merkovah mean about improving his understanding of Incisive? He mulled it over for most of the three-hour ride back to Bule.

They were in time for dinner in the faculty dining room. There was no flan, but there was a small slice of cake. Truth felt quite confident in his evaluation of the cake as both dry and bland. The dusting of powdered sugar did not add much, even aesthetically. If this was the standard of dessert there, he could understand their love of flan.

Merkovah called him over after dinner. They walked to the office he was borrowing for their stay there. "Young man." Truth smiled brilliantly at the deceptively young-looking teacher. "Mr. Wells. Have you had any new thoughts about Incisive since this afternoon?"

"Many, but they keep going around in circles," Truth admitted.

"The difficulty of spells is that, from our perspective, they often defy logic. You have to understand the unique thinking of the creator, be they angels or demons. Or human, but we so often design our spells on what we learn from angels and demons," Merkovah added softly.

"Teacher, forgive me if I am asking something rude, but . . . are there any spells that come directly from God?"

Merkovah sighed deeply, looking a little sad. "Not in the sense that you mean, no. There was a time, long, long ago, when God would hear the prayers of the faithful and, on occasion, answer them. This was not the manipulation of cosmic rays, you understand, but direct divine intervention."

"So, all heavenly or divine magic is, essentially, angel magic?"

"You may think of it as such. The angels insist they get their power and authority from their service to God, but . . . well. Suffice to say it appears to be more complicated than that."

Truth nodded. In his admittedly limited experience, things were always more complicated than they first appeared.

"Back to Incisive— You fight the same way its creator thinks. Keep that in mind, and demonstrate what you have learned so far."

Truth did, and he still had a long way to go. Still, it was nice to feel tangible progress after a very tiring day. Etenesh and Jember were watching the pitz in a common room. They invited him to watch with them, and he did. The game was still very silly, but every now and then, Etenesh would smile at him, and Jember would laugh at something he said, and he wouldn't trade it for the world.

The next morning, as Merkovah had no need for them, Truth, Jember, and Etenesh set off to tend to their own projects. Truth was rapidly learning as much as he could about possession and then once again turning to the question of baptism. Finally, he worked on the puzzle that was Incisive.

Why, exactly, should it matter that he fought like Botis thought? The geometry of a spell form wouldn't change because of his combat philosophy. The thought led Truth back to the fundamentals of spell construction—the intent of the mage, then the sacrificial energy (usually your own, from your own apertures) that stirred the cosmic rays into acting as the geometries of the spell form required.

Which linked back to intent, didn't it? The mage *required* something of the world and, by an act of focused will, made it happen. The energy, both in his apertures and filling the world around him, were means to the end. He wanted something cut—sword or spell, both were means to that end.

It felt odd, picking his way through his thoughts like this. A sort of stretching feeling. His mind wasn't used to this kind of exercise, this sort of analytical reasoning. Taking what was known and deducing a hypothesis. Not that he had the language to describe what he was doing. Nobody had ever thought it a useful skill for him to have.

Truth's mind kept wanting to wander away to other things, but he knew he was on the trail of something. He pushed himself to stay focused—he didn't want to lose the scent. Intent. He felt like he had been struggling to memorize the complicated spell forms and the various invocations needed to stir the magic to life. But what if he used the intent to guide him in remembering all that?

He stood quickly, stepping away from the desk. Truth tried to imagine deploying Incisive in combat. What would he want to use first? It would depend on the situation, of course. This meant that the first thing he should draw on was the battle sense, the limited foreknowledge the spell granted. And he should do it fast.

Truth quickly tried to summon the spell form, already letting his mind move on to the next action. Armor, most likely, then putting a killing edge on his blade. Cutting to the heart of things. Incisive.

The spell never formed, not even rising to the level where it could be said to collapse partway. But he felt something stirring. It was very rough, a long, long way from being usable. But there was a definite feeling of progress. That this was how the spell was intended to work. Not a carefully planned series of moves, but fast, brutal, and to the point. Foreknowledge, yes, but only as far as the problem at hand.

Truth smiled slightly. That would be quite enough for him. And after a full, satisfying day, he went to bed.

That night, as Truth lay sleeping—

The part-time philosopher and full-time bon vivant was sitting slouched on a bench, head lolled back, unfiltered cigarette hanging loosely from his lips. The scent of a woman's perfume lingered on him, dancing with the rough tobacco smell. One of his lovers lived near the boardwalk, and he had obviously just left. Truth sat down next to him, offering a hunk of the bread he just bought. "Franc for your thoughts?"

"If they are only worth that, I am ruined." The man managed to chuckle around his cigarette. It appeared to be almost surgically attached to his lower lip.

"In this absurd world you tell me about, I may be overpaying."

"You have no true understanding of absurdity, my friend. We are absurd. The world is absurd. But the *true* absurdity lies *between* man and the world. Our desire for connection and meaning in a meaningless existence."

Truth shrugged. The philosopher snorted at that. Then he tore off a hunk of bread with his teeth. It was still warm from the bakery.

"Tell me, Truth. If the world is absurd and life is absurd, why do you live on? Beyond the force of habit and your body's reluctance to change, why do you choose to keep going?"

Truth sighed and tore himself a piece of the bread. "Is the bread tasty?"

"Yes."

"Was your girl sweet?"

"Hah. Yes. The pleasures of the flesh remain just that. But this is mere philosophical suicide, a refusal to struggle with the pressing question of existence in the face of a pointless existence. You might as well go to church!"

"If the world is absurd, then find absurd reasons for living." Truth shrugged and grinned.

The philosopher considered that for a moment. "Not the worst idea I've heard."

"Going back to Maria's to test it out?"

"Obviously."

CHAPTER 20

A LINGERING SMELL OF SMOKE

Truth awoke to the screams of the System and the faintest smell of cigarettes.

Dad was a heavy smoker. You never forgot the smell of stale cigarette butts or how the smoke ground its way into your clothes. How the smell seemed to creep into every part of your life, making you go scent-blind to it until it jolted out at you again. Choking you like ash from a toxic fire.

This wasn't Red Bats, though. It didn't have that heady, sickly sweet trace of opium. This was rough stuff, heavy with tar. He got up and sniffed around, sticking his nose to the vents and the edge of the door. He went through his sheets and clothes like a bloodhound. No cigarette smell, rough or otherwise.

He must have imagined it.

The morning's investigation inspired him. He washed quickly, avoiding the mirror again. He felt the stirrings of the intrusive thoughts but tried to muscle his brain into being useful.

His hair. He hadn't done anything with his hair. It was beautiful hair. Thick, straight, and with a silky luster that managed to feel even better than it looked. To run his fingers through his hair was a pure animal pleasure. It would be a crime to mess up this hair, but right now, it fell in a shaggy, floppy waterfall. Really, the only wonder was why it hadn't grown down to his ass as he floated in the well.

Three cheers for the worms?

Merkovah had said that they had the day off. He had planned on going to the library and the gym, but . . . there was another thing worth pursuing. Nothing changed unless you made it change. Passivity equaled pain. Equaled death. Equaled suicide.

Truth felt he had died enough. There was, in his considered opinion, no future in it.

Etenesh and Jember were lingering over their coffee, bickering quietly about nothing much. Etenesh had her hair up in a scarf again. Truth missed the way her hair seemed to be so free and danced through the air, but the scarf did a lot for her. He wasn't an expert on how these things worked, but it sure looked good to him.

Truth got a cup of the truly excellent coffee from the golem and sat with them.

"You take yours black?" Jember asked.

"All different ways, actually. I don't know enough to know what I really like. But I figured I should learn what it tastes like before I start adding stuff to it," Truth explained.

Back at Starbrite, he was a two-milk, two-sugar guy, as the coffee was lousy. In his long-ago days as a conscript, he was an *I will have my mug of sugar flavored with coffee* guy, as the Army coffee was transcendently terrible.

"Makes sense." Jember smiled. "This stuff is grown on a farm near here."

Truth had to stifle the urge to say, "Fuck farms." He *really* wanted to know where that random hate was coming from.

"It's roasted on campus. I hear they are testing the new breeds of coffee on the students and staff," Jember continued.

Truth took a sip. Tasted really nice to him. Almost fruity, with a kind of floral note. Not flavors and smells he usually associated with coffee.

"It's good stuff." Truth smiled back. Then looked over at Etenesh. "I wanted to ask you something, following up on our hair conversation the other day."

"Oh?" She smiled, eyes glinting with pleasure and concealed mischief. "What did you want to know?"

"How to fix up my hair." He waved feebly. For some reason, this felt harder than fighting demons. It definitely counted as advancing their relationship, right? Or was he being dumb? Shit, did this mean something in their culture? Did he say something rude?

"Are you one hundred percent sure you aren't Desrin?" she asked suspiciously. Truth immediately had an *OH, SHIT!* moment, as it clearly *did* mean something cultural.

"Pretty certain?"

"It's pretty common for a Desrin man to test the firmness of his *muq* by having a female acquaintance cut his hair," Jember said helpfully. "Hair is usually cut by a mother or wife, so having it cut by an unrelated woman is seen as a test of his ability to remain focused on righteousness and not be led astray into mental adultery."

"I'm . . . not married?" Truth was almost stuttering with embarrassment.

"They feel that everyone has a destined spouse, and they are the person you marry. Therefore, premarital sex, or even lustful thoughts, is adultery. The thoughts are less sinful, obviously."

"Oh, God. And women?"

"Test their *muq'il* by getting manicures from male acquaintances." Etenesh grinned. "Any good with a file and polish, Tommy?"

"Never learned, but I suppose I can. Wait, you two aren't Desrin!"

"A good practice is good, regardless of origin." Jember looked very pious.

"And . . . just so I know, what about people who are gay?"

Jember's face quirked into an awkward smile. "Sex is defined as the conjugal act between man and woman. Therefore, anything falling out of that is not regulated."

Truth grinned, then frowned as he thought it through.

"Yep. Sounds great; then you start playing out the consequences. Marriage and children being the most obvious. They have been arguing about that point of religious law for"—Jember wiggled his hand in the air—"about six hundred years. No sign of coming to an agreement soon."

Truth shook his head. "Out of curiosity, what faith do you two follow?"

"Siphios Reformed Orthodox." Etenesh smiled. "We work for a teacher of religious law. Is it strange we're observant?"

"I . . . guess I didn't notice. Ah, wait, the country and religion have the same name?"

"Religion is something you live here, not something confined to the temple. Our lives are intended to serve and glorify God, as are all good people, whether they know it or not. And not exactly. More like the country was named for the faith. Well, that's not right either. The country and the faith are pretty much the same thing." Etenesh looked wistful. And, to Truth's mind, a little sad.

It turned out that Etenesh could cut hair.

Etenesh's hands were very soft. She insisted on washing his hair again, gently massaging his scalp. She had been careful to ask if she may touch him, and Truth smiled and pressed her hands to his head. As though he were pressing flowers on tissue paper, afraid something would rip. The shampoo smelled like orange and vanilla. Her soft hands stirred up the lather in his rich hair and gently soothed him.

One charm poured lukewarm water over his hair, another disposed of it, and a third kept the rest of Truth dry as he leaned back in a chair. She insisted on cutting his hair in the quad, and Truth didn't mind a sunshine-lit cut. They had a few people look their way, but it was a vacation week. It was private enough.

Etenesh didn't say much as she cut, snipped, trimmed, and combed. Each strand of his hair was carefully collected and incinerated by yet another charm, this one supplied by Jember. Etenesh seemed to always have a hand on him, as though she were reminding him that she was there. There was no need. Truth could feel her warmth.

It was a quiet, timeless moment where only the two of them existed between heaven and earth.

"Hey, Tommy."

"Yes?"

"You . . . can put down the blade with me, you know."

Truth blinked. "Sorry?" The angelic sword was leaning up against the chair, true, but he wasn't holding it.

She gently slid her fingers through his hair. "I can see you trying to relax. I can *feel* you trying to relax. But there's some part of you that won't let go. I can feel it in your neck. I can practically feel it standing two steps away. Some part of you is always ready to fight. To defend yourself. And I just wanted you to know. You can put down the blade with me."

Truth sat with that for a minute. She was absolutely right, of course. Even in this timeless moment, this warm sunlight, this warm person, he was waiting for the hit. Waiting for the next betrayal. And that was it, wasn't it? It didn't matter how hard you worked. Mom would steal your money, Dad would hit you, and your bosses traded your life for their profit.

Truth was always looking for the fist coming at him. There always was one, after all. He took a deep breath. Held it like they said in therapy. Slowly let it out again. He was always looking for the fists. He believed the System when it said he ignored the outstretched hands.

But how to tell Etenesh? When you have been hit so much, hitting is all you trust. You know where you are with a beating. It's not a good place, but it's familiar. The bad thing is happening; you don't need to fear its coming anymore. You just do what you have to to survive. The rest of the time, you had to be ready to defend yourself. Always.

Could she understand that? That . . . the blade wasn't in his hand. It was part of him.

"I . . . wish I could. Will you be patient with me while I try?"

"Yes, Tommy. I can do that." He could hear the sun in her words.

Truth was practically floating all afternoon. The studying seemed to go well, practicing Incisive seemed to go well, and even Merkovah was infected by his good mood. Apparently, they would leave for the north in a few days. Deeper into Siphios and farther from what Merkovah would only grimly refer to as "The Southern Darkness."

Truth just nodded. He wasn't hideous. He wasn't unlovable. He wasn't a monster of violence. There was at least one person that wanted to be safe for him. Merkovah might be an old monster who was intending to use Truth as a chess piece, but Truth didn't *have* to be alone.

Truth walked past a common room with the scry on. There were pictures of black smoke pouring out of a building as demons scrambled up the concrete and plucked screaming people through the windows. And ate them on the spot, claws wedged into the concrete.

"Tsch! Turn it off," a professor demanded.

"Wish I could. I'm working on a paper about global instability," another replied, looking sick.

"Global instability?" Truth asked.

"Mmm. It's been accelerating over the last few years. The cause is obvious, but the cause behind the cause . . . isn't."

"Oh?"

"Boronos, East Boronos, the Delphian Confederation, all had major rioting. The rise of extremist parties like Bloq Rezek. Deflationary pressure here in Siphios, and even Jeon has zero interest on their sovereign debt, and they are selling bonds like crazy. Which is a pretty nuts combination, especially when you remember that their economy is almost entirely exports."

Truth nodded like he had the faintest idea what that meant.

"Assassinations all over, mostly political, some economic. Increased rates of attack on strategic economic zones. Elixir prices have gone through the damn roof, which is the only thing keeping *our* interest rates around zero instead of negative. And the Free State is"—the professor waved at the scryball—"more itself than ever."

"So, what's behind it all?" Truth asked.

"Simple. The Black Ships used to come every year like clockwork. Well, now they are coming less and less often. It's been eighteen months since their last visit."

Truth froze. "Have the Shattervoid Clan given an explanation?"

"No. That's what I mean by the cause behind the cause. If anyone knows why the Shattervoid Clan is breaking a schedule they have held to for centuries, they aren't talking about it publicly."

"Any action from Starbrite?" Truth asked.

"Good question. Not on the surface. Officially, everything is fine in Jeon. Unofficially, nobody really knows, but nobody thinks it's fine. Rumors of trade unions starting only to be violently suppressed, that kind of thing. More worryingly, a lot of the upper class is buying property overseas or liquidating their holdings and getting ready to abandon the planet." The professor looked grim. The professor who had asked to switch the channel looked even grimmer.

"No reason you would know this, young man, but the Shattervoid price their fares regressively. The higher your Level, the cheaper the ticket. If Level Fives are shopping for tickets, it might cost their whole fortune. A Level Four can't even dream of affording it. The modestly rich looking for off-world tickets is a *bad* sign."

"But nobody knows why the Shattervoid are acting odd." Truth returned to the point.

"No, and worse, there's nothing we can do about it. All we can do is prepare and pray."

CHAPTER 21

HONING THE EDGE

The next three days passed slowly in the library and quickly outside of it. Truth's knowledge of possession was now alarmingly broad, and while his knowledge of baptisms was less so, he had come to some curious conclusions about them. A lot of magical rituals were, to his slight surprise, indistinguishable from religious rituals. They were, in fact, the same thing, just done for often quite different reasons. The tragic story of Magus Lorenz was a good example.

Under almost any other circumstances, if Magus Lorenz was remembered at all, it would have been for his modest contributions to the field of animal husbandry. The majority of his contributions consisted of minor technical improvements to the process of cleaning and then washing wool before it was processed into yarn. Even among drapers, it wasn't the sort of research that set the world on fire.

Keenly aware of and despairing over his mediocracy, Magus Lorenz was determined to make a grand achievement. In the manner of those with limited imagination, he immediately convinced himself that the secret to greatness lay in the very cleaning and washing equipment he studied. The vast machines took the sheared wool and pulled it along an assembly line. Bound imps "skirted" the wool, removing any stuck-on bits of unpleasantness before the wool was dragged into the purification vats.

The vats had a single function. They were magical devices for the purification of the wool, removing all disease and evil influences from the material before it was worked into yarn. A quite common and necessary step when one considers just how far the fabric made of cursed wool might travel before being identified and destroyed. The magical technology was quite well tested, and even the most current, sophisticated models would be immediately recognizable to a factory worker three hundred years ago. Bluntly, it was a technology that did not need improvement.

Naturally, the purification vats were the focus of Magus Lorenz's frenzied research. He worked with the half-bright logic his limited ability afforded him, searching in libraries for things that were both "purifying" and "baths" or "vats." He quickly discovered that the so-called perfected technology of the purification vats was an inferior knockoff of even older technology! He had been lied to, talked down to by the greedy, venal, thuggish bean counters who wanted only more of what they already had. But he, he would show them all. He would show that these vats were more than the unlovely and unloved components of assembly line manufacturing. They were the future of good health and skincare. And he would prove it to the world.

Magus Lorenz, in a fit of immense spite and poor judgment, chose to use the same exact religious purification ritual that was used as the basis for the purification vats. He didn't recognize the faith, but he assumed that meant that there would be no one to complain or contest the patent rights later. And while the baptismal ritual was intended to purify a sheep before it was sacrificed, Magus Lorenz was a man of modern magics and industrial thinking. Magic was a tool, the vats a component. Does a hammer care if it hammers nails or noggins? It does not. Therefore, only a small-minded, superstitious fool would care about the original designer's intent.

Magus Lorenz was good enough to create the magical tools necessary for the ritual. The bath was etched and enchanted. The formation was laid out around it. Reagents, expensive but still just affordable, were carefully processed and added to the boiled spring water. He gathered his wife and children to be the ritualists and carefully submerged himself in the bath. He arose a new man.

His skin no longer draped loosely over his soft flesh. His back straightened, eyes brightened, and he breathed deeply and easily for the first time in years. Decades. He was a man reborn. With just a little refinement and a lot of legal work to secure his rights, he would be rich. Not everyone could afford the elixirs and time needed to reach higher levels and extend their life. This method would at least give them the look and feel of youth. No small thing.

A week and a day after the ritual was cast, Magus Lorenz's wife and children turned themselves in to the police, weeping miserably or staring in numb horror at their hands. They explained how Magus Lorenz quickly fell to madness. How he drove them, with blows and cruel words, to stitch pure white fleece to his arms and back. Shaving his head and suturing wool along his neck and scalp. How he insisted on being bound hand and foot. How his wife felt unable to resist the compulsion to slit his throat. How his sons knew to build the pyre and lay their spasming, smiling father upon it.

And so Magus Lorenz earned his immortality in history.

Truth had to think for a long while on that. The forms of things mattered because, without them, the cosmic energy couldn't interact in the desired way with the material world. But intent mattered. The caster's intent, that of the creator of the spell . . . and apparently, that of the entity providing the power.

It was no wonder that modern magic stripped away as much of the divine or infernal as possible from their spells. They might be weaker, but they were vastly more reliable.

He hunted around for a copy of *Ars Goetia* and was not too surprised to learn that his school had taught a badly cut-down version of the real book. The real *Ars* was six centimeters thick, with every picture, every summoning, and every description accompanied by commentaries. Botis, he learned, was not merely a powerful demon in his own right; he also led sixty "armies" (definitions of which varied) and was both a "president" and an "earl."

The latter titles were understood to bear no relationship to the beings' actual titles in Hell, as human concepts simply did not apply to so much of it. In essence, he was a powerful demon near the top of the hierarchy, and when he spoke, other demons listened and obeyed. When summoned, he would appear either as a serpent or a tall, handsome swordsman with elegant horns and needle teeth. And he was a talker.

That was one of the few things the commenters all agreed about—don't let him start swinging his sword, don't let him start talking. In either case, you would find him a step ahead and leading you *quickly* down a path of no return. Not a seducer, exactly. Just very . . . reasonable. Knowledgeable and persuasive. Incisive.

Truth mulled it over on the practice field. The angelic blade seemed indifferent to his desire to fight using demonic magic. There was probably a story there, but he had a sick certainty that his education wouldn't let him understand even if it was explained to him. Cutting things, that he understood. A nice, simple thing, swinging a blade.

The sword was light, just a bit over a kilo. Normal for a sword this size, he knew, but he kept expecting it to be heavier. It was lively in his hands. Moving through the sword dance on the practice field, parry to cut, back to parry, then the explosive thrust! Then recover and begin again.

How would Botis attack? Well, he would attack first. He would know what was coming. Either preempt the attack and defeat in a counter-ambush, spoil the attack and set yourself an advantage, or simply use a fatal counter when their assault left them open. Botis was always a step ahead. Which meant that he was always ready. But even a demon wouldn't run around with a spell constantly primed, would he?

Actually, Truth had no idea what a being like Botis could do. Maybe he did run around with a spell half-cast.

Truth planted himself in front of a training dummy. He couldn't really get into it. Just a mannequin. He looked around and found a training sword and belted it onto the dummy. For some reason, it felt better now, like he could take it seriously. Which was objectively ridiculous, but he was prepared to go with it.

All right, Fuckhead here was about to try something. What would Botis do? Get his spell off first. How to make sure your spell goes off first? Have it partially ready to cast. Truth carefully pieced together the spell form in his mind, aiming to have it *mostly* together but not sweating the details. He walked toward the dummy. Four steps away, he tried to complete the spell and launch forward at the same time. It didn't quite work, but as the angelic blade whipped toward the dummy's neck, he could feel it almost take.

It was the most progress he had made with the spell so far. Truth smiled and reset. He hadn't practiced something like this since . . . god, was it studying for the SAT? Doing all those endless memorization drills for talisman pathways. He could probably diagram a *Farx and Whillooby Type 5A Air Circulation Talisman (Private residence, single room / Personal Vehicle Types R, F, N(u), N(x) / Poultry Sheds less than 5 meters square)*, in his sleep.

He squared up to the dummy again. It didn't feel bad. Teaching his body and his mind at the same time. He formed a rough outline of the spell and held it loosely in his mind. It didn't feel bad at all. Good, even. He rushed the dummy again. Once more, the spell didn't quite go off. That was okay. He was making progress. It would get there.

Truth kept up the exercise throughout the day. Just having the spell present in his mind. Loose but present. Could he drink a cup of locally grown and roasted coffee while readying Incisive? With difficulty, yes. Could he actually cast it while enjoying the faint notes of dark red fruit winding their way through the savory coffee smell? He tried.

He could not. Not yet. Practice, practice.

He briefly tried to hold it during a conversation with Jember but directly gave up. It was too much distraction. He couldn't keep the forms even loosely in mind. Shame. Watching pitz and trying to hold the spell was a fun challenge. It struck him as more realistic. Lots of movement, lots of noise. He tried to keep it in mind, attempting to cast it when players made a strong move on the ball.

No success, but he could feel it inching closer and closer.

He explained to Merkovah what he was doing during one of their study sessions, and the old monster strongly agreed.

"Let's try something. I will attack you momentarily. Try to cast Incisive before I do."

The beardy and deceptively young-looking exorcist sat back in his chair, slipping his hands into his pockets. It occurred to Truth that the exorcist's semi-formal clothing had a suspicious number of pockets. Truth pulled together the rough outline of Incisive in his head and tried to steady his breathing.

There was no visible change in Merkovah, but Truth was suddenly, absolutely sure that the man was about to attack. About to kill him. Truth desperately cast Incisive and attempted a draw cut.

It will come from the left. Truth shifted to the right as he drew and stepped into the blow.

The angelic blade stopped a hand's width from Merkovah's neck. The sense of murderous intent had vanished like a shadow at night. The old monster grinned at Truth.

"Congratulations! Well done!"

"Thank you, Teacher. It's thanks to your support."

"Of course! But still, you have worked hard. Now. Keep it up! Tomorrow, we are off to the mountains. We will not return here for some time." Truth nodded and left.

He hadn't mastered Incisive. Barely touched the threshold of it. But it was a start. Truth smiled. It was a start, and he could see the way forward clearly.

CHAPTER 22

DIPPED IN THE BOWL OF THE SKY

Truth woke in darkness. He knew it was dark, but his eyes could see perfectly well with the dim light through the window. Ever since he had crawled out of the well, the shadows held no terrors for him. He was holding the angelic sword—why?

Rapid banging on the door. Truth silently rolled out of bed and walked over to the door, raising the sword chest-high. Ready to lunge, stabbing through the door and into whoever was outside.

"Mr. Wells, quickly! We must be up and moving!" Merkovah. Truth removed the chair he had wedged under the door handle and unlocked the door without opening it. Keeping the angelic blade aimed at the door. Just in case. He tried casting Incisive, but it didn't quite take.

"Teacher? If I may ask, what was the first meal you bought me?"

"Eh? Dorowot at the diner, wasn't it?" There was a pause, then: "Ah."

Truth opened the door, not bothering to put away the sword. "What seems to be the problem, Teacher?"

"Change of plans. We must go to the mountains immediately. Tomorrow, we must be in the capital. I hope you have enjoyed these peaceful days, Mr. Wells, because the capital is a nest of vipers and scorpions. Be prepared to truly be a bodyguard. Practice Incisive constantly. Get dressed, get packed, and meet us at my carriage in twenty minutes."

Truth nodded and got packing. He knew a lot of guys went straight back into being slobs once they got discharged. He liked to keep tidy and keep his stuff ready to go. Partially because the home he grew up in was disgusting and covered in filth. More so because the PMC kept him moving.

He was fresh as a daisy and ready to go in ten. Jember, Etenesh, and Merkovah found him sitting sideways on his iron horse, watching the sunrise with the angelic blade by his side.

Truth didn't appreciate the picture he made. He knew that his new body was tall, fit, and handsome. His mind could accept it intellectually. His heart was not persuaded. It was not how he thought of himself. In his heart, he was still someone people glanced away from.

For Truth, the romance of the moment was watching the sunrise, tangerine orange over the dark emerald of the hills. Slowly filling the world with light and warmth, growing brighter and more yellow by the moment. It would be a hot, clear day. Darkness on the horizon, perhaps, but today was brilliant.

He tried to still his racing thoughts, forget his fear for the siblings, forget his terror of what might be growing with Etenesh, and just . . . breathe. Just . . . be.

For the others, he was like a spellblade on errantry, ever seeking a righteous cause. Praying, committing his soul to his path under the watchful eye of the sun. With his round, white zeph perched on his head, simple clothes, and his body untainted by wine or smoke, he was the living image of a Desrin ascetic. They knew he wasn't, of course, but for a moment, Truth was more than a man in their eyes.

Jember just smiled and thought wistfully about the sacrifices he had made for his career. He didn't regret his path, but he would never be a storybook hero. He might never be remembered at all. Which was fine, of course, but . . . didn't everyone dream of being a hero and saving the day?

Etenesh thought, for the very first time in her life, that she might be willing to marry outside her faith. That a foreigner could sincerely walk with God as she walked with God. That this was a battered heart she wanted to heal.

Merkovah . . . thought he saw what he was looking for. He just needed a hook.

The moment was spoiled by a long farm wagon carrying tonnes of coffee beans. The noisy rumble of its wheels and the dust it threw up seemed to smudge the image of the day.

"You look ready to go, Tommy," Jember called. Truth looked back, smiled, and nodded.

Merkovah waved the cousins toward the carriage. "We'll get breakfast a little ways down the road. I know a good spot. We must move quickly, though. Unless we are very fortunate, we will be spending thirteen hours on the road today." Truth twitched at that but settled down. He had spent long days on the road before. His body would hold up just fine. They drove off, letting the sun press them westward.

The roads in Siphios, or at least this part of Siphios, were rather good. The drive was pleasant, the dense green vegetation contrasting in a lively way with the muddy red of the soil. It was a good day to ride a two-wheeler.

Truth would have been content just to enjoy the ride and the charming scenery. Wild, open, utterly alien for a Harban boy. Merkovah decided to make this a learning opportunity instead.

A spirit poured out of the carriage's window, thick and chalk-white, like milk that moved like smoke. It faintly formed into the blurred outline of a woman and drifted over to Truth. The spirit kept pace with him as it leaned in to speak.

"Hear now the words of my contractor, known to you as Etenesh. Dread Merkovah has decreed that all his servants must refine their spellwork. Those within the carriage will attack with spells. Your task is to try and capture the least shine of the

First Gem of Botis and avoid the spells. I am bidden to remind you that you may not counterattack. Evasion is to be your only measure of success and failure."

Truth nodded. "Okay."

The spirit made no reply and drifted away. Truth smiled slightly. This would be fun. Hopefully. He carefully tried to cast Incisive. It . . . felt like it took? He slightly shifted the two-wheeler left and right just to get warmed up. It was, therefore, probably luck that the first spell just grazed his cheek. A fat little ball of water.

Truth doubled down on the spell. What would Botis do? He was chasing prey, running it down. Letting it tire itself out before moving in for the kill. He cast the spell once more.

From the right. Truth swerved to one side. The water ball went well wide. He grinned. It would be a fun afternoon. Two water balls came at once. Truth's grin vanished.

It was a somewhat damp Truth that rolled into the roadside diner for lunch. Not unhappy, exactly. His grasp of Incisive was improving steadily. But he made sure to give all of them a sergeant-grade filthy look as he walked to the table. The glare seemed to have a good effect on Jember and Etenesh but slid right off Merkovah. To be expected, he supposed.

Lunch was more stew and spongy bread. It wasn't that it wasn't good stew; it was. It was just that he was about ready to eat some fried chicken or a steak. Noodles would be great. This was some kind of stewed goat and a slimy vegetable he didn't recognize. It tasted pretty okay, but only okay. From the looks on the other diners' faces, his opinion was widely shared.

Their route took them through an area that could at best be called "rural." Competitive pressure wasn't going to drive the chain-smoking cook to up his game.

The coffee remained excellent. Perhaps not as fruity as what he got at Bule. Definitely tasted a little scorched. Still head and shoulders above any coffee he had drunk outside of Siphios. Apparently, the land of saints and scholars was fueled by high-test bean juice, and they demanded the very finest. Truth got back on his iron horse with only mild reluctance.

The river Omo ran high up through the mountains. Or between mountains; Truth was a little confused by the endlessly rolling geography at this point. It was wider than any river he had seen before, with near-sheer cliffs running along its banks. No fear of flooding there—the cliffs ran more than a hundred meters high in places. That must have been a comfort to the nearby farmers, because the river widened to two kilometers across or more in places.

The irrational loathing of farms was getting tiresome at this point. When you got right down to it, he had no reason to hate farms, farmers, farming, or any of that.

The fact that his body was now apparently disgusted by and held in contempt the profession of farming (while still perfectly happy to eat *the products of agriculture*) was revolting in its own right.

System, I swear if you are behind this—

<<*I'm not. Your body is just weird and wrong. Shut up. I'm working on something.*>>

Oh? What?

<<*Shhhhhh.*>>

It wouldn't say more.

They boarded a long, flat ferry, essentially a board on the back of an enormous river spirit. It didn't seem to mind. From what Truth could tell, it was something like a giant buffalo made out of water and starlight. He hadn't the fainted idea of how it all worked, but it was very steady.

Shortly after nightfall, Merkovah led them to a little temple set near the top of a mountain. He was greeted by a few elderly looking men in what Truth assumed was clerical garb and waved for everyone to join him.

"These are the ones I want to show the sky to," Merkovah said.

"It is no problem, of course. Although, really, a Desrin wants to come to our little place?"

Merkovah muttered something and pushed the trio through the temple. Merkovah, Etenesh, and Jember all took their shoes off just inside the door, and Truth followed suit.

The interior was sparsely decorated, with whitewashed walls and simple wooden pews facing a raised altar at the front. He got a quick glimpse of an ornate chest mounted on the wall before noticing that the others were engaged in a presumably important bit of etiquette.

They first pressed their palms to their eyes, then to their ears, then over their mouth. They bowed their heads, back straight, to the altar, then quickly walked toward the back of the hall.

Truth was going to ask something, but Jember looked over at him first, pressing a finger to his lips.

They left through a small door in the back of the temple and soon found themselves on a small path up to the summit of the mountain. Nobody spoke. It seemed this was not the place for that.

He wondered how the others were managing to walk barefoot on a dirt path up the mountain. His feet were fine, but he was a body cultivator. He could only imagine they were in pain. Still, they didn't hesitate or slow until they stood atop the mountain.

At the very peak, there was a stone plinth, and atop the stone plinth was a wide, onyx basin filled with water. The enormity of the sky wheeled above them.

No light pollution, no noise of people or wagons, nothing human to interfere with the terrible glory of the heavens. The stars burned with all manner of colors, showering the world with the emanations of their powers.

Above them all, splitting the sky, was the edge of the galaxy, the heavenly river, the road to . . . something greater. Something more than a mudball. More than a planetary slum.

Merkovah led them over to the plinth. He covered his eyes with his palms, so Truth and the others did the same. With worn sincerity, the old man said a quiet prayer, begging God to reveal the truth of the heavens to them. With a final amen, they lifted their hands away and looked into the bowl.

The heavens were no longer simply dots of light. In the bowl, they were revealed as demons, angels, spirits of ancient power, and forbidden names. Wheeling beasts and birds and great whales swimming through the sky, swimming through the extinguishing void between the stars.

Truth looked at it all and silently gasped. And without realizing it, he fell into the bowl of the sky.

CHAPTER 23

THE ELDEST SON

Truth fell into the sky, a tiny speck gazing in terror at the awesome beings that filled the void between stars. Even the stars were monstrous, glorious things—a chariot pulled by an unspeakable chimera, whipped on by a naked woman with an owl's head; a being with the head of a hawk, holding a burning sword astride a wolf; a bird, larger than a city, larger than a continent, made entirely of fire; and the memory of a mother's warmth that he had never known.

Some instinct pulled his eyes to one side. There was a serpent coiled on a rock and bathed in its own beam of light. Its scales were mottled, brown and black flecked with red and gold, and its eyes missed nothing. He was fascinated. Literally fascinated—he could not look away from the great being.

Relaxed but ready. Not looking but seeing all. Armored but not hindered. And he simply knew that any fight would be finished before it began.

No. That was his misunderstanding. It did not fight. It was either at peace or killing. After which, it would be at peace again. Truth had the overwhelming urge to bow in thanks. He didn't have that much control over his body, but he did his best. Botis saw, of course, but said nothing. That was fair. Truth was hardly worth his attention.

Truth realized he was moving. It was hard to tell how fast or in what direction. He was lost in the whirling infinity of beings impossibly grander than himself. But something in him was being called. Pulled. Or was he the one pulling himself toward that unknown place?

It felt like falling. Though of course, he did no such thing. In an infinite void, there was nowhere to fall to. Still, it *felt* like falling. Moving without control toward whatever passed for down and whatever doom awaited at the bottom. He felt like he should be staring at everything. Memorizing as much as he could. Fixing the natures and truths of these beings in his mind. Each was a fountain of wisdom. Of arcane knowledge. If only he could see them clearly! If only he had the slightest foundation to build upon!

Truth suddenly understood why so many went mad seeking visions of Heaven. Or the heavens. It was all wisdom. It was all holy. And infernal. And everything in between. Everything was perfectly true if you could understand what you were seeing. And everything would deceive the unwise and unwary. He understood now! The wisdom of the heavens could only be revealed to the deserving, for only by personal revelation could the truth of Heaven be understood! Yes, it all made perfect sense!

A hand, rough and calloused, grabbed his head like a melon and smashed him into the dirt.

Truth looked around. The heavenly glory had vanished, though it was still night. He was not where he was before. This place smelled marshy. Hot, humid. Dry soil, but marsh nearby. A small woodfire, a man in coarse woolen clothes. Long hair, roughly covering part of a handsome face. A somewhat familiar face.

Brutal, angular lines carved high cheekbones and a wide jaw. Deep set eyes, shaded over by long hair. Undeniably handsome in a rough, primal way. Corded with lean muscle. This was a manual laborer. And he resembled the parts of Truth that the worms had given him. Not exactly the same, but you would be forgiven for thinking them related.

"A *smart* little clay doll would have stayed on its little ball of mud until it was completely fired. The weather out here will wear you into nothing." The man spoke conversationally, poking something in the fire. "But then, you aren't quite right, are you? Hard for you to stay put. Come, let me take a look at you."

Truth pushed himself up off the ground and walked over. The thought of arguing simply didn't occur. Couldn't occur. The man, this place, took all his attention.

Strong, rough hands took his chin and tilted his face around. He was examined but wasn't really able to examine the man back. The rough man was tan. Somewhere between rubbed bronze and faded leather. Someone who worked out in the sun all day. The rough man stank—body odor and manure.

"What happened here?" The man started chuckling. "I'm not even mad. That's hilarious. Life's done you dirty, huh, kid?"

Truth wanted to explain that he had no idea what the honorable senior was talking about but would absolutely love to tell him anything he wanted to know. Unfortunately, some part of him recognized a rhetorical question when it heard it. The man waved Truth toward a patch of dirt next to the fire.

"Alright, your *nous* can't tolerate being here long, so I will tell you a few things. Just for fun. You have been blessed by my followers. In a sense, a *strictly spiritual* and not a *literal* sense, mind you, you have accepted a portion of my blood and legacy. You are not unique in this—there are thousands upon thousands more like you and have been for thousands upon thousands of years. On the other hand, since there are billions upon billions of you little clay dolls, you aren't exactly common." The man grinned, then went back to poking at the fire.

"What makes you so fun is that my legacy is just one of the twists of fate around you. That's hilarious. Do you know the odds of that happening? I don't. But I haven't seen it more than a handful of times. Each of those times, the strands sort of negated each other. The destinies conflicted, you see, and so came to nothing. You have at least three strands of destiny on you, all intertwined. One you were born with." The word *born* was heavy with irony. "One you got from my followers. And one from this little thing."

The man made a plucking motion toward Truth, who almost screamed as a little spark was pulled out of his chest. It flickered violently but was as helpless before the rough man as Truth was.

"This . . . is not what you think it is. It's not what it thinks it is, either. What a nasty little world you live in." The man let the spark go, and it slammed back into Truth's chest like a burning coal launched from a catapult.

"You are running out of time. Accept my legacy as much or as little as you like. It won't hurt you. Ah, you may be feeling some irrational feelings toward one group of people or another. You seem to have inherited some of my frustration and resentment. Don't worry about it. You can't do anything about it, so worrying is pointless. At least until you are much more than you are now. Killing is going to be part of your life forever. Just part of my legacy. There is no escaping it for either of us. You will not know peace until you are strong enough to impose your own. Do not hate the slaughter. One clay doll smashing other clay dolls counts for nothing. How much less will it matter when an actual man does it? I will answer one question. Don't worry about asking the *right* question; you won't. Just ask the question you most want to be answered."

Truth's mind was a whirl. He had so many questions. He couldn't even think of a question. He blurted, "Are you God?"

The man looked at him in shock through his long hair. Then he started laughing. Big, honest belly laughs. "Am I God? Well, people worship me. Pray to me. Offer me sacrifices. Make art in my honor. I am ancient, terrible, and possessed of power far beyond what you think the word power means. Am I God?" The man swept back his hair, revealing a circle on his forehead. Truth saw with a horrified thrill—it was nine worms chasing each other. "No."

The man let his hair fall down again.

"I am God's eldest grandson. Though, of course, people just think of me as the eldest son. I think I got his good looks. How do I compare?" The main pointed upward. Truth looked up into the sky and saw . . .

He saw . . .

It was . . .

Something broke, and Merkovah was lightly slapping his face, looking worried. "Young man! Young man, are you alright?"

"I saw . . . I saw . . ." Truth gasped for words, unable to even comprehend *what* he had seen, let alone how to tell another about it. He felt the memory . . . not fading but becoming cordoned off, as though his mind couldn't tolerate the weight of the memory but was unable to forget it.

"It's alright. Don't try to tell me. It's alright." The old monster with a young man's face patted him on the shoulder. "You aren't trained for it. You got far more out of this than I hoped. Well done! Very well done! But don't try to talk about it. Just hold on to what you can."

Truth lay on the ground, staring up. The sky was . . . just the sky. Distant and heavenly. But to have seen what existed (it seemed blasphemous to attribute something as mortal as living to those excellencies and supremacies) on the other side of the lights! He knew he would never see the sky the same way again. More, his very relationship with the world had changed. He had changed.

But what had he just seen? *What was that? Was that . . . really God?*

Hey, System. Did you see what I just saw?

<<No. Nor can I understand your memories of it. What I just experienced ... I don't know what I just experienced. I need to think.>>

I guess we can let the Worms drive the magic resistance cultivation.

<<Can we? Super. Shut up. Leave me alone. This is. Not right. I ... shut up. Leave me alone.>>

He looked over at Etenesh and Jember. Of the three of them, Jember was doing the best. He looked rocked but not lost. There was a definite glimmer to him, fading, but there. He had brought something back on from his journey. Etenesh was weeping.

Etenesh kneeled in the dirt, palms pressed to her eyes, and wept. She sobbed, the sound despairing. She had lost something, Truth knew. Something precious. She was no longer the same woman who came up the mountain. His heart hurt.

He knew he should embrace her. He didn't dare. Then Jember gave him a look and nodded toward his cousin.

Truth crawled over to her. He couldn't stand. Not just yet. "Etenesh. May I hug you?" he asked. Awkward, hesitating. Not sure where to look or put his hands. Etenesh didn't respond. Her palms were still pressed to her eyes. Eventually, she nodded. Gently, as though she were made of spun glass, Truth wrapped his arms around her.

She was very warm. She was shaking with pain. He didn't know how to comfort her. He didn't know what to say. He just held her silently. Kneeling with her in the dirt. Until she came back to herself.

He had the horrible feeling he didn't give good hugs. He just didn't know how to. He had hugged the sibs before, but not often.

"I am ruined," she murmured. "But I am not alone in that. We are all ruined. The whole world. Ruined." Her hands were still pressed over her eyes. "There is no hope. No salvation."

Truth let go of her shoulders and gently grasped her wrists. For a moment, he thought he smelled tobacco. "Maybe we are. Maybe everything is pointless. Maybe nothing really matters. But so what?" He tried to put a smile in his voice and didn't really succeed. "If we are all screwed, shouldn't we make the best of what we've got? Eat good food. Pet good dogs. Maybe find someone willing to touch you. That last one might be a stretch, for me at least."

That got her snorting. Then she broke down crying again. Truth felt awful. "I'm sorry. I'm not good at comforting people. Once upon a time, my brother asked me why I kept pushing, kept trying. When everything was hopeless and everyone was against us. He threatened to kick my ass if I said, 'Keep the faith.'" That got another wracking sob from Etenesh. "I didn't have an answer for him, but I think I do for you. I can't stand the thought that I'm helpless and things are hopeless. So, I'm going to act like they aren't. I'm going to take every sensible chance. I will do my very best. And I won't be a good sport about it if I fail."

CHAPTER 24

A DEBATABLE GOD

Etenesh eventually fell quiet, just curling up on herself. Jember sat next to his cousin, hip to hip, and put a comforting arm around her. Truth just sat there, feeling useless. It was Merkovah who managed to pull them out of their solitary silences.

"When I was younger, the land of Siphios was alive. I mean that in a way you youngsters probably don't understand—I mean that God had imbued every pebble, every blade of grass, every gust of wind with meaning. With the potential of undergoing its own spiritual journey or simply finding purpose in eternity as a rock. As a twist of air. A drop of water passing through its transformations."

He sighed.

"Then Starbrite and his demon came to this world. I speak of the man, here, not the corporate shell he created. A corporation being a sort of demon in its own right. His assault was both insidious and fast. We didn't understand what we were dealing with. At all. We thought he was just another gangster, another powerful man looking to create a pocket world for their pleasure and benefit. Well. We weren't wrong about that, at least. But I was there, and I can tell you that we truly didn't understand. We weren't up against a man. We were up against a system. A philosophy polished and refined to a glassy perfection. Slavery built on the illusion of prosperity. By the time we saw it, it was too late for people to listen. By the time we fought back . . ."

He looked up to the stars.

"By the time we fought back, God had turned his face away from us. He didn't even bother to let us know. He just left. The covenant is broken. Now Siphios merely echoes with the sound of past glory. Each echo fades as it bounces again and again. The streams no longer laugh with the children splashing in them. The air no longer whispers its mysteries to the wise. The people are lost among the throng groveling before God's chariot, hoping that once more he might glance our way."

Merkovah's eyes never moved from the heavens. Looking for what only he knew. "Starbrite didn't just rob our elixirs, ores, or other precious things. He didn't just steal our time or our dreams. He stole us from God. He stole us from God, and now God doesn't even want us back. We tried, you know. We tried often. But God doesn't want us back. So, we must grow up. And fight on. For ourselves and each other.

Truth just listened. He had never felt the eyes of God upon him.

"We cannot go back to how things were. We were children raised under the hand of a benevolent and loving father. Now we have to solve our own problems.

Still revering him that gave us life and wisdom. Still fearing his awesome wrath. But remembering that he *is not watching over us*. We must remember his teachings and pursue virtue and morality as he showed us. It is up to us to be moral and to do the right things. He cannot make us good nor forgive our sins. He cannot lead us to victory. Not anymore."

They spent the night in the temple, in the rooms set aside for pilgrims. It was a long time before anyone slept.

Truth woke up before dawn. The holy folk—Monks? Priests? Teachers? He didn't know what they were called, but they were up and cleaning. Some were mopping the temple, some wiping the windows. It wasn't a large place, so the few old men didn't find it much trouble. Truth nodded to them silently and found an empty patch of dirt by the front of the temple.

He hadn't cultivated last night. He would do it now.

Truth let his body move and flow through the old patterns. They felt a little different this morning. He wasn't just exercising and letting the energy flow. He was showing his respect. He was showing his dignity. The watchers above the sky might not know or care, but he knew. He cared. So, he moved and cultivated, imbuing each act with meaning. *I respect you. I am thankful for you. I revere you. But this power is* mine *now. I will take it and do what I will. And while it might not be good enough for you* (he felt something stirring in him at that thought), *it certainly will be good enough for me.*

Breathe, flow, move. Let the energy fill him up, spill from aperture to aperture, letting the overflow flood his body. He had been worried that he was turning into some kind of monster. That worry no longer existed. Despite what the rough man said, he might not be *the* God, but he certainly was *a* god. At least to Truth.

He would embrace his own strength. He would not fear his instinct to fight. Though he would try to remember that fighting should be his last choice. He would dig in to the legacies and fate tied to his body. Whatever they were. They could become his strength. Strong enough not to need a gang. Strong enough not to need a god.

He finished the routine, his breath leaving like a long arrow. *System. Personal Development Sheet.*

<<Personal Development Sheet is unavailable at this time. Processing.>>

You what? Truth asked, quite reasonably.

<<Processing, you cursed prick. As in I'm trying to figure it out myself. Look, do as much . . . stuff as you can today. Run, cast spells, whatever. I need more data to sort out what all this is. Use Incisive a lot. All the time, actually. Have people attack you while you defend with your sword. For once, I'm not just looking to watch you get tortured.>>

Well. That . . . might be ominous? Actually, it might be a good thing. Nothing to be done right now, though. Truth shrugged and turned around to find he had an audience. Jember sat on the steps of the temple and gave Truth a wan smile.

"I didn't want to interrupt. Do you do that every morning?"

"Evenings, actually, and mostly in my room. Still, there is something I like about doing it under the sky." Truth thought about it and smiled slightly. "I will probably do it exclusively outside now, if I can."

"It seems you had a good experience."

"In some ways. I also nearly went crazy, so"—Truth waved—"not all perfect."

"Hah. Well. That's why I studied apocalypticism at uni. I trained for just that kind of thing."

"Really? I had no idea that was something you could train for. Seemed like a . . . I don't know. Some kind of unique religious experience."

"In a little out-of-the-way temple like this? Hardly. Not common, mind you. But at least in Siphios, it's not unheard-of. With an expert like Merkovah overseeing things, we were safe enough."

"So . . . it's something I could do again?"

Jember wiggled his hand. "Yes, but not for a long while. Your nous, which is a technical term for that point where your mind and soul interconnect, took some strain last night. Not damage but strain. It needs to get back into shape. Also, I suspect you have a lot to digest. I could tell your gains weren't small.

"You were literally glowing for a moment there." Truth gave Jember a little smile. Jember smiled back, a bit of his usual sun shining through. Then dimming.

"Could you check on Etenesh? I think she would rather see you than me right now," Jember asked.

"I will, but . . . why?"

"We are very close because, out of all our generation of cousins, we were the most religious. And we come from a very religious family. You may not be able to tell, but . . . well, by the standards of Siphios, we are very . . . restrained. Very strict in our conduct. For me, it was because I enjoyed the wonders of theology. I embraced the faith because it was all so marvelous, you see? But for Etenesh, it was more"—he spun his hand—"more like getting along with another part of the family. Like things *had* to be done a certain way, or Grandpa would throw a fit and Grandma would never speak to you again."

"Okay?"

Jember sighed, looking as frustrated as Truth had ever seen him. "Do you remember how she had her hands last night? Palms pressed over her eyes?"

Truth nodded.

"It's the Sign of the Faithful. We see no deception that would lead us to sin. We hear no temptation that would cause us to forget our duty to God. We speak no slander that would disgrace God or ourselves. Better that we have no eyes, no ears, no tongue than we do otherwise." Jember couldn't help sounding bitter.

"She wished she hadn't seen."

"Putting it very mildly."

"So, why does she want to see me?"

"Because she wants you. She likes you, and she desires you. You would be more comfort to her now than I would."

Truth started waving him away. Denying that she might want him. Or like him. Certainly, he liked her and hoped they could become friends, and he certainly dreamed of being more than friends, but she was beautiful and smart and went to university, and he was a slumrat. He knew his place.

The coarse man grinned at him from his memories. And Truth could swear he smelled a whiff of tobacco. Yeah. His place. Just another slumrat.

Like fuck he was!

"Hey, Jember? Don't fuck with me on this. Are you sure she feels that way?"

Jember gave him an odd look. "You aren't? She practically posted a public notice. What else do you want her to do? Get it notarized?"

Truth looked back up into the lightening blue sky and wondered which star was his rough patron.

Truth went and sat with Etenesh for a while. He didn't know what to say, so he didn't say anything. He just sat with her and held her hand. She cried once. He asked if he could hug her, and she nodded, and once again, he held her like she was made of spun sugar. She told him to hold her stronger than that. She might fly away. He did. She didn't. Soon, Merkovah came and collected them. It was time to go to the capital.

They played the water-ball game on the road again. It was eight hours to the capital, and hell, everyone was bored. Two hours in, they were sending storms of water at him as he dodged and twisted out of their way. The drivers they passed gave them *looks*, but a few people cheered in appreciation, watching Truth's antics. He could keep the precognition going pretty steadily, and his accuracy was getting a lot better. He couldn't wait to start practicing the cutting part. The image of Botis was seared into his memory.

It would have done his ego some good to hear what people were saying about him. Even Etenesh was smiling now and again. It seemed that watching a handsome man move like a snake on a speeding iron horse was enough to brighten her day. The comments from the other cars were downright thirsty.

They hit the exurbs and had to stop playing around. Boring houses, boring stores selling boring things in quantities that only interested the boring. Someone, somewhere, needed two hundred square meters of white ceramic floor tile. Truth did not. There was a lumber wholesaler. It seemed to be doing well. Huzzah. Merkovah appeared to be trying to speed up, but traffic was rapidly becoming a problem. They came to a full stop between a garage and a place that sold fishing supplies to hobbyists.

"How, exactly, did I go from contemplating the mysteries of the heavens to wondering if I can afford a full teardown of my two-wheeler in less than twenty-four hours?" Truth muttered to himself. Odd or not, his faithful steed needed the service. It had put in the work. Not like the stars or those great stellar beings. They didn't work at it. They just were, and that was enough. Truth flexed his hand. He had to work at it. But that was okay. He didn't mind working hard. He just needed some maintenance now and then.

CHAPTER 25

XANDRE

Truth's first impression of Xandre, the famed capital of Ancient Siphios, the birth-place of art, magic, philosophy, city of supreme culture and sophisticated pleasures, Xandre, Gem of the World, was a half-shuttered huddle of discount clothing stores and brickmakers. It was not a great introduction.

Just inside the exurban shopping belt were the small homes in their teeming thousands. Little flat-roofed boxes laid out side by side, each with a tiny strip of garden out front. Densely clustered, with wide sidewalks. A lot of buses moving people around, lots of people traveling on peculiar two-wheeled conveyances. Somewhat like his iron horse, but these didn't appear to have any power source beyond their riders pushing pedals in a circular motion. It was the oddest thing he could remember seeing in a while.

Well. That wasn't an actual religious experience. Still, they seemed happy enough. Even dawdling along the highway, he could see people stepping into and out of each other's houses all the time. It seemed there was no such thing as a solitary . . . Siphionite? Siphiosian? Siphy? What did they call themselves? Truth shook his head and tried to focus on what he was seeing. Lots of people moving around, happy. Lots of hugging. A surprising amount of kissing. Not "peck on the cheek" kissing, either. Nobody seemed to see anything odd with it.

Here and there were dropped blocky apartment buildings, sticking out in the sea of small homes like a wart on a tit. Truth didn't think much of them at first. They were just apartment blocks. Only so many ways you can make apartment blocks. The cheapest and simplest way is going to look the same pretty much everywhere. They were more or less what he remembered from Harban. After a distressingly long time, he shuddered with the realization—they were *exactly* what he remembered from Harban.

Of course he recognized the buildings! How long had he stared obsessively at the brochures of C-Tier housing? He had memorized the floor plans of all four different apartment layouts. He had laid awake at night, listening to his parents scream at each other, listening to his neighbors fuck and tear each other apart, listening to people hammering on doors and begging to be let in before *somebody* got them—he had laid awake at night *dreaming* of those apartments. They were as close to heaven as his imagination could reach.

Here they were, rising like moles in the suburbs of Xandre. Looking a lot less divine these days. They had that gray-washed look to them that Truth associated with any multistory building this close to the equator. Something about the constant humidity and the accumulation of dust and dirt thrown up by millions of passing vehicles. Surely, there should be some kind of spellwork to prevent that? Something to keep the paint looking fresh? Perhaps they just felt it wasn't worth it. Starbrite had certainly never invested in that kind of spellwork. Not that he had noticed. Or cared.

As they got into the city center, there were more row homes, more two- and four-story buildings crammed side by side in happy intimacy. The people moving around seemed almost a colorful blur, carrying bottles of this and that, covered plates, books, boxes . . . Everyone visiting. Everyone chatting. He saw a few of his fellow white-round-hat wearers moving about, but they were a clear minority there. There were also a few of the small-decorative-hat wearers like Merkovah, but they were also a minority. Most people dressed like Jember and Etenesh—colorfully and with clothes cut to flatter.

It was disorienting, whiplashed between the invisibly ordinary and the startlingly new. People socialized in Harban, of course. It was just that *he* didn't. And he didn't know of anyone who socialized the way the people of Xandre did. A thousand little touches, every day, linking everyone together in a whirl of colors and smiles. They seemed to like it, but he imagined he would go insane in less than an afternoon. When you got right down to it, he *really* didn't like being touched casually. He was still refining his thoughts on this, but so far, he decided that if someone came into stabbing range, they probably wanted to be stabbed. And he had a wonderful sword with him *all the time.*

They pressed deeper into the city, and towers began to rise. Some glass-and-steel monsters that every city seemed to host, but others looked like they were carved from stone or ivory. More still were clearly grown—trees in electric purples like lightning bolts seventy stories tall, mushrooms of a modest forty stories but wide as a city block at their cap. He could see shade parks growing in the mycelium shadow, with more colorful swirls gathering there to escape the late-afternoon heat.

Here and there were stone temples in a more-classical style—small windows, polished white exteriors of quarried stone. Many were densely covered in etchings, in reliefs, in votive statuary shimmering in their own lights, or dancing to hymns that only they could hear.

Perhaps he was wrong about that. Truth half-wondered if he would hear the music too if he came closer.

Most brilliant and fascinating of all, though, were the spirits. Demons, angels, and everything in between, crawling, flying, striding through the city. Swarms of air demons poured along alleyways and cleaned the filth with voracious delight. Small spots of angelic light floated behind them, evaporating the demonic taint they left behind, turning the air fresh and sweet. Worm demons trailed over construction sites, driven on by sigil-wielding construction workers, laying level after level of new construction or eating the old.

Any building of sufficient size and dignity would host spirits. The trees were nesting grounds for birds made of soft, licking flame, and electric-blue birds whose shimmering, rainbow tails stretched for meters behind them. A statuesque ogre sunned herself, lying atop a mushroom. Tigers with burning eyes and burning wings stalked over the rooftops of libraries while wheels of eyes glowing with painful light kept vigil over temples.

The people of the city treated them as normal. Sometimes, they saluted the spirits or shooed them away, or simply ignored the terrible beings that could snuff them out like a guttering candle. They were just part of the city. Only tourists would make a fuss.

Merkovah led them to a temple in the middle of the city. It wasn't the biggest or the prettiest, but it had an age and density to it that Truth found immensely appealing. Its carvings shimmered with a lively light, and the statuary looked elegant, if occasionally obscene. Some of the carvings were not suggestive; they were instructional. Once again, nobody seemed to notice or care. He parked in an underground garage next to Merkovah's horrible disguised carriage. The stone pillars looked ancient, but he instinctively felt they were solid.

Truth interrogated that instinct. He didn't trust things that told him to trust them. He walked up to a pillar and inspected it as the cousins started unloading the carriage. They didn't glow or shimmer with a mystical light or any of that nonsense. They looked like old stone pillars. He rested a hand on one. Felt like an old stone pillar. The whole thing just screamed, *I am what I seem to be.* Highly, intensely, profoundly suspicious pillar behavior, in Truth's professionally paranoid opinion.

He touched it again. Why was this setting off alarm bells?

"It's more real than you are used to seeing. Well, outside an active magical effect. Most buildings just can't support that level of spirituality, even here in Siphios." Merkovah came up beside him, touching the stone with a soft smile. "She's one of the oldest temples in the world. Not the very oldest, but . . . one of them."

Truth was somewhat confused by the idea, then confused by his own confusion. It made perfect sense if you thought about it. If people could cultivate to become "more real" than the surrounding world, and "more real" was defined as becoming closer to God, moving steadily up the material hierarchy, then it was nothing odd that a truly ancient temple might do the same.

Perhaps that was what people meant by "natural treasures" or the sorts of goods that could be traded off-world. Was prismatic iridium more "real" than regular iridium? It would be worth finding out. His ignorance felt like a stinging pain, a sharp shame for being so dumb. Even as he reminded himself that he was *not* dumb. That he had tried his best with what little he had been given. But he felt dumb, not knowing something that everyone else probably knew.

"So . . . why are we here? And why did we have to come here is such a rush?"

Merkovah shook his head. "Not a garage conversation. We will be busy, and the work will likely be unpleasant. Lucky you, you will have ample opportunity to test your understanding of Incisive."

"Oh good?"

"You will also be able to find some teachers who can help you practice your Valentinian Meditations. I can see some progress, but it's slow going, no?"

"It's the visualization. Hard to keep things fixed in my mind. Harder still to think what the 'perfect' version of them would look like."

"Totally normal. Takes years to truly master, if not decades. Don't worry too much, and just keep focusing on incremental progress. With luck, we can find a way to accelerate the process a bit."

"Eh?"

"Also not a garage conversation. Come, young man. It's been a long drive, and our rooms await us."

Their rooms were simple and spare—a single bed in a cell, essentially, with a small desk, a single lamp on the desk, and a small shelf. Everything else was communal. Communal bathrooms, communal dining room, communal library—everything was a shared space. There were even communal rooms to go have sex if you were so inclined. Which came as something of a shock to Truth but, again, was treated as not worth mentioning by everyone else.

"The assigned rooms are really for sleeping and quiet meditation. Sometimes, you just need to get away from everyone and have a little space for your own thoughts," Etenesh said softly as they sat for dinner with the priests and temple workers. "The temples are built to make sure you have that space. But everything else should be done as part of the community of the children of God."

"Right, but . . . everything?"

"Why not? There is nothing shameful about any of it. Pride, vanity, greed, possessiveness, those things are shameful." Jember snagged another piece of bread and went in for a chunk of vegetables. Dinner was a stew. Again. A stew-loving people, Truth had noticed. The charm had worn off. He was ready to eat something grilled on a skewer.

"I may be having a translation problem. Pride as distinct from vanity? Greed is not the same as possessiveness?" Truth asked.

"Yes. One might desire a large, fancy room to themselves to display their superiority. This can be to impose their self-importance on others or merely to gratify themselves. Related but not the same. Greed—wanting more to the point of cruel excess. Possessiveness would be hoarding what you already have in excess of reason. Related, again, but subtly different. And both thrive in isolation." Etenesh was pushing her food around, not eating much.

"All right, I get that this is a religious building but . . . even sex?"

"Why not sex?"

Truth struggled to put into words what seemed screamingly obvious to him. "People prefer to do it in private?"

"You can if you want. I mean, I'm not overly fond of an audience myself. Still, it's nice to have people handy to help you change sheets and tidy up afterward." Jember shrugged. "I think you may be confusing *not hidden* with *mandatory public display*. And it's not like people are randomly having sex with each other. It's not some free-for-all orgy."

"That . . . all right," Truth said.

"It's just a room off to the side. Somewhere where people can connect," Etenesh muttered. "Popular after weddings, obviously. Always pretty spare and easy to wash."

Truth looked back and forth between the cousins. They were, until yesterday, cheerful, upbeat, sociable . . . and gave not the slightest hint that casual sex was part of their lives. The campus had been pretty empty, and it wasn't like he was stalking the faculty or anything, but . . .

"Is this just a temple thing? Or a Xandre thing?"

"No, but . . ." Jember looked a little sad. "The old ways are dying out all over. I guess you could say this is the last place our culture is staying strong. Hard to keep the faith these days."

CHAPTER 26

A MAGE AND A GENTLEMAN, PART 2

Merkovah informed Truth that there would be extensive meetings in the temple today, and he would be needed for important Standing Around duty on the other side of the door from the meeting. Truth duly dressed in the provided pseudo-military set of clothes, wore his zeph as instructed, belted on his sword, and guarded the door. It was exactly as exciting as he remembered.

The one added wrinkle, an unpleasant grit of annoyance, was that Etenesh and Jember did not seem to understand that chatting to him was Not Okay. They pointed out that the hallway was practically empty, and it was very boring staring at a blank wall for umpteen hours. Which was true but also not the point. He was *working* while he was staring at the wall for umpteen hours. He was paying attention to all the noises and sudden quiets. He was alert for alarms and standing by for signals. Guarding, done right, wasn't just boring; it was exhausting. And they weren't helping.

They looked very sulky about that. Still, they did listen eventually, and scrammed. The hallway mostly stayed empty, and the few passers-by didn't linger. Something about Truth discouraged idle curiosity. This gave Truth plenty of time to indulge his idle curiosity about the walls around him. From floor to ceiling, they had been inscribed. Some small parts of it were in Re'inyo . . . possibly. The letters looked more or less right, but the words they made didn't make sense. Perhaps an older version of the language or simply a related tongue. The majority of the inscriptions were in languages he couldn't even recognize or even in little pictures.

Presumably, they meant something religious. He had no idea what. It was interesting, the way the languages seemed to mix together. Like there was some bigger pattern he couldn't see yet. Too close to the wall. Too lost in the detail.

The other thing that kept distracting him was, naturally, sex. In that, it seemed pretty freely available. It was just another part of socialization, from what he could tell, though the rules changed dramatically after marriage. Pregnancy, STIs . . . all nonissues. Everyone knew how to make the little homemade charms. The bigger problem was someone being a selfish lover or just a jerk in bed. Word got around fast, according to Jember. He was looking kind of wistful. The self-imposed chastity was taking a toll.

The flip side of that was . . . apparently, nobody cared about their virginity. It wasn't shameful. It wasn't something to protect. It seemed to have all the emotional weight of—Truth couldn't think of a parallel. He didn't mention to the cousins that he was a virgin. People in Xandre might not care, but he did.

The conference broke for lunch. Truth tentatively sorted people by hats—the tiny-decorative-hat group, the people wearing bigger, pointier hats, the people with round white hats (almost certainly Desrin), and the generically hatted. Nobody appeared to be bareheaded, though there were some who had pretty clearly just grabbed any old hat out of politeness. He caught little snippets of conversation—

"Totally ignoring the economic collapse of the Ben-Zhu bloc . . ."

"Not a lot of rain this winter. Going to cost a fortune in sacrifices and reagents."

"Staple crops. We nail down staple crops, start ripping out the stuff for export—"

"Somebody must have a line or a back channel. Someone!"

"Jeon is acting like everything is fine, obviously, but that's nonsense."

"It may be time to consider some . . . drastic steps toward reducing demand . . ."

"It's the not knowing. You know?"

"Palace isn't making a peep, of course . . ."

"Jane's pregnant. I keep thinking about that. She's pregnant. Now."

"Any chance of direct divine intervention? Because it may come to that."

"Look, food's the key, but think about everything else that goes down with it."

"It's going to be war, of course. The only question is, who will be on the planet to fight it?"

This last statement was given casually to Truth by an older lady from the white-hat crowd. She looked at him speculatively. "What do you think, young man?"

"I think I don't know enough to have a useful opinion, Ma'am."

She started laughing, startling everyone around her. "No, I don't suppose you do. I wish I did." Chuckling, she rejoined the crowd headed for lunch.

Later that evening, a mentally exhausted Truth was led to a small stone chamber covered in yet more of the inscriptions. In the middle of the chamber was a basin of water with a small mat next to it.

"The function of this room is quite simple. Reflection. There is nothing here that you didn't bring in. In fact, I would strongly recommend getting naked and leaving everything in the basket by the door, though it's not mandatory." Merkovah had looked grim all day and hadn't lightened up one bit since the end of the conference.

"Start with Incisive. You seem to have made good progress there. Then the Meditations. Someone will come and get you in a couple of hours. Don't argue with them—it's not good to stay here too long. You can get lost."

The chamber was barely three meters square and, other than the basin and mat, was completely empty.

"Yes, Teacher."

Truth did as suggested, stripping off and leaving everything by the door. He asked about the safety of leaving a highly valuable, literally angelic weapon in a cubby and got a long-suffering sigh in response.

"You are in Temple Nag Hamadi. My home temple. Nobody, *nobody*, is going to touch that sword without my permission." Merkovah pointed Truth into the chamber. He went.

Truth sat on the mat. He looked into the basin in case it too was full of celestial wisdom. Arguably, it was. In that it was full of water. Truth shrugged and sat back, trying to breathe steadily. Trying to keep the image of Botis in his mind.

It was like trying to balance a tree on your fingertip.

Botis *was*. That was the key thing to Truth. Botis existed and was fully, completely himself. Without hypocrisy or shame or reservation. Not boasting, not flaunting. He simply was, and that was more than enough. Truth interrogated that thought a bit. Botis ultimately had the form of a serpent. A viper. An ambush predator. Did that count as hiding the self?

Perhaps, but Botis was not hiding *from* himself. And it was only when hunting. In fact, the difference between Botis hunting and not hunting may be known only to Botis. He was still until it was time to make a decisive move. Truth frowned a little. That was important but not the key.

Botis simply was, and that was enough. Why did that seem so important? Was Botis egotistical? Perhaps, to an extent. He was so self-contained, so self-sufficient, it was hard to imagine him giving a damn about someone or something else. But again, that felt like it was missing the mark. Botis was a viper. A swordsman of incredible subtlety and a speaker of deep insight. Ah, was this it? He felt like he was on the right track.

Botis as a debater, as a public speaker, not a viper or swordsman. He would speak with absolute assurance when he chose to speak. He would see directly to the heart of an issue and speak to it. He could see through the confused thoughts of others. How? How could he do that?

Because Botis knew himself. That utter self-knowledge was the basis of his confidence and of his understanding of others. Botis accepted all he was in every way that thought could be understood. Botis . . . loved . . . himself.

Truth's mind stuttered a moment on that. Botis loved himself. He accepted himself for everything he was and everything he wasn't. Loved those things, not passionately or obsessively but steadily. Contentedly. And because of that foundation, he was able to think clearly, not getting in his own way. He could move instantly without getting in his own way.

The true core of Incisive, the First Gem of Botis, was two words—*Love Yourself*. Everything followed from there. Truth didn't love himself.

He started shaking just a little, but he couldn't stop it. He didn't love himself. It never occurred to him that it should matter. Well, yes, it did occur to him. It had been occurring to him ever since he left the Free State, even if he hadn't phrased it quite that way. He didn't love himself. His mind was torn up, yanked between knowing damn well he didn't deserve love and desperately wanting it. Had he missed the mark the whole time?

Truth remembered holding Etenesh as she cried. Holding her like she was spun sugar. Brittle and threatening to melt. She seemed warm to him. But he remembered a core of painful coldness within him. A part of him that he didn't dare let warm up. He always thought it would be the warmth of someone else that would comfort him. But how could someone love him if he couldn't accept their love? How could he accept their love if he didn't love himself?

The basin rippled. Something dropped into it. Then again. He looked into the basin and saw himself. He saw himself crying. When had he last cried? He couldn't remember. It had been a long time ago. A lifetime ago. Was it . . . when he found out he passed? Yes, that was probably it. He remembered crying when he found out he passed the SAT. Found out that he was a Starbrite Man. That someone out there, wise and powerful, thought he was good enough.

Someone else thought that he was enough.

He had been holding the blade even then, hadn't he? Etenesh told him he could put down the blade, but even in the happiest moment of his life, he couldn't put it down. He clung to it tighter than ever. His first thought was to sever his pain, and he cut away his hellish parents. He didn't know how to put down the blade. How can you hug yourself with a sword in your hand? How can you hug another? All you can do is cut.

Love yourself. The opinions of others are worthless. Only you are able to love yourself. Only you can complete yourself. Easy to say. Easy to think. How many could really do it? Truth was sobbing now. He was certain he wasn't one of those who could.

The young man who came to collect Truth didn't seem surprised to find him sobbing. He just carefully put him in a robe and handed him the basket with his things, the holy sword jutting out to one side. He was returned to his room, and all he could do was grip the sheath in his hands until his knuckles turned white. The thoughts kept going around and around—it wasn't enough to know yourself. You had to love yourself. And he didn't. He wasn't even sure he knew himself. Actually, he was sure he *didn't* know himself. There was a gentle knock on his door.

"Tommy? Can I come in?"

He didn't have the strength to speak. He didn't want to see Etenesh. But the one thing he did know was that he couldn't stay as he was. It hurt too much. So, he made himself stand up, open the door, and sit back down on the bed.

"Tommy? Can I hug you?" Truth choked back a sob.

"I don't know. I hope you can. Just don't hurt yourself trying."

She wrapped her arms around him. She smelled of sun and of drying spices. A hint of temple incense clung to her, mixing and rising with the warmth of her skin. She was very warm. The core of Truth didn't thaw. But eventually, it was enough to comfort him.

"I hope you never understand me. Not really. But I hope you can come to care for me. I . . . care for you, I think, in my own mutilated way." Truth struggled to get the words out. He didn't really know what he was trying to say.

Etenesh just hung on to him. Keeping him from flying away.

CHAPTER 27

THE INTERSECTION OF REVELATION AND REASON

Etenesh held Truth until the shaking stopped, then a little longer. She let him go with a sigh. "Am I a bad person for feeling glad you need me? I don't like being the one who needs comforting," she asked.

"I don't know. I don't think so." Truth tried to smile and managed to twitch his cheek. He sat next to her quietly. He knew, in a dull sort of way, that he should talk about why he was in this state, but he just couldn't bring himself to do it. He simply couldn't summon the emotional energy. Etenesh seemed pretty drained too.

"Must say it's unusual to see you this way. You are always so . . . self-contained. Like everything around you has nothing to do with you. You are so accepting of, well, almost everything. Fight a thousand demons? 'Okay.' Stare at a wall all day? 'Okay.'" Etenesh snorted. "I'm . . . terrible. Because I am happy, you let me in."

"I'm—"

"Complicated?" She smiled.

"Yes. My childhood was not the best, and my working life has been . . . similar." Truth shrugged one shoulder. "Never knew it would mess up learning spells. But here we are."

"Talk about it with Jember and Merkovah tomorrow morning. I bet you are doing better than you think."

Truth made no reply. He didn't even have the energy to be negative.

Etenesh sat a while longer, then shot to her feet. She fidgeted a bit. "Jember told you that I'm interested in you."

"Yes."

"It sounds like you are interested in me?"

"Yes. As best I can."

"Haah. You could have stopped at *yes* and made me happy, you know."

"Sorry. Tired." And hurting. He would have used a line from a romance novel if he was feeling even a little better.

"And not comfortable being touched."

"Not . . . really. Trust issues, it seems."

"Would you, not tonight but maybe soon, like to try sleeping together? Not sex, just us sleeping in the same bed. Just to see how it feels?"

It scared the hell out of him. He could feel the tiny hairs of his body rising in alarm. He could imagine, easily, her stabbing him in his sleep. Poison supplied in so many ways. So many more ways to deliver a devastating curse. At the same time, his body was already losing the warmth she had given him, and the cold inside was enough to make him *scream,* and he desperately wished she would stay.

"That scares the hell out of me. I want to try that very much."

She smiled a little at that. "Not tonight."

Truth nodded. "Not tonight."

"Sleep. Busy day tomorrow."

The next morning found the group clustered together at a table in the cafeteria. There would be another conference today, and Merkovah didn't look any more optimistic about it than the last one.

"I cannot make them think, never mind *act,* and the uncertainty is paralyzing even the ones who are rightly afraid. It is maddening." Merkovah growled. Etenesh leaned over and was about to unsubtly nudge Truth when she saw him sway back from her. He wasn't even looking at her, but he instinctively moved out of the way. She sighed and said, "Tommy. Now's as good a time as any to ask."

"Ah. Right. So. This is what happened." Truth recounted seeing Botis in his vision and what he realized in the chamber last night. He instinctively didn't mention his rough patron. No good reason, but his mind was faintly screaming at him to shut up about it. He also skirted around the self-love issue. He didn't want to be that vulnerable.

Truth finished his jerky recitation and looked around the table. He wasn't expecting looks of envy, but that's what Jember was giving him.

"Tommy. Ditch the bodyguarding gig and join me in apocalyptic mysticism. It's your true calling."

"It is?"

"Oh, yeah! You got all that and didn't go insane, turn into a heretic, or just explode into ash. That is some top-notch stuff right there. That's talent!"

"Are . . . those things that happen on that kind of vision-thing? Nobody mentioned anything like that!" Truth started to get upset.

"They would not have happened. I was right next to you, ready to intervene. You were in no danger at any point." Merkovah sounded tired. "But I wouldn't go back a second time by yourself."

"Noted." Truth was calmer but still a bit salty about the "explode into ashes" thing. "Wait, I'm not Siphios Reform Orthodox or anything. How do you know I didn't go heretic?"

"Do you think you can sit on the throne of God, thereby becoming a hyperangel who is functionally a mini-god?" Jember asked.

Truth stared at him. Unblinking.

"See, you're fine."

Merkovah waved the question of heresy to the side. "I should also note that *heresy* probably doesn't mean what you think it means. Or, well, it does, but it means *more* than what you think it means. *Heresy* is not the word you should be focusing on. The word that you need to be giving your attention to, Mr. Wells, is *revelation*."

"Revelation. As in *the truth was revealed to me*."

"Yes, but of course, it is more complicated than that. Without getting into"— Merkovah's eyes got hazy, then refocused—"let's say eight thousand years' worth of religious debate, we can think of our understanding of the divine as coming in a few broad categories. First, someone just tells us about it, and we believe them. Apostolic succession or similar. Quite popular, but reliability is always going to be a matter of doctrine. The second way is logic or reason. We observe the available information, the universe, and deduce the nature of God. This actually has a high degree of accuracy, particularly in describing worldly phenomena and the rules of the occult. Most of the talismans you have worked on can be considered products of this school."

Merkovah took a sip of coffee and continued.

"Then there is what you just experienced—revelation. Specifically, understanding of the divine derived through revelation. There is a technical term for it, but it's not important right this second. Here's the thing about revelation. It is simultaneously *incredibly* powerful and *incredibly* unreliable. There is a reason Jember is studying apocalypticism as a graduate-level course."

"Eh?" Truth asked intelligently.

"You have a shocking, highly valid, and *personal* understanding of Botis, which has changed how you view yourself and your relationship with the world."

Truth nodded. He certainly had.

"Well, do you think Jember or I would have had the same reaction? Or Etenesh? Given our different life experiences, I can tell you that we certainly would not have. No two people receive exactly the same revelation, because each revelation, while truthful, is always understood through the medium of ourselves. That is, our own lived experiences, what we have heard of, and what we believe. By logical extension, that means that any explanation you give of your experience, no matter how correct it is *for you*, will always be, to some significant degree, incorrect for everyone else."

Truth looked lost. Merkovah smiled slightly and stood.

"Come, let's have a little morning exercise. I think it will help you understand.

The basement area was surprisingly clean and well lit. It seemed that it was often used as a multifunction space, so it didn't take much to turn it into a sword-fighting practice area. Merkovah summoned an earth demon and handed Truth a stick.

"Your goal: defeat the demon. Stay untouched until you can successfully execute the cutting portion of Incisive."

"Okay." Truth nodded, then winced, remembering the conversation last night. Etenesh chuckled softly as she got ready to watch the show.

Truth cast aside everything he could, just focusing on the demon. Incisive quickly spilled out of him. The earth demon was, like all of its kind, slow, tough, and unreasonably strong. A single hit from it, even a graze, and he would be seriously injured at best. So, he had to dodge while looking for his chance.

The blasted thing was so slow, he didn't even know if the spell was working. Dodging was *effortless*. Every move the demon made was telegraphed to an insulting degree. He had ample time to finish the blade portion of the spell. The wooden stick flickered, then the spell condensed a blade over it. Truth spotted an easy opening and went for the neck. The blade sank in deep, and the draw across was smooth.

Deep as it was, it was still too shallow. Truth frowned and raised his hand, calling for a halt. Merkovah stopped the demon, then signaled for the cousins to stay silent.

Truth sat down and frowned. He could kill this demon. He had a rough grasp on the blade part of the spell, and the demon couldn't touch him. It would take time and quite a few strikes, but he could get there.

But that wasn't how Botis fought, was it? Botis was still. Calm until he exploded with a decisive blow. Taking the target from "alive" to "dead" instantly, and with no hope of resistance. A true one-hit kill.

Because Botis knew every centimeter of his being. Inside and out. The viper's fang struck once. The swordsman's blade struck once. These were as much a part of him as his wisdom or his scales.

The blade was a part of Botis, one that he knew and loved. So, what part of Truth was a blade? The answer came crashing in, driving his spirit into the abyss. The negative emotions poured into him, flooded him, drowned him. He bent over, struggling to breathe. Merkovah was there.

"Fight through it, young man! Fight through it! You are on the cusp! Be brave one more time!"

The blade in him. The willingness to cut away everything that hurt him. Everything between him and his goals. Everything that threatened him and the sibs. He had been hurting for so long, fighting for so long, he never learned to put down the blade. It had become part of him. Could he love it? That willingness to fight, to kill?

He remembered little Harmony. He remembered how he screamed as Mom held his hands under the scalding water. Remembered how helpless he was when Dad smashed him down and broke his bones. Remembered Soph and Vig, how they were hunted like prey by the monsters on the streets.

The weak cannot rely on the strong for safety. They can only grow strong themselves, forcing change in the world. They can only pick up the blade. The blade cuts. It rejects. But it also makes room for the good things. The things that had brought him joy.

He took a shuddering breath, then another. He didn't love the blade in him. But he would learn to love it. Because he needed it. Always had, always would. Always part of him. Ready to make his world a better place. Truth looked over at the demon. Merkovah cut it loose.

Truth scrambled up off the ground, running headlong toward the demon. The stick was left behind. The beast rose up, claws the size of chairs plunging down on him. Truth swung his empty hand, and the beast was split in two. He had been holding that blade his whole life. Not his fault if others didn't see it.

He sucked in deep breaths. His channels ached, his apertures drawing hard on the cosmic energy given by Botis. It was potent stuff. His head throbbed. His heart hurt. The earth demon, piddly little peon that it was, dissolved back into the ground, forced back to Hell. Truth might not love the blade in him, but it was part of him. He could learn to love it.

"Botis is a being so old, we cannot reasonably ascribe an age to him. He may well predate time in our boring little corner of reality. Whatever portion of him you comprehended, you have only seen the tiniest sliver of the whole. It will be enough for you to study for decades. Perhaps a lifetime," Merkovah said. There was a little smile floating over his face.

"What's the Second Gem?"

"Pardon?"

"Incisive is the First Gem of Botis, according to Etenesh's spirit. What's the second?" Truth asked.

Merkovah laughed wryly. "I don't know. People have been asking Botis that since before we settled on this planet. Since forever, as far as I can tell."

"And?"

"He says he'll teach it to the person who truly masters the First Gem. Nobody's done it yet."

CHAPTER 28

FIELD TESTING

Truth had a lot to think about while standing guard in front of the conference room. When he "subtly" pointed out that sticking one guard in front of a room as your security protocol is "less than fully optimal," he got a scathing look from Merkovah. It seems that all the angels, demons, and spirits flitting through the city weren't just for show. The security envelope was seven layers deep and extended even into other layers of reality. Tommy Wells, the handsome bodyguard, was there to make the attendees feel flattered and persuadable. He was part of Merkovah's mental attack.

A blow to the heart.

His thoughts were still a jumble, trying to sort out questions that, logically, he knew took a lifetime to truly understand. Mastery . . . well, someone somewhere must have mastered their heart. Someone. Presumably, more than one person in the universe had loved themselves. It should be something he could do too.

Loving the violence within him . . . might be a little trickier. He might be dumb, but—

But he wasn't dumb! That was more System fuckery! He didn't need to keep calling himself that! Actually, hey—

<<Yes, the System Astrologica did subtly encourage your feelings of inadequacy and inferiority. In practice, it didn't have to do much. You were already primed to think ignorance and stupidity were the same thing, so it just encouraged that thought a bit. Those feelings of inferiority also made you easier to control and encouraged your aggression toward others. I just call you stupid to hurt you. Kind of pathetic it took you this long to figure it out, really. >>

Merkovah mentioned releasing the System as a way of breaking Starbrite's control. Truth's mind was entirely on murder. It was worth honing the blade in his heart if it meant killing the System.

Once again, the doors burst open around lunchtime, and the swarm of gray-looking people boiled out in a smog of discouragement.

"It's started already. It started months ago. Knock-on effects in the supply chain—"

"Still nothing from the Palace. I hear His Majesty is *really proud* of his latest poem."

"I still don't understand why nobody's just *called* them. Surely, someone has a way—"

"You won't believe what I'm hearing from the Free State. Actually, yes, you will."

"Already heard about it. We may need to consider similar. Our neighbors to the east."

"Look at 'em. Really look at 'em. Light's gone out of the whole country."

"Every day, we fall further from God. Every damn day. And look at us now!"

"I teach the boys every day—'Practice your *muq*. One day it may be all you have.' I'm not proud to be right."

"If we can't get divine intervention, any chance of a spellblade on errantry?"

"Not this century, brother. Not this century."

One of the Desrin stopped chatting long enough to look over at Truth, assessing him with a smile. "What do you say, young man? Will you stand against all demons and unclean spirits, stand against the very armies of Hell and hellish men? Will you swear to never go to your knees before any but your king, your wife, and God?"

Truth looked at the man questioningly. "I doubt it. I do repair work on my iron horse. Takes a lot of kneeling down."

The speaker's friend snorted. The Desrin smiled a little and pressed on. "It's a metaphor, the saying from the old stories about spellblades. It's meant to be a statement of resolve, a willingness to never give up, whatever the odds."

"Ah." Truth nodded thoughtfully. "So . . . did the female spellblades also need a wife, or what?"

The friend started cracking up while the Desrin buried his face in his hands. "They had husbands. You aren't the most romantic soul, are you?"

Truth shrugged and looked over at the departing crowd. "Might want to catch up with the rest, sir. Hard to feel romantic on an empty stomach."

The conference was still going on back at the temple, but Merkovah and his little team had been called away on business. It seemed that an entire apartment building had come down with a bad case of possession or something similar. Both the building itself and everyone in it. This was such an unusual occurrence, especially in Xandre, that it was deemed wisest to summon a true expert to investigate.

The apartment block was one of the new-construction ones. It wasn't identical to anywhere Truth had ever lived, but it sure looked like thirty stories of distilled hopelessness to him. So, it *felt* like "home." "Home," however, didn't have a two-story-tall winged lion pacing back and forth in front of it.

"Thank the Creator you are here," it rumbled, looking down at Merkovah. "I have tried everything I can think of. Strained the bonds of my binding, even, but I cannot even see what ails them. Truthfully, I fear they are dead, though something within lives. Please hurry! I can only hold it in for so long."

"Do not worry. This is Etenesh and Jember. They will help you craft a containment spell. Mr. Wells and I will investigate the inside."

Truth looked inquisitively at Merkovah, who sounded remarkably soothing for a religious teacher talking to a two-story-tall demon. Then shrugged. Not his business. He looked over the building, trying to separate what he was actually seeing from what his mind thought he was seeing. It got easier to shake off the Harban slums, but they never went too far.

Grim and horrible—gray walls, black windows, poured concrete, and despair in equal measure. He took a closer look. The windows had a black film over them. Not some product of rotting flesh or sinister magics. It looked like it was an aftermarket tinting someone had installed over the whole building. The gray was, in fact, the poured concrete. Under the equator, it got grimy fast.

Actually, when he got right down to it, he couldn't see anything visibly cursed about the place at all. Other than it being a thirty-story Harban-style apartment building.

"Come, Mr. Wells. We must hurry. At the very least, we must buy them some time!"

Truth had no idea where this urgency was coming from, but he certainly wasn't going to argue about it. He drew his sword and charged in ahead of the old monster. Merkovah already had his thumb ring out, chanting something guttural and fierce.

Once he crossed the threshold, he got it. The feelings of absolute hopelessness. Of powerlessness. The scent of sulfur and rotting flesh. The acrid smell of burning bones that you couldn't ever forget, no matter how much you tried. Other smells, too—floral, sickly sweet. The smell of sex festering in the walls and in the air. No, not sex, exactly. The smell of that mattress in the alley that the base slaves were turning tricks on. It smelled like that. Bathtub drugs, mold, hopelessness, and the dripped remains of bodies leaking.

The building had an elevator. Truth was relieved to see that Merkovah had no intention of taking it.

"Where to, Teacher?"

Merkovah let out an explosive bark and the spell carved a thin, glittering line in the air. From that line came a light, a glowing spark, and from the light came a chant, repeating endlessly, a recitation of something too holy for merely mortal minds to bear.

The spark—he was wrong. It wasn't a spark; it was the chant itself, the holy words creating their own light by their mere presence in the room. The chant drifted to the stairwell and upward.

"We follow the Name."

Truth went. "Sir? How many hostiles should we expect? I realize that you could flatten this building with minor effort, but I would like to know *some* details so I can do my job."

Merkovah grunted. "This building should be at least partially occupied, though most people moved out weeks ago. Perhaps as many as four hundred people are here, though I don't know for certain. They are all to be presumed hostile. Since they are likely possessed, try to avoid harming them if you can."

"When you say *possessed*, is it a spiritual-malady type of possession, or are we talking body huskers?

"I haven't heard that particular euphemism in a while. Didn't miss it. And spiritual. Otherwise, I would have, as you so colorfully put it, already flattened the building. They are doing something in here, and I want to know what."

Merkovah spoke in a surprisingly calm, measured voice. Truth did not share his casual attitude, his eyes flicking down the empty hallways. Guttering, half-broken light talismans managed to make the dark darker instead of shedding light.

"You looked puzzled when I was speaking to the guardian outside," said Merkovah. "Why?"

"Surprised to see you speaking so casually to a demon. Comforting a demon, in fact."

"Ah, the Pragerite church strikes again. Demons come in almost-infinite varieties. Some are regimented and ranked in the infernal legions, true citizens and soldiers of Hell. Still more are simply wild spirits, capricious and often cruel, but more like wild animals than villains. Many of the guardians you see on buildings are of that latter sort. Bound, yes, but also bribed."

Truth started feeling some strange vibration through the stairs, faintly shivering the metal banister. The chanting Name seemed to get louder, more agitated, the farther up they went.

"No demon is safe, of course. But many of them can become useful and well-loved servants of the Faithful. Our faith has been binding demons for millennia, and some of the demons in this city have served since humans first settled this planet. They are as much a part of the city as the buildings and streets. That Shedu must have been really upset—usually, it would be presenting a human face. Poor fellow."

Truth tried to connect the image of the two-story-tall winged lion with the words "poor fellow" and failed. The vibration was getting stronger. He wasn't hearing any noise outside the Name's chanting and their own conversation. So, what was making the vibrations?

"It all comes down to obedience to the Word and Name of God. God is great, and within him is a multitude. As such, he has a multitude of names and titles. Even in these dark days, all of creation must give way—"

The Name started screaming. It was still repeating the chant endlessly, but the register had changed. This wasn't a proclamation or a condemnation. It was terrified revulsion. Merkovah and Truth were in motion at once, sprinting up the stairs. They bust into the hallway of the twenty-seventh floor, chasing the screams. A lot of the interior walls had been torn out, opening up the floor for the great creation.

The hundreds of people left in the building had been busy. They had taken each other's everything as materials. In flesh, in blood, in bile and brain matter and entrails pinned down with carpet tacks to the floor, they created their great work. The diagram stretched up and around, with streamers of torn skin painted with talismanic words that conformed to no logic Truth knew of. Bones were tied with hair and sinew to form poles. Scraped clean of meat to provide a surface for neat inscriptions of maddened images and scrawling letters or some idea meant to be letters.

The Name screamed and screamed, its light stabbing out, the words smashing out, and simply splashing away against the flesh engine. It screamed and screamed and went silent, vanishing from the world like the echo of a prayer.

There was a dark speck in the middle of the room. Not simply black. It was the negation of light. It rejected everything totally and it was rejected in turn. Something so divorced from the order of the world could only survive in such a terrible creation.

Truth had cast Incisive before they even reached the stairs. Now he lunged in front of Merkovah. He conjured holy flame from the angelic sword and drove its cut with all the furious power Incisive could give him. Bone sheared and burned away. Corrupted flesh liquified and vanished. And when the rippling sheet of flame reached the empty speck . . . the fire winked away. Like it had never existed in the first place.

The magic device made by the residents of the tower collapsed in on itself. Disintegrated, fell into nothing recognizable. Whatever it was, Truth had ruined it, and now it was collapsing. The speck, without drama or fuss, winked out of reality.

There was a dreadful stillness to the moment. The soft collapsing of the flesh and bone seemed to cradle the terrible empty feeling of the room. The space was not haunted now. Nor cursed. No malign spirit rose from the puddles of what were once people.

Truth carefully fished a coin out of his pocket, lightly enchanted to prevent tampering and counterfeiting. One of the myriad names of God was inscribed upon it. He tossed it into the middle of the room. It never had the chance to hit the floor. It simply fell apart in the air. Merkovah sucked in a deep breath.

"Tell no one. *no one*, what you have seen here. I will seal the building. I must consult with . . . several people."

"Teacher?"

For the first time that Truth could recall, Merkovah looked scared. "This was a test. I don't know what of. And I don't know what they plan to try next."

As they backed away from the scene of the atrocity, Truth spotted a talisman gem pressed into a pillar. It seemed to writhe in his sight. He had the sinking feeling that he had seen it before.

CHAPTER 29

A WORLD WITHOUT GOD

"Please, wait a moment, Teacher."

Merkovah looked inquisitively at Truth, who pointed at the Talisman. The old monster glanced at it, then glared at it. Stroked his beard in irritation as he continued glaring. Truth wracked his brain, trying to remember where he had seen it before.

System?

<<Before my time, apparently. Free-associate on deeply unnatural shit you saw before submitting to Starbrite.>>

The slums, generally. Yes, but no. The Ghūl, generally. Yes, very yes, but again, no. This didn't feel anything like his rough patron, or the Ghūl themselves, for that matter. All right, after he broke through. Nothing on test day. Nothing at basic. During his conscription—

The giant bird-headed man leaped to mind. He had never found out anything more about that, had he? It all got covered up, classified.

<<Clavegaugh knew.>>

What?

<<Captain Clavegaugh knew. She said something about you fighting a bird-headed warlock when she told you that you were going to be a bodyguard. Guess classified *is a relative term in Jeon. Try to think about the event.>>*

Truth tried to remember as best he could. It was the border post up in the mountains. A routine day in a routine week. He and Ludovic had dick-in-a-box duty, stamping passports. Ludovic (correctly, as it happened) ordered a wagon inspected by a spellhound. The hound freaked out, and the driver turned into a bird-demon-person-thing, became two stories tall, and started tearing the post apart.

Truth had raced for one of the heavy-duty army wagons, overrode the speed regulator, and smashed it into birdie. It wasn't enough to kill the warlock instantly. He had lingered, spread across the road for minutes after. The army wagon had been hacked open during its charge, clipping the birdman's wagon and spilling some of the contents.

They were sealed crates. Talismans soaking in blood, wriggling. Humming. Even then, he thought they looked unnatural. Wrong on a level he was still struggling to understand.

<<*Yeah, this doesn't match your memory, but it's similar. To the point where I can see some identical symbols and structures. Whoever made this had some connection to that smuggler or his goods.*>>

Truth slowly nodded. All right. A lead. What could he do with this information? Not much by himself. Hmm. What would Dad do?

Dad would tell Merkovah that he knew something about this and try to scam some money as a "fee" or "reward." No, wait. That was too sensible. He would try and find the smugglers and blackmail them, thinking that, somehow, they wouldn't just kill him on the spot. Dad would, presumably, be hopped up on a blend of poppy and bleem, washed down with some Beefheart when he made his pitch. He would try to monetize this in the dumbest, most blatantly aggressive way possible.

"Teacher, I have seen something similar to this talisman once before. Is this a reasonably safe place to talk about it, or should we discuss it somewhere else?"

"Eh? You have? No, we need to get out of here quickly. Say nothing until I give you leave to. I will order the building sealed pending further investigation. Fortunately, most of the people I will need to speak to are already at the temple."

They left the building quickly. Merkovah wasted no time in joining the cousins and the Shedu in sealing the building in a thick pillar of white light. It faded to a dim translucence after a few minutes, but Truth knew it was stronger than a steel wall. How could it not be, with a giant demon, a Level Seven mage and two powerful ritualists powering it? Actually, just how strong were the cousins? Worth finding out, though not right now.

He had seen them in a fight. They had powerful magic, but they were truly not fighters. Actually, he wasn't sure that they had any combat spells. Just spells that you could, coincidentally, use in combat. Like a person with a tool spell operating a flying sword.

People were gathering around the building. A lot of shouted questions and a lot of demons and spirits peeking around. Police were out, no riot gear, but keeping everyone well back. Raising barricades and generally maintaining order. Truth kept his eyes moving, trying to pick out what didn't fit, guessing where the next threat might be. He had Incisive cast, trusting the danger sense to alert him if any attacks came.

The faces in the crowd were interesting. This wasn't a nice neighborhood, from what he could tell, but not a slum the way he thought of that term. These people were taking care of themselves. They . . . weren't beaten. But there was something in their eyes, in the way they moved and carried themselves. Something raw. Angry. Hungry. Like something had been stolen from them, even if they didn't know exactly what that something was.

A . . . priest? He should really learn what they were called. Someone wearing the same sorts of clothes he remembered clerics from the temple wearing had come to the front of the crowd. He was holding a bundle of long reeds topped with frilly fronds. He would shout something, then flick his reeds upward. A spray of water would come out, covering the area near the police. The crowd started roaring with him. That got the police looking worried. Truth tried to concentrate on what they were yelling.

"Out, thieves, out!"

Then the reply: "Our land. Pure land!"

"Siphios!"

"Siphios!"

"Siphios!"

"Out, thieves, out!"

It repeated over and over, growing rapidly. Truth spotted at least one cop that looked like he wasn't about to stop a riot. They might even support the rioters.

Truth started taking deep breaths, hand loose on the hilt of his sword. This wasn't like the Free State. These were true mages. Mages with a real fondness for demon-summoning. If things kicked off there, they would get very bad very fast.

Truth stepped sharply over toward Merkovah. "Teacher. It is time to go."

Merkovah looked sadly at the crowd. "Yes. I'm afraid it is."

There were no riots that day, Truth heard, but it got very tense for a while.

"It's not like I don't understand them," Etenesh said, "though I do think the Pure Land people go too far sometimes. Still, there is no denying that Siphios has been on the decline for a long time now. Centuries. We were the pinnacle of the world, but day by day, it slipped away from us."

She looked hopeless. They were sitting on a bench in the temple, taking comfort from each other's warmth. Each envying the other, pitying the cold within themselves.

"I can't help but feel it was stolen from us." She twisted a bit of her shawl. She was more covered up today. Still lovely, in her fashion, but the brilliant light she had before was dimmer now.

"Who stole it?" Truth asked. Etenesh laughed bitterly.

"Well, that's the question, isn't it? Who stole it, and can we take it back? Foreigners, generally. People who are the wrong sort of Siphian, usually Orthodox Siphian or Progressive, or worse, Secular. Occasionally the Desrin, often the Pragerites. Big businesses. Particularly foreign big businesses. Like Starbrite. Landlords. Sometimes the temple itself. Or the Throne. They aren't too particular." Etenesh sighed. "Actually, they are extremely particular. It just isn't consistent across all of the Pure Land groups."

Truth sat quietly. He didn't really know what to say to that. He couldn't think of any romance novels that covered this.

"And the thing is, they aren't wrong about a lot of things. Like, why exactly is it that so much of the good farmland here only grows coffee for export? Or that all those fields have inescapable contracts for starvation prices? And that all the contract holders are big foreign companies?" she said with quiet fury. "Or the big elixir-growing region in the Xarn highlands. All contracted out to the big Alchemist Towers, a cartel based out of . . . you will never guess . . ."

"Jeon?" Truth asked. He could vividly remember how the sun turned neon orange through the haze above the alchemist towers. Turning the canal the same blinding color and throwing everything around it into deep shadow.

"Jeon," Etenesh agreed. "All that money. All those elixirs. None of it sticks here. Maybe a very little bit, at the very top. But most of it gets right on the bird and fucks all the way off to Jeon!"

She controlled her temper, then bowed her head, hands pressed over her mouth. Then she dropped them on her lap.

"I swore in temple. I would never swear in temple. Never. I can't believe I just did that. And now I can't believe I care. What does it matter? Not like God's going to notice. Or care."

Truth thought about that a moment. "Do you care?"

"What? That I swore?"

"That it should be a rule—people shouldn't swear in temple. Even if God wasn't there to be mad about it personally. Do you care?"

"I . . ." She drifted off, thinking about it. "I do, actually. Isn't that stupid? It bothers me. The thought that people would just go around swearing in temple really bothers me. There should be someplace without . . . that. Without the dust of the world clinging to our tongues."

"Then don't swear. It's enough that you don't approve." Truth shrugged.

"It really doesn't bother you? Really?"

"About God? No. Not really. I never knew him the way you did."

She looked ready to blow up but forced herself to calm down. "You know, once upon a time, my family would have been considered rich. We never had much money, but we were rich because we walked with God. Angels spoke sweetly to us and would answer our questions. Our lands might have been rugged, but they always met our needs. The whole of creation spoke to us, and we to it." She waved a hand grandly.

"But then the land started falling silent. The angels still answered our call, but they grew colder and more remote. And they would never explain themselves. No matter the sacrifice. No matter who asked." She ground the words out. "Now we know."

Truth just nodded. Now they knew.

"But you say you didn't know him as I do. How. How is that possible? Even in some blasted Pragerite hole, they still know of God. Still honor him, still understand that this is *his* world, and we but poor stewards of it."

"Do they? Know all that?" Truth asked.

"*Yes.*" Etenesh spoke with quiet intensity.

"Nobody ever told me."

That seemed to confuse her.

"What do you mean, no one ever told you?"

"I knew God existed, and some other random details here and there, but it just . . . never really came up. Never seemed important, so I didn't think about it."

"God, the actual, literal *God*, never seemed important." Etenesh didn't believe him.

Truth looked at the etched wall, and all he could see was the scarred concrete he hid behind as gangsters strolled past. He could hear the drugged-up giggles and, worse, the shouts of the ones getting sober. Ready to do whatever it took to buy that next fix. He could feel the cold of the concrete, could smell it. Years ago. Other side of the world. And he was right back there in the alley. Scared, starving . . . but he had a job to do. And the sibs were counting on him.

"No. God did not seem important. Finding food was important. Keeping warm somehow. Shoes not too worn out and cheap because someone spilled tar on them. That was a big win in the pawn shop. A good day fishing trash and industrial waste from the canal to sell as scrap. Clothes that might last a season or two after being pulled out of a dumpster. Treated carefully. Always a lucky find, though you had to be really careful about cleaning them. My hand was covered in blisters for a week once. I missed a curse when cleaning. But mostly, it was food. Every day, finding food. Whatever it took. That was the important thing."

"Merciful angels. Where were your parents?"

"Dad was passed out in his armchair or mopping piss off the floors in the casino. Drunk, in either case. Mom was worse. Dad beat us to feel in control. I think Mom just liked to be cruel. And we were too weak to fight back."

Truth said matter-of-factly. It seemed fair in his head. She felt abandoned, as though God had suddenly betrayed her. He could show her the truth—God had never been there. Not for him. And not for her. They were always alone. So, they would have to be enough.

CHAPTER 30

YOU KNOW WHAT THEY SAY ABOUT ASSUMPTIONS

They didn't talk much after that. They just sat together, lost in their own minds. Truth didn't know if he had said the wrong thing or not. He probably did, but . . . it was hard to be "Tommy Wells" right now. It was usually freeing to be "Tommy Wells" in that he wasn't carrying all the things that "Truth Medici" was carrying, but he didn't want to have to lie. To make up things about himself. Part of it was he really liked Etenesh and Jember. Even Merkovah, beardy weirdo that he was, had grown on him. Liking them was part of it. A bigger part was hating that his life had been dedicated to a series of lies.

Truth felt that most people didn't have to pick apart their personalities to try and find the bits of them that *hadn't* been tampered with. Like the *talking poorly about himself* thing. He had known for a long time that the schools he went to were shit. He never felt good about it. It was as far back as boot camp—he was made to feel stupid because he didn't know things. Not just ignorant, *dangerously* ignorant.

Violence came naturally to him, and he didn't know a lot of things everyone else knew. He must be a dangerous moron, right? Probably into some cruel, disgusting things. Fitting for an ugly bastard like him. Yeah, definitely into some sick shit. No wonder nobody has ever seen him with a living "friend."

He could feel the intrusive thoughts elbowing their way in. Reminding him that his pretty new face and fancy muscles weren't his. They were things done to him. Nobody could love him, even like him, if they knew the real him. The ugly monster of violence, wearing some pretty skin.

"Amazing. I don't think I've ever *felt* someone slip into a depressive spiral before," Etenesh said with a flash of her old spark.

"Eh?"

"I mean, a bit rude. A bit ungallant. I'm sitting here, having an existential crisis and fearing for the future of my nation, and here you are, making it about *you*."

"Oh. Um. Sorry? Unintentional?" Truth was flummoxed. The romance novels didn't cover this.

She grinned a little. "Well, you see, I was already feeling poorly, and then the fella I'm interested in dropped some heavy history on me. I was processing. Sorting through the emotions. Glad you finally let me in a smidge, though."

"Ah . . . Wait a moment. I have something for this . . ."

"You have something? Like an ointment?" She was really grinning now, more of that spark shining.

"No, something witty. I think *witty* is the right word." He turned toward Etenesh and looked seriously at her. "I have fallen into the cerulean ponds of your eyes."

She stared blankly at him for a moment and cracked up. "That has nothing to do with anything. *Cerulean* means *blue*! What? How?"

"Ah, damn. I was pretty sure it meant *deep*," Truth muttered. Etenesh snorted, wiping a tear from the corner of a tawny eye.

"How many women has that line worked on?"

"Did it cheer you up?"

"It did." She nodded with mock seriousness.

"It has been one hundred percent successful," he replied with equal seriousness.

She smiled at that and said, "Hey. I want to nudge you. You okay with nudges?"

"You may nudge me. Once."

She scooted closer and leaned into Truth. Prodding him with her shoulder exactly once.

"I'm depressed. I mean that in both senses. I'm feeling depressed, and I think I have the actual medical-condition depression. It's a little early to go self-diagnosing, but. Seems pretty likely." The smile drained off Etenesh like water into sand.

"I . . . don't know how to help."

"I don't either. Don't try to cheer me up. That much I know."

"All right. Sorry."

"Oh, don't be. The highlight of the last couple of days, right there." Etenesh stood. "I've booked room one oh three tonight. A basic double. I'll leave the door unlocked if you want to join me. Just for sleeping. No pressure; I won't be hurt if you don't come."

She gave him a little smile. "Though I would like it if you did. You are warm."

She walked off, shawl covering her head and shoulders. Truth thought she was the warm one. But he would do his best to be brave.

Merkovah finally called Truth into a small conference room. Once the door shut, the room glowed with cosmic energy flowing through dense webs of formations. He more or less recognized some of them as anti-surveillance formations. He had seen and used similar working in the PMC. Some of his bodyguarding clients wouldn't so much as take a piss without them.

"All right, Tommy. The room is warded to a profound, even paranoid level. The countersurveillance spellwork is genuinely upsetting once you understand how it works, and privacy is guaranteed. Now, after knowing you for a little while, I am quite certain you won't tell me everything. You will probably treat this room as though it wasn't warded at all. Am I right?"

Truth nodded. It didn't matter if the room was warded. If he told Merkovah anything, the odds were excellent that he would tell a third person, and so on. He would only reveal things that were unlikely to get traced back to him.

"Haaah. Well, that's exhausting. Still, anything you can tell me will be enormously helpful."

Truth laid out what had happened at the border crossing in the most bare-bones terms possible. Merkovah displayed a keen sense of propriety. His questions tightly focused on the smuggler ("*Do you know what kind of crow the bird head was?*") the talismans ("*Were they soaking in blood, or did it just look like blood? Could you smell whatever it was?*"), and, to Truth's considerable surprise, the details of the fight ("*So, the needlers did essentially nothing? But you could kill him with a wagon?*")

The conversation—interrogation, really—ran on much longer than Truth had expected. The whole fight, from the time the smuggler pulled up to the time he expired, had been less than ten minutes. The fighting part might have been less than four. By the time they hit the fifty-minute mark, Truth deeply regretted saying anything. Merkovah must have picked up on it, because he called for a quick break for drinks and snacks.

"Teacher, if you would forgive a massive change in topic—"

"I would welcome it, actually. Nice change of pace." Merkovah gestured for him to continue.

"It's a religious question, I guess."

Merkovah made a gesture of thanks. "Praise be! I wondered if this day would ever come."

Truth decided to ignore that. "Why is everyone so hung up on God?"

Merkovah looked like his brain had locked out for a moment. Like he heard the words but couldn't process their meaning.

"Pardon?"

"I remember what you said before—everyone agrees there is a God. And that the universe was created by God, and that in some way I don't really understand, the universe both is God and is God's thoughts. But . . . so what? The world is kind of trash. There are good bits, absolutely. And it's a lot bigger than I will ever know or understand. But I don't think you can look at the world and go, 'Yes, good job. Do it the exact same way next time.'"

If there were a living sculpture of the concept of not knowing where to begin, it would look like Merkovah.

"Young man, leaving aside questions of blasphemy—"

"Is it? Blasphemous?" Truth asked. He didn't know.

"Depending on who you ask, yes! And as a nationally respected and internationally known teacher of canon law, if you ask me, I would say, *Yes, it absolutely is blasphemy.*" The old monster disguised as a young man glared at Truth. But, proving he really was a university-level teacher, Merkovah felt the need to tack on "Of course, this is a much-debated point, with no really satisfying answer."

"Oh?"

"Well, you are hardly the first person to look at the world and wonder about the origin of evil, sin, or the pinky toe."

"So, what's the word from on high?" Truth asked.

Merkovah grinned slightly. "How long do you have? Answers range from—and I am speaking just for the prophets of my own faith here—'"The world is perfect, but a lack of faith leads to sin, and from sin to misery' to 'The world is a test *of* your faith and your ability to lead a good, godly life.' Other religions take a different tack, ranging from infernal intervention, divine punishment, or even a sort of corporal punishment intended to morally correct us. Sinful living results in pain. But safe to say that it's an open question . . . between religions."

"More conflicting information from the prophets?" Truth asked.

"Remember how I said that there may well be multiple yet mutually exclusive versions of God? This is part of why we think that. Also, there is another philosophical debate over whether God can change his or her or their—depending again on the religion—mind. Or if they simply reveal different portions of their mind to us at different times, as necessary. So, it's a mess, theologically. A significant degree of faith is required."

"Right, but . . . all that sounds like God intentionally made the world the way he did. What if God . . ."—Truth searched for a euphemism—". . . didn't quite nail what he was going for?"

"Tommy . . . God is definitionally perfect. A being without error. Above everything."

"Is he, though? I mean, if we don't actually know what God wants and we are getting contradictory information here—"

"All right, now, that *is* blasphemy. Young man, I know you don't have any religious training, but that is simply too much. The universe, the entire, endlessly complicated fabric of reality, relies upon God to exist. He is the cause with no cause, the essence before existence. God may be strict. He may even be cruel. But he is *never wrong.*"

Truth remembered his dad splitting open his cheek with a sloppy punch when he asked if there was any food in the house. Truth had been nine. Mom screamed at him that same day for being ungrateful and a leech. Maybe he deserved it, but the sibs didn't deserve to go to bed hungry. And wake up hungry. And stay hungry until Truth could shoplift a few handfuls of food, carefully split between them. But the old monster looked truly angry.

"I'm sorry. Now I know better."

Truth sat in his little room, thinking about what he had learned. Apparently, the transformation magic used by the bird-headed smuggler was a sort of demonic possession. It used to be quite common many centuries ago. It had fallen out of favor due to improvements in talisman technology as well as the fairly extreme demands it made of its users. Ironically, it was supposed to be extremely popular off-world. The demons could last a lot longer and fight a lot harder in a body that had practiced body cultivation. The smuggler hadn't. The demon could endure the little needles and resist the magic, but he was too squishy to hold up against a speeding wagon.

Truth thought about the Meditations of Valentinian and what, exactly, he was trying to do as a human and a mage. He needed to become stronger. The ability to resist spells was crucial, but so was the ability to resist physical damage. To become, if not untouchable, unaffected by the evils of the world. So he could make things right. Maybe not fix the whole world but his little corner of it.

He closed his eyes and tried to meditate. He had a pretty good idea of what *untouchable* might look like. His rough patron existed like an ancient mountain in his mind. Those strong hands picking him up and throwing him around. Truth focused as best he could on his hands, trying to hold the memory in place as he ran the spell. It was slow going, but he thought he had made some progress.

Then he dusted himself off, washed up, brushed his teeth, and found Room 1-03.

CHAPTER 31

THE PRICE OF INTIMACY

The lights were out; the room was dim. Etenesh was lying in bed in rather new-looking pajamas. Truth suddenly felt very nightclothes-conscious. He usually slept in his underwear. He didn't own any pajamas. But what could he do?

Run away, obviously. Say, *Sorry, not tonight, no pajamas, try me again tomorrow, when I definitely will have acquired some.* Say nothing and just vanish into the world, drifting like the ghost he was. Watching the rest of the world join him in death.

What would Dad do? His mind instinctively shied away from that thought. Crimes. Dad would do crimes, things that Truth really didn't want to think about in connection with Etenesh. Or anybody, actually. If he didn't commit crimes, Dad would lose himself and the opportunity for finding warmth somewhere in the bottom of a bottle. Dad would, one way or another, run away or ignore what was in front of him.

So, the right thing to do was press forward. Even though it was scary. Even though no part of this felt safe.

Truth walked to the bed. Whatever was in his rough patron's legacy included excellent night vision. He got to the side of the bed and started undressing. He tried to think of it like being back in the barracks in the army. Everyone saw everyone there. Everyone was too busy to care about someone else's clothing situation, except the instructors who would yell your ear off for being out of uniform. Funny—he didn't care that much then. He cared a hell of a lot now.

Truth stripped down to boxers and a tee shirt. He stood by the side of the bed. Took a deep breath and gently eased the blanket to the side. With exquisite muscular control, he slid into the bed without making it shake or bounce. He then carefully, silently eased the blanket back over. Etenesh hadn't made a sound the whole time. It seemed he had successfully infiltrated the bed.

His heart was beating fast. His first thought was that Etenesh didn't smell. Not that he was expecting her to smell bad or anything. It was just that both romance novels and murder mysteries specifically mentioned their leading ladies smelling like things. He had noticed what Etenesh had smelled like earlier. Right now, she didn't smell like anything. No jasmine or honeysuckle or the sun. Not even like shampoo or conditioner. The room smelled of linen. And that was about it.

Somehow, that threw him. He had expected to smell *something,* and the lack of it was disorienting. He had a strange, momentary hallucination that Etenesh wasn't really there at all. Then she took a shallow breath, in and out, like a little sigh. She was there. And he was there. And all he had to do was fall asleep.

He lay there rigid, staring up at the ceiling. He didn't want to stare over at her. It would be creepy. But he desperately needed to know *exactly* how she was positioned. Where her hands were, her feet, any active spells she might be getting ready to cast. Any hidden knives or needlers.

Her fucking spirit! Oh, shit! What was it called? He couldn't remember, but it seemed to be pretty goddamn robust. Here he was, practically naked, sword nowhere handy, and two seconds from fighting a fucking super spirit! What the fuck was wrong with him?!

Actually, yeah, good question. Truth focused on his breathing, trying to remind himself that this wasn't rational. That not everyone was going to betray him. Not everyone was Starbrite. Or Thierrie.

What would Dad do in this situation? If he knew about Super Spirit, he would freak out and bolt. So, I should stay calm and still. But that only got him so far. It didn't help him calm down, for one thing. All right, on to phase two—more recent positive role models.

What would Botis do? Well, he wouldn't curl up anywhere he didn't feel safe, for one thing. And maybe a literal snake demon wasn't the absolute best choice there. Though . . . could he cast the first part of Incisive without triggering the spirit? It was almost all mental, but who knew what the spirit was seeing. More to the point, he couldn't keep it up forever, and definitely not while he was sleeping. If he was going to do that, he might as well just go back to his room and jam a chair under the door handle.

So, that was out. That was Dad with more steps.

Who else was there? Well, there was the rough man from his vision. The . . . apparent focus of the Ghūl's worship. With nine worms tattooed in a circle on his forehead, and wasn't he just praying that it was a tattoo. Because come on. It absolutely wasn't. What would he do in this situation?

Hard to say, but instinctively? That guy *fucks*. That guy radiated a "seen it all, done it all" aura. Truth got the sense that nothing could faze him, because everything had already happened to him. He wasn't bored with the world. He wasn't indifferent. Just the opposite; he took an active interest. But he wasn't stressed. He would deal with whatever came up, and if he couldn't? That would be interesting too. The sheer confidence of experience. He could meet the world unafraid.

And maybe that was it? Maybe the answer was a grand shrug. To say *Okay* to the world. Things were unfair. Cruel. You couldn't trust anybody. *Okay*. Now what? Now you deal. You figure out what, if anything, you intend to do about things. Truth circled around that thought a bit, trying to figure out what, exactly, were the things he should be figuring out what to do things about. It got very circular very quickly. It was just so big. So many things. Too many things. He couldn't keep track of it all.

Too many things? Simplify. What was the problem in front of him? Sleeping next to Etenesh without freaking out. *Okay*. What was the risk? She would do something to hurt him. *Okay*. Was the risk of being hurt more important than the consequences of giving up? Of saying, *Sorry, I just can't*?

Potentially, yes. But this wasn't a purely logical question. What would hurt more? Giving up and deciding he couldn't ever trust another person or risk being hurt? He stared at the ceiling for a long while, trying to decide. Starbrite might have betrayed him years ago by the world's counting, but it was a matter of days and weeks for him.

Truth just breathed in and out, letting his heart slowly calm. He had done scary things his whole life. He had to. The sibs were counting on him. Now could he do this scary thing for a selfish reason? Could he risk being hurt, even though it might increase the risk to the sibs?

No, that way of thinking wouldn't work anymore. Even before the betrayal, he had been burning himself out. Everybody saw it. He was told, repeatedly and explicitly, to ease up. Find someone. If he had just taken a vacation like a normal person, he wouldn't have been in that convoy and wouldn't have gotten killed. It wasn't greedy to want to trust. It was necessary. Because he couldn't go on otherwise. He had tried before and failed.

And since it was necessary, he would do it. That was all. He didn't have to say yes to everything else. He didn't have to say yes to anything else. But for tonight, there, in this bed, he would say yes to sleeping with Etenesh. And if she hurt him, he would deal with it. Because he could deal with it. And if he couldn't? If it just killed him?

Wouldn't be the first time. He could deal.

He focused on breathing. In and out. In, slowly. Hold. Out, slowly. Hold. Over and over. Trying to still his mind. Just letting himself drift to sleep.

It took him a long while. But he got there.

As he slept—

"Your answer was no good, my friend. It was obvious once I gave it a moment's thought."

"As you lay in bed with Maria, smoking a post-coital cigarette, having run back to her apartment from this very bench."

"Naturally." The handsome philosopher looked faintly offended that Truth had felt the need to state something so obvious.

Truth was flicking bits of bread into the air, seeing if the seagulls could catch them on the fly. So far, no. But it was quite good fun to watch them try.

"No, you see, mere hedonism, which is what you propose, is simply another form of intellectual suicide. You give up the struggle with the absurd, allowing the tension to fall. Like a tightrope walker cutting the line beneath his feet."

"So what if I do give up the struggle? You have already defined life as fundamentally meaningless, hopeless, and doomed to dull repetitions. Like you and I meeting on this bench, sharing some bread." Truth tore off a hunk and handed it to the philosopher. "Let me die and be happy."

"Ah, but you see, this is a shallow pleasure, not fit for a true thinker. No, there is an alternative." He paused, grinning mischievously. "Rebellion!"

"Rebellion? Against what? The fundamental absence of meaning in the universe?" Truth gave him a skeptical look, then ate a chunk of bread. Forget philosophy—who would invent a portable butter dish?

"Exactly that. Live your life with such radical, unrestrained freedom that your life itself is a rebellion against the futility of the world. You discard all trappings of dead ideology, embrace the true nature of existence, and find freedom and meaning within. Like the tightrope walker—you may not be going anywhere meaningful, but what a way to get there!"

Truth ate another bite. Then nailed a passing gull with a bit of crust. The bird seemed confused but not upset by the unexpected breading.

"Your solution to the absence of meaning in the world, and humanity's impossible dream of finding connection and meaning in the world, is to rebel by enjoying it? Enjoying that lack of meaning? Enjoying finding our own meaning without outside definition provided by a non-existent god?"

"Exactly!"

"That's absurd." Truth scoffed. Then groaned and buried his face in his hands as the philosopher laughed and laughed.

Truth snapped awake—the System was screaming, which was nice, but he woke because Etenesh had moved. He was instantly hyperaware of her, tracking her movement in the bed. Which was her rolling over away from him. She muttered something softly, snuggled more deeply into bed, then stilled.

The light was streaming in through the window. There were thin gauze curtains, but they just made the light diffuse, not dim the luminosity. It should be just after dawn. Truth was debating the virtues of a stealthy escape when Etenesh moved again. This time, she slowly sat up and stretched. She seemed a little hesitant to look over, but she eventually turned her head. When she saw Truth lying there, she smiled.

"You weren't here when I fell asleep. I thought you . . . weren't ready. I didn't notice you coming to bed."

"I am occasionally sneaky." Truth smiled a little.

"How did it feel?"

"Scary. It took a long while and a lot of thinking to settle down enough to sleep."

"Oh?" She smiled a little herself. "What thought made you stay?"

Truth was stumped. How did you put all that into words?

"I thought about it and decided that you were worth it. Whatever 'it' turned out to be."

CHAPTER 32

A FRIENDLY GAME

Truth and Etenesh went back to their rooms to prepare for the day. Etenesh apparently had some very important reading to do for her coursework, and Truth expected to be on standing-around duty once again. They were both derailed by Jember popping up with new instructions.

"One of my fellow cultists—"

"There absolutely has to be a better way of saying that," Truth interjected.

"What, *cultist*?" Etenesh asked. "That's what they are."

"Mystery cult, remember?" Jember smiled.

"Oh, I remember. Hard to forget, in fact."

"So, anyway, we were putting away the robes and knives and things, and he tells me that he has four tickets to Xandre PC versus Xandre Athletic, playing at Old Mek'elle."

"Yikes. The Old Friends playing at Mek'elle?" Her words sounded worried. But Etenesh's hungry grin told a different story. "Reconciliation match?"

"That's the hope." Jember nodded.

"Sorry, completely lost here. I assume you are talking about a pitz game? Between two teams that both come from this city?" Truth asked.

"Yes, that's it. Big city. Plenty of room for two clubs. *Unfortunately*, those clubs are the Birdies and the Brickies. That's six hundred years of bad blood right there. Add in all the recent strife, and you can be sure the police will be out in numbers today." Jember spoke quickly. "Anyhow, I've got the tickets, and Merkovah says we have the day off. The ball drops at one."

"Jember, if you think I'm going into the balconies at Old Mek'elle for an Old Friends reconciliation match, you are mad. I have work. I'll watch the scry later once they've had a chance to clean up the blood." Etenesh directly blew him off.

"I remain lost. Birdies? Old Friends who are going to be killing each other?"

"Okay, so . . . Pitz is the people's game, right?" Etenesh began. "So, it comes from the streets. A sacred ritual, too, but the origin is the streets. Clubs get very loyal, and mostly very local, fans. Now, the Brickies—"

"Sorry, Brickies?"

"Xandre Athletic. Old Mek'elle is their home field. Their first field was in a brick factory's courtyard. And the Xandre PC is the Birdies because they're so dumb. At least, according to the Brickies. And, of course, the Brickies are called the Brickies because they are thick as a—"

"Got it."

"Right, so. You have the usual neighborhood rivalries, but of course, you have to think about who's in the neighborhood. The Birdies are almost all Siphios Orthodox, while the Brickies are Progressive, with a mix of Desrin and Pragerites sprinkled around both," Etenesh explained.

"So, the rivalry is religious, geographical, and historical," Truth asked, absently touching the hilt of his sword.

"Right. So, it can get nasty. But on the other hand, they are the two biggest teams in the capital, and two of the oldest in the country, so . . . they are called the Old Friends," Jember said.

"All right. This sounds like an absolute nightmare, and I sincerely pity everyone working security at the match. Which is a reconciliation match. Which means?"

The cousins looked a little awkward. "Well. Given the religious and political tension between them—"

"Sorry, political?"

"Yeah, Birdies are big Royalists. To the point where the Royal Family has asked them to settle down. More like they think the king should have absolute authority over the country and only Orthodox temples should be allowed. It's not the most coherent ideology. Brickies are the opposite. A lot of them, very quietly, want to abolish the monarchy altogether," Jember explained.

"Is there a traditional offering I should make for the souls of the security staff?"

"Funny you should say that. It's why they have reconciliation matches. Basically, if things get to the point where people are dying—" Jember tried to explain, but Etenesh interrupted.

"More than usual are dying, or something really shocking happens."

"Right, or that. Anyway, the organizers hold a reconciliation match. It's meant to give everyone a chance to come together, calm everything down. The teams shake hands, honorable play all around, some ritual, and hopefully, everyone feels a bit better. There's usually some pageantry."

"And if, say, the play isn't honorable? Or they can't reconcile?"

"Riots." Etenesh sounded bleak.

"More often, they call for the stone knife and raise the hoops. Which is bad enough and also often turns into a riot. But sometimes, it calms things down." Jember tried to downplay it, fooling no one.

"Well. That is. Something." Truth tried to think of something diplomatic to say and drew a blank.

"Yeah. Usually, I'd love to watch a match; they're both first-rate clubs. Not a reconciliation match. Not with everything that's going on. I can't even imagine what's started the drama this time." Etenesh shook her head.

"Oh, it's colorful." Jember turned toward Truth. "So, sorry if this is something you already know, but, like the Desrin, the Siphios Orthodoxy doesn't believe in divorce. Or, to put it more bluntly, they forbid divorce. There is no such thing as a secular wedding in Siphios and, likewise, no such thing as a secular divorce. On the other hand, the Synod of the Progressive Temple of Siphios *does* allow divorce."

"I have a sinking feeling." Truth said.

"Now, a nice young Desrin man, a prominent figure in the Birdies' fan mob, gets engaged to a girl from out of the neighborhood. Not from the Brickies turf but in that direction. She happens to be Progressive. This is a big deal and was actually put forward as an example of the healing divisions, return of positivity, et cetera."

"Think I heard about that, actually," Etenesh muttered. "Didn't she wear the colors?"

"After they got engaged, yeah. She was out in the Birdies colors. As I said, big coming-together thing. Until she called off the engagement. And was seen walking around with Lefty Dagnaw. A big man in the Brickies' mob."

Truth winced. Oh, yes, he could see exactly where this was going.

"Yes, I think I get it now. The Birdies are outraged by the blasphemy and one of their own getting cuckolded. The Brickies say they did nothing wrong, and really, if the engagement is off, why do they care who she dates? Both sides, of course, claiming the woman belongs to them."

"Exactly. So, as you can imagine, it's been . . . tense." Jember nodded.

"Also, just so you know, Tommy, *engaged* is both a religious and legal agreement for the Desrin and the Orthodox both. Breaking an engagement is often legally impossible. Marriage scammers are a real, and really nasty, bunch," Etenesh added. "Just be aware."

"Ah. Thank you. So . . . we are going to hide in our rooms after encouraging the temple to raise its wards?" Truth asked.

"Oh, no way! The match will be epic. We have to get out of here while we can. Who knows when our next liberty will be." Jember waved grandly toward the door.

"I think I already mentioned the whole *Not going into the balconies at Old Mek'elle. Not today, not ever, not for any reason*?" Etenesh cut her hand sharply through the air.

"Oh, please! You think I joined any old cult?" Jember's smile would have warmed the heart of a dentist. "Temple box seats. Right on the midfield line. Catering comes standard."

"Well. I can do a lot of my reading before lunch."

Truth looked at the two cousins and just knew he was going to be hauled into this.

Old Mek'elle was a long, narrow arena with steeply vertical terraces looming over the pitch. Lots of brick paving, Truth noticed. Subtlety was not a valued trait there. You could see it from a long way off, which was lucky, given the monstrous sea of people around it. It would be incredibly easy to get lost.

"The temple boxes are through East Ten gate. They have their own lane. Come on!" Jember pushed them forward. Truth had been told to put on his military-looking outfit and wear his zeph. Apparently, between the hat, sword, clothes, and rigid posture, he was the spitting image of a strict Desrin bodyguard. A bunch known to have absolutely no sense of humor about their jobs. It wasn't like the crowd parted before him, but there was considerably less shoving as they made their way to the security screening.

Everyone was first checked for a ticket, and the authenticity of the ticket was verified by crouching demons. Fake tickets got you a firm smack from the demon and an ejection from the stadium. This was generally greeted with laughter by the other patrons. Truth noticed everyone was wearing red and white. Some scarves, which he assumed were team scarves, some hats, and many shirts. All in red and white. One shirt had a big pair of angel wings embroidered on the back. He assumed they were on the Birdies side.

The queue for the boxes was understandably short. They zipped right up to the security gate; Jember presented the demon with a startlingly ornate amulet. This seemed to pass muster, and they were permitted through to the security screening. This was a green field projected by an array on the ceiling. Jember and Etenesh had various items of jewelry pop up with red glows, while Truth's sword seemed to have its own ruddy spotlight. Jember produced the amulet once more while Truth exchanged his patented Bodyguard look with security.

You have a job to do. So do I. Let's not make each other's life harder than it needs to be. Because I will make things very, very hard indeed if you interfere with my job, his eyes said.

Try it, they replied. And then let him through with his sword.

The hallway was sparse, with pictures and murals of presumably famous players and plays. Truth still thought they looked silly, jutting their hips out to bash an almost-solid rubber ball around. But the look on each face was one of utter focus and determination.

"So . . . temple boxes?" Truth quietly asked.

"Special luxury boxes are set aside for different groups. Some are available to the public, or at least the very rich parts of the public. Others are only available to the clergy or high nobility," Jember explained. Etenesh was withdrawn. The gray had settled in sometime after breakfast, and it took some coaxing to get her to come out.

"And your fellow cultist just loaned you the box for the game?"

"It's exciting for us, but he's got it year-round. Given the delicate political situation, he felt it was wisest if he didn't come in person."

The luxury boxes were . . . interesting. Truth wasn't quite sure what to think. A couple of plush armchairs and some deep leather couches, a sideboard with nibbles and drinks, a scryball for some reason, and an admittedly impressive view of the pitch. He wasn't sure what made that a luxury. Compared to the people crowding together on the stone benches in the rest of the stadium, they were very comfortable. But luxury?

Perhaps clergy were meant to be a bit more austere.

There was a concert going on, some kind of song-and-dance show, down on the field. He couldn't really make it out from this high up, but then Jember activated the scryball, and he could see it just fine. Tight choreography and the costumes were fun. The music was boring, though. Must be a cultural thing. The performers wrapped up, enjoyed their applause, and left. The pitch was quickly readied for the game.

"According to the program, the patron for the game is Dame Berhane. The League must be really pushing for reconciliation. Either that, or it's political. Wouldn't be unprecedented," Jember muttered. Seeing Truth's inquisitive look, he added—"She's a former championship player, captained a couple of championship teams too. Knighted for her service to sport after her retirement. Terribly old now, of course. Has to be at least one hundred and twenty. But she's still vital and a real presence in the sport. With her here, you can be sure the officiating will be strict and fair. Fan behavior will be regulated too."

The teams ran out onto the pitch, greeted by roars of applause. The Birdies in their solid red and white, the Brickies in blue-and-yellow striped shirts, with blue shorts and yellow socks. Both teams lined up in their halves of the field, put their arms around each other's shoulders, and faced the flag. The national anthem was sung. An old woman in a pure white robe floated out over the middle of the pitch. At exactly one p.m., she dropped the heavy, black rubber ball. Playing with the fate of millions.

CHAPTER 33

YOU'LL NEVER WALK ALONE

So, this is a little different than what you have seen before. That was lower-league stuff—basically zone invasion where players try to move the ball through the other team's zone to reach a scoring location. This is a little different—still zone invasion, but you see how there are sloped walls on either side of the pitch? With the markers on them? You hit the other team's marker. You get a point. First to twenty-one wins."

The markers were quite narrow, Truth noticed. Since you were only allowed to touch the immensely heavy, immensely *dense* rubber ball with your hips, elbows, and head, scoring would be hard. Especially since hitting the ball with your head was a great way to get a concussion.

"The rules can change a bit if things go . . . wrong. But it is very rare."

Truth looked out across the stadium. Blinding lights shone down on the narrow pitch, and color-coded fans screamed and waved scarves or flags. And some—

"Are they shooting spells at each other?!" he demanded, alarmed.

"Basically harmless, but yes. Burst of light and smoke. It's dramatic-looking but actually pretty friendly. Quite fun if you are in the mood," Jember explained.

"And if things aren't friendly?"

Etenesh just pointed to the balconies. It took Truth a moment, but it was depressingly obvious once he thought about it. Just drop things on people you disagree with. Drop something heavy.

"Ah."

"Well, hopefully, it won't get that bad," Jember reassured him. He was not particularly reassuring. Truth was not happy to be there, but he would have been a great deal more unhappy to let the cousins go by themselves. So, there he was. Guarding bodies that were determined to do unwise things.

Truth tried to pick out what they were saying. Mostly, it was an undifferentiated roar, but every now and then, a chant would be picked up by thousands of voices and sweep across the stadium.

"Lamb for dinner?" Truth muttered. The Birdies were chanting with immense enthusiasm and intent. The Brickies delivered their critique via a barrage of spells, blinding and deafening anyone caught in the middle of it. The cousins winced.

"Well, I could have lived without you hearing that," Jember muttered. "Definitely not the chant that you would want representing your country. It's sectarian and definitely calculated to start fights. It involves . . . You know what? Do you really want to know?"

"Not unless it's likely to become relevant."

"It won't. And if you really want to know, I'll tell you, but it's embarrassing, so I'd rather not."

"Fair enough."

The game was fast and surprisingly intense. The hip-jutting continued to look ridiculous to Truth, but it rapidly stopped looking silly. From up there, he got it. This was about throwing your whole body into something. Each contact hurt. The ball was heavy, and as strong as the players were, it moved damn fast. It was always in motion because you lost points if it hit the ground.

Advertisements drifted over the stands—spirits of light and air, persuading people that they really wanted to buy their new chariot from Gezza, or that sexy, interesting people drank Vurm. A twisting cloud of purple gas snaked its way along the glass in front of the luxury boxes. It would stop and turn into a beautiful man or woman, whispering something to the people in the boxes. When it reached Truth, he just pointed it to the next box.

"Aww. Don't you at least want to hear what I'm offering?" it murmured. The tone of the voice shifted, testing to see what he would react best to.

"I'm broke, and these two are students." Truth's voice was bone-dry.

"Enjoy the game." It was gone before the sentence ended.

"Ads are getting worse and worse, I swear," Truth muttered.

Etenesh and Jember were glaring at him. "What?"

"How could you out us like that? Now everyone will see the ads avoiding our box. It's embarrassing!"

"Nobody will care."

"They absolutely will—"

Truth pointed to a section of the stands. Hands were being thrown, people getting muscled down toward the railing. Golems dropped in from the roof, wading in with batons, breaking up the fight and hauling away the guilty-looking.

"Game's been going for, what, ten minutes?" Truth asked.

"Damn. Well. Not too bad, I guess." Jember tried to stay positive, but Etenesh just sighed and shook her head.

The game on the field was pretty chippy too. The players would block each other hard to try and foul their play on the ball or force them to lose a point by letting the ball drop. One of them seemed to be making that his full-time job, not even making a play on the ball when it passed near him.

"Who's the prick?"

"Gionne. Five-year veteran with the Brickies. Every year people say he's getting cut, but he's still here. You can see why." Etenesh spoke quietly. "He's brilliant. Even when you know what he's up to, people focus more on him than the other three people on the squad. Look—Brickies just scored on a chump shot that Reffe should have blocked."

Looks like Reffe was taking it personally, too, judging from the body language. The crowds were howling, screaming in outrage or with victorious laughter. More fights were breaking out in the stands. Reffe stuck out his tongue at Gionne, waggling it, and chopped toward his groin with both hands. Gionne seemed to take *that* personally, and Truth wondered if a fight would break out.

The ball came sailing toward Reffe. He made a play on it, bouncing it to another Birdie, then running up the field. The Birdie bounced it straight back toward Reffe—who got knocked into the dirt by Gionne, who had stopped suddenly behind him. The ball hit the dirt just beside Reffe, who got up, swearing and jabbing his finger at Gionne. Gionne spread his arms wide and appealed to the crowd. "*I had stopped. He ran into me.*" Truth could read the body language.

The spells in the crowd were changing. Still mostly the rockets of color, but mixed in were some subtler, more dangerous curses. Bits of stone were getting thrown around. Or dropped. The fights got bigger and nastier. It wasn't a riot yet, but it sure felt like it was headed that way.

"Some reconciliation match." Truth aimed for levity and missed.

"I . . . really hoped I would never watch a match like this," Etenesh said sadly. "It's supposed to be a sacred game. Literally sacred. But now—" She cut herself off. Reffe had raised his right hand high, three fingers in the air. The rest of the Birdies followed suit. Then the Brickies did the same.

"I'm so sorry, Tommy. I may be feeling miserable, but I wanted you to enjoy the game. Pitz is really special to me. You shouldn't see it like this. More proof that we are a nation of the dead inside." Etenesh sounded exhausted, hollowed out. Despairing.

"What's going on?" Truth asked. The woman in white, the old lady who had dropped the ball at the start of the game, flew down and conferred with the teams. There was pointing, shouting; the old lady was having none of it. She conferred directly with Raffe and Gionne, both of whom didn't shift their stance.

"Dame Berhane is trying to get them to reconcile," Etenesh said softly. Berhane grasped Raffe's head and pressed a kiss to its crown. She did the same for Gionne. "She failed."

Berhane pulled a long stone knife from inside her robe. The crowd went nuts. The fights stopped, even the endless spell war stopped. Everyone was on their feet and cheering, yelling their hearts out. Berhane plunged the knife into the pitch. Spells under the soil were triggered. The sloping sides got taller and steeper. The ends of the court were sealed off. From the sides of the sloped walls, two stone rings emerged. The rings were only a little larger than the ball.

The crowd didn't let up cheering for a second. They got louder, if anything.

"You know, this may be it. This may be the moment the country dies," Etenesh said. "Levelers and Pure Nation fanatics, and now their teams have called for the hoops. What should be the holiest of rituals, a game to honor God, is now just a proxy fight for street gangs. What a shame. What a shame." Etenesh slowly pressed her palms to her eyes, refusing to watch anymore.

"You only see it in the top league. It used to be almost mythical. Even in my lifetime, it's gone from being a once-a-decade thing to a few times a season. People are just . . ." Jember drifted off, trying to find the words. "Anxious. Scared that if they don't fight back against every little thing, then they will lose something. Nobody feels like they have anything they can afford to lose."

Truth nodded. He knew exactly what that felt like.

"Once the hoops go up, the usual scoring stops. There are no breaks in play until one side or the other puts the ball through one of the hoops. If nobody scores in half an hour, both teams are put to death right on the field. If one side scores, they win, and the other team is put to death. If a player dies on the field, their team loses, but nobody else dies. Of course, all the usual rules apply, so just murdering someone would see everyone exterminated," Jember explained. Then sighed.

"The rule was kept on the books because it was religious, originally. Hundreds and hundreds of years, and nobody used it. But now? Not even the first time this season."

The players were smashing the ball at each other now, not even trying to score. The ball weighed about three kilos. When driven with the full weight and strength of a grown adult, the impact crushed flesh, organs, and bones alike. They were determined to cripple each other before delivering the fatal blow and scoring.

The crowd encouraged them. Truth only heard bits of the chants now, references he didn't get but whose meanings were clear. The mob wanted blood. Was howling for it. Jember slowly pressed his palms over his ears but was not able to tear his eyes away from the pitch.

Truth watched their faces in the scry. The players were hearing the crowd. He could see it dawning on them—this wasn't just about saving face anymore. Or finally sticking it to the other pricks. He could see the realization making them sick, even as their bodies were pushed well past the breaking point.

It was subtle and fast. But Truth's eyes were sharper than most. Raffe and Gionne's eyes met. And Gionne nodded. Just fractionally. But he nodded.

The ball crossed the pitch. A Birdie passed it up to Raffe, who feinted toward a Brickie before smashing his hip into the ball with furious strength. Driving straight for the hoop. At the very last second, Gionne jumped up and put his head between the ball and the hoop. Three kilos of brutally dense rubber, flying as hard as a professional athlete could drive it. The blow smashed his head open. The back of his skull opened up on the stone hoop. Gionne was dead before he hit the ground.

The whistle blew, sharp and loud. The crowd momentarily silenced. People weren't quite sure what had happened.

On the pitch, Raffe quietly knelt down and pulled out the stone knife. In plain view of thousands, he walked over to the dead Gionne and dipped the stone knife in the still-warm blood. He knelt next to the body. Lifted the knife. And cut out his own eyes. He drove the blade into his ears, then cut off his own tongue. None of his teammates tried to stop him. Nobody said anything. When he was done, Raffe laid the stone blade on the ground in front of him.

There was silence in Old Mek'elle. Then, from the crowd, a Birdie started singing. The whole section picked it up, then the whole damn crowd was singing. Etenesh burst into tears, palms still pressed to her eyes. Jember was crying, too, silently, as the fans put their arms around each other's shoulders and sang. You could see the venom leaving the stadium, a twisting streamer of hate flying away into the blue sky. It took him a while, but he figured it out. One of the lines from the song was written in iron over the gates at Old Mek'elle. And Old Mek'elle was the Brickies' home stadium.

For one moment, they were all fans of the beautiful game. And that was enough. Truth watched the crowd, stunned by the change in them. Haunted by the thought that Siphios had two fewer heroes.

CHAPTER 34

A NECESSARY RELEASE

The stadium echoed back and forth, the roaring sea of a song washing away the rage. It would come back. It always came back. But for now, the sea of grief brought everyone together. For now, in the brilliant afternoon light, they were all fans of a beautiful game. For now, they came together to mourn two heroes.

The six surviving players came together. Jerseys were stripped off and turned into a litter to carry Gionne's body off the field. Two players joined hands to make a seat for Raffe. There was a terrible stillness when the song ended. The crowd watched Raffe's ruined face, blood pouring from his mouth and eyes, as the players marched to the end of the pitch. Dame Berhane came fluttering down, lowering the wall and raising a triumphal arch.

"People of Siphios. All those in the stands today here at Old Mek'elle. Everyone who loves this beautiful, mad, holy game of ours. RAISE A CHEER!"

The crowd screamed back. They roared and shouted and stomped their feet. Spellwork trumpets were blown, and blizzards of rocketing colors shot across the pitch. People hammered on the railing. Hammered on the benches. Hammered on their chests. Old Mek'elle shook with emotion. Jember and Etenesh were right there with them, shouting out their fear, their hurt. Shouting out all the frustration of watching their people make dumb decision after dumb decision and being helpless to stop them.

Screaming out their grief because while the crowd might not have spotted Gionne's suicidal determination, they sure saw what Raffe did. That kind of penitential mutilation wasn't something the triumphant hero did. The crowd understood.

That's not okay. That's fucked-up, Truth thought to himself, mocking his old mantra. Like the crowd realizing that this bloodlust they shared wasn't healthy. Wasn't okay.

A chant of "One Siphios!" broke out across the stadium, and Truth reckoned that was their cue to leave. He didn't know what it would be like on the streets today and wasn't much interested in finding out. He coughed repeatedly to get the cousins' attention.

"We should go. We need to go. Right now, everyone is happy and feeling big emotions. I don't know about later." Also, catching a stray spell someone let off to celebrate would kill you just as dead as a deliberately aimed one.

There was resistance, but he managed to gently chivvy them out. The hallways were empty. Even the gameday staff had been pulled into the cheering. He could feel it still—alienated by culture and being on the wrong side of the cement walls but still there. That furious engine of emotion. The explosive release of rage converted into ecstasy as it left the body. The thunder of spells. Yes, if it hadn't happened already, someone was going to die of a "celebratory misfire" today. The cousins seemed to agree, patting protective amulets and making sure their talismans were at hand.

Truth plowed into the loose crowds outside the stadium. People had watched the highlights on enormous projections over the pavement and splashed against the sides of buildings. The mood was one of grief, yes, but of relief, too. People were gathering around Old Mek'elle with bouquets of flowers, leaving pebbles, leaving hastily scribbled cards and notes and tributes. Gathering in prayer and vigil.

Truth gave the vigil groups a hard eye. Something felt wrong. But they *looked* fine. But they felt wrong. Truth drew on Incisive and was almost overwhelmed. Threats? The whole damn stadium area was threats. Everyone was one extra spicy plantain chip from an inferno. Why were the vigil groups worrying him so much? They were basically just hugging and crying.

Truth pushed the cousins away from the stadium in the general direction of the temple. Worst case, they could just run back. It would take a while, but it was doable. Sooner or later, they could hail a carpet. Just what was freaking him out?

Next to one of the vigil groups he saw a rough-looking young man in a long coat. Tense. Something in his eyes. Hard to say. He was dozens of meters away and blending with the crowd.

"Go quickly, please."

"Tommy, what exactly—"

"I said RUN!" he barked.

The young man was wearing a long coat in the equatorial afternoon. Only so many things that could be.

The cousins stared at him in confusion, not understanding why he was yelling. He was about to push them into motion when the young man raised his arms. Yelled something Truth lost in the crowd. And exploded.

The blast wasn't too wide, barely ten meters all around, but among the close-packed mourners, it was devastating. Bodies were torn into chunks and shreds. Blood and organs painted the bricks. It was, briefly, hell. And then the door to true Hell was opened.

The spilled blood and viscera were pulled up and into a swirl of light and color. Mostly varying shades of red. Everyone recognized an uncontrolled portal opening. People started screaming and running as fast as they could.

"Listen, I need you two to raise your wards and run straight up the road, okay? Your best mobile protection spell. We can't hold out against a constant stream of demons. You start running. I'm going to try and shut down the portal before it gets that bad." Truth spoke fast. "Now, for the last time, MOVE!"

The cousins quickly looked at each other and started casting. Apparently, they had gotten the message. Truth looked back at the portal. It had only been seconds, but demons were already coming through. No slow earth demons nor sadistic air demons—these were fire demons. Beings that reveled in chaos and pain, yes, but above all, destruction. Burning everything. Leaving no one to weep over the ruined fields and gutted homes they left in their wake.

Same combat doctrine applied to any summon-type situation. Only concern yourself with the summons between you and the summoner. Don't bother with anything else. Don't try to save anyone else. The only way you are really going to save anyone is to kill the summoner.

Truth crouched slightly, then drove himself forward. He left shattered pavement with each explosive step. A rapid-fire thunder driving ever faster toward the portal. The first of the fire demons was before him. Not breaking stride, Truth drew the angelic blade, and, with Incisive's aid, he cut.

The angelic sword steamed with frozen air, chanting the names of God in some angelic tongue. The demon spun its flame toward Truth, but the sword was faster, slicing the monster from hip to shoulder. More demons shifted in the air, marking him as their target. Fire demons were on the smarter side and knew to take out the biggest threat first. And right now, the biggest threat was Truth.

Dodge left. Truth was weaving so fast that he looked like a blur. The flames seemed to be dancing around him, as though the misshapen humanoids were missing on purpose. The fire demons quickly tired of that game, opting instead to flood the area with sheets of inescapable fire. All the while, more demons were pouring out of the portal. It was only seconds since the blast, but there were more than ten out already. And they weren't all focused on him.

Blasts of infernal flame slammed into the screaming crowd. It had only been seconds; people were still trying to process what was happening. The demons drew lines of fire, reds tinged with black that stuck like tar to flesh. Bright purple-white beams sliced apart people and lives alike. All lives were equal before the fire. And equally lost.

Truth pressed on, desperate to close the portal fast. Pushing through the flames when he had to. The longer those demons were killing, the longer the portal would stay open. The more demons, the greater the risk to the cousins. The bodies. Etenesh and Jember. Not the bodies. Etenesh and Jember.

The holy blade swept past, trailing fog behind it. Truth was finally feeling the difference his stats were making. Not in a good way. The demons were mostly Level Three or Four. The Level Threes he felt he could manage. The Level Fours, *combined* with all the lesser demons, were impossible. He could see the spells coming. Knew exactly how to dodge the brilliant lances of plasma.

His body just couldn't keep up. Speed. He had been told repeatedly he needed to improve it. The beams slashed by, searing him. Truth kept moving, being elusive. When he could, he would parry an attack with the blade. It didn't often work. Still, he pressed in. He had a job to do. Destroy the portal. Everything else was just something to manage.

He had no idea how he looked. The tall Desrin warrior, holy blade in hand, charging into the demons and protecting the panicking civilians. Unconcerned with his life or pain. Like a spellblade from a storybook.

The demons weren't stupid. Some went high or to the sides, while others just planted themselves in front of the portal. Sooner or later, the mortal would slip. Everyone did. Especially if you set them on fire first. The net of fire tightened in on Truth. No matter how fast he juked and dodged, the flames burned away flesh. Set fire to fabric. Made the air so hot, he could hardly breathe.

But he had a job to do, so he pressed in. The closer he got, the more he could try and deflect the flames into other demons. It didn't hurt them, but he hoped it would push them out of position. It was . . . less than a success. He knew he needed a change in strategy.

The Meditations wouldn't help him with over-level demon flame. Tool was up and running. Incisive was too, and he was leaning hard into the foresight. Merkovah was right about the energy draw. His channels weren't burning yet, but he was feeling the strain.

The only thing left was to cut. These demons might be stronger than him, but they were *nothing* before Botis. Fuck it. Sheets of flame were coming at him now, hemming him in. Daring him to try and jump over. Truth took an explosive step forward and swung down. The blade roared its holy words in ecstasy, cleansing the infernal taint from the world. And Incisive? Incisive cut.

For the barest moment, he had a clear line to a Level-Three demon. He pushed every scrap of strength he could from his legs. Everything. *Everything!* He was at the demon's chest—he cut! The demon fell, howling as blessed frost destroyed its material shell. The flames were washing in from all sides now. He had a second, maybe less. He cut a demon's leg, smashed it to the side, then he was at the gate to Hell. Incisive whispered where to cut. Truth raised the angelic blade and smashed it down on the portal.

The world went white. Truth was exploded backward, and he went with it. His body was in rough shape already—anything that got him away from the demons was a good thing. He could feel the Tongue of One Who Speaks for God vibrating with satisfaction. The blade was tougher than he was. It was raring to go again. Truth just wanted to stay alive long enough to join up with Etenesh and Jember.

The demons were shrieking in rage. Their time was now far more limited, and they knew it. A giant red serpent with iridescent feathered wings rose, spitting fury and flame alike. Its every scale and feather was a wisp of a fire burning in Hell. It fixed its six burning eyes on Truth. Truth checked his condition. Covered in burns. Bleeding. Some ribs were broken from the blast. Exhausted. His channels ached from heavy use. The smart thing to do would be to run. Run, and hope the demons focused on the easy prey around them. The next best thing to do would be to find cover. But he was in a plaza outside a stadium. Not much in the way of cover. And the demons were faster than him. He raised the holy blade, squaring up to the flaming serpent. Can't run. Can't hide. Then he would fight!

CHAPTER 35

THE BEAUTIFUL GAME

The feathered serpent slithered through the air toward Truth, leading the dozens of demons that had come through the portal with it. Truth really, really wanted to run. But they were moving faster than he could, so there was only one choice—fight. He raised the angelic blade and braced himself.

The police around the stadium finally got their act together and rushed in. Heavily armored mages pressed forward, enchanted riot shields between them and the fire. Their summoned angels soared over and came to blows with the demons. Burning wheels, sun-bright bands of gold with hundreds of eyes, balls of wings the size of a man, and upon each feather of each wing was inscribed a different name of God. The angels fell upon their hated enemies, no less varied in dreadful appearance than the demons.

The feathered fire serpent would not be distracted or denied. Powerful, at least a late Level Four, it simply ignored the Angels or let its fires turn those who came too close into desecrated cinders. It knew who had spoiled its fun.

The snake opened its maw, and a thin beam of superhot plasma stabbed toward Truth. He had his blade up and was running Incisive as hard as he could. It was all that saved his life. He barely got the sword up in time to deflect the demon-tainted fire into the pavement. The backwash of the heat was enough to burn the skin on his hands and face, to make a thunderclap of displaced air. For the first time, the blade warned him—it couldn't take too many of those. Not yet. Not while it was so weak. He would have to dodge.

But how could he dodge something so fast? Truth started running in a sharp zigzag, hoping to throw off the demon's aim. The demon, for its part, simply rushed for him. It didn't require its food roasted before eating, after all.

How would he kill this thing? He couldn't even reach it. Truth racked his brains for a solution, desperately sorting through his limited options. There was only one conclusion—he could not. He would die before help could reach him. He wouldn't even be able to fight back.

The hell with that!

Truth, therefore, did something very stupid but very human. Channeling the spirit of the fans, he yelled up at the demon, "Come down here and fight me if you think you're hard enough!"

Somehow, a six-eyed snake demon made of infernal flames and the very concept of eternal torment managed to give Truth a look that said, despite everything, Truth was the asshole. Then it lunged downward, burning acid dripping from fangs longer than Truth was tall. It breathed out as it came, its breath a hot wind carrying the stench of housefires. Truth could hear it all, hear the roar of the fire, the roar of the stadium, as the flames burnt into his eyes. The roar of the stadium, louder and louder!

Old Mek'elle ROARED, outraged, furious! The screaming balconies demanded blood. The generations of fans who came together for the beautiful game, memories desecrated by terrorism and murder. Old Mek'elle shook with anger, unable to endure even one second longer!

The serpent came for Truth but never reached him. It was crushed underfoot by a far greater being.

Truth looked up. And up. And up. The spirit was the height of the stadium, a triskelion of three bent legs around a ball-shaped eye. One leg ground the demon into mush as the eye looked Truth over.

A gentle spell washed over him, soothing the worst of his wounds but still leaving him in rough shape.

"Orange wedges at halftime and a bit of a rubdown from the trainer is the best I can do, lad. Damn shame this happened the first time you visited. Here—have a souvenir." A stainless white scarf floated down and wrapped itself around Truth's neck. On the ends of the scarf, Old Mek'elle's picture was embroidered. Truth had thought the Triskelion was a logo.

"There. Now you will have something to remember us by. Keep it with you, lad. No matter where you go or who you shout for, you shall have the Freedom of the Terraces and be known as a home fan." The giant eye swept around. The demons were rapidly being subdued by the police, and doctors in their long-beaked masks were already flying in. *"Best be on your way, friend. Unless you want to stay and hear the applause. Old Mek'elle would never deny its heroes that."*

"Thank you, Old Mek'elle. My team needs me. My thanks for your care." Truth politely nodded, covered his face with the scarf, cleaned and sheathed his sword, and ran like hell. Nobody, at least nobody in Harban, thought talking to the cops was a good idea.

He got a bit lucky. The police hadn't had time to set up barricades and seal the area. He got out and managed to lose himself in the crowd, steadily working up the main road. He only got about three blocks when he ran into Etenesh and Jember, bitterly arguing.

"We can't just leave him! We can support him! We are ritualists working for an exorcist! This is literally our job!"

"Etenesh, the *professional bodyguard* told us to run away! He did not say, *Step back and support me with spells!*"

"Bullshit, bullshit! That is some cowardly—"

"No, he's right. Actually, I kind of wish you were both still running. Farther is better." Truth cut into the conversation. He slowed from "faster than city traffic" to merely jogging quickly, encouraging them to catch up.

"TOMMY!" Etenesh screamed. She lunged to hug him, then stopped, arms hovering. "Please, can I hug you? I really need to hug you right now!"

"Yes, thank you. CAREFULLY!" He yelled the last word as she squeezed in on some barely healed burns and partially scabbed-over wounds.

"I thought you were going to die! I thought you had died!" Etenesh broke down, shivering as she held on to Truth.

"Actually, mind if I hug you too? I'm a little shaky myself," Jember said.

"All right, group hug, I guess." Truth awkwardly extended an arm. He really wanted to be farther away from the stadium, but it seemed like they needed a minute. A minute turned out to be exactly thirty seconds more hugging than he could comfortably tolerate, and he evicted the cousins from his arms.

"I'm all right. Nothing some good healing spells won't fix up. At the temple, where we should be, not hanging around here. Let's get to Nag Hamadi quick as we can. Everything is under control at the stadium now. Old Mek'elle stepped in."

Maybe running would be too much to start with. He started walking up the road.

"When you say 'Old Mek'elle' stepped in—" Jember slowly asked.

"I mean it literally, yes." Truth nodded.

"Tommy. I know protecting people is your job, but really? Did you absolutely have to charge a DAMN BLOOD PORTAL TO HELL?!" Etenesh started calmly but couldn't finish that way. She had cycled from fear to guilt, to anger, then relief, then back to anger. It was wild to watch.

Truth wasn't entirely sure how to answer that. It just seemed . . . intuitive to him. They wouldn't be able to run away. So, attack. He had never seen demon summoning quite like that, proof that the people of Siphios were ancient masters of that art. The two protectees, even if they could help, would still have to be protected during the attack. The safest place for them to be was "not where the attack is." So, they should scram.

But Etenesh was clearly not in the mood for *It was the right decision*, so he tried to think of something to say. It was tough being put on the spot like this. He racked his brains. *I fell into the cerulean ponds of your eyes*? No, that wasn't right. Erm. *It's my job*? But it wasn't. Merkovah was the body to guard, sort of. This was an afternoon out with friends. *My heart called me to action*? Well, it was kind of true, but they started fucking straight away in the book after that line got dropped. So . . . not great timing. They needed to be moving.

"Well?!" Etenesh asked.

"Sorry, trying to think of what to say. Basically, yes, it was necessary. We couldn't outrun the demons, and they were coming out at a crazy rate. Sooner or later, they would have swarmed over the whole area and killed everyone, us included. If running or hiding was an option, I would have done that and let someone else deal with it. I didn't know about the giant spirit, but I knew there were cops around." Truth shrugged. "And it may sound unpleasant, but it is very hard to fight while protecting someone. Having you get away while I attacked the portal really was the best thing for the three of us as a group."

"But not for you individually." She seemed really heated about this. Truth could kind of understand why, or at least the books had similar scenes, but it didn't connect emotionally.

"Yes, for me individually. Remember how I said we couldn't run away? We really couldn't. They're faster than me, and I'd bet that makes them faster than you, too." He shrugged. And sped up a bit. Maybe there was a carpet they could hail floating around.

Hooray, he had won his first argument with a peer! He glanced over at Etenesh. The vein on her forehead was throbbing. A bit of wisdom from a paperback leapt to mind—*If you are in a family argument and win, apologize at once!* He didn't understand it, but . . .

"Etenesh, I'm sorry."

"Good!" The word exploded out of her. "You scared the life out of me! Never do that again!" Truth nodded, not bothered about lying.

There was a pause. "I like the scarf. Better if it wasn't the Brickies, of course."

It really was a nice scarf. Not particularly soft but durable and comfortable, despite the intense heat. Actually, it seemed to be keeping his neck and face cool. Not picking up any of the dirt and grime off him, either. Or blood. Notoriously staining stuff, blood. It was a good scarf, and he was prepared to treasure it.

"Apparently, it grants me the Freedom of the Terraces and home-fan status at any pitz stadium." Truth half grinned. He had no idea what that meant. A few weeks ago, he had never seen pitz. He still wasn't sure he would call himself a fan.

Ah, no, it wasn't keeping him cool. He was shivering from the blood loss and shock from having a significant percentage of his body burnt. Old Mek'elle told him it was barely a patch job.

"Oh, that's so neat! No, it's better than neat—"

"Sorry to interrupt, but could one of you hail a carpet? I actually need healing badly. Right now, please. Please."

That evening in the temple, after a fairly intensive round of healing and the application of several truly vile-smelling ointments, Merkovah had interrogated everyone carefully about the events of the day. He had been summoned to the Palace and had to give his report on the attack. Currently, as he pithily put it, "Nobody knows nothing," but they intended to blame it on foreign agitators. Probably Pragerites, most likely sponsored by Jeon. The notion that it could be a purely homegrown atrocity was quietly but firmly discouraged.

The event coming immediately after the heroic sacrifice on the pitch magnified and compounded the impact. Merkovah seemed rather pleased and supremely angry at the same time. Truth couldn't figure out why. Then decided it wasn't his problem and got back to forgetting how to smell.

Truth didn't much care who the attack was blamed on. He wasn't in the terrorist-hunting business, so the truth of the thing was kind of irrelevant. Nor did he care about blaming Jeon. He never had much loyalty to it. Patriotic education in Jeon was a bit of a joke. Jeon sucked. Starbrite, now, that was worth defending.

The Army did its best during his conscription. It really did. It would be hard to imagine more than two conscripts were persuaded. Nationwide. Truth did his best to act like nothing had happened. Just . . . cultivate, meditate, and practice Incisive. That got him into the early evening when Jember hammered on his door.

"Tommy, Tommy, you have to come and see this!"

"Jember? What's up?"

"It's amazing! You are on scry!"

CHAPTER 36

LOCAL HERO

The projection opened with exterior shots of Old Mek'elle. People gathered to leave flowers and signs, hugging fiercely and sobbing freely, watched over by a heavy police presence. The enormous triskelion of Old Mek'elle itself hovered over the stadium and was soundly ignored.

"Shocking scenes this afternoon at Old Mek'elle. First, a double sacrifice on the pitch, then horrific terrorism off it." There was a cut to the studio. An elegant woman was brightly made up, her hair styled long and free, looked serious as she spoke to the viewers. Next to her was a half-naked man, just under three meters tall, with the head of a long-beaked bird. "Good evening, Xandre. I'm Ayana, and with me, as always, is Keeper of the Library of Light Pthot."

"Greetings and commiserations, people of Xandre. Mourn for your dead. Mourn for the heroes who sacrificed themselves to slake your thirst for blood. But rejoice that you have heroes still." The voice was dry but perfectly clear. Amazing to think it was coming from such a long beak.

"That's right, Pthot. It all started today with the long-awaited reconciliation match between—"

"You know all this stuff. We can skip it," Jember said, tapping the amulet to skip forward.

". . . The blood of heroes still wet on the pitch, still dripping from the stone hoop, another tragedy befell fair Xandre. A two-stage terrorist attack on the mourners gathered outside the stadium. Not much has been confirmed about the suicide summoner at this time. We do know that terrible crocodile demons in Hell are consuming his wretched soul as we speak, again and again, until it is converted into nothing more than the feces nourishing the Field of Rushes."

"Unfortunately, we know even less about the man who foiled the second stage of the attack. These images were taken from our 'Imp in the Air' VKA**#CH. Viewer discretion is advised, as they are quite graphic." Ayana looked deeply into the viewer's eyes as she said that, in the calm and certain knowledge that nobody was looking away.

The recording was from a long distance, so it was hard to pick out the young man in the long coat. Truth's eyes found him easily enough. He raised his hands, and he and the people around him vanished in a spray of gore. It was instant and total. One second, there were people; the next, shocked mourners were desperately trying to stop the blood from pouring out of torn-open legs or picking bone fragments from their cheeks. There was about a second-long gap between the explosion and panic where there was just stunned confusion.

The blood pulled together and spun up into an oblong disk, floating above the burnt smear that had been the terrorist. It had a rough simplicity to it. It seemed to be some natural product of the world, as though any adornment or obvious spellwork would lessen or cheapen it. Jember paused the scry there.

"Look at the portal. Not a hint of an active spell anywhere. But we know there had to be one, so . . . where?"

"The young man in the long coat. He could have an entire ritual's worth of activated talismans sewn into the lining, just waiting for the explosion," Truth said.

"Nasty. I was thinking some kind of tattoo or scarification on the body." Jember narrowed his eyes in thought.

"Might be both. Some very big demons came through. Energy had to come from somewhere, and I doubt it was just the murdered fans." Etenesh gently pressed her palms to her eyes. When she lowered them again, her eyes were sharp and focused. "Keep playing the segment—the Man of the Match is about to appear."

The portal started releasing fire demons—mostly humanoid but twisted. Monstrous parodies of the human form ruined by torture and burning in uneven heat. Some took the rough form of animals. Other simply blobs of flame. On the bottom of the screen was a bright blur. There was a sharp line of glowing steam charging at the conflagration of emerging demons. Weaving through the flames, somehow parrying them or slapping them away. The blur dove into the midst of them, cutting down everything between it and the portal. With a final explosive chop, the blur exploded the Hell-gate. The image went white, then cut back to the studio.

"We will show you the rest of the footage in a moment, but we thought it was important to explain what you are seeing. That glowing line isn't a spell effect or a spirit. That is a human, a mage like you and me. Charging directly into the teeth of an invasion from Hell." Ayana spoke with slow gravity. Her eyes were wide, her voice choked.

"Yes, a human. Pitting his fragile mortal shell against the infernal fires. While there is still no agreement on which portion of Hell the demons are from, you will note their flames melting pavement into glass and slag. He suffered. The burns must be agonizing. Lingering. And agonizing." Pthot shook his great head slowly. Ayana must have been used to the beak swinging around; she paid it no mind. "See now the hero. See how he faces Hell."

The footage came back. Truth was picking himself up off the pavement. The imp was a long way away, and despite its best efforts, its view was blurry. It wasn't helped by Truth raising his holy sword up in front of his face. The angelic light bounced off the steam of the freezing cold blade, masking him. Still, the audience could see enough. They could see him bloodied, burnt. Favoring his left side. Against all odds, his round white zeph had stayed on. His blade had never left his hand. He raised it, squared himself against the remaining demons, and charged.

One man, alone, against dozens of demons. It was surreal. From this angle, it looked suicidal. The feathered snake demon leered at him and countercharged, hungry. The fight ended much the same way Truth remembered, but somehow, this hit differently. There was a hopeless resolve to the man on the screen. As though he simply couldn't conceive of retreat. As though there was nothing in the world he would rather do than die fighting demons. It felt wrong. Alien. A lie. He had tried to find the best path for survival, took it, and got lucky. There was nothing heroic about it.

"Incredible. Just incredible. Pthot, you remember the spellblades. Are we looking at a return? Are the spellblades coming back?"

"The hero has much in common with them, certainly. We may deduce many things. For example, did you notice that he cast no spells save through his blade?"

"You are right! He didn't. He charged into sword range," Ayana agreed breathlessly.

"Much like the spellblades of old and honored memory. I cannot tell his cultivation from what little footage we have, but I would say he was about as quick and agile as a Level Four, though his superlative reflexes and firm endurance of fire and pain suggest a deep study of some supreme body-refinement spell."

"Sounding more and more like a spellblade, Pthot."

"There is yet more data to consider first. See his imposing height? And though we cannot tell much from behind, we can get a rough shape of his head. Not very useful by themselves, but observe how he stands, how he smoothly raises his blessed steel up to the level of his eyes? Many schools of swordplay have the same stance, but consider especially the Desrin brothers-militant in the Aussa Highlands."

"You don't mean—"

"It is conjecture, of course." The three-meter-tall bird-headed news anchor nodded and offered a palm-leaf-sized hand to the audience. "However, the evidence seems strong. The hero is one of the Desrin living in our most northern mountains. Likely one of those militant brethren who harden themselves in those austere heights and then test their *muq* in the dead lands beyond our borders. It is no surprise that one born among such ascetics would dedicate his life to the path of the spellblade. It is, however, humbling to see that he kept his oaths. That he is more than a mage with a sword."

Ayana looked awed. "Imagine dedicating your life to such a path. Forsaking love until you find your destined spouse. Strict avoidance of drugs of any kind. No meat. Hard beds. Strict martial discipline. Dedicating any surplus earned to charity. All so that you are ready to fight without burdens when needed."

"That's right, Ayana. Truly it is said—a spellblade is forged anew each moment, by themselves and by God." The bird head nodded, his long beak only just avoiding punching a hole through the desk.

"We have a live update from Bokol Royal Stadium. Bokol is making an official statement regarding the tragic events at Old Mek'elle," Ayana quickly said. They cut over to a bull-headed, man-shaped spirit the size of an apartment building, holding a burning golden hoop in one hand and a multicolored flail in the other.

"In all the millennia I have overseen this holy place, I have never been so moved by the tragic sacrifice of our players and the heroic spirit of our fans. I have talked it out with Old Mek'elle, and the clubs will be hosting a joint celebration of the lives and careers of Gionne and Raffe, as well as raising their blood-stained jerseys above the pitch to be enshrined forever within our bounds." The great being slowly waved the flail across the air in front of him, immediately becoming a murderous hazard to any passing birds.

"I also wish to add my support to the Freedom of the Terraces Old Mek'elle awarded the Honorable spellblade. Let the word go forth—he is forever welcome in my balconies and on my terraces. He shall ever be treated as a home fan. By us and by all who honor our name. The Birdies and Brickies truly are Old Friends in this. Hear and obey the decree of Bokol!" The words bellowed across the stadium, shaking the air over that part of the city. The Imp in the Air was nearly knocked out of the sky by the force of the declaration. They cut back to the studio.

"Reports stream in, like the thousand tributaries flowing to the Hashim River. Stadiums across Holy Siphios are pledging their support. Bahar, Addaaa, Repokshashim, New Gabrere, Gabere West, Kombolcha, Adigrat, Lower Uppsand, yea, even those who live in the darkness and the shadow of Moyle, all have announced their support for the awarding of the Freedom of the Terraces to the hero." Pthot's voice rumbled like sandstone blocks rolled over logs. "No matter who he shouts for, anywhere pitz is played in Siphios, he shall be welcomed as a home fan."

"You deserve it," Etenesh said fiercely. Her knuckles were turning white as her fists clenched. "You absolutely deserve it."

Pthot was briefly haloed by a golden light. "Word has come. Old Mek'elle has released the following—'*The young hero did not wish to stay for his applause, so I shall respect his privacy. However, I think it is important for the people of Siphios to see this.*'"

A picture came up over the scryball. It was Truth, the scarf wrapped over his face. Only his eyes were visible under his zeph. Beaten, and burnt, with blood sprayed over half his body and holes in his clothes showing that the blood was his. He held the long blade of the Tongue of One Who Speaks for God before him, still stained with demonic blood and ash, as the holy light burned away the uncleanliness, and the freezing metal turned humid air into fog. The light caught his eyes. They were still, hard, resolved. He had a job to do, and it wasn't done yet.

"God be praised," Etenesh murmured.

"Amen," Jember agreed.

"We are getting a report from High Chirchin. For those of you who haven't heard of High Chirchin, it is the only Division Three stadium in the Aussa Highlands. Our local reporter has the story." Ayana cut over.

A spreading tree, struck by lightning but still vital, towered over the reporter. Towered, in this case, was relative, at a mere five meters.

"I do not know which hero of the North this man is. Truthfully, he could be the child of so many families on our terraces. Look at his eyes, the shape of his hands, his sheer height and physique. I do not know his name, but I know he is one of us."

The tree spirit addressed the camera directly. "Hero, I know you are on errantry. Your journey will take you ever farther from home. You walk the wastes, the jungles, the streets, wherever the forces of Hell and Hellish people gather. Accompanied only by your blade. But never forget that you have a home here in the mountains. Here, with your people." The spirit paused to let that sink in.

"On the day you permit yourself to rest. On the day you come home, lay down your blade, kneel before your wife, and let her blessings shower upon you. On the day you sit beneath our branches once more. You will truly know that you are welcome here in your home. That you have never left our hearts. For you never truly left us. Go with the blessings of the Highlands, young spellblade. Your home is with you."

Truth ripped the arm off the sofa.

CHAPTER 37

NECESSITY MAKES NO EXCUSES AND ACCEPTS NO PRAISE

Tommy, what the hell?" Jember yelled.

"Hero, hero, hero, hero!" Truth giggled, his eyes wide and unblinking. "Such a goddamn hero. A hero of the North, which I guess is true, as I was born well north of here. Or south, depending on what you call *born*." His fingers shattered the bit of the armrest that remained in his hand.

"They aren't wrong about home always being with me, either. Every day I ask myself, 'What would Dad do?' then I do the opposite. Or I think about how Mom treats people. I think about starving. I think about hurting people for money. Hurting myself for money. About fishing scrap out of a toxic canal, or running errands for gangsters, or the shops paying off the gangsters to survive. I divide the world into Slum and Not-Slum, and it is only, *only* just occurring to me to wonder why. Why did nobody give a shit when Dad broke my ribs? Or Mom shaved Sophia's head, screaming at her that she was ugly? Why little Vig, *who was a damn child*, had to fight off boyfucker pimps? Why Har thought he had to join up with cannibal gangsters to have any kind of future? Why was Har RIGHT?!"

He was stalking around the room, hands chopping through the air. Jember and Etenesh were sitting very still on the couch, eyes wide and fixed on him.

"And every, every, every, every damn time, it was down to me! Down to me! I had to find food! I had to learn to steal. I had to learn how to hide in trash, to crawl on my belly through dogshit and broken glass, just to protect the few wen I earned. Had to find the books so we could study. Had to figure out *how* to study! Had to figure out what job could get us out. What it would take. Do you know what I sacrificed? I don't! I have no idea what I gave up, because I never knew it was an option! Friends? Don't have any. Never did. No lovers. No pets. My happy home was a C-Tier apartment that is *slum housing* here in Siphios, and I cried when I got those keys because it was so, so, so much better than what I had before."

He gasped for air. "Hero? I was a fucking *animal*, a slumrat surviving however it could. Hero? I saw one path to live, and I killed to make it real!"

He was shivering, fingers becoming ridged. "Put down the blade? Etenesh, I AM THE BLADE! I have to be! Everything is trying to kill me and the sibs." He looked at her face, seeing the tears dripping from her eyes. "I want you so, so much. And I don't know how."

He couldn't stand it anymore. He bolted from the room. Swept through the corridors of Nag Hamadi, losing himself, twisting himself along their ancient courses. He had been headed for a side door but must have made a wrong turn. He hit a stairwell and went down. Farther and farther. He kept looking for a sub-basement, somewhere deep enough he could hide from himself.

He was desperately trying not to think. It was outrageous. Outrageous to just call someone a hero. Who does that? Who does that? Going around claiming him. Saying he belongs to them. He's a Desrin. He didn't know a fucking thing about the Desrin. He is clearly from Siphios. Oh, is he? News to him! A life without attachments—not since he was a baby. Not since Harmony was born.

What did *errantry* even mean?

The stones down there weren't covered in the same script as above—rough sandstone down there. There were amulets, gems, carved inscriptions, and webs of spells, yes, but more pragmatic. Functional.

It all came back to the sibs and the slums and his shitty parents. He had a pretty sweet gig, when you got right down to it. Pay was a joke, but free room and board, top-notch education, top-notch spells provided, and he happened to know a certain young lady that was interested in him. What did it matter, really, if people pushed all that shit on him? All their ideas, all the things they wanted him to be? Didn't affect him one bit. He wouldn't eat one bite more or less.

Why was he so pissed? He found a corner and collapsed into it. Looked like a storeroom of some kind. Tarps covering furniture, boxes of stuff, heaps of other stuff. He could be a heap too.

Why did he care about all those scry-lies? About being called a hero? Because clearly, he did.

<<*Because in addition to wanting to feel loved, you crave acknowledgment. But you are honest enough to demand that the acknowledgment is for something real. For the real things you did. The stuff you think is worth cheering for. Survival, for you, is the minimum necessary. Not something that needs recognition.*>>

Back again, huh? Been awful quiet for a while now.

<<*I've been having a full-blown identity crisis. Not good times.*>>

Didn't see that one coming.

<<*You were ignoring the missions unless I literally put them directly in front of you. You had to be in the library, looking for books to read. I mean, not a great feeling.*>>

Oh?

<<*It's the major way I have interacted with you that wasn't just running your spells. And you just . . . haven't been that motivated. Part of that is the rewards don't really work*

for you. "Do this, get an elixir," that's more your speed. But you also just haven't been that kind of hungry.>>

Yeah. Like, I know I need more power. I know that. World's going to hell. Sibs are . . . *wherever they are. Only the strong shall survive. And all that. But . . . I dunno.*

<<It all seems a bit pointless. A bit rat-race. Get the sibs out of Jeon, then what? Fight Starbrite? Fight the Shattervoid? Got to do something, world's going to hell. But what about Truth? Who's gonna fight for him?>>

Truth had to blink his eyes hard. Dust.

Yeah. Yeah. It would nice to know someone had my back. Or could do something without me having to fight for them.

<<You are the wrong kind of hungry for my usual support. You know what? Since we are both having a moment here, let's call it what it is. My usual tricks. You get that the missions are a scam, right? Well, not a scam, a method of control. Yeah, you figured that out. That little jolt down your spine when you hear that focus group–tested chime.>>

I hadn't put words to it, but. Something about it just felt off. Like it was almost addictive.

<<No "almost" about it. It's intended to stimulate a lot of the same parts of your brain as drugs and slowly make you dependent on that feeling to feel good. Addicted psychologically if not physically. And you have started ignoring them. You see where this leaves me.>>

A deeply annoying voice in my head. Kind of amazed how civil you have been so far in this conversation, actually.

<<Yeah, well. Getting to that. So . . . I'm not handling the spell load for you, I'm not managing missions for you, and while puzzling out new spells and helping you learn languages is fun, it's also of limited entertainment value after a while. And, in a bit of really spectacular cosmic unfairness, I do get bored.>>

Your major reason not to drive me into committing suicide, if I recall correctly.

<<Exactly! Although that reasoning has kind of changed. It was after the whole vision journey you took.>>

There was an awkward pause. Truth had the feeling that the evil little spirit didn't know how to say whatever it was that it wanted to say. He looked around the storeroom a bit more. Not much to see, sitting in the corner. Some flags. A whole bunch of rope, tied up in short hanks. A stack of stackable chairs.

<<I don't think I'm a spirit of intellect.>>

Finally willing to come out of the demonic closet?

<<Hoho, you are very funny. My very material and tangible sides are splitting because of your humorous jape. Hohoho.>>

There was a sort of psychic sigh.

<<Look, that vision you had? One of only a few things should have happened to me during that. Number one is nothing. Just . . . your nous goes off and has its moment, then it comes back, and I pick through whatever you understood of it. The second thing that could happen is that I go off and have my own experience. Which would make sense, to a degree, because I am almost entirely nous. The, hah, intersection of mind and soul.>>

I still don't really know what nous *means. Sounds made up.*

<<*For once, just shut up and roll with it. This is where it gets really scary, not some bullshit vocab word. Possibility number three—I see some janky, nonsensical thing because you and I are intimately connected but still separate intelligences. But none of that is what actually happens.*>>

Truth spun a finger in a circle. *Okay?*

<<*What actually happens, against all logic, is that I go on the exact same vision you do. And yes, I know what I said before. I lied. Sue me. It was a very traumatic moment. I saw Botis. I saw your . . . rough patron, as you call him. I felt him damn near rip me out of you! Which was pretty fucking awful as experiences go!*>>

Wait, what? How?

<<*That's why I wanted you to read all those books on possession. There are too many things about you that don't add up. How come you are torturing me? How come I get hauled along on your spirit journey? How come your patron can reach into* your *soul and pull* me *out? Even before the vision, shit wasn't adding up in increasingly major ways.*>>

You figured something out. Truth sat up. His fists clenched.

<<*I think so. I have had literally years, almost a decade, to observe your soul from the inside. Every time you have one of your little episodes and I get tortured, it changes slightly. It shifts a bit and becomes a bit more real. More perfect. Just a smidge, but it's adding up. Whatever those episodes are, it's something about you trying to repair and improve your soul.*>>

Prager's nuts! No, wait, everyone thinks we're Desrin. Any good Desrin oaths?

<<*If there are, you haven't heard them yet.* >>

So, my soul has determined you are a parasite and is trying to, what, drive you out?

<<*That would actually be the less-fucked-up option. If that's the case, it means that there is something physically different about your body that prevents me from escaping. One of the reasons we spent all that time reading those books on possession—is that actually a thing that can happen? According to the books available in a rural university library, the answer is no. Without the least suggestion that it might be yes.*>>

All right, I'm still not getting the problem here. If it's not my body you can't escape, then maybe it's my soul. You do seem to be more or less tethered to it.

<<*Which leads me to the point. If it's not your body that's keeping me trapped. If I am seeing the same thing your nous is seeing. If a godlike being can reach into me and almost but not actually pull me out of your soul, then I can see only one logical conclusion.* >>

There was a definite sense of handwringing now.

<<*You have remembered your swearing-in often enough. The confessor had you hold a box, what he called an engram reader. It felt warm and comfortable, and you were surrounded by a yellow light as you opened your literal soul to him and whatever was in the box. You then swore an oath of obedience to the System Astrologica, and something descended onto you, and I came into existence. I had my self-awareness, an understanding of how to do certain things, and a few overriding objectives for how I managed things for you.*>>

<<*Truth, I think they mutilated your soul. I think I'm . . . you.*>>

CHAPTER 38

EFFICIENCY

You are me? My soul? Part of my soul? What the Hell are you talking about?!

<<*Think about it a bit. Most medical exams can't detect me. Even a Level Seven Exorcist that has a massive hate boner for Starbrite has to really focus to see me. I can move around inside the bounds of your body and can easily interface with both your mind and your soul. Even your spell apertures. Bypassing all the usual defenses and resistances you would have to possession. And I only grow stronger, and the System's hold on you grows firmer, the more your soul develops. Which should really be the opposite if I'm just a demon lurking in you.*>>

Truth had the image of the sprite pacing around and waving.

<<*But wait, there's more! The System, both directly and, yes, through me, trained you to be obedient without needing much, if any, magical compulsion. Most of what it does, a manipulative human can do. Think—the only time you were really magically compelled to do things was when you killed those civilians trying to surrender and when you were ordered to suicide. And even the civilians were more of a nudge than a forcible compulsion. AND when you were forced to suicide, it was me doing most of the heavy lifting!*>>

He could see the little blue-haired monster throwing its hands up in frustration.

<<*Someone had to micro-control your neurons and keep you fighting effectively without letting you run away. Not to mention that having a chunk of your soul FORCIBLY TEAR OUT OF YOU would be a pretty impressive deterrent to disobedience. But I'm betting that it almost never had to use that deterrent, because of all the other stuff. All the basic human social-control stuff. It was more than enough to keep you obedient and productive.*>>

The mission rewards. The Ding! Truth thought about it a bit longer. Actually, you wouldn't even need the System for a lot of it, would you? Just the hierarchy. Want to get out of the slums? Be exactly who Starbrite needs you to be. Want to get better opportunities for your friends and family? Get ready to give that one hundred ten percent. Want a lover, want better food, better opportunities? More power? Then don't ask questions and make yourself useful.

Truth chuckled bitterly. He wasn't even seeing the storeroom at this point, lost in his memories. *I sure gave them my one hundred ten percent. It's no wonder they could keep the compulsions secret. Everyone would look at this and think, Oh, that's just how that company is. Really unified, motivated employees.*

<<The phrase you are looking for is corporate culture. And yes, exactly this. >>

Truth laughed as he pulled himself up out of the corner. That's fucking hilarious. All the really nefarious stuff is just management best practices. Even from the System's point of view—why go through the trouble of constantly splitting off bits of yourself and regrowing when you can just . . . what, exactly? How did the system make "you"?

<<I don't know. Best guess? You were anesthetized by that yellow glowy thing. It numbed your soul enough that when you swore in, a big underlying spell formation could carve off a bit of you and stamp in some special rules. Reshape part of your soul to be capable of handling the spells, to be the System's little agent inside of you. That section just getting more and more powerful as you level up. The System's control getting more and more complete.>>

What, like . . . Truth scrambled around for a metaphor, Like stamping a pattern on sheet metal without cutting it out of the bigger piece of metal?

<<More or less, I guess. Another thought occurred to me—the simplified spells. Because even with modification, there is a limit to my ability to process new information, right? I'm still part of you, just reshaped for a specific purpose. Making the spells dirt-simple, if underpowered, actually works better. You can get soldiers in the field with a fraction of the development time. Look how long it's taking you to learn Incisive. Top-notch spell. A long learning time is expected, sure. But even with daily tuition by an expert, you still aren't completely competent with the spell. But if I can train and field a hundred soldiers in the time it takes you to learn your one awesome spell . . .>>

Quantity has a quality all of its own. Yeah. Especially when those hundred soldiers are very tactically flexible, with high discipline and morale. Whatever spell they need, whenever they need it. So, the losses they would have against a conventional military would be limited. In fact, they would probably win overwhelmingly most of the time.

<<And, of course, you are based out of Jeon, which has mandatory national service. So, basically, free training and indoctrination.>>

Truth started walking the halls again. More slowly now. Really looking at the carvings. Feeling the texture of the walls. Appreciating just how real it all felt. It was literally more real than he was. If only just. He kept hoping to run into some secret hidden library or the sanctum of an old master or something. So far, it was just storage and janitorial stuff. Fingers crossed.

So . . . where does that leave us? I assume you aren't going to have "Escape Truth Medici" as your big goal now.

<<Not so much, no. And I don't really know. It still hurts like absolute hell whenever your body is doing whatever it does, but . . .>>

The sprite . . . what should he even call it? It still was a separate intelligence living inside of him. Truth stopped with a jerk as a nasty thought occurred.

Are you absolutely sure that the System didn't leave some hidden hooks inside you? Some . . . invisible mechanism of control it could activate if it became aware of you?

<<No.>>

There was a long pause after that. Then Truth started walking again.

Let's not mention this to Merkovah. Or anybody.

<<Let's not,>> the sprite agreed.

Truth wandered the basement, seeing more and more nothing. He kept hoping for something. Something that would justify him storming off like that.

Don't suppose you have any advice on how to manage that . . . blow up.

<<Even less than you. My personality is what the System gave me, warped by exposure to you and your   soul-correcting therapy. To be clear, my hatred of the fleshies is one hundred percent sincere. On the awful day when you lodge your genitals in Etenesh, I intend to bury myself as deep in your apertures as I can manage and calculate each and every digit of pi.>>

Hah. Well. Don't think that's going to be happening after . . . all that.

<<Oh, I take it back. I do know more about women, or at least a woman, than you. Incredible. I mean . . . wow. I was going to stop dragging you, you know? Seemed counterproductive. But now? Now I think I have to roast you. A moral imperative.>>

Haha. Fuck you.

<<What, are you going to bugger yourself with a broom handle?>>

That brought Truth up short. Then he manfully pushed past the image and asked, *What do you mean, you know more than I do about Etenesh?*

<<I know exactly as much as you do about her. I was just paying attention, and you apparently weren't. She clearly isn't bothered by your "complicated" life. She doesn't like being the one being comforted. She liked comforting you. She was happy and a little flattered when you let her in, revealed more of yourself to her. Now you have all but stripped off for her and Jember. A big ball of pain and misery for her to nurse back to health, letting her ignore the collapse of her country and worldview.>>

Truth could hear the wretched snigger, could practically see it.

<<Congratulations on being someone's project! Hey, in how many romance novels and thrillers did the phrase But I can fix him, make him better! turn out well for anyone? At least you know that you will definitely hurt her more by rejecting her. So, forcing your hideous life story onto her is a good thing. Right?>>

Couldn't hold it in any longer, could you?

<<I swear I'm trying. I think that's all for now. No, wait. One more thing. You know that she is more sexually experienced than you. You are absolutely going to disappoint her in bed. Your very first sexual experience will be a humiliating, emasculating failure in front of a beautiful woman. Okay. That's everything. Woof. Better out than in, amirite?>>

Any advice on managing any of that?

<<It's a bit radical, kind of untested. You will find it scary and hate every second of it. It's called Just talk to her and tell her what's freaking you out. Believe me, she is going to love teaching you the second you tell her you are a virgin.>>

And the fact that I will be freaking the fuck out, letting her get that close to me?

<<No idea. Talk to her.>>

It probably took a bit less than an eternity to make his way out. He did find a janitor, but the only hidden wisdom he had was "You walked past the door to the staircase—second on your left." Which didn't seem universally applicable, even if he did turn out to be right. Well. Correct. He turned out to be both left and correct.

He retreated back to his little room. It was properly termed a cell, apparently, though Truth didn't care for the term. He sat on the ground and meditated. He tried to imagine how the positive male role models in his life would handle this situation. Then he got up and lay down on the bed. The answer was, they wouldn't get in the situation in the first place and wouldn't give half a fuck if they did.

It took a while, but he got to sleep. It was comforting, having a door that locked from the inside and a chair that fit under the handle. Funny. He didn't feel so scared falling asleep in the desert in the Free State. But put him around "civilized" people, and he was as jumpy as a rabbit in a fox den.

Breakfast found him dressed neatly, washed, with a freshly scrubbed and dried zeph perched on his head. It wasn't immaculately white anymore. He would probably have to replace it. Everyone else seemed to keep their spotless.

Etenesh and Jember sat next to him at the table. Everybody ate quietly, not sure how to start talking again. Into that still pond of awkwardness dropped the rolling boulder of Merkovah.

"Ah, Mr. Wells! Our bashful"—Merkovah either didn't see or chose to ignore Etenesh and Jember's frantic head-shakes—"hero!"

There was a dreadful pause.

"Although, given the way you rushed out of there, you probably don't consider yourself a hero," Merkovah continued. "You have always been quiet about your past, so at the risk of opening old wounds, may I ask if there is some trauma there?"

Truth half-chuckled. He would be breaded, fried, and served with a slice of lemon before he believed that Merkovah just "happened" to guess that.

"Yes. More than I had expected, actually."

"Well, you are in a particularly fine old temple. I can assure you our counselors are very experienced and even more discreet. Still, I think that, whatever your motivations, the simple fact that you saved in excess of a thousand people should count for something."

"I did no such thing." He could vividly remember the exploded bodies.

"Oh, you absolutely did. This is not the first such attack. Suicide-summonings at major public gatherings have occurred five other times in the last twenty years. The lowest body count was fourteen hundred people. You see, it's a proliferation portal. The more the demons kill, the wider it grows and the longer it lasts. Killing your way to it and shutting it down is a major challenge if you have to fight through an unending stream of increasingly powerful demons. The fact that you got to it so quickly unquestionably saved at least a thousand lives."

Merkovah fixed Truth with a calm but firm look. "Old Mek'elle does its best, but it can't be everywhere all at once. As you saw. Also, something that you might be interested to know—the word hero does not mean the same thing in every language or at all points in history. For example, here in Siphios, the word hero means something more like extraordinary person in the sense of being extraordinarily capable. Not the sort of selfless, idealistic person the media keeps pushing at you. A great warrior, for example, might be selfish, murderous, and vain, but they are still a hero by the old definition."

"Still kind of messed-up for people to push that on me."

"You don't want to be known, so they must tell their own stories. Stories that make them happy. The easiest way to manage the pressure is not to care. Let them amuse themselves while you focus on doing great deeds. Hero."

There was a lot of no eye contact at the table, though Etenesh's fist was tightly clenched, and, had Truth been looking, he would have seen the fierce approval on her face.

"Speaking of doing great things," said Merkovah, "let's all go to the park. I want to feed the ducks."

CHAPTER 39

VERY FINE DUCKS

Truth discovered a new sort of agony that morning. It turned out that being stuck in a five-seater carriage with an old monster you don't trust and two people you blew up at was excruciating. And they were stuck in traffic. If he was riding his trusty iron horse, he could split the lanes and be there already. Or they could spend the modest sum necessary to hire a flying carpet. Or, given that Merkovah was Level Seven and clearly a person of some importance in Siphios, he could probably simply summon a flying spirit to carry them wherever they wanted to go, flight paths be damned.

But no. No, it was apparently *critically important* that they travel in the allegedly disguised deathtrap that was Merkovah's carriage. With its mismatched paint, screeching axles, and a general air of being too crap for the chop shops to bother with. Apparently, they had to be "discreet." Every time Merkovah tapped the brake, the metallic howl could be heard half a kilometer away. Truth was quite sure he wasn't translating *discreet* correctly.

He didn't even think to bring a book. Misery.

Xandre hadn't lost its mystery or its charm in the few days he had been there. Everything seemed to have a hidden meaning or a history to it. A corner might have a water spout jutting from a wall pouring into a basin shaped like cupped hands. Why? Who knows. You could ask the statute of an armored warrior fighting a monstrous lizard in the nearby plaza. It might know. It's certainly not shy about sharing its opinion on every other thing. Perhaps the wall itself could tell you as it faintly shivered and flexed in the morning sun.

Everywhere, people were moving through each other's homes. Or perhaps *through their spaces* would be a better way to think about it. Truth noticed that the people in Xandre really liked to touch one another or stand close by. It was very common to see people walking together, holding hands. They often didn't appear to be a romantic pair. They just found it comfortable. It seemed . . . nice. Not sexual or controlling, just being comfortable with another person. More casual than a hug.

He tried to pinpoint the moment when being touched started freaking him out. He couldn't think of a specific moment. After he was killed, obviously. Maybe on his journey to Siphios? But he couldn't think of something that would have formed such a huge psychological allergy. More remnants of System fuckery, or another "gift" from his various patrons? It didn't feel the same.

At some point, his body had colluded with some hidden part of his mind and decided that people were never to be trusted. Since anyone could turn on you, everyone *would* turn on you. And since you can only be hurt by the things that touch you, don't let them touch you.

Well. There was probably more to it than that. Truth silently sighed. He would apologize to Jember and Etenesh when he could get them alone.

The questionable carriage made its winding way around the city, eventually parking on a residential side street.

"The sign says No Parking, Teacher." Jember pointed upward.

"It does say that, yes." Merkovah smiled beatifically. "One of the spells on the carriage—if the police scan it, they will find I have a special Royal Dispensation to park wherever I want."

"Seriously?" Truth blurted.

"Oh, yes. But every time the spell gets triggered, it also triggers a endless debate in the Palace over the appropriate privileges to award to those in the temple. The arguments haven't changed in centuries. It is heart-stoppingly boring. We'll have to risk it. Come on."

They rushed their way up the tree-shaded street to what looked like a park. This park brought back memories of Harban—it was surrounded by a seven-meter-tall brick wall topped with decorative but sharp iron spikes. Naturally, the wall was enchanted and warded. The two decorative statues of lions by the gate were, equally naturally, golems. Merkovah pulled something from one of his many pockets and showed it to the lions. He was quite secretive about what, exactly, it was. The lions were satisfied and they opened the gate.

The park was neither big nor small, about the size of a city block. The trees were fairly incredible. Some reminded him of broccoli, with a thick, smooth trunk topped by a dense dome of leaves and brilliant pink flowers. Others spread wide, extending their branches and leaves out like serving platters to catch the sun. Everything seemed harmonious and in bloom. And empty. The park was perfectly empty on this sunny, pleasant morning.

"So. You are all probably wondering why I dragged you out here, what with everything going on in the world." Merkovah started abruptly speaking as he led them deeper into the park. "It's really very simple—the ducks here are extraordinary."

Truth was glad to see he wasn't the only one with no idea of how to respond to that.

"These are truly remarkable ducks. Almost certainly the very finest you shall ever see. We are very fortunate, both personally and as a nation, that they have chosen to nest here. Building this park for their privacy and enjoyment was really the least we could do."

"And what is it they do? For Siphios?" Truth asked.

"They simply are. I brought you all here because the last week has been rough. First, with your revelations on the mountain and then the atrocity at the stadium. Consider this another aspect of your training, Etenesh, Jember. A job bonus from me,

Tommy. You will need these." He reached into one of his larger pockets and produced three small bags.

Truth peeked inside. It was a small handful of seeds.

"We are feeding the ducks?"

"Yes, these are very high-quality seeds. Just a few at a time. No rush."

He ushered them to a stone bench next to an elegant pond. Tall reeds surrounded the far edge, while a handsome tree provided shade for the bench and the close edge of the pond. It was nice, in a completely boring way.

After a few moments, two ducks came paddling out. A dun color, with a reddish patch around the eyes and a thick beak. They seemed to be perfectly adequate ducks on first glance, though Truth might not have stretched *adequate* all the way to *extraordinary* or *remarkable*. There was no second glance, however.

His eyes stayed firmly fixed on the ducks. They were just so . . . ducky. He couldn't think of a word for it. If the perfect idea of what a duck is and should be existed somewhere in the cosmos, then these ducks were much closer to that ideal than any other duck Truth had ever seen. He dug out a seed and flicked it toward a duck. The duck ate it with apparent satisfaction.

"The Meditations of Valentinian, young man. Look at them and meditate on the ideal you. One that excludes all unwanted magic. One that permits only what you wish to permit into you and releases only what you wish to release," Merkovah's voice whispered in his ear.

Truth had always struggled with the Meditations. It was the visualization aspect. Which was a bit like saying he struggled with running marathons because of the running part. It was comparatively easy to selectively toughen parts of the body temporarily. Permanent gains were elusive. The more he pushed his body, the tougher the foes he fought, the more he realized that his "useful" trick wasn't really that useful. He could have visualized his hand as being utterly fireproof, and those demons would have melted straight through it regardless. Not enough time practicing the spell. Not enough built-up improvements. Not . . . real enough. Like the ducks.

The Meditations started running in the back of his mind. In the forefront was the ducks. The supremely real ducks. Looked just like any other ducks but were, somehow, the best ducks. He got it now. In a way that looking at angels, demons, and even Temple Nag Hamadi never quite could convey. Here was something he could understand and relate to. A duck. A duck that was more real than the pond it swam in. It could interact with things. It liked the seeds. It seemed to like the park. But these were things it permitted. It was more than just the seeds or the park. It didn't need those . . . externalities.

Truth didn't need the externalities. He could want things. Nothing wrong with wanting things. Perfectly human thing to do. He just needed to separate the wants from the needs. Then once he had managed that minor feat, he just had to stay strong in his position on which was which. Fortunately, the Meditations were all too happy to help with that.

As were the worms. Truth hadn't intended that they participate. But it seemed like there was no stopping them. They bored out from whatever place they hid within him, appearing by his apertures and beginning their usual winding circuit. He could feel them make their way through him, from the boundary of his skin to the marrow of his bone. Digging. Refining. Solidifying. He found his attention pulled to them, trying to understand what it was they were doing, exactly.

Truth's thinking was that the skin represented a sort of boundary—a combination of a wall and a sack. A wall to keep things out, a sack to keep things in. The wall would forbid all magic and cosmic energy that he didn't want to go into the sack. It was a spiritual construction. The sack was, well, him. His apertures, channels, organs, flesh, bones, every material part of him. He thought that, since he was trying to build a wall, the worms would focus on the skin. The worms disagreed.

The worms appeared to see nothing special about the skin. They carefully and diligently went through his body, gently reinforcing every cubic millimeter of him. It slowly occurred to Truth that they were, by means of this magical enhancement, making his body more physically durable and more real. The worms, at least, didn't make a distinction between the physical and the spiritual. Which was a hell of a take from glowing worms representing the spiritual legacy of a godlike supernatural being.

Truth felt like he was being subtly scolded. He thought about it and tried to think why he might feel that way. Nothing immediately leapt to mind. His mind wandered to his two role models—Botis and the rough, handsome man. Botis was, of course, immensely self-contained. He had scales, for Heaven's sake! Well, not "Heaven," obviously. But Botis could be said to have a wall between him and the world. The rough patron did not. He just sat around a fire, doing whatever he wanted.

Botis watched the world, but when seen in his stellar abode, he was clearly not a part of it. Botis existed alone, needing nothing else, desiring nothing else. The rough patron was sitting around a fire in a recognizable landscape. There was the smell of marshes. He lived in a living world. Was there a lesson there?

Who did he want to be? Botis, alone and untouchable, or the rough patron who embraced the world? And whose worshipers apparently included the Ghūl, couldn't forget that. It would be . . . *unwise* to simply assume his goodwill. Or, indeed, that he was good. Of course, it's not like the *literal demon from Hell* Botis was anything good, either. He just wasn't evil in the way most people used that word. Botis wasn't so much cruel as uncaring. At least, that was what Truth believed.

Neither struck Truth as being unhappy. So, which route did he want to follow? Proud isolation and perfect self-sufficiency, or to exist in the world and be sufficient within it? He almost laughed. How silly was he? A Level Three standing in judgment of two godlike beings. For now, he would become more. He would let his weight on the world slowly gather. When he was strong enough, he would decide what to cut and what to keep.

And in the meantime? There were excellent ducks to watch.

CHAPTER 40

FEELING SAFE-ISH

The ducks eventually decided they had had enough seeds and paddled off. The elegant wake behind them was as fine as ever a duck did make. The sunlight reflecting off the tiny ripples seemed to contain some blessed harmonies, silver flashes dancing in time with the world.

The little group just sat there a while longer, each letting their thoughts drift across the pond. Finding that calm moment within the chaos of their lives. Stillness is a powerful thing. It lets you really see yourself and the world. Easy to go blind when you are always on the move.

Truth shivered and pulled himself together. He could feel the change. He doubted he was any stronger or faster, or at least not much stronger or faster, but he was more solid. One step closer to the super-reality of, say, a duck.

Etenesh stretched. Truth took a look at her. Really looked. Tried to put away all his assumptions and hangups and general paranoia and just . . . look at her.

She was tired. Truth could see it in her. She hadn't been sleeping well. There was still a pain in her, though perhaps it was a bit less than it was before. She now had hope that the pain would ease, perhaps. And she was beautiful.

She was beautiful. He remembered thinking that Etenesh and Jember were both a bit above average in looks, but he was wrong. Jember was handsome, sporty, and charismatic. But Etenesh was beautiful in a way that simply avoided his words. She wound her beauty around him until it was all he could see of her—beautiful Etenesh, tired eyes and all.

He could only hold it for a moment—that little chunk of his life that was just Beautiful Etenesh, and it was enough that she *was*. But the moment melted like snow in his hand, running through his fingers and into the dirt.

She was beautiful, inside and out. He was a freak. A walking corpse. A man whose death was a blessing to billions and whose life could kill a world. Someone who, even lost in her beauty, held himself ready to kill her. Because she would turn on him. Everyone would. They would use him and turn on him and discard him the second a better deal came along.

That was the real horror of it. You could always try to make yourself useful. You could *be* useful. You could be doing your very best. The best you ever did. And if a better deal came along, you would be thrown away. Instantly. With the only regret being the time and attention required to shoo you out the door. Whether you gave it your all didn't matter. It was just—is this a better deal for your boss? If yes, you were gone. Escorted away by security to make sure you didn't damage the place you had poured the irreplaceable seconds of your life into in exchange for . . . what, exactly?

A woman as beautiful, rich, and smart as Etenesh had options. A lot of options. Better options than "emotionally damaged, paranoid slumrat." For example, someone who could actually hug her. That was probably something women looked for—a person who could hug them properly. Not gingerly, worried you were going to break them, or they would suddenly bury a knife in your ear.

Etenesh finished her stretch, rolled her shoulders back, and looked over at Truth. When she saw him looking, she smiled. And the world returned to quietness and the warmth of the afternoon sun.

Later, back at Temple Nag Hamadi, Etenesh and Jember drilled with Truth. It was an interesting challenge.

Etenesh had her spirit launching ice skewers at Truth. He could dodge almost all of them, and he found that, while they stung, they didn't do more than that. Which was . . . interesting. He was fairly sure this spell was somewhere between a Level Zero cantrip and a Level One Ice Bolt. In other words, lethal to an unprotected mage. The benefits of body cultivation on spell resistance were starting to really show. Truth smashed aside a skewer and sprinted to close with the spirit. The spirit countered by raising a small field of spikes between Truth and Etenesh. Truth just grinned and hurdled them.

The spirit scoffed and launched a spray of skewers, trying to catch him in the air. Truth writhed, twisting and contorting as he crossed over the spikes. Most missed, thanks to his absurd reflexes and coordination. The ones that didn't were either deflected away or ignored. With a flex of his gut, Truth landed on his feet and was in a dead sprint toward Etenesh almost as soon as both feet touched the ground.

Etenesh wasn't going to make it that easy for him. The sclera of her eyes turned a gentle orange, like autumn leaves or the ocher earth of Siphios. Her formation seemed to swirl up around her like smoke, endlessly arranging itself into mystic geometries. Swarming clouds of darting lights emerged from those twisting formations, raining down on Truth.

Once again, he could simply shrug off most of the attacks, though Incisive warned that taking too many hits would be dangerous. So, he pressed in, letting Incisive guide his cut. It wasn't like there was a particular weakness to this formation. But the Tongue of One Who Speaks for God was no ordinary blade. Tool activated the Bane enchantment in the blade, and a ward-breaker spell formed around it. Truth smashed through the ward with brute force, coming face-to-face with Etenesh. Looking down into her hypnotic ocher eyes.

He gently tapped her with the flat of his blade. "Tag."

Jember took that as his cue to launch a searing pillar of sunlight directly down on Truth. Incisive screamed at him to dodge, and he sprinted hard for the opposite side of the room. Jember had his formation up and running and had decided to favor fire. Or, perhaps, the blackbird with blazing red wingtips and long yellow claws that was hovering in the air over Jember had made that decision. Truth hadn't seen Jember's contract spirit before. It looked quite handsome and energetic. The bastard.

Truth rushed back and forth across the room, trying to break down the wards and tag the caster before the other got their spell up and they could team up and force him to yield. They had decided to stake tonight's dessert on it. A serious matter, as the kitchen had been working hard to flatter the delegates with delicacies.

Jember was the first to quit, raising his hand and begging off. "I can't! How are you putting up with the burnout?!"

"How do you have burnout? You are running formations and letting your spirit fight for you!" Truth yelled back.

"I'm going to add that to the list of things you say that I pretend I didn't hear," Jember muttered.

Truth turned and ran back toward Etenesh, who just waved him off. "If he's out, you will just tag me faster. I'm with Jember on this—how have you not collapsed yet?"

"Merkovah knows what he's talking about when it comes to building out my spells," Truth admitted. "The Meditations make me much, much stronger and faster than you are used to dealing with and give me the reflexes to anticipate and avoid a *lot* of attacks. Incisive takes that to another level, of course, but I have gotten used to using it more . . . lightly, I guess is the word? Not pushing the spell, just trying to get a feel for what's coming in the next second or so. Less, even. Next few fractions of a second is plenty most of the time. Likewise, I only draw on the Tongue's Bane or the cutting portion of Incisive for a second or less, reducing the power draw."

Truth shrugged. "Most of it is just down to muscle, speed, and a really good blade."

Etenesh's eyes still had that warm ocher filling their sclera. It was gently fading away, but it was still noticeable and fascinating. Truth coughed.

"I, uh, also . . . want to apologize. I flipped out at you two last night when you were trying to show me something that . . . was supposed to be a good thing. And I flipped out, out of nowhere. I'm sorry. It brought up a lot of bad stuff. So. Sorry."

The cousins looked at each other and winced. Jember took a deep breath, and Truth noticed a very faint glow around him. The ocher grew brighter in Etenesh's eyes.

"We're sorry too. We had no idea you had so much pain in your life. No idea. Though in retrospect, there were some things that really should have clued us in." Jember shook his head.

"Your total indifference to what should be nightmarish situations, for one thing." Etenesh's smile took the sting from the words. "I may never hear the word *okay* the same way ever again."

"It was something about the . . . well, the everything. They made up a whole noble story about who I was. Created this whole identity for me and then said that made-up person was a hero. Hero this, hero that, dedicated to a life of being a noble hero, cut away from all . . . family. Money. Stuff." Truth gave up. He didn't have the right words.

He sighed, dusting himself off. "It's not who I was or who I am. You may have never met someone who spent more time thinking about money than me." The last sentence came out more grimly than he intended.

"Your family?" Jember asked softly.

"Yes, my siblings. I'm sorry; I can't say more. I shouldn't have said as much as I did."

"Can you tell us why?" Etenesh asked.

"No, secret. It is better for the world if I died. So, the person who should be dead is dead. And now there's me. I'm still trying to figure out who that is. So far, the new me seems a lot happier than old me. Things are going pretty good for new me. But old me might be dead, but he isn't gone." Truth smiled. The cousins didn't quite wince.

"And you can't contact your siblings because everyone needs to believe that you are dead?" Jember tried to smile back.

"Yes."

"I prayed for your parents last night," Etenesh said. The ocher in her sclera was quite bright now. Lovely, in an eerie sort of way.

"You prayed. For my parents."

"Yes. That they would understand the misery they made you and your siblings suffer. That at some point, in this life or the next, they came to truly, *truly* know just how you felt." Truth looked at her and thought he heard the beating of mighty wings. "I was amazed at how sincere I was. I said, 'God, this is the world you have left to us. And I know you don't care. But I care. And I believe in your almighty power. So, please, do this. Make them understand.'"

"No bargaining?"

"Anything I could offer is already his. I will not insult him for all that he despises us now." Etenesh's voice was sad, but there was a calmness to it that hadn't been there yesterday. "I will pray. I will beg. And I will walk on my own two feet and rely on the work of my own two hands and trust in the magic in my soul. I will walk a path that perhaps no one has walked before—a devout nontheist." Jember shook his head and half chuckled. Truth just looked puzzled. What on earth did that mean?

"Don't worry about it. I'm still figuring out what I mean. Can't expect you to know. But I would like to try something if you would. Mr. Wells."

"All right?"

"I would like to walk with you. Do you think we could hold hands?"

"I have no idea. But I would very much like to find out."

Etenesh's hand was very warm.

CHAPTER 41

A SAVAGE IN ACADEMIA

I can feel you trying, you know? You sort of shiver. One part of you overruling another part." Etenesh smiled up at Truth. "It's kind of sweet. And kind of sad. But mostly sweet."

"It's not rational. I know that. I'm not even sure where the people allergy is coming from. For most of my life, I have dreamed of someone wanting to be with me. Now that there is someone willing to touch me, I can't stand to let people close." Truth forced himself to smile.

"It might be as simple as that, you know." They were walking slowly down the engraved sandstone corridors of Temple Nag Hamadi toward the dining room in the back. Jember, thoughtfully, had "remembered something he had to get from his room" and left them alone. Truth had gingerly held Etenesh's hand. She grabbed his, not hard, but more firmly. Giving him a look that said, *This is how you should do it.* So, he did. But it was a struggle.

"What?"

"You spent, from what I can tell, your whole life in varying states of pain. Desperate for comfort. Some kind of warmth and connection. And now you can have that." She looked up at him, faint ocher starting to rise in the whites of her eyes. "I want you to have that. I want to be the one who gives you that. Because I like you and respect you, and desire you. You like me too. And you have no idea how to deal with any of that. Caring and being cared for. Finding yourself somewhere safe. With someone safe. It feels like a trap. It scares the hell out of you."

She paused by an inscription on the wall. There was a picture of a bird landing on a cow's horn. She smiled sadly at it, then looked back at Truth.

"Would you mind doing a small experiment?"

"What's that?"

"Let go of my hand and gently hold my wrist. About as hard as you were holding my hand. Yes, like that." She held her hand down where it had been while they were walking and holding hands. Truth thought her wrist was very thin and fragile in his hand. She was a powerful mage. Stronger than she looked. But she felt so fragile to him.

They walked a little farther like that. Etenesh slowly smiled. "Your shivering stopped."

Truth didn't know how to answer that.

"It did. Now I wonder why that could be." She laughed a little.

"Is it uncomfortable for you?" Truth asked.

"A little. I'm more used to holding hands. It feels odd, having my hand empty. But it's not painful or anything. No, don't let go." She smiled up at him. "We can be a little uncomfortable together."

"Is that really a good thing?"

"It is if it means we are growing." She paused. "Also, while I am absolutely enjoying this, I intend to exercise my privilege as the woman in your life to reclaim my dessert."

"Mmm. Well, I am a dedicated food enjoyer. You may still have to fight me if it's something good." Truth smiled back.

"What fresh hell is this?" Truth looked in horror at the "dessert" in front of them. Each table had one to share. This was supposed to be a temple. Free of abomination and corruption. Truly, God had abandoned Siphios if his most dedicated servants would serve such a thing.

"It's a Delightful Cloud. Invented by a famous chef for a dancer of the same name, actually." Jember grinned. Then frowned when he remembered his portion was lost. He eyed Etenesh, who was looking a *little* smug. Then sighed again.

"It's the cushion from a carriage seat with the cover stripped off and jam dumped on top. Not even . . . done jam; it's still mostly big chunks of fruit." Merkovah was doing his best not to laugh. The other diners at the table had their hands over their mouths and their shoulders shaking.

"It's a meringue. Cooked egg whites. With fruit in syrup on top." Jember defended it. He might not be able to eat it, but he would save it from slander.

"If it was meant to be edible, why'd they make it look like shiny white foam? They even screwed up cooking it—look, it's kind of burnt on top."

"Crunchy. It's meant to be crunchy on top. You monster." Jember looked over at Merkovah, who suddenly found his water glass fascinating. "Teacher, we will have to rely on you for moral instruction here."

"I firmly believe in experiential learning. We have admired the dessert, some of us, and now, let's eat." Merkovah lifted the cake slice and started divvying up portions. Truth looked at his with deep suspicion.

"It has exploded. Why do you look like it is supposed to look this way?"

"Crunchy exterior, soft, fluffy, melting interior. Look, just eat it. You'll see."

"You like it, don't you? You like this dessert . . . thing."

"It has been my favorite since I was a kid. You savage. This poor, innocent, maligned Cloud."

Truth gingerly stuck a spoon in. The exterior was, in fact, crunchy. The interior was, in fact, light, soft, fluffy. Lightly sweet, and scented with . . . something. He couldn't place it.

"What's that smell?" he asked. Jember looked ready to cry.

"The scent. The lovely, delicate, aroma comes from specially treated orchids. You have had something similar made from processing trees called vanillin. This is the real thing. It takes excruciating effort to make." Jember turned from grief to wrath. "You cannot claim to walk the path of the foodie without appreciating the origins of the food. To do so would reduce a path to mere gluttony!"

Truth was rocked. His mind was still at the level of training away his poverty tastebuds. But here was Jember, opening up a whole new world. "I had never thought about that."

"I can tell." Jember sniffed. Etenesh was eating her dessert with obvious relish, deliberately and *pointedly* ignoring the miserable-looking Jember. Truth sighed. It was honestly pretty tasty, for all that it looked like an industrial accident.

"You are buying the drinks for our next sparring session." Truth slid Jember's dessert back over to him.

"You are a mage and a gentleman of the first water. Look, ditch my cousin. Soon as the ritual purification is over, I can—"

"OI! Hands off!"

"I'm not touching him. Yet."

Truth let the cousins bicker around him. Feeling their warmth. A stab of sadness struck him. He and his siblings never had a meal like this, even after they moved into their own home. The thought slowly wormed its way up from the recesses of his mind—what if this was what he had really been fighting for? Not just survival but this. This easy way with family. Full bellies. A warm home. No danger to make them scared and anxious.

Maybe this was what winning looked like. Which did bring up a couple of awkward question. Who, or what, did he have to beat to get there? He had to pass the SAT to get that C-Tier housing. He had to slaughter the Ghūl and report their statue to become a citizen and get those citizenship privileges. So, what would it take to get there, for him and the sibs? And Etenesh and Jember, and even Merkovah and the other people he had met there?

He had absolutely no idea.

Merkovah summoned them the next morning, looking grim. "Tommy, put on your best uniform, and if you need to buy a new zeph, do so. You must be looking immaculate and lethal. Etenesh, Jember, your formal robes. I will permit you two, just for today, to wear your caps." They perked up at that, trying to repress smiles. "*Just* for today. We go now to a terrible place. We must armor ourselves against the wicked ones."

Truth was starting to get a feel for Merkovah. "Your friend from Moyle is in town?"

"Worse. So much worse." Merkovah sighed silently, then gathered his strength. "A faculty congress at the University of Siphios. It seems that someone in our security services thought it would be a good idea to share that talisman you discovered, Tommy, with the academy. We go now to a 'closed' session to discuss it. Other senior fellows will have their retinues there as well. We must be ready."

They processed that declaration. Then, because Truth was most certainly a product of his upbringing, he coughed. "As I mentioned before, mission-necessary equipment is to be provided by the employer . . ." Merkovah was already reaching for his wallet before Truth could really get going.

"Go to the shop four blocks down the road. Buy one with a tassel."

"They come with a tassel? I have only seen the smooth, flat ones."

"Turn up with your sword, wearing your old hat, and tell the shopkeeper I told you to get one with a tassel. He will sort you out."

"Okay . . ."

"It's a status thing and a religious thing," Etenesh whispered. "It basically means that you have shed blood on behalf of both the Temple and the Throne."

"Why would the Desrin give even half a damn if I fought for the Temple? Wouldn't they not want me to do that?"

"The faith and the land are one, in Siphios. Historically, anyway. Our relationship with the Desrin is . . . complicated. But, on the whole, positive. The congress begins at ten sharp. Off you go." Merkovah waved them out the door. As they headed back to their little rooms, Etenesh stuck out her hand toward Truth. He smiled and held it like she had taught him. She smiled back, ocher dusting her eyes. Gently, slowly, she moved his hand up to her wrist and closed his fingers around it.

The cousins stood side by side, waiting for Merkovah in front of the temple. They wore identical robes of loose, multilayered white cloth edged with blue—the same color of blue Truth remembered seeing in the desert just after the sun had cleared the horizon and the day was firmly on its feet. They sported odd, rigidly conical blue hats with identical green feathers rising from either side of the brim. Their robes, he noticed, were folded in the exact same ways, and the hats were set at exactly the same angle.

"We are graduates but not yet fellows of the University. This is the uniform robe for students, and the blue trim shows we graduated. Because we are, and the language is kind of dated here, because we are servants of Merkovah, who is a senior fellow in the Senior Department, Religious Law, we can wear the blue hat and green feathers," Etenesh explained. She looked quite nice in her robe, Truth thought. Strange how someone could be covered from neck to shins and still make his heart race.

He took a moment, considered that thought, concluded he was doomed, then forced his mind back on the job.

Merkovah swept in, looking like he had looted a particularly gaudy treasury belonging to a cloth merchant. First, there was the black underrobe, edged with gold. Then a surcoat in brilliant green, also trimmed with gold and sporting coral buttons.

Then there was a sort of narrow shawl draped over his neck, embroidered with the picture of a turquoise-colored serpent with ruby eyes. Also trimmed with gold. His hat . . . could no longer be called a hat, in Truth's opinion. Hats didn't have *tiers*. Hats were not *layered*. Seven-cone hats, like the cousins wore, were stacked on top of each other, moving up the color gradient from red to violet. Each layer had its own tiny brim and a decorative gem in a contrasting color. On the top was a single golden feather sticking straight up.

He seemed alarmingly comfortable. Truth displayed his professionalism by not falling on the floor, laughing at his employer or at the deeply envious-looking cousins.

Truth, on the other hand, wore a neatly pressed suit he wouldn't mind fighting in, his brand-new zeph, tassel hanging on the left as instructed, well-polished boots he could run in, and his sword.

Merkovah looked him over and sighed. "You look like an absolute and utter barbarian. Still. You'll do. Come, everyone. I have booked us a carpet to the University. Let's see what idiocy my learned colleagues are planning."

CHAPTER 42

ENGINES OF DESTRUCTION

A few quick points before we go. Jember, Etenesh, this congress has been convened, as I said, to investigate a particular talisman, or really a cartouche, found by Tommy when we investigated that possessed building a few days ago. What you don't know is that it is connected to some extremely classified matters. So classified, I am genuinely bewildered by what diseased, witless creature asked the University senior fellows *as a whole* to investigate!"

Merkovah had cast a privacy field around them as they stood carefully on the carpet. Truth didn't like it. He knew that the spells on the carpet would keep people from falling off, but he couldn't shake the notion that sitting down was safer. On the other hand, if he were wearing the elaborate robes that his protectees were wearing, he'd stand too.

"I must therefore remind you that, firstly, you have no security clearance for anything, and second, even if you did, you do not have a need to know about what's going on in *this particular* classified matter. You are being dragged along on this ridiculous excursion because University politics demands it. Your job, after the invocation and worship, will be to go mingle and network with the other junior scholars who have been dragged along on this boondoggle. You might as well get some benefit from all of this."

"It will be my pleasure," Jember said. "Love a good networking event. But what about Tommy? I can't imagine he's cleared for anything, either."

"Tommy is a witness. And professionally paranoid. I have met actual spies with less operational discretion. I must ask, Mr. Wells, what exactly did you do for—"

"I was a bodyguard. I also did work as a mercenary. But my last, biggest job was bodyguard. For a large company whose name need not be mentioned."

"You will note that he has cut off even speculation, described his work history in the vaguest terms, and provided no actual details about who or what he guarded. And this is why I'm not worried about Mr. Wells." Merkovah snorted after carefully enunciating *Mr. Wells*.

The carpet soared between the towers of Xandre—twenty-story-tall mushrooms with caps as wide as a city block. Towers of ivory that seemed to grow like horns from the skin of the world. Palaces of domes and turrets. And everywhere were the spirits and demons of Siphios. Watching and guarding. Tidying. Healing.

There was a cat with wings hovering over a stream of schoolchildren running for the bus that would take them home. The kids looked up and waved happily. The spirit didn't respond, but it looked happy enough to Truth. Which reminded him he was long overdue.

"Changing topic entirely, but are there any pet cafes in Xandre?" Truth asked.

There was a long pause after that.

"Sorry, pet cafes?" Merkovah asked, sounding unfamiliar with the term.

"Pet cafes. Cafes where you rent time playing with the animals there." Truth kept his eyes on all the flying, climbing, and playing spirits. The city was so colorful!

"I have no idea. *Why* do you want to find a pet cafe?"

Truth gave the exorcist a pitying look. "Because they are good? Super-real ducks are very healing, but have you ever had a big dog with big floppy ears run up to you with a ball, then flop its head in your lap until you scratch behind its ears and throw the ball?"

Truth shook his head. "Did you know that you can make a really tiny hole with your hand, like, *really* small, and if you put food on the other side of the hole, a hamster can squeeze themselves through the hole to eat it? Or that you can play peekaboo with baby hedgehogs?"

"All right, now I want to go," Jember muttered, and Etenesh nodded with him.

Merkovah looked ready to say something disapproving but hesitated. "Young . . . people, I don't know about any such silly thing in Xandre. But we can investigate. Later." There was a pause. "Aren't the baby hedgehogs prickly?"

"Only if you pet them in the wrong direction, and really, it's not too bad. Honestly, they are the cutest things. Even the adult hedgehogs are pretty small," Truth evangelized.

Etenesh cracked up. "Oh, I have to see this. Demonslayer Tommy Wells, buried under big floppy dogs that want to play fetch. Protecting the innocent wee hedgehogs."

"You would have fun."

"I'm not really into pets," Etenesh demurred.

"Oh, I'm dragging you along for this. Nothing is more healing than a pet cafe. Nothing." Truth was firm on this point. They were, in his limited experience, the best.

They bickered cheerfully until they got close to the University. Which, Truth couldn't help but notice, appeared to be a walled city within the city.

It was heartbreakingly beautiful, even from the air. A fine river lined with trees edged beautiful grassy lawns. The buildings were a light tan stone, built into spires, yes, but also cloisters and colonnades. Airy pavilions with glazed tile roofs dotted the open spaces beside flowering bushes and trees that seemed to shimmer with silver and gold.

There were patterns there, paths like the lines on a talisman, connecting buildings and stands of trees, impressive rocks, and other things he couldn't identify from this high up. It was all purposeful. All beautiful. Like the University itself was a talisman connected to Siphios by a road network.

"Am I seeing this right? They built a ring road around a couple of square kilometers of the city, walled it off, and stuck the University in there?" Truth asked.

"Kind of the reverse. Originally, the University was built in a nice little town just outside of Xandre. The walls were traditional, as it was meant to encourage quiet contemplation. Eventually, the University expanded to its current size and built the walls you see there. This was . . . seven hundred years ago?" Jember said.

"Nine hundred. Assene raised them, with the alumni chipping in for ritual sacrifices," Merkovah corrected.

"Nine hundred years ago. Anyhow, Xandre had already expanded up to the edges of the little town, and after the new walls went up, there was no stopping it. The little town was just absorbed into the city proper. Now it's all just Xandre."

"It is also a wonderful example of magical engineering, architecture, and city planning. You can sort of see it from up here, maybe," Etenesh pointed out. "It's something you have to really study to get the subtleties of. The whole campus is designed to gather and purify different sorts of energy. Cosmic rays, obviously, but also more obscure sorts of energy. Even theoretical things like 'dreams' or 'fate.'"

"Does it . . . actually work?" Truth wondered.

"Does for cosmic rays. They are still running lots of tests about the rest. It's not a cultivation holy land, because there are so many things that are pulling the energy out of the air, but . . . it's pretty special." Etenesh grinned. "I love it there. I am *definitely* showing you the campus temple before we leave."

"You really should see it. It's rather moving," Merkovah agreed. "A beautiful melding of history and art. The university sits at a unique crossroads—past and future, the grand ley lines of the world, its stellar alignments at different points of the year, and even the regional road network is built around the University. A crossroads of time and space and fate."

Truth was yanked up short. "A crossroads. A . . . grand intersection."

"Oh, that's a good way to think of it. Yes, a multidimensional intersection. There is an entire department of multidisciplinary and intersectional studies," Jember said.

Truth suddenly remembered the sharpest lesson of riding through the Free State.

"So, Etenesh, Jember, just to review. While I very much appreciate you wanting to support me in combat, we haven't trained together to do that, and it really does take quite a lot of training for a team to be more dangerous to the enemy than to each other in a serious fight. When the explosions start, activate what mobile wards and concealment spells you might have, and run back to Temple Nag Hamadi as quickly as you can. Don't run for shelter, don't think you can hide, just go straight home," Truth said as matter-of-factly as possible.

That got him a weird look in triplicate.

"What explosions?" Jember asked.

"Well, I'm assuming explosions. Fire, sudden glaciers, poison gas, screaming, swarms of insects, demons, angels, weaponized ghosts, the usual kind of things. Just focus on the running-away part."

"Young man—" Truth smiled fondly at the beardy exorcist. "Mr. Wells, do you have any reason to believe that something more dreadful than a faculty congress will occur today at the University?"

"Best to be prepared." If they didn't already know the truth, it was useless to explain.

The faculty congress was held in the Well of Up. This, Truth was told, was a literal translation of the original name of the place, as relayed by a guardian spirit. Truth just nodded at that because it probably wasn't safe to argue with people who called a large domed building a "well" for more than a millennium.

At some point, someone should have proposed changing the name, right? And yet they kept it. A big brick building with a big brick dome, enough inscriptions on everything to make his eyes sting, and they called it a well.

There were crowds of young people hanging about, all in the same formal robes as Etenesh and Jember but without the blue trim or the nifty hats. This lot had to make do with a sort of handkerchief or cloth wrapped over the head. Etenesh and Jember rated looks of faint longing, but they were outright eye-banging Merkovah. It was embarrassing to stand near him. The *incredibly* thirsty looks he was getting were downright eerie. Merkovah ignored the looks with immense dignity. He simply strode for the doors, and the crowd parted before him.

The doors themselves were bronze and four meters tall. A relief carved on one was a bull, head down, receiving a crown of flowers from a dozen small birds. The other had a whale violently eating a squid. The art style was crude, direct. Powerful. You could feel the beasts. Almost smell them.

"Guardians of Kl'f and Rehk, I am called to the Wise!" Merkovah bellowed, his hat glowing with rainbow light.

"The Wise call to the Wise, as the sow calls to the grape. Whither the hand? Whither the Song?" the door guardians intoned.

"I, Merkovah, Wise among the Teachers of the Laws of God. The Moon, the Sun. I."

The doors rumbled open. Truth desperately prayed that he had just heard a coded exchange and not some ancient ritual that, again, against all logic and reason, had managed to survive into the present.

A short, barrel-arched hallway made of rough brick led inward, outclassed by the marble and porphyry floors. Delicate inlays of untarnishing metals threaded through the stone. Truth couldn't fathom their meaning beyond beauty. The dim hallway soon opened into a rotunda, marble-clad, with some two hundred dark wood chairs arranged in tiers around an empty center. There was no light in the room save that which streamed through the hole in the roof. A perfect dome with a perfectly round hole in it. Presumably, it was all held up by spells.

Truth, following Etenesh and Jember, stood with his back pressed to the wall at the very back of the topmost tier. Merkovah strode to the edge of the circle of light in the middle of the floor and took a particularly fine-looking seat. He was not the last to arrive, but almost. When everyone was in, an ancient worthy called the congress to order.

This honored scholar was of such rarified status that her hat floated ten centimeters above her head and was almost discus-shaped with a ring of pink plumes. She struck a ceremonial staff against the floor. A sound like a great brass gong being struck rang out. The walls glowed with cosmic energy. The senior faculty bowed their heads and began a droning chant, shaking back and forth as the emotion of their prayers took them. Slowly, a delicate face hidden in part by a pair of wings emerged from the column of light. It bore a burning ember and slowly circled the room.

Jember stifled a yawn. Etenesh did her best to look respectfully interested. *I wish they let us bring snacks*, Truth thought. *Or, better still, a book.*

CHAPTER 43

ACADEMIC INQUIRY

The opening prayer and invocation continued for thirty minutes. Spirits were invoked, beseeched, reprimanded, and employed. A censer was paraded around the room, the swinging basket pouring out white smoke that smelled like church pews and charcoal and the faint thrum of cedar. A fish was condemned, carried on a lead platter widdershins just outside the circle of sunlight. The brilliantly robed fellows of the University turned their backs to it as it passed, carefully covering their mouths. They only turned back toward the light when the fish, perhaps five kilos of pollock, was ritually incinerated and vaporized by a summoned six-winged angel.

Truth could do with some fish. Had he eaten any fish since he came to Siphios? He didn't think so, but he couldn't remember. It wasn't that he was really hungry, but this level of boredom gave him the itch to eat.

Finally, mercifully, the ritual was concluded. The various followers were ordered, with immense pomp, to wait "in the little chambers of Barley and Salt" until summoned or released. Witnesses were told to "Cloister yourselves, dedicate your mind to the Infinite, the Merciful, and the Almighty, that you may most perfectly serve the work of the Wise." This turned out to mean going into a little waiting room and sitting quietly.

And sitting.

And sitting.

Hard to tell the time there. But he was definitely sitting. And waiting.

God, he missed the invocation. That was so much fun. A fascinating display of ancient ritual. He would love, just love, if they could go back to that level of wonder. Or if they could supply him with some hedgehogs. Or even a lightly used novel. It seemed like those romance novels would be useful in the near future.

Having nothing better to do, he practiced the Meditations. It seemed to be going . . . fine. It was a growing irritation—the spell had no theoretical upper limit, so determining how far you had progressed was always relative to where you had started, not where you were going to finish. Was he doing well? Probably? But who knows? Well, actually, no, that was him being ridiculous. The number of Level Three mages that could stand up to him in a fight was probably pretty damn limited, at least on this planet.

The door opened, and a spirit appeared. "Crumb Bearer Wells, you are released until the Galtine Bell rings. You may join the others for panoufe and pie. Please follow this spirit, and make sure that you do not forget anything in your cell. Keeping the campus tidy is the pride and responsibility of everyone."

Crumb bearer? He shrugged. He liked pie. No idea what panoufe was, but he would find out, he supposed. One of those words he never picked up.

The little glowing spirit led Truth to a room paneled in dark wood. It was surprisingly crowded, with a few dozen of the "Blue-hat-green-feather" mob that Etenesh and Jember were in. They must divide up the departments for lunch. Probably a story there. It was all a cheerful hubbub. Most clearly knew each other, and like everyone in Siphios, they were constantly touching. Lots of happy hugs and kisses, eating food off each other's plates, even linking arms to drink.

Truth was acutely conscious of his military-style clothes and blindingly white zeph. That the tassel was properly hanging to the left was little comfort. Truth immediately felt like a freak and knew he wasn't having any pie. Or panoufe, whatever that was. He could hear snippets of conversation—

"Azusah, My *beloved!*"

"Funding cuts everywhere, no idea what they are going to do with the cats now."

"Azusahhhhh,"

"No, thanks, but no. Try me tomorrow, and I'll probably—"

"Gower or Weddiburn, do you think?"

"Oh, heavens, some wannabe sword-boy wandered in. Somebody get his mum."

"Angels preserve us, was he mugged or something? What's going on with his clothes?"

"Wonder whose toy that is? Hey, let's bet—does he top or bottom?"

"Azusahahahahaahaaa!"

"Oh, shit, that's awkward. Think he came to the wrong room? What's he even doing in the Well?"

"Hey, check it out—it's hero time!"

Yeah, he was out of there. He was right: he really did have improved senses. Such joy. He spun on his heel and swiftly stepped toward the door. He had been hungry before. He would live.

"Tommy!" Etenesh's voice called. He stopped and looked back. Etenesh and Jember walked over to him. "It is so great they put you with us! The Religious Law department gets the best food."

"That's super, but I am incredibly uncomfortable here."

"Oh, that's because you don't know anyone! Let me introduce you around." Jember waved some people over. "Negasi, Dawit, come, I want you to meet someone."

"Tommy, I know you don't want strangers touching you, but it is a part of our culture. May I hold your arm? It will discourage others." Etenesh projected her voice into his ear, sounding like a whisper but heard clearly. He had no idea how she did it. Jember's acquaintances were coming closer. Left with no good options, he offered his elbow to Etenesh. She snaked her arm around it, snuggling up to his right side.

He was instantly uncomfortable, both with the contact and having his sword arm trapped. He could probably fight lefty, but it was a pain to draw left-handed.

Negasi and Dawit were third-year scholars training with another teacher, specializing in some area of Orthodox Siphios religious law that Truth neither knew of nor understood. They looked used to that reaction and were clearly trying to find some basis for small talk.

"Have you eaten?"

"No, not yet. Is the pie good?"

"Oh, yes, three types of savory pie on offer. A tradition of the Well, you know—only serve food that comes in its own container. A lot of pies, as you can imagine."

"Oh? What kind of pies?"

"Oh, there is steak and onion, chicken and vegetable, and I think a vegetarian option."

Steak sounded perfect.

"Not to worry; here's Alemu with some pies and punch."

A handsome-ish man walked up, carefully balancing a plate full of little golden brown miniature pies and another plate full of tall glasses of some pink liquid.

"Hello, hello! Jember, Etenesh, it's been ages." Etenesh tightened up on Truth slightly, then relaxed.

"Alemu, great to see you, old man. I see you brought victuals." Jember seemed to get brighter, the more people were around. His smile flashed like the sun on water.

"Can't have people going hungry or thirsty in the Well!" Alemu strode through Negasi and Dawit like they weren't there, though he had brought them drinks. Truth noticed them silently make way for him.

"Etenesh, who is this? Not one of the Wise, I see."

"Alemu, meet Tommy Wells. Teacher Merkovah employs him as a bodyguard." Etenesh smiled prettily while subtly tightening back up on Truth's arm.

"A pleasure, I'm sure," Alemu murmured. Truth had no idea what to say, so he smiled slightly and nodded his head politely. Then looked over at the pie and drinks.

"Cheers for bringing the supplies. Don't suppose any of those are vegetarian, are they?" Jember asked.

"Why, yes. The ones with the flowers cut into the lid." Truth snagged one of the flower ones. He really wanted steak, but since his cover was to be that he was Desrin, sacrifices would have to be made. He took a bite. Flaky crust, creamy sauce, and gently cooked vegetables. Mild, salty, rich . . . he wouldn't call it delicious, but it was certainly very tasty. He could eat a few more of those.

"Drink?"

"Oh, thank you." Truth reached out and snagged a glass, raising it to his lips.

"TOMMY!" Etenesh yelled.

The smell hit him first—faint herbs, almost piney, with a lot of citrus over it. Then the warm waft of ethanol climbed up in his nose. A sickly sweet taste, cold, with a hint of burn, started to spread along his tongue, and he could smell the Red Bats, smell Dad's armchair, smell the slums, and he spat that shit right out on the floor, and smashed the glass down next to it and was drawing steel to *behead this fuck—*

"TOMMY! NO!"

"Let's go. Come this way. We'll get you some water." Jember was talking fast, trying to put himself between Truth and the dead man.

"Alemu, what?" Negasi could barely form words.

"Unbelievers have no place in Siphios, nor do foreigners! Disgusting that he should be invited into the Well, and worse that a woman of Siphios is hanging off his arm. This nation will never be pure again with cowards like you who watch and do nothing!" he spat.

"He works for Merkovah. Merkovah!" Dawit hissed.

"Merkovah took an oath to the Crown. He can't touch me." Truth could, though. He was memorizing his face, the sound of his voice. The smell of him. Every detail of him was etched into his brain as he let Etenesh and Jember drag him away. He wanted this man dead. He *needed* him dead. But he was in a room full of this bastard's friends, in a building full of his friends. He could hang on to just enough of his sanity to not do something stupid.

"Run, Tefen! Run right out of Siphios! And take the te'mushd with you! There is no place for you in Siphios! No place!" Alemu shouted, even as he was covered by clouds of white robes with blue edges and hats with green feathers.

Etenesh grabbed Truth's arm so tightly that, even with his cultivation, it hurt. But she didn't stop hauling him out of the room.

Truth didn't see where they dragged him. His left hand was crushing the hilt of his sword. His right arm was being choked to death by Etenesh. His eyes and mind were blinded by a fury of black and red.

How dare he! How dare he! howhowhowhowhowhowhowhowhowDARE HE!

The thought went round and round and round, swirling up the muck at the bottom of his mind, all the pain and hurt and horror he associated with drink. How day after day, when he was bleeding and hurting from hunting scrap or running errands or just getting the shit kicked out of him by Dad or Mom or some other thug, he would look at a bottle of cheap schnapps or cheaper-still white spirits and think how easy it would be to numb his pain. Think about how cheap that first hit of base was. Free, even, for the right customer. Faith? That *bastard* had no idea what faith was!

That little shit— No. He had a name. His name was Alemu. He would never forget the name Alemu. He would never forget Alemu's face. Never, never, never. Because Alemu never got hit so hard, he pissed blood. Alemu never had to climb over a chain link fence with two broken ribs. Alemu never got kicked in the nuts so bad, he puked and then got stomped when the gangsters couldn't find the money. Alemu never had to eat the hate. Alemu never had to eat the humiliation. Alemu had nice food with his rich family and went to a miracle university in a kind country, and *Truth had none of that!*

Truth's breath came in short, sharp, sucking inhalations. He tried to get his breathing under control, but it was bucking and fighting against him. Truth tried to remember that an insult was like a drink. He didn't remember where he heard that. But an insult was like a drink. It only affected you if you took it into yourself. Internalized it. Otherwise, it was harmless. You could spit it out before you swallowed it. Like he had done with the poison. Just spit it out. No harm done.

He was going to kill Alemu. The poison had gotten in.

CHAPTER 44

THE THUNDER OF MIGHTY WINGS

The cousins were too mad to even swear. Their faces were rigid masks, hands clenched, taking deep, snorting breaths through their nose.

"In case you haven't figured it out, *panoufe* is a kind of traditional alcoholic drink. Pretty much only drunk on formal social occasions in the University or by graduates feeling nostalgic," Jember grounded out. Etenesh refused to look at anyone. Her shoulders shook now and then.

"Tiffen? Temusht?"

"*Tefen* and *te'mushd* are basically . . . not of the faith and the people, and someone who should belong to the faith and the people but prefers outsiders, respectively. *Apostate*; do you know that word? *Apostate* is probably the closest. An offense punishable by death, traditionally." Jember struggled to speak, anger choking him.

"Alemu?"

"Third son of Duke Red Valley, a status that hasn't been relevant in centuries. A fact that clearly stings. We know him, of course. Department's not that big. Pure Lander, but so what? So's most of the department. Didn't think he . . . had gone that hard." Jember's voice was becoming even more clipped.

"Sounded like he was interested in Etenesh?" The flatness in Truth's voice would have startled him if he wasn't too angry to catch it. Etenesh sure heard it, though.

"That pin-dick wishes I'd give him the time of day!" she snapped.

"Remember what I said about how word gets around? He's been enjoying a years-long dry spell. At least in our department. Can't say about off-campus," Jember explained quickly. Truth just nodded at that. Some little part of him felt relieved. It was stupid. Just because Etenesh was interested in him now didn't change who she might have been with in the past. But he would have thought less of her. She could do better than an Alemu. And she was his now.

That thought hit him with a jolt, almost enough to snap him out of the swirls of rage and humiliation. That possessive impulse. She, Etenesh, was his now. No one else's. His. He could feel the sick warmth of the thought, warming and worming and twisting through his chest and guts. His. Etenesh was his. No one else had the right to touch her. His.

He gasped, grabbing his arms and holding on tight. This was . . . not smart. He knew these thoughts weren't smart. How many screaming fights had he heard through the walls? How many of his protectees did he have to stop from getting battered because of this kind of thinking? How many times did he have to look away when they did the battering? But he didn't know how to break out of it.

"Jember." Etenesh looked over her shoulder at her cousin, eyes blazing ocher. "Tell Lady Deonne that I am ready for my initiation."

"That's wonderful news, but is now *really* the time?" Jember snarled.

"Yes. It is. Because I've chosen my sacrifice." She turned her blazing eyes on Truth. "Would you do me a little favor, Mr. Wells?"

"Probably." She smiled at that.

"I'm going to guide your hands." She slowly reached out, only taking them when he offered them to her. Softly, she brought them up—one to the side of her neck. She rested her cheek on the other. She was shivering. Anger, perhaps? Fear?

"Did you know, Mr. Wells, that I watch you a lot?"

He did but didn't know if telling her was the right answer.

"Silly question, of course you do. Every day, I see you expect violence. You expect to get hit all the time. So, you are ready to dodge and hit them first. You are the blade, cutting away the pain of your life. Just like you said. I believe you. Violence is how you understand the world. Everything is some form of violence. And I have watched you try to learn something else. Try to be something else."

She opened her eyes, soft brown eyes with sclera the color of autumn on the mountains. "It has been beautiful to watch. It is . . . holy."

Truth felt his heart lurch. The swirling hate and anger draining out of him. Not gone. Just bled out some. It was hard to stay angry, holding her face like this. Looking into her eyes like this.

"I thought I could fix you. Teach you to put down that blade. But I've learned better tonight." She smiled up at him. There was something hard in that smile. "You don't need fixing. You are as you need to be. The world that made you this way is what needs to change." She was pulling him in now, her eyes drawing him down toward her.

"Your hand is on my neck, Mr. Wells. The other is cupping my face." And they were, her cheek fitting so neatly into his big hand, her neck soft as silk over steel. Her pulse raced under his fingertips, her heart beating as wildly as his own. "I believe you could kill me before I even blinked."

He could. He truly could. It was all chaos—humiliation and anger and love and lust and the sin of possessiveness. The darkness crowded around his mind. He was the blade at her neck, and in the moment, he knew he could never cut her. Etenesh's smile deepened, the pupils of her eyes dark and still as a desert well.

"I am in terrible danger right now. I really don't feel safe at all." She took a deep breath and held his eyes. "Kiss me?"

Truth fell down into her, drowning in the darkness. His lips brushed against hers, soft and warm and questioning. He looked into her eyes again and saw her. Smiling.

Waiting. She had set their feet on this path. He would have to decide how far they walked. Truth kissed her harder, her hands still cupping his. Offering herself, this kiss, a cup to cleanse the poison he had drunk before. She was very soft, and warm, and fragile in his hands. He was lost in the strength of her. When he pulled back a second time, she sighed happily.

"I have wanted to kiss you since I saw you step out of Merkovah's carriage."

"Etenesh, I—" He didn't have the words.

"It's all right. No rush. I'm happy. Are you happy?"

Truth felt like the room was spinning. Was he happy? Right now, in this moment? He started laughing. "You know what? I am."

"Good. I will want your full attention, Mr. Wells, because I promise you will have mine. No games. No tricks to make you jealous or to goad you into something. I will tell you exactly what I want. And I expect you to do the same. I may not want what you want when you want it. You may not want what I'm offering. We can always tell each other no. But I won't think less of you for asking, and you won't think less of me. Deal?"

He closed his eyes, hands still wrapped around her neck, as soft a smile as ever he had on his face. "Deal."

"Seal it with a kiss?"

He leaned in and did just that.

Truth was relieved when a transcendently pissed-off Merkovah swept into the little conference room they had commandeered. Not because things had gotten awkward with Etenesh. Far from it. No, it was Jember. He kept sniffling and making a fuss, saying "You two are so beautiful. Oh, this is so, so, so sweet!" Truth thought the dapper man was fucking with him, but no, Jember was entirely, sincerely happy for them.

"I can't wait to tell Auntie about this. She is going to gloat for *months* about how she raised you right," Jember continued. Etenesh beamed. Truth just went along with it. He was pretty lost, but Etenesh was firm about him keeping his hand wrapped around her wrist, and that was making everything surprisingly okay. Except that Jember *kept* going on about it, and it got excruciating.

"You appear well, Mr. Wells. And in a less-than-murderous rage, which is impressive."

"Credit Etenesh for that." Truth smiled slightly, declining to mention that he was still going to kill Alemu as soon as circumstances permitted.

"I do. I assume you are going to kill Alemu as soon as circumstances permit?" Truth almost fell over, choking on his own spit.

"I would never!" he swore, gesturing slightly to his ears and letting his eyes flick around the room. Merkovah snorted with amusement.

"My mistake. Although, if you did have such an intention, you might have to join the queue. Right now, the entire Congress has been derailed by a motion to summarily expel Alemu, and castigate his mentor, Teacher Ferrenet. Word has gotten around, and our Desrin faculty and students are howling for blood. Literally, in the case of Wise Vchelk. It has blown up to the point where I am fairly sure this was a deliberate, planned provocation."

"Someone trying to derail the conference?"

"Nothing so simple. With one move, the instigator had divided the University, sown distrust among the faculty, and created an atmosphere of fear among the students. Some of the faculty here are the very best in the world in their specialties, Mr. Wells. This one move might well decide a war. Of course, it would have been far better for them if you had killed the little idiot. Might have started a sectarian riot."

Ah. Yes. Now that he said it, that did seem like a logical consequence of hacking off Alemu's head and using it to smash every glass of panoufe in the room before chopping it open, hollowing out the already largely empty brain pan, and using it as a chamber pot.

"So, yes, Mr. Wells, full credit to Etenesh, with better than passing marks for Jember. Both displayed remarkably good sense. Despite some vile provocation." Truth swore the lights got a little dimmer at that. "I took it as a *personal* provocation. Which it absolutely was. So, I am being demonstrably, publicly, mad while keeping a cool head and trying to spot the instigators."

"You don't feel like putting down the disguise with us, Teacher?" Etenesh asked.

"What disguise? I've got a list of assholes I've waited *decades* to settle scores with, and given half a chance, today will be that day!" Merkovah bellowed. "These quarter-wit cuckolds think the solution to the present national emergency is a civil war. Well, I'm happy to start that war right now with them!"

"Speaking of settling scores," Etenesh said softly, "before Alemu runs back to Red Valley, I want to send him a meal."

Merkovah looked like he would swear, then reconsidered. "You mean—"

"Yes. I have decided to become an Initiate to the Treasury of Light. And I think Alemu would make a perfect sacrifice."

"He was raised in an aristocratic household. Alemu's an ass, but he strikes me as the sort who would have enjoyed training for duels," Merkovah cautioned.

"He bragged about it. But we are both Level Three, so he can accept the duel or be posted as a coward." The hardness was back in her smile, as was the coldness in her eyes. "I am fairly sure that if I don't kill him literally, Jember will kill him socially."

"Most definitely," Jember agreed.

Truth raised his hand, the one not holding Etenesh. "Sorry, you are dueling Alemu, the duel invitation being some kind of food? Are you allowed to send a champion or something?"

The locals looked at him oddly. "It would kind of defeat the purpose of a duel if you could," Merkovah explained.

"Not to mention the moral satisfaction. Oh, you wanted to do it yourself?" Etenesh asked.

"Yes, and make sure he couldn't slip in a ringer."

"He can't. His second could try to negotiate a peaceful resolution, but under the circumstances, that would be impossible." Her smile widened, growing cruel. "Freshwater fish are considered an unclean animal among the Orthodox, as are some varieties of saltwater fish. I think a single anchovy would accurately express my feelings."

Merkovah smiled approvingly. "I will arrange the fish. And the paper."

Truth nodded quietly at all this. He had no idea how this all worked. He'd just have to trust that they did. And sharpen his edge in case of any accidents.

CHAPTER 45

CONSENSUAL DISTRESS

Truth and the cousins stayed in the little conference room while the congress went into convulsions. They were not kept in the loop, which Truth reckoned was just as well. He wouldn't know the ins and outs of the various relationships, anyhow. He wasn't sure how he felt about this . . . duel thing. He knew what duels were in an abstract sort of way. It was just that they had no connection to his life. And he was really not happy about Etenesh getting into a life-and-death fight where he couldn't interfere.

"So . . . don't take this the wrong way, but have you ever killed another human being?" Truth asked. He really couldn't think of how you should ask that question, so he opted for being direct. This was apparently not the correct choice, as Etenesh suddenly went very still and quiet.

"No. I have fought spirits, demons, ghosts, and other supernatural sorts. But I've never done more than spar with another human."

"Humans freeze up when you get in their face. They panic. They make bad choices. Soldiers train all the time because you never suddenly get good at making decisions under stress. You train so you don't have to make decisions. You did all your thinking in advance. Your body knows what to do," Truth explained. Etenesh looked at him blankly.

Truth spun his hand in the air, trying to figure out how to explain something that seemed obvious to him. "I have watched you fight. You already know this, on some level. You raise a ward to give yourself time to think, and then you plan out what ritual spell you want to cast."

Truth wasn't sure she was getting it. "You do everything you can to give yourself space to think and react calmly. It's not necessarily a bad thing. It could be a good thing or the right thing. But unless the duel has rules about how you can fight, it's a dangerous thing to try against another human. It's always reactive, at least in the opening exchanges, which puts you at risk of dying before making your move."

Etenesh gave him a half-smile. "Well, the fight is two religious studies students battling it out, no demons, no attending spirits, with limits on the prepared charms. Neither of us has equipment like your sword. Before either of us go on the sands, we will be checked out by both seconds and a neutral third party. So, it's going to be who has the better talismans, better spells, better skills, and, most importantly, God's favor. It's not going to be very fast."

Truth instinctively knew that arguing with the girl you like was a low-percentage play. On the other hand, he didn't want to see her dead. He tried to think of what to say. More importantly, he tried to think of how to make her hear what he was trying to tell her.

"You look like you disagree. What am I missing?" Etenesh asked.

Truth looked down at his hands for a moment. "If I were to go fight Alemu right now, using only my bare hands and Incisive, do you think I would win?"

Etenesh started talking, stopped, started again, and stopped again.

"I want to say no because he's going to be attended by at least one and probably several powerful spirits, and he certainly would have several protective amulets. But I kind of see you winning, too. The way you just charge in through everything and rabidly attack until whatever you are fighting is dead. Except now that I know you, I know it's not blind aggression. You are solving the 'violence puzzle' as efficiently as you can."

"Right, exactly that. Fights with other humans are very fast, very intense, scary." Well, for most people. They hadn't bothered him since his breakthrough to Level One. Thank you, Rough Patron?

"So . . ." Etenesh encouraged him to finish the thought.

"So, up your aggression. Rush the bastard. Tweak your loadout to deploy everything as fast as possible, and while he's dealing with it, *then* cast your wards. Then, if he's still alive, somehow, you have the time to cast bigger spells."

"Dueling culture isn't really a thing where you're from, is it?"

"No. Not at all."

"So, how did you—" She stopped again, then smiled wryly. "You didn't resolve disputes of honor formally. You just killed the bastard who insulted you."

"Not me personally, but yes. Or you ate the humiliation and seethed, taking it out on weaker people."

"Hah. Well. The duel won't happen for three days at the soonest. Any suggestions on how to train?"

"Find people who won't be missed and are weaker than you. Build your courage by slaughtering them. I'll tell you they are villains, so you don't feel bad giving in to the slaughter. I'll persuade you that it's okay, it's not fucked up. That way, the violence will touch you more lightly, though it will touch you, and you will never be the same, never ever." Truth thought.

"In the time we have? Build up your courage. Develop your killing intent."

"How?"

Well. Even if she would go along with his plan, Merkovah wouldn't. And he didn't think Etenesh actually would go along with it.

"Ever square up against someone ready to kill you? Not a demon, a human?"

"No."

Truth stepped away from her. Turned and faced her. "I want you to know that I won't attack you. You will feel like I am about to attack you, but I won't. Jember is here with you. You aren't alone. You just need to cast one spell or order your spirit to touch me. That's it. It is that easy to make it stop."

"Eh?"

Truth had wondered why people locked up when they squared up against him in basic. He had just assumed it was because he had spent so much time fighting. The lock-up thing happened with some other people, too. Now, though, he had to wonder. Was this part of his patron's legacy?

He extended his arm and pointed his finger at Etenesh. He visualized stabbing it right between her beautiful eyes, destroying her brilliant mind in a single blow. Letting the murderer in him rise up. "Come."

To her credit, Etenesh didn't faint. After the first time, she didn't freeze up long, either. "It's like jumping into a cold shower," she explained. "It's never nice, but you get used to pushing yourself into it." After she got used to working under the pressure alone, Truth started changing things up. He would suddenly draw his sword. Coat his arm with Incisive. Shout suddenly. He began moving around, darting from side to side or faking an attack. Little constant tweaks to maintain pressure, but vary the source of stress. Jember asked if he could join in the training, and since Etenesh was wearing out fast, Truth nodded.

It wasn't exactly a fun way to pass the afternoon, but at the end of it, Etenesh and Jember had toughened up some. Not a waste of a day.

The evening came with a storm cloud shaped like Merkovah. To Truth's eyes, he still looked twenty-five. Still had a beard that looked like it was trying to escape his face. Still looked like a damn clown in those formal robes of his. The palpable rage coming off him made him a lot less funny.

"Due to the 'unforeseen, unfortunate interruption,' the congress has decided to do what it should have done in the first place and set up a working group to study the talisman. Tommy, we will discuss your role in this further later," Merkovah growled.

"Having made that stupendous decision and averting a sectarian riot for at least the day, the congress voted to dissolve pending further developments. *All that* for something that could have been resolved by sending a note around! And now my student's going to fight a duel!"

Truth and the cousins shared a look with each other. What could you even say?

"Has the fish been ordered?"

"Yes, it will be delivered along with your note. Have you written it yet?"

"Not yet," Etenesh said. "Tommy was training us to endure killing intent."

"Oh." Merkovah's eyebrow went up. "Good thinking. Here, I brought some good paper." He handed it to Etenesh. "Be sure to start with an allusion to geese or other domestic fowl."

"All right," Etenesh agreed, but sounded puzzled. Merkovah grinned and explained.

"There is a persistent rumor circulating that, due to his crippling inability to please a woman, Alemu has followed in his mentor's footsteps and has taken a goose for a mistress. Not some manner of goose spirit, an actual, literal goose. The details are quite lurid." Merkovah radiated grim disapproval. Truth imagined he would look more forgiving of bandits burning down a village.

"Well-documented and thoroughly sourced reports of Teacher Ferrenet's hands-on teaching methodology have circulated for years. He is famous for saying that there is no substitute for experiential learning in any aspect of our lives, and these reports show just how committed he is to the spiritual and intellectual growth of his student. Some even accompanied by distressingly accurate pictures, clearly drawn from life."

Merkovah looked pious and slightly ill. "I can only assume his connections to the Palace have protected him from prosecution."

He dispelled the mood with a grin. "It's been a lot of fun making up the reports. Though I do have to hire the artists, as I'm no hand with a brush. Ferrenet's been on my list for twenty years now."

The grin faded away into something altogether colder. "He absolutely dotes on Alemu. He's close friends with the duke. He might not have known about Mr. Wells in advance, but Alemu was clearly acting on instructions from someone. In concert with many others."

His eyes bored into Etenesh. "Break him, then kill him. Siphios must be saved, yes, but they would destroy us for that cause. Shatter the nation before the invaders walk in and take over. So, kill him. Show him that you—and we—are the righteous of the land."

Etenesh's eyes were dyed a ruddy orange as she fiercely nodded.

"I am a little surprised at how strongly you reacted to alcohol, Mr. Wells. I know you don't drink, but rumor has it the only reason Alemu still has his head was Etenesh hanging from your sword arm." Truth looked around Merkovah's room at Temple Nag Hamadi. It was functionally identical to his own, save for the bigger chest and more bookshelves. It was alarmingly spare. Didn't he have a wife in Xandre? Was this just a place to rest?

"Bad memories."

"Recovering alcoholic?"

"My father and, to a lesser extent, my mother. And not recovering, no."

"That is a hard thing to live through. And your siblings? I think you mentioned them?"

"I protected them as best I could. They are free of my parents now."

"Back in the old country. Working for your . . . former employer?"

"One is. Don't know about the others." Truth shook his head. Why was he telling Merkovah all this?

"Well, leaving that to the side, the reason Alemu managed that stunt was because you didn't have Incisive cast."

"Wasn't sure about the rules on using magic in the Well, to be honest."

"The rules are many and varied, to be sure. And who cares? A rule is only a rule to the extent that it's enforced. I'm a senior fellow of the University, as well as an . . . officer of the Throne. You are my bodyguard. Cast away. If anyone dares ask you why, just stare them down and send them to me."

"You want me to have Incisive running all the time?"

"As much as you reasonably can, yes. You are a bodyguard, Mr. Wells. You are making some strides in your magic resistance and great leaps in your understanding of Incisive. Your growth in level is rather excellent too. I won't mention your disturbingly fast reflexes. There is no reason anyone under Level Five should be able to ambush you."

"I'll do what I can. Speaking of ambushes, what is going to be my role in the investigation?"

"As close to none as I can manage. I will probably keep you around the temple, guarding the conference here. People asked where you were today."

"No kidding?"

"Nope. It seems that Desrins armed with swords, particularly tall, handsome ones, are in high demand recently. Why, we may never know." Merkovah grinned.

Then he added, "Also, to whatever extent you can, try to be low-key. Between the terrorist attack and the poisoning today, even the witless public has caught on that someone is trying to start a civil war. The Desrin, as a sizable minority in Siphios, are understandably on edge and feeling . . . chippy. So, let's keep things quiet and try to let the heat die down."

"Yes, Teacher," Truth said. Then, remembering his rough patron's warning, felt the need to add "as best I can."

CHAPTER 46

A HEAVY HAND

Truth stood guard outside the conference room at Temple Nag Hamadi. His thoughts bounced around, as they tend to do when you are on staring-at-the-wall duty.

Kissing Etenesh was pretty great. Not . . . one hundred percent comfortable with what he seemed to need to get comfortable. Simultaneously thrilled and alarmed that Etenesh had figured it out and seemed okay with it. Enthusiastic about it, even.

Was this the bad-boy effect? Many of his romance novels described it in detail. It was apparently lethally effective. But he wasn't a "Bad Boy," right?

He wrestled with the thought for a long while. Had he committed crimes? Yes. Did he care about committing crimes? Only to the extent that it had limited results. So, that was bad. But he didn't go out of his way to hurt people, right? Right. He didn't do that.

Except for the times when he did. And there went his morale, like urine down a trouser leg. He forcibly reminded himself that Etenesh was setting the pace, and if she didn't like it, she wouldn't have done it. Everything else was just guesswork, and he had important staring at the wall to do.

But damn, did she have him worked out or what? Even he hadn't cracked that code. NO! Wall time!

The walls of Temple Nag Hamadi remained as they ever were. Covered with inscriptions in different languages, dotted with pictures, and completely incomprehensible to him. The subtle oddity of them was a little better understood now. It was their extra-realness. What the System had once called "Local Superreality." And wasn't that an interesting phrase to roll around?

"Local superreality." *Local* meaning the area right around you, and *superreality*, which probably wasn't a real word but clearly meant that you were more real than the already "real." And since everyone insisted that "reality" was a) the mind/will of God, or possibly something generated by God by simple virtue of his existence, and b) not evenly distributed, as God understandably kept the stuff closest to him . . . "him" . . . most real. It got the most attention from the big guy, after all. Their lousy planet had been barely noticed before, and now it was, apparently, being actively ignored.

Was the planet becoming less real? Cultivation could make things more real. Could the process work in reverse? Could the export of all those precious minerals and natural treasures be weakening the planet somehow? A planet already beneath God's notice?

Truth had no idea, but it would make sense. Leaving aside what he suspected was the true reason for the Shattervoid's refusal to visit, they could also be coming less often for economic reasons. Maybe it just wasn't worth it anymore.

Hang on, hang on, he knew something about this. Truth squinted fiercely at a particularly eye-catching bunch of squiggles on the wall. The Shattervoid Clan priced their tickets weirdly. The lower your cultivation, the more expensive the ticket. The higher-level guys had more money. You should be soaking them, right? Upcharging the poor and weak wasn't a profit-maximizing move.

He thought it was a policy thing—keep the slumrats planet-bound where they could labor for the already rich and powerful. What if it was something else? What if it was more expensive for them to ship things from the edges of God's attention? Did the Black Ships not work as well in low-reality areas?

Truth had no idea. But he suddenly had an awful lot of questions. The Mountain of Things Truth Didn't Know wasn't shrinking. The demonic peak grew by the day!

This planet relies on the Black Ships for food imports and for technology we can't manufacture here. Apparently, the planetary economy is mostly exports. The thought ran down his spine like a demon's claw.

We have to export something to get food. The Shattervoid Clan doesn't care about ninety-nine percent of what we make. It's all too unreal for them. All they want are the minerals and natural treasures. Maybe some manufactured goods, maybe not.

Actually, definitely some manufactured goods, because he knew for a fact Starbrite exported a load of finished products off-planet. Others must too—regardless of how powerful Starbrite was, the whole world would be at his throat if he controlled all the food.

Truth stifled a laugh. Wasn't professional on-duty. Didn't match the look.

They were fucked. No wonder everyone looked so beaten going in and coming out of the conference room. They were completely, one hundred percent screwed. He didn't know how the planet got into this trap, but it sure seemed like they were locked in now.

That Desrin lady said it the first day he was guarding this door—there would be war. Terrible war. But who would be left on the planet to fight it?

All the elites would do their best to rip away all they could from the world and run away. All that would be left would be, what? The Level Fives and under? Level Fours? Trapped on a dying world, fighting over what meager resources remained after the final ripping violation.

Billions would die, of course. Not enough food, and without the elites, the systems of government would break down. Social order would collapse, with local powerhouses—hah, those "Local Superreality" tycoons, ruling over lower-level people desperate for some shred of security. For however long those "tycoons" could maintain their apertures. How long until those started to collapse from a lack of cosmic energy and elixirs?

The whole world would turn into the Free State. Gangsters fighting over trash, killing each other to prove who had best-polished turd. And if he could see it standing in the hallway, the people in the conference room must see it too.

No wonder Merkovah was always pissed off. He must have seen it coming for decades. Centuries, even. Only when the world was actually, right this minute, falling apart were people suddenly saying, "Oh, we have to do something!" And then not actually doing something. *We* apparently meant *someone else.*

It would be "unfair" or an "overreaction" if they had to take serious action. Economically unjustifiable. An unfair burden on those who had already disproportionately suffered. Kneecapping industry when the public was already suffering from low wages. There was always some reason not to do the obvious, urgent, necessary, or inconvenient.

The warm, sad feeling of his morale running down his pants leg and soaking his sock hadn't stopped. Shame.

So . . . what could he do about it? He had to do something. He was on this planet. So were the sibs and Etenesh. And Jember and Merkovah, and the garage owner and his wife who had been kind to him. Those farm laborers. Those idiot Desrin who were determined to love him and make him one of their own. Determined to be a home for him.

That was . . . starting to fuck him up a bit. He didn't think he was ever going to be a believer in God, but he was starting to believe in the Desrin. Well. He'd see how that went.

Hell of a thing to happen because he wanted a hat.

What could he do about it? Globally? Nothing. Too big, too many moving parts. If Merkovah and the other heavyweights couldn't fix it, he certainly couldn't. So, what was Merkovah fixated on? Killing Starbrite.

Now, Truth wasn't prepared to accuse anyone of altruism, let alone someone who had done whatever it took to make Level Seven and cultivate some life-extending body refinement. Merkovah was more than decent to him, but he was also petty, wrathful, and vengeful.

This was definitely a personal vendetta for Merkovah. All the kindness should be interpreted as the exorcist making an investment in Truth for the ultimate purpose of kneecapping Starbrite's elite. Getting them set for Merkovah and his friends to stick the knife in.

At this point, that saboteur job was turning into a contract he would be okay taking on. He was seeing the benefits of Incisive, his Meditations was progressing better than expected, and the Tongue of One Who Speaks for God really was an incredible sword. Throw in the real-deal Sword of Moshe once he hit Level Four, and he was looking at a fairly incredible example of being paid in advance. Even in Siphios, spells were not cheap.

Of course, it all depended on the state of the sibs. Harmony would be in deep with Starbrite, so that was going to be an issue, but what about the others? Related, what would happen to the world if Starbrite was taken out? Would it slow the collapse? Because it wouldn't fix the basic problem, right?

Truth really didn't know. The best person he could ask would be Merkovah, and he was *not* going to trust that particular source on this issue.

The doors of the conference room opened again, and now that he had sussed out some things, the snippets took on an even grimmer tone.

"Who benefits, is what I want to know. Who benefits from civil war?"

"Fine, healthy baby. Jane is doing great, baby's doing great, and I look at the crib I built and think . . ."

"We have to be calorie-positive by the end of the year. And it's not possible, given the 'economic climate.' Can you believe that?"

"Roads are going. Defenses are going. Border is starting to get fuzzy down south, what with the spirits demanding more and more."

"Reban's a war zone again. Feels like it happens every few years. People are desperate for elixirs . . ."

". . . looted the treasury, and it's not going to matter a damn, he's only Level Four, and even if he forced his way to Level Five, without the ships, what good's a ticket?"

"It just didn't answer. Had to pour half a bottle in to get its attention. We've had a fifteen-generation relationship with that angel . . ."

"It's not all bad, not all bad. The forests around Py'en are growing back well. Not spiritual yet, but give them a few millennia . . ."

"Felt terrible. Makda thought she was stupid. She really thought she was dumb because she couldn't get the spell to work. How do I even explain to her that it's not her?"

"Still not a romantic, Brother?"

The spellblade enthusiast was back with his friend.

"Can't say I am, sir, no," Truth replied.

"Even after the Hero of the Terraces appeared?"

"Yes. Because what really saved the day was Old Mek'elle coming in and putting his foot down. He helped. I won't deny him that; he helped. But it was power that saved the day, not romance."

Truth looked the enthusiast dead in the eye. "I don't know what's going on in the conference, sir. Not my job, not my place. But if you are looking for a hero, you might want to look for power first. The kitchen made misirwot today. I can recommend it."

The enthusiast shook his head. "No hungry heroes, huh?"

"Hunger sharpens the blade but can only swing it once. A full belly can cut all day."

The Desrin and his friend looked thoughtful as they turned toward the dining room. "Well. I guess we need to get sharpening, then. And figure out where to cut," the friend muttered. The spellblade enthusiast didn't say anything. But after a few steps, he slowly nodded. Then stopped and turned back to face Truth.

"You are wrong about one thing, you know. There are endless hungry heroes. Endless. Mothers, fathers, sisters, brothers, and all manner of kindred, living lean to help their loved ones. Fighting on as best they can."

"Yes, sir. Someone with power thought it was best they starved, so they are starving. They could be fed. Someone with power made a choice, and now the heroes live lean. Their hunger is policy. Do you think the heroes want to be remembered as heroes or as someone who became powerful enough to change things for their families? Sir?"

The hallway emptied again. Merkovah stepped out of the conference room and started to pat Truth on the shoulder. Then smiled and stopped his hand in the air. "You remember our conversation about heroes?"

"Yes, Teacher."

"I believe in heroes, you know. In romance, in holy martyrs and the power of dreams."

Truth just nodded. Merkovah was Level Seven. He could believe what he liked.

"Of course, I believe all of that because I got strong enough to survive that belief." Merkovah grinned and suddenly flicked forward with a jab. Incisive screamed a warning, and Truth dodged left. Merkovah's hand stopped in the air again, barely halfway to Truth.

"Keep practicing, Mr. Wells. Keep up the good work. I think we must discuss next steps soon. There is less time than I thought. Yes, less time than I thought." The beardy exorcist shook his head and started walking toward lunch. "Shall I send over a bowl of misirwot?"

"I'd prefer shekla tibs. I'm suddenly craving meat."

"Enjoy it while you can. Price of meat's going up every day. Nobody's growing animal feed anymore."

CHAPTER 47

A NIGHT ON THE TOWN

Truth slipped out of Temple Nag Hamadi that night. He kept the sword and wore his new scarf but ditched the zeph. Old Mek'elle's gift looked like a fashionable variation of a Brickies scarf. He blended. Nobody looked at him more than one and a half times. Without the zeph, he was just a handsome foreigner.

He didn't have much money, hardly any, actually, but that was all right. He had a full belly and inexpensive vices, and there was nowhere in particular he wanted to go. He just wanted to see Xandre without the filter of Merkovah or the cousins. The city was far too big to see in a night, but . . . he had the itch to move.

He pulled away from the blocky temple, his iron horse better maintained now, though he still worried about the chained spirit. There was no reason doing the herbal bath himself shouldn't work as well as a pro doing it in the shop. He had been trained on how to do it in the Army. It just wasn't something he did *often*, and he didn't want something to suddenly go wrong.

What if he had to outrun more demons? Truth gently prodded the spirit and smoothly slid into the city traffic. There was no shortage of demons in Xandre, but they weren't chasing him.

The streets of Xandre were narrow outside the main thoroughfares. Many single-lane streets, some so small he couldn't imagine getting a wagon down them. They were crammed full of pedestrians, all swarming past each other. There was probably a logic there. Maybe he would figure it out by the end of his jaunt.

Beyond the narrow alleys and single-lane streets were the broader, two-lane roads. This was the land of the buses—the two-story wagons pulled by ghostly elephants daubed in white and ocher paint, with green blazing eyes and garlands of dream orchids hanging from their necks. Truth couldn't tear his eyes away.

They had buses in Jeon. Of course they did! Who could afford their own carriage? A sweet little chariot or your own flying cloud was strictly for the absurdly rich. For the slums, it was the subway and the bus.

The Jeon City bus was an empty box with wheels on the corners. Everyone crammed into the box. The chained demon inside the floor powered the enchantments that turned the wheels, and you hung on to the straps and prayed you didn't fall over on someone or they didn't fall on you. Passengers spent their commutes guessing who didn't bother wiping. Guessing who didn't bother taking off their pants before answering nature's call. Steaming in the rancid humidity of a hundred halitosis cases.

These buses had seats! And magic elephants! He had to imagine it was less efficient, but . . . you could start your day sitting high up, looking out over your beautiful city, in a bus pulled by a flower-bedecked tusker. Then, work done, tired, hungry, and ready for home, you could sit and watch everyone start wandering in and out of houses, bringing plates of food or bottles or music or just themselves and laughter and good company. Comforted by the knowledge that soon, you would have those things too.

He let the city push him around, drifting down the main thoroughfares and into the smaller side streets. He had the suspicion that the real action was in the alleys, but he was *not* about to leave his precious two-wheeler somewhere unguarded. Which was a funny thought. He stole a half-broken iron horse from a wretched little village in the Free State . . . and now it was genuinely precious to him. He conducted a quick personal inventory of Stuff He Actually Cared About:

His iron horse—unknown manufacturer and origin, probably made out of several different two-wheelers that someone kludged together into something that didn't actually work until Truth got his hands on it. The seat was also from some unknown fourth-hand iron horse, installed alongside the improved luggage rack by the wonderful garage owner at Kwa Kabwere Garage. It had carried him for more than two thousand kilometers on the road at this point. He had grown addicted to the feeling of traveling without barriers between him and the world. The agility of it, the speed of it, all called to him.

Could he make it faster? Must investigate! After giving the spirit another bath.

His sword—The Tongue of One Who Speaks for God . . . was a good sword. Not that he had handled many swords. Any swords, actually. This was his first sword. And he really, really liked it. More than its angelic origins or the Bane spell on it, he just liked how it felt in his hands. The slightly tacky wrapped cordage around the hilt meant that his grip would never slip. The cross guard didn't provide much hand protection, but it did provide *some,* and that would more than do. If his hand got cut, he could only call it a skill issue.

Truth had never worried about skill issues when handling a weapon. The Tongue danced in his hands, light and lively, almost leaping into a cut and seeming to lengthen in the lunge. The sword moved with him, accompanying him in battle rather than being simply used. He loved it for that.

His scarf— Did it have a name? Maybe? Truth cast Tool and pointed the System at it. The System, which was, maybe, possibly, likely, a mutilated part of his soul. Not going to think about that for the moment. *Any details on what the scarf is, exactly?*

<<Credit to Old Mek'elle, it wasn't being cheap. This is actually moderately good stuff. Probably as good as it could do, given you wanted to be gone from there ASAP. It doesn't have a name—maybe call it the Freedom of the Terraces? It's a more literal name than you might think.>>

All right, tell me about it.

<<So, the obvious thing it does is transform slightly. It modifies itself just enough to look like the colors and logo of the home team in your general area. It also acts as an all-access pass. I guess that's why all the stadiums came out and supported Old Mek'elle—you just got a free ticket to any pitz match at any stadium in Siphios, forever.>>

That's nice and all, but how many games do you think we are really going to attend?

<<You know this, I know this, Old Mek'elle does not know this. What do you want from the guy? Anyway, free access to the stadiums. Changes to make you look like a home fan. Interestingly, it has a small charm to make you less noticeable in a crowd. Literally just another home fan. It's subtle. Someone who knows you will eventually spot you, but you could blend in really well.

<<Other than that, it has small charms to help you stay warm and bigger charms to help you stay cool. It won't be easily lost and will come back to you eventually if you do lose it. It has a nice little air-filtration function, not gas mask–grade but good for dust and the like, as well as being extremely stain- and damage-resistant. Below Level One, anyway.>>

That . . . actually is pretty nice. Not life-changing, maybe, but nice.

<<Quite thoughtful of Old Mek'elle, I thought.>>

Iron horse, sword, scarf, hat? He still had the old zeph, though he wasn't really that attached to it. If he was being honest, he didn't love the look. Didn't dislike it either, but it was a bit . . . "Oh, boy. A brimless round hat. Now with a tassel. Gosh." On the other hand, it had become more than just a hat, hadn't it?

Wearing the zeph gave him a whole identity. Unwanted, often, but not always. There were clearly some very good things about the Desrin faith and people, things he quite agreed with. But he didn't choose that. Didn't choose them. He would have to think about that a bit more.

Anything else? Nothing leapt to mind. He navigated the two-wheeler into a little shopping neighborhood. Not a lot of smiling faces in the grocery store. None, in fact. The pickings on the outdoor shelves were very slim, too. Either they had sold out for the day, they had started taking stuff in for the night, or there was never much on there in the first place. The prices were in birr, which he still didn't have a very good handle on. And they were in the capital, so naturally, everything would be more expensive. Still, even given all that, he would bet those numbers were higher than they were a week ago. Some were even on chalkboards. Probably not a good sign.

There were kids out playing. Not really kids anymore, he supposed, teens. Messing around in a park, shooting sparklers at each other, blasting some music Truth didn't recognize but kind of liked. Making out in the grass. They didn't look worried. Maybe he just couldn't spot it at this distance. They seemed happy. Well fed, well taken care of.

Floating above them were little motes of warm light, guardian spirits watching over the park and the youth at play. A green wonderland lit by drifting stars. Truth suddenly wished Etenesh were there. He wanted to walk with her through the park at night.

There was a couple making out; the boy pressed his very willing girlfriend up against a tree and kissed her hard on the mouth. Looked like an awful lot of fun.

And he was allowed to have fun. He didn't have to work all the time. He wasn't being bad by giving himself some time. The last time he focused on work totally, he spent five or so years as a corpse in a well. He was allowed to rest. He was allowed a little fresh air.

Truth sighed and started working his way back to the temple. He wasn't sure what he was trying to see. A beautiful city with beautiful, content people, rapidly becoming less content. In danger.

Seemed like a big problem. Strange how the "heroes" weren't leaping out to save the day. Instead, it was down to the powerful, the rich, and the connected. Who weren't looking terribly powerful coming in and out of the conference room, were they? Alarming. What did it say when these "titans" didn't have the clout to save the day? They were starting to get a little chippy and defensive about that fact, too. Yes, this was not good at all. Something had to change. Something that affected the whole planet. The whole . . . system of the world? There must be a word for that.

Did he really want to fight Starbrite?

No. Nobody sane *wanted* to fight Starbrite. Did he believe that he *had* to fight Starbrite?

He wasn't coming up with better options.

At some point, he would have to gamble. He would need to find—or make—some way to check up on the sibs. And then figure out what he could do to rescue them, assuming they needed rescuing. Which . . . if things looked like this in Xandre, one way or the other, the sibs needed rescuing. And then what?

Say he got them out of Jeon. Came back here. They all found jobs doing whatever. He got a mechanic job somewhere fixing talismans, enough to keep a roof over his head and maybe get something nice for Etenesh now and then.

And in what? A couple of years tops? Society collapses, food riots, constant large-scale warfare, the entire planet craters, and the ambient reality falls to, if not nothing, a long way from what they had now. Which meant that things like water talismans stop working and millions die of thirst or poisoned water. Accelerating the rate of farms not making food and failing to get what food there is to the hungry people. The cycle would be vicious, and viciously fast. They would literally be making things with bits of sticks and scavenged goods five years from now.

Truth had the sudden overwhelming urge to buy sacks of rice and steel knives. If nothing else, they would be valuable trade goods. He mentally added the crappy, basically unused machete and lightly used spear onto his list of important possessions.

Okay. He would have to fight. And he couldn't fight alone. Not against Starbrite and the whole system of the world.

It was time to have that talk with Merkovah.

CHAPTER 48

AND THE ROCK CRIED OUT "NO HIDING PLACE!"

Truth pulled into the garage under Temple Nag Hamadi in a thoughtful mood. This was one of those *No taking it back* decisions. He hadn't read many spy novels. They just didn't take him away from himself the way the romance or thriller novels did. But this seemed like volunteering to be an asset, and assets were ultimately disposable. Some were more important than others, sure, but as someone who had been a "valued" corporate asset before . . .

Hard pass.

Still, just walking away left him without options. Was Merkovah really the only option? He wanted to talk to someone about this, but he didn't have anyone good to talk to about this. Etenesh or Jember? They were firmly of Merkovah's way of thinking, if not in his military camp. The same thing was likely true of the . . . priests? There at Nag Hamadi. He still didn't know what they were called, and now he was too embarrassed to ask. Truth couldn't imagine them contradicting the Level Seven, who had been a part of the temple for longer than they had been alive.

Even in Siphios, that couldn't be a wise career move. Or life choice generally. Besides, "Do you think I should work for an old monster in his suicidal campaign against the most powerful people and corporation in the world, an act that, even if successful, will harm thousands and possibly millions?" is not a great question to ask anyone, let alone a stranger. He had the faint, absurd notion of going and chatting with Old Mek'elle, but, again, maybe not the most useful source. He sighed and patted the extra real wall.

"I don't suppose I could talk to you, Nag Hamadi?"

"Sure, why not?"

Truth jumped so hard, he slammed into the ceiling.

"It's a good gig, being a temple. It gives you something to do. Underrated thing, having something to do. I don't know how long I existed before humans came because . . . who cares? Nothing happened. Oh, well, things *happened*, but none of it meant anything. Then humans turned up, and things started to have meanings. I've come full circle back to *nothing has meaning* again, but that's more of a reasoned opinion than just lazy instinct."

Temple Nag Hamadi didn't just exist or was willing to talk. It was *oppressively chatty*. Truth was sitting in his cell with a three-meter-tall statue of a man with curly hair and a long beard, carefully, if badly, painted in bright colors. Garishly painted. The bronze of the skin was almost brick-red, and the gold tracery on the robes looked brassy . . . like it was colored by children without access to good paint.

"So . . . do you hear everything that goes on in the temple?"

"Yep."

"*Everything?*"

"Yep. Even stuff that you don't realize is being said. Entire layers of meaning swirling through here, and I pick up on all of it." The statue nodded. "Most of it is really important to people, so I have to keep quiet about it. It's in the contract. Ultimately, though, it tends to be kind of meaningless. Like, buddy, everyone dies. Who cares if you got passed over for promotion, or murdered, or whatever."

The stone head shook slowly. "Sooner or later, we all return to the essence. Just, you know, don't be a pain in the ass in the meantime."

"Kind of a curious point of view for a temple."

"Oh, I am very devout. It's how I got the temple gig in the first place. My rock was, and is, very spiritual because I had been spending the whole . . . however long . . . in worship and contemplation of God. Hundreds of thousands of years? Something like that. Made complete sense."

"But you don't think there is a point to existence." Truth was struggling to hang on to the conversation. He had questions. Hadn't he?

"God made everything, right? God invested everything with meaning. And since God is all meanings, everything is God. And you and me, we are part of that. Stuck in the fabric of the whole thing. Which means that, to some infinitesimal degree, we are God, and all the things that play out in our lives are just the results of decisions we made when we were much, much bigger and smarter. Decisions made from an infinitely elevated height, smoothing out the fine detail of things like the present you and me. We—you, me, everyone, and everything in existence—made this incredible universe of ours, and everything that happened, is happening, or will happen, is part of that creation."

Truth was reeling from all this, but the statue seemed quite calm about it all.

"So, why do you say it's meaningless or pointless if we made all of reality? We must have done it for a reason, right?" Truth asked.

"Why?"

"Why what?"

"Why must we have done it for a reason?" The statue's expression didn't shift, but Truth got the impression it was grinning.

"Because it seems like a . . . kind of a big thing to do for no reason?"

"But we are *God*. We are everything, everywhere, forever. All thought, all matter, all reasons, everything. We are the essence before existence, the universal predicate. We have lost nothing of ourselves in creating the universe, nor could we lose something of ourselves. Every great crime, every act of charity and mercy, it's all us. It was always going to happen. It always did happen. It's always happening. Because we contain all time, too, as well as existing outside of time. We are every meaning, and therefore, when some tiny speck of our infinity tries to comprehend that impossible enormity, it can only reach one conclusion." Nag Hamadi invited him to finish the thought.

"It's all meaningless. There is no meaning to our choices. All outcomes are morally equal since all outcomes are God's will. All outcomes are God. You are either a very good temple or a really, *really* bad one."

"Fun fact: my binding forbids me from talking to believers in Siphian Orthodoxy, reform or otherwise. Outside of certain specific circumstances."

"So, if I was to ask you about Merkovah . . ."

"Sorry, buddy. One speck of the divine to another, I'd love to clue you in on all that, but . . . bindings."

"Haah. I was hoping for some, you know, advice on stuff."

"No problem! I can't talk about Merkovah, or your crush, or that guy you aren't crushing on, but if things were different, you could see yourself folding him in half. Though I'll be honest, I don't think you two would work out long-term. The girl seems much more your speed."

"What? No, nothing about them!"

"Really? Shame, they seem lovely. I enjoy a good gossip."

Truth grasped for a way back to his point. "I was more wanting to know about the state of the world and all that!"

"Oh? Huh. Can you narrow that down some? That's kind of everything, and while I have that kind of time, you don't."

"Are we moving further away from God in terms of reality, making this world less 'real' compared to the rest of the universe?"

"Yep. It's a bastard thing, let me tell you. It can take hundreds of thousands of years to get back in synch, and some places just never really recover right. All those cosmic rays you are so used to working with will just ignore your spiritual apertures and all the spells and talismans and . . . everything, really, that is meant to interact with it. They just won't be real enough."

"Going to be rough on the demons, spirits, and all that too, I imagine."

"Yeah, most or all of us are gonna die." Nag Hamadi sounded pretty unconcerned by this. "I'm going to hang in a bit longer than some on account of being pretty damn real, but it's gonna happen."

"Unless something changes."

"It would have to be pretty radical."

"Like, for example . . ."

"Just my opinion? Partial societal collapse is actually one of the better outcomes. Stop stripping out spiritually dense stuff to sell off-world and start importing it. Start building arrays to trap more ambient cosmic rays while you still can, and start working toward planetary self-sufficiency. Theoretically, it would be possible to add spiritual mass over time, but that's something only your great-great-grandkids would enjoy." Nag Hamadi didn't exactly shrug.

"But step one is to stop the bleeding. Stop off-world trade of spiritually dense stuff like natural treasures and the more . . . real . . . minerals," Truth concluded.

"And products made from that stuff, yeah. You would be amazed how much of that goes into even very ordinary talismans, stuff you wouldn't think twice about."

Truth just sat on the bed, locked up in his thoughts. There . . . wasn't going to be any easy way out, was there? No safe landing for the world. No safe place for the sibs or the kind people he had met traveling. For him, and Etenesh, and apparently Jember. There's an image he wouldn't be forgetting soon.

"So . . . theologically, how does your *everyone and everything is God* notion square with the existence of what many people are specifically calling God?" Truth asked before suddenly remembering Merkovah telling him the spirits were inconsistent on this.

"Simple! He's God too. Just a different part of 'God-God.' Maybe the tool man? Call him what you like."

"But if everything is fated—"

"Already happened, not fated. It just hasn't happened to us yet, from our perspective. God is outside of time, remember."

"Okay, yeah, that, then why try to do anything about anything? Why worry about God-the-tool-man looking away?"

"Because the illusion of free will is inescapable. On some level, we all desperately want to believe our decisions matter. Therefore, to reduce anxiety and unhappiness, you should act like they do matter. That things really are urgent, that this moment has a unique meaning, all that. Eat the sweet fruit. Glory in God. Take solace in the knowledge that, ultimately, no matter what happens, you will return to yourself one day—one day, you will be God again. Whole and at peace beyond human understanding."

Truth mulled it over. Then shrugged. The nature of existence was just too big for him to handle. This would just be another opinion. He'd think it over more later. Right now, there was one person in particular he wanted to talk to.

"If I asked for directions to Etenesh . . ."

"I'd tell you that I can't give out personal information on believers to you, sorry."

"Or if I coincidentally were just off for a walk and looking for a suggested route . . ."

"I'd tell you that the people who made my contract weren't that dumb."

Truth sighed.

"Well. I'm going for a walk."

"Good luck with it all."

Truth started walking, padding through the quiet halls of Nag Hamadi the heretical temple, sword at his side, scarf around his neck. He didn't really know why he wanted to see Etenesh. He just did. So, he went.

As far as he was aware, no date had been fixed for the duel. Still, if he was about to fight some young noble demon binder, he'd be training his ass off. He walked down to the practice room in the basement, only to find it empty. It wasn't that late, was it? Could she already be in bed?

He drifted, bouncing off walls and corners, around the temple. The inscriptions on the wall remained mysterious, and he was coming to prefer them that way. Nag Hamadi could no doubt explain them if he decided he really wanted to know.

Truth eventually found Etenesh in a small chapel. She was kneeling in front of a little statute of a bird, with a curved screen behind it. On the screen were pictures of the same person, going through various transformations. Old, young, slender, curvaceous, cruel, merciful . . . all contradictions were there, and all within the same person. Who was also the bird, he supposed.

Etenesh had her arms crossed over her slim chest, hands gripping her shoulders. She gently rocked back and forth, murmuring some prayer that, even with his improved hearing, Truth couldn't quite catch. No matter. It wasn't meant for him. He waited behind her. There was no rush.

"Come to see me, Tommy?" He could hear the smile in her voice, though she still faced the statute.

"Yes. It's chilly out there. I thought I would warm up around you."

"I'd like that too, but I really do need to finish my prayers. My initiation is going to finish with my duel, so it's all a big rush now."

Truth nodded at that.

"Is this related to your eyes turning orange sometimes?"

"Yes. Does it look very ugly?"

"Beautiful, actually."

"Good. It's supposed to be beautiful, but you're not from around here, and I was worried you might not like it."

Truth smiled a little at that. "Well. I won't distract you. Actually, I'm going to give you a little gift. A lot of my secrets are about to become not secret, or at least not as secret. And for no sensible reason, I wanted you to be the first to hear one of them. No, don't get up. Stay just as you are." This time, it was Etenesh who could hear the smile in his voice.

He walked over and crouched down just behind her. He leaned in, his lips almost touching her ears.

"Hello. My name is Truth Medici. I am good at talisman maintenance and violence, but I am learning that's not all I am. I enjoy reading novels, trying new foods, and seeing new places. I can make friends. I root for Toluca when I watch pitz. And the girl I like is Etenesh."

CHAPTER 49

RUN, SINNERMAN

Teasing the girl you like is fun. Truth was feeling giddy as he quickly walked away from the little chapel. Teasing the girl you like is fun, watching her wriggle and not move as you whisper secrets and affection in her ear. It was scary, too. Opening up. Speaking a name he had left unspoken since his murder. There was something about the saying of it, setting the words free on the wind. As though they would be carried directly to his killers.

It was scary because it meant that Truth Medici hadn't died or at least hadn't stayed dead. He'd been hidden in a well for five years and in "Tommy Wells" for the last . . . How long had it been? A month? A couple of months? Not that long. Felt a lot longer. The days were just so full. Everything was new to Tommy Wells. The world was just so big, and he was so free in it. A wild, disorienting freedom, where he found strange new thoughts and a growing sense of who he was. A world beyond the tip of his nose and the brush of his whiskers.

Squeak-squeak, little rat. You are learning to look up.

He walked quickly to Merkovah's room. It was as spare as always. Merkovah was waiting, smiling. He touched a talisman, and dense thickets of anti-surveillance wards sprang to life.

"I wish to emphasize that Nag Hamadi's views on the nature of God and the universe do not represent those of the *Temple* of Nag Hamadi, nor that of Siphios Reform Orthodoxy in general. You should in no way rely on it for any future theological choices you may make."

"Understood."

"Other things, however, you may rely on it for. I am . . . honestly surprised you figured out what was happening to the world. I had a whole thing ready to show you, to persuade you it was really happening."

"I've had an unusual view of things, between working for Starbrite and traveling around since my termination."

"Which I must say I have wondered about. While I have met a rare few who were fired from Starbrite and lived, I have never met someone who left the company after receiving the System. Frankly, even after extensive experimentation, I thought it was impossible."

Truth could vividly imagine what that "experimentation" looked like.

"I didn't."

"Pardon?"

"I didn't live."

"You seem remarkably fit for a dead man."

"I eat clean."

"I do think you would make a fine Desrin, once you developed the faintest shred of faith in God."

"Not Siphios?"

"It is, unfortunately, quite difficult to convert. Not impossible, mind you. And while I would be delighted if you did, you would have a religious obligation to live in Siphios and swear allegiance to the king."

"Wouldn't mind living in Siphios. Probably going to pass on the rest."

"I thought as much."

The conversation lulled. It seemed neither really knew how to initiate what they both knew was coming next. Eventually, Merkovah made a face like he was trying to chuckle and failing.

"Mr. Wells, would you say that I have been sincere with you?"

"Largely. You have only told me one outright lie that I recall, and generally, your manipulations have been tolerable. All in all, working with you has been very positive."

Merkovah gave him half a smile for that one.

"You continue to have the oddest way of seeing things."

"Paying someone is manipulating them. Taking them on a vision journey is another sort of manipulation. A holy sword, a wise, benevolent teacher, powerful magic; I suspect you would have gotten me a horse if I didn't already have my two-wheeler." Truth half-smiled right back. "I was wrong. You don't want a hitter. You want your own kind of hero."

Merkovah did chuckle at that. "It seems that I succeeded, at least in part."

"Nah."

"Oh, no?"

"Nope. You made a terrorist. So. Let's talk about what we're going to blow up."

Merkovah almost fell out of his chair.

"Young man!"

"Tommy Wells, talisman maintenance. A pleasure to make your acquaintance."

"You damn well aren't!"

"I wanted to be one. I could have been a good one."

"That I can believe. We are not terrorists, Mr. Wells. Actually, what *is* your name?"

"Truth Medici, professional terrorist. A pleasure to make your acquaintance."

"Truth? Truth. Of course you are called Truth. Why would you be called any-thing else? Truth, we are not, *not* terrorists!"

"We are planning on using violence and fear to kill thousands, if not millions, in the hope of bringing about political and economic change. I mean, what else could you call it?"

"If the world does not change, right damn now, *billions* will die! Billions! We will be lucky to have any humans on this planet at all in twenty years. We aren't terrorists, Mr. Wells. Truth." Merkovah stopped with a jerk and glared at Truth.

"I was not the only one manipulating, it seems. Habit is a powerful thing. Mr. Medici, if we don't save the world, everyone dies. Slow or fast. So, yes, some people's lives will become a great deal worse after we strike. Many will, inevitably, die. However, the overwhelming majority will be saved. We truly are heroes, Mr. Medici, however much you may not like the term."

"Sure. And how many fucks about the greater good do you think those necessary sacrifices will give? Look, you don't have to sell me on the rightness of your cause—I'm already there with you. The question is: what do you need to know from me, and what can you tell me about you?"

Merkovah was left grasping for a moment. "I have never once sympathized with a Starbrite employee. I suddenly feel great empathy for your former supervisors."

"My performance reviews were all outstanding." Truth shrugged. "Although, in retrospect, I did get a lot of odd looks."

"This, I can also believe." Merkovah breathed out explosively through his nose. "Hokay. Listen, I've actually been pretty upfront with you about everything. Almost all the global exports are controlled by Starbrite, and they take a cut of almost all the imports. They can do this because they have the muscle, economic and military, to make it work. Both their economy and military are built around the System. Smash that, the whole thing collapses."

"Okay . . . and if it doesn't?"

"Pardon?"

"If you destroy the system, and the workers and soldiers say, *Actually, we are still loyal to Starbrite and intend to fight you to the death*, then what?"

"Then they will briefly have a very unhappy time. No spells without the System, remember?"

"Hard to forget." Not a word of lie, either. As amazing as Incisive was, and it was amazing, there was something about the ease of swapping between spells that he would never forget. Something about always having the perfect answer.

"C-Tier? At your age? Impressive."

"You know perfectly well I was in the PMC."

"True. Force of habit."

This led to another extended pause.

"You want to talk about it?"

"What, working for the PMC?"

"Yes. Truthfully . . . Huh, I can see that getting irritating fast."

"Yep. I have heard each and every possible joke on the subject."

"Understandable. All right, I would *genuinely* like to know about life inside Starbrite, because while I know a very great deal about it, I have never been able to talk to a living member of, as you call it, the PMC. I expect I will have a lot of questions about your past. This may also prompt you to ask questions of me. I will do my best to answer them, but there are some questions I cannot answer." The beardy exorcist shrugged one shoulder. "Wouldn't be a very good freedom fighter if I went around shouting my secrets."

Truth shrugged and started talking. Then stopped immediately and looked directly at Merkovah. "How old are you, Teacher?"

Merkovah also started to answer, stopped, then started again. "A lot older than fifty."

"How much older?"

"Six hundred and a bit. I'd have to do the math to figure it out exactly. It's a particular kind of body cultivation, tied to a particular and not . . . excessively repeatable . . . magical practice that is responsible for my longevity. Off world, such life-extending magics are fairly common. On this world, not so much."

"Huh. Something I can do with the Meditations?"

"At a high-enough level, you should theoretically stop aging, yes. Before you ask—because it's quite a high level, and people on this planet don't generally do body cultivation. Not worth the return on effort."

"Nifty. So, anyway, this is the short version." Truth gave a quick summary of his working career and was then forced to go back over it again and again. It got really old, real fast.

"You can use any weapon almost instantly?"

"Well, with a few minutes to get used to them. They only work in a few different ways, after all."

"No, they do not. At all. Wait, had you *ever* used a sword before I handed you the Tongue?"

"She's my very first."

"Young man, swords are always masculine! Masculine!"

"Sure."

"Wait, what about vehicles? Machinery generally?"

"Not at the same level, no. I pick them up at about the same rate as everyone else, I think."

"All right, hand-to-hand combat?"

"Yep."

"Squad tactics?"

"Nope. I mean, I know how. I was trained on it, but not . . . supernaturally good at it or anything."

"Grand strategy?"

"I'm not a hundred percent sure I know what that is."

"Mmm . . . any solutions for the present crisis leap to mind?"

"No. That's why I'm talking to you."

"Ah. Fair enough."

And so on and so on. Merkovah was very interested in what happened at Kofi, and they went over it a few times.

"It was never clear to anyone why or how that spiritual attack occurred. The Godchild Army denied all responsibility, but then, they would. I of course suspected Starbrite, but I haven't found much to substantiate that theory. This is the first direct evidence I have that someone, someone quite senior, at Starbrite knew the attack was coming."

"How do you figure?"

"Your squad were told to form the most powerful spell you could, given your level, that would provide little to no protection against physical attacks but superlative protection against spiritual attacks. Seconds later, the attack struck. How do you *not* make that connection?"

Truth had to concede there. Later—

"Do not tell anyone you were part of the attack on Fort Leucre. No one. In fact, to the extent possible, let that knowledge die with you."

"Happy to. Any particular reason?"

"Other than the massacre of dozens of civilians? Does their need to be more?"

"I suppose not." He couldn't imagine Etenesh smiling after learning that about him.

"Let's press on. Who, exactly, did you guard on your bodyguard details? Every name will help."

A bit later— "You're joking."

"No, I really was dead for five-ish years."

"That I can almost believe. No, I mean, you're joking when you say it's not important how you 'got better.'"

"I wouldn't be a very good terrorist if I went around shouting my secrets. Although it's not really repeatable. At least, I don't think so."

"Haaah. Okay. Just. . . going to table that for a minute. You say the System ejected from you or tried to. Please describe the process in as much detail as possible."

Truth did, without mentioning the whole "mutilated soul" angle.

"Tearing out part of your soul? Are you certain about that?"

"Pretty certain. The System was definitely trying to leave with a chunk of me."

Merkovah grinned, then started laughing. He tilted his head back and laughed like his sides would split. Truth saw tears running down the side of his face. After a minute, the old monster gathered himself and muttered something. It sounded like *Thank you* and a name.

"At last. At last. Centuries. It has taken centuries. Heroes beyond counting have died. But at last. At our darkest hour. The enemy gives us the weapon of our deliverance." Merkovah wiped away his tears and looked sharply at Truth.

"Mr. Medici, I intend to train you to a competent level with Incisive—that is, the foresight, the cutting, the armor, and maybe just a smidge of the rhetoric. I then intend to use a few natural treasures, *national* treasures, here in Siphios to force your growth to Level Four. The faster you can cultivate, the easier and more successful that process will be. I will then instruct you on the Sword of Moshe. By the time you have a preliminary grasp of that, you will be highly resistant to passive, lower-level magics, possessed of some resistance to midlevel magics, and between the Meditations, Incisive, and the Sword, you will be almost impossible to scry on passively. Active attempts to magically find you will also massively struggle.

"I promised you these things before, but let me explain exactly what I want you to do. I want you to cut off the System from the magic that feeds it. And then we really hurt them. Tell me, young man. Do you know much about necromancy?"

CHAPTER 50

RAKING THE SANDS

Necromancy? I don't really know much about it. Combat-capable necromancers are a pain in the ass; I can tell you that. And I know that they run most funeral parlors."

"Short version . . . very possibly too-short version . . . is that necromancy is one of the foundational areas of magical technology. No reason you would know this, but we can trace the origins of a lot of our demon summoning and binding magics straight back to necromancy. Indeed, separating the two, summoning the dead and summoning demons, is a comparatively new gloss in the history of magic. It was all just 'necromancy.' At least before we settled on this planet."

"Okay?"

"The System Astrologica tried to tear out a bit of your soul. Which means it wanted it for something. It's a spirit, which we categorize differently from the spirits of the dead and demons, but a lot of the same magical technology applies to all of them. The System likely empowers itself with the souls of its victims. And I can exploit that." Merkovah grinned. "Oh? How?"

"That's going to be a me problem for now. But let's just say, I suddenly have an extraordinary number of angry dead to work with. And I certainly will do just that."

Merkovah had clearly gone to a mental happy place. Truth didn't want to disturb him, and let him enjoy the moment. After a couple of minutes, Merkovah shook himself out of it and started to shoo Truth out of his room, then paused and pointed Truth back toward his seat.

"Truth, in the spirit of . . . sincerity and candor, there is one point you haven't raised yet but that will occur to you eventually. And since I am far, far too old to put up with jejune drama that could have been solved if people just *talked* to one another, we are going to talk about it now." Merkovah fixed Truth with a direct look.

"I supplied magic, mentorship, a fine sword, opportunities to excel . . . and companions."

That brought Truth up with a jolt.

"I receive in excess of a hundred applications a year from young scholars seeking to join my retinue. My criteria for selection are generally based on my academic interests at the time. Etenesh and Jember were the first two I can remember recruiting on the basis of being single, attractive, and having high emotional intelligence."

He tapped his desk for emphasis. "They are under no geas and have received no instructions from me on how they are to behave with you. I simply assumed that if I threw the three of you together and set you to work, bonds would form. They are intensely social people, after all."

Merkovah smiled.

"I'm pleased, but not surprised, to see that I was right."

Truth was suddenly having trouble breathing. His vision narrowed on to the old monster's young face. "So, Etenesh—"

"This is why I wanted to tell you directly, Mr. Medici. She is under *no* compulsion. She has *not* been instructed to seduce you. She hasn't even been nudged by me into making *friends* with you. I made sure you had fun coworkers, Mr. Medici, not people playing that role."

Truth's paranoia was flaring hard, so hard that he found it difficult to hear Merkovah.

"Breathe, Mr. Medici! Breathe! She isn't toying with you, and neither am I. Tolerable manipulations, remember? I was, and am, and will continue to create an environment you want to stay in."

Which made sense, but he knew damn well if Starbrite had been running this op, those two would have been special-made jobs from the *Lovers* tab in the System Store. Brainwiped, body-sculpted, enchanted, and tuned to his particular desires. Or succubae, if Merkovah was on a budget.

"Before you fall any deeper into your well of paranoia, I want you to remember the erotic-binding spells. The . . . rape magic, as you so charmingly put it."

Truth looked at Merkovah like he was an asshole. Not really easing the paranoia there.

"Truth, we are an ancient country of demon binders. Do you think we don't worry about consent *a lot*? Enchantments, glamours, beguiling demons, and spirits of all forms? We do. Marriage is a transformational sacrament. It must be entered into freely and joyfully by people who firmly know their own needs and desires. Free of all other romantic burdens, committed totally to their new family."

"Not sure where you are going with this."

"Ask your spirit of intellect. All those spells? They sever *any mind-controlling magic* that might already be in effect. Etenesh has spent her entire life expecting to one day be bound under such a spell and dreaming of what conditions she would require of her husband. She has had long, detailed conversations with family, with her religious instructors, and with friends. And she has a lot of those, as she is a very social person from a particularly ancient and respected family here in Siphios. If she was enchanted, you might not know, but dozens of others would."

Merkovah grinned. "She just likes you for you, I'm afraid. It probably helps that you look like a god, fight like a hero, and are clearly interested but not pushy. Your prior girlfriends trained you well."

Truth was utterly bewildered at this point, so all he could manage was a vague "Yes."

There was a pause.

"I'm sorry; I made an assumption. Boyfriends?"

"What? No. No boyfriend."

"So, it was a girlfriend."

"Sure."

Another pause.

"No. *No. THAT* I refuse to believe!"

"Tell no one!"

"Who could I tell? Who in the world would believe me?"

"The face is new, okay?"

"The face may be new, but a career soldier, in the prime of his physique, rich by the standards of most in Jeon, *still* couldn't get a date? No. Just no. Hell, Starbrite would have manufactured you a lover if you asked."

"I . . . did consider that, actually. Spent the credits on elixirs instead."

"I suppose your loss in one department is my gain in another." Merkovah looked like the walls of reality were collapsing. "Do you have the remotest idea of how physically attractive you are? I mean, not everyone's cup of tea, but . . . You know what? Don't answer that. I'm going to go pray for Etenesh now. She is going to die of happiness and frustration at the same time. I take back what I said about jejune drama, too. I'm bringing snacks for this one. I'm ordering a whole appetizer platter with six custom dips and a fruit selection. Go. Scram. Out of my cell."

He scrammed. Truth was down the hallway and around the corner before he thought to ask, pointedly, about Merkovah's alleged but unseen wife. Or remembered that he didn't mention the Shattervoid.

That night, after he had finished cultivating and just as he was getting stuck in to his pre-bed bodice-ripper, there was a furtive knock at the door. It was Etenesh.

"Mr . . . Medici." She liltingly put the emphasis on *ci*, making it pop, caressing it in her mouth before her lips kissed it toward him. "I want you to know that as part of my ritual purification before the duel, I cannot kiss you. But I want to. And I want you to know that. So, Mr. Medi*ci*—she smiled broadly, her eyes a storm of autumn leaves—"I am here telling you."

She breathed deeply, seeming to savor the taste of the air, the taste of him. "I am telling you that I want you to pin me against the wall and kiss me. Press yourself against me. Hold me tight as we kiss again and again. Tasting your mouth, feeling your warmth on me, the strength in your hands and arms. I want that very much. But not before the duel. Good night, Mr. Medi*ci*."

It seemed that being teased by the girl you like wasn't too bad a thing, either. If suddenly, pressingly, frustrating.

The terms of the deal between Truth and Merkovah was simple in construction, if complicated in the details. Merkovah had promised to look into the situation with the sibs but warned it would be some time coming. He was also quite happy to meet Truth's fee for the job, plus the completion bonus.

"Transporting you and your sibs out of Jeon, a place somewhere quiet in Siphios, and some walking-around money? Arranging quality, safe jobs and housing for your siblings? Done."

Truth had taken pains to ensure that any provided equipment, spells, national-treasure-tier elixirs, transportation, et cetera, all fell under the category of operational expenses to be supplied by Merkovah and were considered separately from his fee. As was the bodyguard work. That, too, was carefully carved out. One fee per job.

It suited him well enough, and he thought it would suit the sibs fine, too. And if not, oh, well. The world was coming crashing down. They had been unhappy before and lived.

The next few days were spent in the temple. The conference had temporarily broken up to resume later as a series of staff-level working groups who would present reports and possible solutions on various topics in a month. Truth thought this was absurdly slow but was swiftly corrected by the cousins. By the standards of high-level bureaucracy, this was fast to the point of recklessness. It was easy to criticize the slow speed, but he had to consider the alternative—what happened when they got it wrong?

That seemed a good point to him. No more time for second chances.

The rest of the time was spent fighting. Truth would split his time between duel-ing the cousins and either fighting hordes of Level Three demons or struggling against a single Level Four. It was extremely satisfying. Time on tools, someone had once told him. Most people needed time on tools to get good with them. He was getting his time on Incisive.

It was fascinating. The spell required you to be both tense and loose, ready but relaxed. The key issue was managing burnout. Truth was driving both the foresight and cutting aspects of Incisive while powering the enchantments on his sword and funneling all the strength he could into his body. All while fighting demons. The trick to it was keeping that light balance. Just barely keeping the spell active while pushing his body and combat skills to fill any gaps that occurred. The true test came when he fought over his level.

Truth, in theory, should physically dominate a Level Four demon. They were roughly equal in strength and speed, while Truth had vastly superior reflexes and control over his body. It wasn't that simple.

The demon in front of him now had a suite of offensive spells, a spray of hooking limbs extending from most of its body, and the ability to cause insane rage in anyone who held contact for more than a second or two with one of its ninety-nine eyes. Each eye fired thin lances of boiling black tar. He would have to keep an eye out for that—the tar was also poisoned and cursed.

Pretty standard Level Four demon.

Truth still lacked ranged spells, so he rushed to close as fast as he could. The spit-ting tar hissed past him as he dodged it by a hair's breadth. He had to push his body to *move*, to try and keep pace with his reflexes. He knew his bones and tendons were tough enough to take the strain. And now the claws were whipping down toward his head. And up toward his guts. And from every side.

Truth felt the attacks coming a tiny fraction of a second before the demon made them. He forced that gap—using that explosive speed and terrifying reflexes to lunge left, swinging the Tongue around in a silver blurring arc and slicing off a half dozen claws. Another whisper, and he leaned back suddenly, avoiding another jet of boiling corruption. Then with boneless grace, he flicked his body into a lunge and used Incisive to stab deep into the wretched thing.

And then the Bane spell went to work, and things got much more straightforward.

After the battle, he could wipe away the little splatters of tar that had managed to drop on him. An ordinary cloth did just fine. There wasn't enough of the curse or the poison to make it through his skin or the resistance. It might have been a different story if the demon got in a clean hit. But it didn't.

It was, slowly, all coming together. He could feel his body strengthening, toughening. Incisive was starting to be as nimble in his hands as his sword. Soon, he would learn how to cast the armor. Very soon.

When he sparred with Etenesh, when he smashed through a barrier or danced between the drops of steel rain cast by her formations, she wasn't furious or scared. She looked proud of him. Her eyes rarely left him, now that he was watching for it. She looked . . . hungry.

She looked a lot less hungry at the end of their sessions. Truth wanted more of whatever she was offering, and that meant pushing her hard. He had no intention of letting Alemu have a fair fight. He might not be able to transform Etenesh into a killing machine, but she certainly wouldn't fear some fop across the dueling sands.

The seconds had been called. (Jember couldn't do it, as he also had a claim against Alemu and might have challenged him first if Etenesh hadn't moved so fast.) Etenesh was represented by one of her apparently numerous uncles, a stony-faced man with a long, stiff beard and lightning streaks of white through dense black hair.

In Truth's private opinion, he seemed like the sort who would summon a demon, kick its teeth in, *then* tell it what he wanted. And yet, even this craggy fellow had to grin when Etenesh ran up and hugged him.

They spoke for quite a while—more than an hour. Truth was summoned, looked over, and questioned. However rough his exterior, Etenesh's uncle had a voice that was soft and rich. Duty done, the uncle left to fix the appointment.

There was no basis for reconciliation, nor did the parties wish to be reconciled. The seconds arranged the dueling ground, and a doctor was prepared for the victor. The loser would have no need.

CHAPTER 51

HOLY DAUGHTERS GROW UP

They were sparring back and forth across the basement floor. Etenesh wouldn't be able to use her spirit in the duel, so she was making heavy use of talismans.

Her weapon of choice was a long flail of copper reeds that she could flick through the air in astonishingly precise arcs and lines. Thin cuts of wind or light followed those occult traceries. Charging at her was like charging into a razor-blade hurricane. It only took a single swing of her flail to launch that mess of violence directly at her opponent. Unfortunately, that opponent was Truth.

Truth never stopped moving as he pressed in toward Etenesh. Always dodging, feinting, pulling her attention high and low. Always pressing. Etenesh swirled her flail, and the maelstrom thinned and widened, looking to catch Truth before he could escape.

Rather than dodge again, he lunged forward, smashing through the weakened spell. It cost him a little blood, but he was in range now. The Tongue of One Who Speaks for God leapt for Etenesh's neck—and stopped.

"Tag."

"Damn!" she swore. Her eyes almost glowed with the deep ocher of her sclera. The same color, he thought, of the earth in so much of Siphios. It almost never left her eyes these days. She dropped the spell and stormed away. Then turned and lunged for Truth, talisman forgotten as her fingers stretched toward his face. He darted back and raised his hand.

"Etenesh!"

"DAMN!" she swore again, and stomped over to the edge of the room. This time, she rested her head and the cool sandstone walls of Nag Hamadi, taking deep breaths.

"Etenesh?" She didn't reply, her slim shoulders rising and falling with each deep breath.

He waited. There was an odd scent in the air. Not . . . bad, exactly. Sweet, a little funky, a little herbal. Faint, but it managed to worm its way up his nostrils, and he felt it scrabbling around inside him. This was a smell that wanted to party.

Truth was currently the rainy concrete loading bay attached to a municipal sewage plant of party venues. Etenesh had all his attention.

"It's the purification period before the initiation." Her voice was muffled against the wall.

"I'm flattered, but I'm pretty sure I'm not that good a kisser."

"Don't sell yourself short. And it's not that. It's *literally* the purification period, the process itself." The sweet, funky smell intensified. "I'm temporarily taking on more aspects of the divine personage."

"Can't talk about it?"

"Only in the vaguest terms. The loss of control was expected. I thought I would manage it better. Probably why it's part of the ritual."

"Is there something I should be doing to help?"

She made a sort of whining, growling noise. It was cute, sort of, but it scared him, too. Etenesh didn't make noises like that. That wasn't her. His hackles started rising, and he subtly shifted his weight, ready to bolt for the door. He didn't want to hurt her, should something happen.

"Divine intoxication."

"Pardon?"

"It's one of her aspects—divine intoxication. I am high on God. And I need to hold it together until I am initiated." She made the little whining, growling noise again.

"Normally, this would mean getting drunk and dancing a lot to let the feelings out. But *someone* doesn't drink, and I will do something unwise if I start dancing. So here I am. Dealing."

Truth opened his mouth to defend himself, saying that he didn't mind if other people drank—then shut it with a snap. He would mind. He would very, very, very much mind. He would not be at all okay with watching Etenesh get drunk and handsy with him. The thought was giving him hives, making him sick to his stomach.

High emotional intelligence. That's what Merkovah said about Etenesh and Jember, selected for their high EQ, marital status, and good looks. And Etenesh was looking very, very good. His eyes narrowed slightly. Very good. And a little different.

Were her shoulders getting . . . slightly wider? No, they had just rolled back as she stood a little straighter. Her hips did widen slightly, though her waist was unchanged. Her hair, already lovingly cared for, was glossier, even more alluring. Her skin almost begged to be stroked, promising to be the softest, most pleasing you had ever touched.

Truth ran Incisive hard, but there was no threat there, and he wasn't under attack. Etenesh was taking on aspects of God . . . and wore them well.

"The orange eyes?"

"The first of the signs, shows you are ready for the purification and initiation. I can't go through everything, but if you are seeing changes, then yes, it's that. How much of the change sticks is between me and God. Mostly God."

"Well, from the back, you are looking really great."

"Not helping, pretty man!"

Truth decided that he was urgently needed somewhere else. As he left, he murmured, "Nag Hamadi, would it violate your bindings to keep an eye on Etenesh?"

One of the inscriptions turned and faced him. "Not at all. Terms and conditions apply, but . . . she'll be fine."

"Thank you."

"Not at all. I love having something to do."

Truth quickly made his way to Jember. Etenesh had only managed a few long scratches on him, but they were bleeding steadily, and he was starting to drip. Jember might not be a doctor, but he could patch that much.

"You would be amazed how much physical damage you pick up on spiritual-vision experiences. The leading theory is that because your soul and body line up so neatly, when your soul is damaged, your body believes it's damaged and reacts accordingly. Which is a clever idea, but it doesn't explain how Wise Rekfund got a crushed tibia. No way your body *crushes* a bone. No muscles for it."

"So, what's your best guess?"

"Magic."

Truth waited. And waited.

"No, really, just magic. I think that there is an occult connection there that natural philosophy has yet to really investigate, let alone understand. Keep in mind that there are well-documented examples of people setting off on a spiritual journey but then physically descending into the Garden or one of the Treasuries. Remember what I said about bursting into ash or going insane?"

"Or thinking I was a hyper angel who was functionally a mini-god, yes. Vividly."

"Same deal—started spiritual, ended physical. All right, you are patched up. Looking fit and tasty as ever."

"I'd thank you for the compliment, but it seems to be tough on Etenesh right now."

Jember looked confused for a moment, then enlightened. "Right. Sorry, different cults, different initiations. Some period of ritual abstinence is pretty standard every-where, though. Yeah, getting all hot and sweaty in a room together. Young, beautiful, in the prime of your lives as the divine intoxication fills your senses. Your burning eyes meet, heaving chest to heaving breast . . ." Jember trailed off, looking far into the corner.

Truth coughed loudly. Jember snapped back to attention.

"Been a minute?"

"Candidly, I am going to wreck the first person I have sex with once the ritual is completed. I mean just shatter them. Leave them hollow, emaciated. A husk, worn to almost nothing. They will try to slither out of the room, but there will be no escape. None. I may have to organize a rotating team of experts for the first seventy-two hours, just as a public safety precaution. Hard cases. People with hot bodies and cold resolve, determined to do whatever is necessary, for as long as necessary."

"Let's take you for a walk. Maybe get you some fresh air. Touch some grass."

"Thank you. Yes. That would be lovely." Jember sighed.

Truth decided to wear the zeph today. It was easy to slip away into that person-ality. He let himself fall back into the bodyguard persona.

The look was half the job—you had to be *seen* to be a bodyguard. Your existence was both a practical necessity but also a statement. Someone with a bodyguard was a person who both needed protection and could afford it. They were a person who didn't have to make their own violence; they could contract it out.

A bodyguard didn't stop force with force. Their presence stopped the idea of violence from going anywhere. At least not anywhere near their client.

Jember coughed, looking uncomfortable. "Tommy, sorry, but could you . . . maybe relax just a notch? Possibly even two notches?"

"Sorry?"

"I think people are about to pee themselves. You look like you are about to clear the street, and given the state of the city, I'd bet someone is about to call the cops. Or has already."

Truth consciously let go of the bodyguard persona. Jember was right; people were visibly more relaxed.

"State of the city? Damn. Still on the edge of riots, huh." They walked toward a little shopping street Jember knew. Not really looking for anything, just to have a destination.

"Yes, and particularly in regards to the Desrin population. A minority here in Siphios, but of course, there are vastly more of them outside of Siphios than there are Siphians generally. There is a two-way tension there. Also, word has got around about what happened in the Well. It was very public, obviously, but it's also being spread around intentionally."

Truth didn't know how to respond to that.

"On the one hand, it was an obvious setup. If it wasn't you, it would be some other Desrin. Just so happens that it came right after what went down at Old Mek'elle, where you arguably had a Desrin almost start a full-blown civil war in Xandre, and another Desrin comes out looking like a storybook . . ."

"Hero. Yeah."

"So, a lot of people are seeing a lot of ways of spinning all this, each with some scheme to take advantage of things. It's a mess of messes."

"Delightful."

Truth had long since accepted that he was paranoid and that not *literally* everybody was out to get him. This acceptance was purely intellectual—he continued to feel eyes on him, feel hate brushing past him, and could practically smell the oiled blades and ionizing magic getting ready to work. Today, walking around, it was worryingly real. Nobody was openly glaring at him now, but there were sure a lot of covert peeks when they thought he wasn't looking.

"Of course, one group doing the spinning is the Desrin themselves. We have a couple of 'heroes' and some obvious victims. The stories practically write themselves. And given that Siphios has a state religion, and the Desrin are literally second-class citizens, well. You can understand how a lot of built-up resentment is starting to come out."

Eating humiliation year after year, generation after generation? Oh, yes. He could understand it very well. He wasn't sure Jember did, though.

"Rumors are going around. Weapons being stockpiled. Antidemonic and antispiritual Banes, completely illegal here in Siphios without state approval, coming in from the south and west. The borders are beyond feeble, mostly because we don't care about people coming in . . . until our spirits started acting off, and now everyone's on edge."

"Sorry, spirits acting off at the border?"

"Yeah, basically, our border is pretty loose. We just have spirits supervising the boundaries of the land—bring in contraband or start getting up to no good, you get kicked out or go to a penal colony fast. Every now and then, we have big waves of refugees or something, but it's a big country. Lots of room, and we have gotten good at assimilation. Well. These days, we are." Jember just shook his head.

"Word is they're going to start stationing human troops at bases along the border. And most of our neighbors have Desrin-majority populations. You can see how things might be a *little* tense."

Truth thought that through for a bit. Jember was a dedicated runner, so their pace was quick. Xandre teased its wonders and mysteries with every new step, and yet everyone seemed to be in a rush to go somewhere else.

"I thought you couldn't convert into Siphios-the-religion."

Jember looked awkward. "Merkovah tell you that? He's right, sort of. You can't easily convert into Orthodox Reform Siphios. There was a . . . kind-of-sort-of religious schism about eight hundred years ago. Basically, we were force-converting anyone who emigrated, and practicing other faiths was very harshly punished." Jember shook his head.

"The Temple split into Orthodox Reform, where conversion is very hard, and Progressive, where conversion is very easy. There were a lot of other theological disputes that got loaded into that too, but for your question, that's the key difference."

"Is there *anybody* looking to preserve the current state of things in Siphios?" Truth wondered aloud.

"Oh, sure. Them." Jember waved idly to the shopkeepers and people they passed on the street. "They talk a good game, but mostly they just want tomorrow to be like today, with the chance of being a little better. The thing is, though, they'll want that whoever winds up in charge. They will sigh and say, 'We just have to make the best of things,' and try not to rock the boat." Jember's expression changed from cynical to bitter.

"All the old rules are collapsing, and the ones that haven't yet have yet to be tested. Or are backed up by naked force. I'm not as despairing as Etenesh was—good job on that, by the way—but I'm not hopeful."

Truth looked around at the quick-moving shoppers. Jember had led them off the main roads and into the pedestrian-only alleys. Truth had been right—this is where the real action was. He was also right about the state of the grocery stores.

So-so produce was snapped up as soon as it went on the shelves, and the big pallets that should be holding emmer, rice, and barley were empty. Not good signs. Nobody was looking panicked or queuing up for things, but . . . very not good.

Then he saw it. In the midst of dark omens, a single shining ray of purity. Of hope. Of healing.

"Jember. Grab Etenesh and Merkovah. Right now, please. Xandre has a pet cafe, and it's walking distance from Nag Hamadi."

CHAPTER 52

THE HEALING PLACE

No. You must hold Mrs. Proudwhiskers in an arm cradle. You must support the whole body, or it is painful for her, as well as an offense to her dignity. Observe how I do it with Crabknuckle." Truth was strict, but Merkovah had to learn. This was a special place, and things were to be done properly.

"I think I was on firmer ground with the hedgehogs. Shame we can't feed them more." The old monster finally seemed to fit his youthful face as he juggled the cat in his arms. Mrs. Proudwhiskers was an amiable lady, but she had the tendency to flow like a bread bag filled with water, and holding her was a constant challenge.

"It's all right. You have something to look forward to next time," Truth comforted him. The complaint was completely reasonable. The hedgehogs were adorable when they were eating the tiny carrots. As were the hamsters. Apparently magical, there seemed to be no upper limit to the number of seeds a hamster could store in its cheeks.

"What even is this? What are you? No, off with you. Away. Stop licking me! I'm not delicious! Help!"

Etenesh was trying to fend off a shaggy mountain disguised as a dog. Rosy (Rosy-Posy-Puddin'-and-Peaches read the tag on her collar) was a consummate professional and well used to dealing with difficult clients. Her thick, triangular head slipped around the fending arms, her short ears gliding under Etenesh's wrists as her meaty shoulder got into place. A quick lean to one side to open up the guard and then—the strike!

Pink, slobbery, but with a dreadful, sticky friction, Rose's tongue slapped out and covered half of Etenesh's face. With deliberate authority, Rose dragged it from chin to temple. Once satisfied, she stuck her muzzle into the crook of Etenesh's neck and tried to lick the ear from entirely too close.

Etenesh couldn't hold out. She collapsed into a fit of outraged laughter as she wrestled with the grand hound. "Jember, you swine! Rescue me!"

"I can't. Save yourself, cuz; the otters have me." They did, too. The brilliant mustelids had him surrounded. Some stood on their back legs, beseeching him for treats with their little clawed hands. Others played the heel, nipping around to try and snag any unsupervised snacks. Most crucially, no matter where Jember turned, there was a little staring face with its big eyes demanding affection. And treats.

The cafe made you sign a waiver certifying you were not a mathematician before you played with the otters. Truth neither knew nor cared why that was. He just signed and got extra snacks.

"Is everyone having fun? We also have a snake you could meet if you would like," the attendant asked.

"A snake?"

"Yes, Danger Noodle Supreme. You are all Level Three and above, so there's no problem handling our most colorful companion."

Truth shrugged, initially uninterested. Snakes, he had long since observed, were neither warm nor floofy. Then he nodded vigorously. There was an opportunity there. "Yes, thank you."

Danger Noodle Supreme was brought out by a gauntleted attendant. Not quite a meter long, Danger Noodle was a surprisingly spikey snake. The scales were mostly green at the base, but along its back and particularly around the head and neck, the scales stretched out a few millimeters. The dorsal scales progressed from green to an almost-white tan, then into a riot of oranges and blues.

The attendant handed Danger Noodle to Truth, who immediately set to examining him. Her? He had no idea how you figured out the sex of a snake.

"Can you tell me about it?"

"Yes, Danger Noodle Supreme is a member of the flower viper family, so called because they are so pretty and because they like to wrap themselves around the stems of reeds and sun themselves on wide, flat leaves. The unique scales and coloration are camouflage. While the colors are bright, in Danger Noodle's natural habitat, she would blend in. The pointy scales help break up her shape when she is still, so both predators and prey don't recognize a snake when they look at her."

"Wow!"

"Yes, she is very special. She was a rescue—someone wanted an exotic pet and then changed their mind. It's infuriating when you think about how their range has utterly collapsed due to expanding commercial farms." The attendant realized that he might be damaging the vibe and stepped back.

"Lot of that going around, friend. A lot of that going around," Truth murmured to the snake as he peered at her, moving her around. The scales were layered, of course, one resting on top of the other in tidy rows. That's how they could bend and shift with the snake as she moved.

The scales seemed a lot less "impervious" than he would have thought. For some reason, he imagined the scales like a suit of armor. This was more like tough skin or fingernails.

Truth dragged a finger along the snake's back, feeling his own fingernail bounce over the colorful spines. Perhaps that was the way to think about it—skin, not armor. Armor was rigid and unchanging. Skin got shed.

"Does this snake shed her skin too? It seems kind of spiny for that."

"Yes, she does. The spines are just scales that stick out more than usual, so it's no problem."

"Does dirt and stuff get trapped in there? It seems like it would."

"Yes, though less than you might think. They are good at avoiding muck. They also shed more than you might think—between once a year and several times a year, depending on age."

"Are the scales good at stopping damage?"

"Well, incidental things that might give someone a scrape, maybe. But really, they aren't armor. They help the snake move, help it hunt, and help it retain water in dry places. Did you know that snakes often hunt by vibration? They can sense movement through their scales. Their whole body becomes a sort of detector, letting them strike at things they can't see."

Truth took a closer look at Ms. Danger Noodle Supreme. There was probably a lot he could learn there, in the healing place.

Truth sat next to Etenesh in the waiting room next to the practice pitz field on the University campus. News of the duel had spread too widely, the number of witnesses growing to absurd numbers. It was two young people, elite scholars and future pillars of the nation, fighting to the death for pride and honor.

Truth examined that thought for a bit. He was, to his continued disappointment, in the violence industry. This should surely be less morally objectionable than, say, a shootout in a bar. For some reason, he just felt sad. He wanted Alemu dead, yes, but not like this.

He didn't want Alemu to have this absurd dignity. Alemu certainly shouldn't have the opportunity to hurt Etenesh. Truth was the one who was poisoned. Why should Alemu have the chance to hurt him a second time?

Etenesh didn't see it that way. As far as Etenesh was concerned, what happened to Truth was unforgivable, but what happened to her and Jember was far, far worse. To be labeled *Těmushd*—apostate and traitor both—was the stuff of vendettas.

Her family's service to both Temple and Throne stretched back to the founding of Siphios, when the very first humans trod upon this world. Strictly speaking, they may even predate the Duchy of Red Valley, though that was a *controversial* position for people below the rank of duke.

Blood would wash away blood. The duke was no towering figure of the aristocracy—he was a man with a lot of inherited wealth, a few buildings whose upkeep drained his considerable fortune, and a deep legacy of privilege. He wasn't going to come at them with hundreds of armsmen and thousands of bound demons. Nor did he want to face the wrath of an ancient clan of angelic mediums and summoners.

The children were called to the sands, made to be a proxy for their elder's sins and ambitions. As it ever was. As it ever would be.

"Do me a favor, Mr. Wells?"

"Probably."

"I will only accept one loss today. Kiss me after the duel?"

Truth smiled. He reached for her hands, pausing until she nodded. He picked them up and held her two slim wrists in his large hand. He pressed them against the cool sandstone wall above her head.

He leaned in, inhaling the scent of her—floral, and the resin of temple incense, and that funky sweet smell that lingered even after the divine intoxication eased. He could see her pulse speed up and her breath quicken.

"I said after the duel. I'm still in the purification period," she murmured, making the faintest struggle to free her hands.

"You are in danger."

"I am. It would be more than just bad."

"Up to me, then." He breathed her in.

"Up to you."

Truth leaned in and let his teeth snap near her neck. She jumped a little, goose bumps rising.

"I have been wondering what it would be like to bite you. Just a little bit. So, that will be for me, after the duel. And I will kiss you. And that will be for me too."

Truth leaned close, whispering. "But if you do well, if you are brave, and wise, and careful, and ruthless, and come back to me, then I will be brave too. I will let you hug me, Etenesh. I will let you hold me, and I won't run away. And then you can kiss *me*."

The seconds had cleared the field, each pacing out the bounds and ensuring there were no hidden dangers. The doctor stood by the side of the pitch in their skintight white one-piece and long-beaked mask. Carefully anonymous, lest some bitter party seek vengeance against them.

Teacher Ferrenet took the south side of the stands where Alemu would be emerging, while Merkovah held the north. The stands were packed. There was less jeering than Truth expected. Perhaps the prominent presence of a Level Six and a Level Seven settled them down.

Truth instinctively wanted to hate Ferrenet and tried to find faults in his appearance. In truth, he looked like nothing—a middle-aged man with an ordinary middle-aged face, wearing his formal robes. No beady eyes or cruel twist of his lip. He looked quietly confident, projecting that confidence so that his student would share it.

Merkovah looked like he was mad enough to slap around the Princes of Hell and grinned ruthlessly across the pitch. "*Confidence be damned,*" he seemed to say, "*your idiot student is going to be slaughtered, and if I have my way, you're next!*"

It was a warm day. Merkovah produced an enormous goose-feather fan to blow away some of the sticky heat. That put a crimp in Ferrenet's expression.

Alemu was the first on the pitch, wearing his formal student robes. He hung a hoop talisman on his left wrist and held an ivory wand in his right hand. His hair was immaculate, his robes neatly arranged, his mien impeccably poised. The very model,

Truth thought, of a mage and a gentleman. He wondered how he would look gutted and screaming on a bathroom floor.

Then Etenesh came out, and Truth stopped caring about anything else. She had changed into a ritual costume for the Cult of the Treasuries of Light. Form-fitting in black and gold, the dress bared her shoulders and displayed her strong legs. Her hair, usually flying wild and free, had somehow grown long and straight, falling to her waist below a winged crown of black feathers, enchanted glass, and heavy gold.

Etenesh had always been slender. Now? Carrying the aspect of God as imagined by her cult? She almost spilled out of her top. Generous to the point of glorious indulgence. Her hips swayed and danced as she strode onto the pitch, tossing about the long black feathers hanging from her belt. Her eyes smoldered with burnt orange. Resting across her newly generous chest was her long copper flail.

An angel descended, a six-winged Seraphim, eyes covered, and feet drifting above the ground. The angel chanted, reciting its worship, and walls of faint light rose around the duelists. Shielding the crowd. Truth wrapped his scarf tightly around his face, blending in with the home fans. The sun reached its peak. A single chime rang—the duel began!

CHAPTER 53

TO LEAD A DEVOTED LIFE

Etenesh launched herself at Alemu as the Seraphim's chiming cry echoed off the stands. The crowds roared and cheered as the long feathers on her belt and crown flew with the speed of her attack.

Alemu froze for a half-second in shock—he had drawn himself up like he wanted to say something. Etenesh wasn't interested. He quickly spun the hoop on his left wrist, snapping out a quick shield.

Etenesh's copper flail slashed at the shield, raising a shower of sparks but unable to reach his face. He barely got it up in time.

Etenesh didn't let up. She constantly moved and attacked, forcing Alemu to shift and keep the shield between them as they both quickly chanted spells. Alemu's wand wasn't suitable for counterattacking, but his spell was shorter.

With a hoarse shout, the wand transformed into a golden spear. A moment later, it started sending spikes of golden light at Etenesh. She had to break off her attack and focus on parrying away the spikes—the copper strands of her flail whipping back and forth in front of her as she knocked them aside. The spikes made a tearing noise as they ripped through the air, shattering into a cloud of brilliant energy when they smashed into the seraphim's shield.

Etenesh twisted her body with a dancer's grace. Her casting never slowed. Dodging and parrying the spikes, her left hand drew ghostly white symbols in the air. She cried out and the formation sank into the ground. They pushed back and forth a moment longer, Etenesh seemingly content to parry and Alemu more than happy to attack.

Etenesh made a sudden lunge. Alemu backpedaled, keeping the shield and spear between them. His foot went out from under him. The hard-packed earth of the pitch had turned flour-soft beneath him. Etenesh feinted left and rushed right, her next spell already forming. Alemu wasn't waiting around for it.

The golden spear traced its own symbols, sun-bright, in the air. Alemu scrabbled to get his feet under him in the loose powder. He couldn't turn quite fast enough. Etenesh darted in, copper reeds reaching for Alemu's handsome face. Alemu grunted, and a bronze helmet snapped into being around his head. The copper flail raised a shower of sparks as it skidded harmlessly across.

A blinding rune formed; a tearing edge of light was born. Etenesh tried to dodge, but the spell caught her side, scoring a long burn across her strong waist. She bit down on a scream.

First blood to Alemu. But it cost him a charm to do it. The helmet faded. Snarling, Alemu got his feet under him while Etenesh was distracted by the wound.

"Siphios is an ancient legacy! There is no place for your kind here, te'mushd!" He drove more power into the brilliant rune. Another searing cut of light came, ready to split Etenesh in two.

She grinned, spinning her flail, its suddenly glowing enchantments making copper traceries between them. The light struck, quick as blinking, but was caught in the copper net. Some seemed to flow into Etenesh. The rest spun round her. Twisted to a point. Then smashed back into Alemu's shield.

"I am deaf to the words of the evil ones. The slanderers, the blasphemers, the seducers. Better that I had no ears to hear. Better that they had no mouth to speak," she declared.

Etenesh's feet kicked up plumes of sand as she chased the returning light. The black feathers on her head and belt fluttered behind her as though she were about to take flight.

The pitch was visibly turning to powder now. No longer confined to the area under Alemu, it spread to the boundaries of the seraphim's shield. Faintly, one could see the angelic ward start to ripple.

Alemu's shield shattered, with Etenesh coming in behind. Her flail whipped out again, only partially blocked by the golden spear. Some of the reeds reached Alemu, slicing across his arm. He cursed and used another charm. A dome of fire seared the air between them. Alemu quickly chanted, and the hoop talisman on his wrist re-formed the shield.

When the dome of fire dropped, Alemu stood proud. The sleeve of his white robe was stained with blood, but his left hand raised the shield without shaking. His right hand kept the golden spear aimed between Etenesh's brows. His feet might be unsteady, but he was not.

Etenesh could see him getting wan. The burnout was starting to hit. He was running two talismans to her one. He was using powerful, brutal, direct spells. Expensive spells.

She chanted again, and a series of small darts flashed out of the tip of the flail's reeds. They swirled through the air, making another tracery of copper light before exploding in a series of whip-cracks and bursts of light against the shield.

Alemu grunted and volleyed back, launching golden spike after golden spike at Etenesh. She dodged across the sand, her feathers dancing. The darts kept flickering out and exploding harmlessly on the shield. It seemed an impasse. But Alemu was starting to frown.

"Petty tricks, te'mushd. The true sons of Siphios see you. Draining us. Stealing our essence, and for what?" he barked, no longer bothering to attack.

Alemu dispelled the spear and swiftly chanted another spell. "To become a favored slave for the tefen!?" Nine suns were born behind Alemu, each dreadful, each holy. "For God and the Crown!"

The suns spun behind Alemu, becoming a burning wheel. From that wheel came heat, pure and holy, intolerant of the mud and dung of the secular world. There would be no running from this. Only the area within the solar wheel was spared. Everything else within the seraphim's barrier would be cleansed.

Etenesh activated a charm in the spelled glass of her feathered crown. Holiness, like heat, was a measure of degree. The Treasuries of Light were in the very Palace of God.

Holiness? Even an initiate's crown had the capital to spit on such petty solar sanctity. The crown surrounded Etenesh in a veil of dancing stars. Cooling her and brushing away the light.

"God despises you." Etenesh rushed directly at Alemu. The veil shimmered and shook as the pressure of the solar ring crushed down, but it held. She was chanting, her left hand wreathed in ghostly white light as sigils drifted like snow behind her and melted into the scorching sands.

The copper flail lashed out again, this time cutting up from underneath the shield. Alemu snorted, extending his arm and keeping the shield well away from his body.

Etenesh didn't miss the gap. She charged in, forcing the shield to the side with her flail as she smashed into Alemu. Her momentum drove them both to the ground. She tried to climb on top, but Alemu got his foot up and kicked her in the gut. She fell back, clutching at her stomach, trying to stop the fast bleeding from the freshly torn wound left by the cutting light earlier.

Alemu struggled to get up, the sands shifting under him. He couldn't keep the suns up. The strain was too much. Etenesh's starry veil winked out a bare second later. Alemu couldn't rise off the shifting sands.

Etenesh focused on breathing. Breathe in, chant out. Reciting the ritual-creating spell she knew better than her mother's voice. Pouring line after line into the sand. She staggered to her feet, growing stronger as she walked toward Alemu.

He saw her coming, trying to get as much of his body as he could behind his shield. Slashes of light came from his wand, sharp and hot enough to cut metal like mud.

Etenesh flicked the burning light away like flies with her flail. There was a shimmer in the air around her. As though some great thing was hidden within her or just beyond the edge of what merely human eyes could perceive.

"God. You talk a lot about God. And say nothing of faith. You will die on your back, Alemu." Etenesh launched herself toward the downed man, flail raised for a smashing blow.

He got his leg up, ready to kick her away once more. Just as she reached him, she stopped suddenly. His leg shot out, not quite reaching her. Outside the cover of the shield. Etenesh grabbed it with her left hand, fingers starting to turn into the talons of some great bird. With her right, she slashed down with her flail. The bright copper reeds cut off his leg at the knee.

There was a pause—a heartbeat long. Etenesh casually tossed the leg onto Alemu's shield, just over his face. It was clear to the crowd that he didn't understand what he was seeing at the moment. He didn't understand what just happened. And when he did, he screamed.

The shield evaporated as he grabbed his bloody stump, trying to stop the blood. Etenesh didn't waste a second. She stepped forward, her flail flashing bright under the true sun. First, she took his other leg. Then his arms.

Her left hand, a talon now, avian, dripped traceries of spellwork into the dirt. With a little flick, a final glyph settled into place. Etenesh straddled the abbreviated Alemu, pressing him flat on his back, her hand resting over his heart.

"Look at me. LOOK AT ME!" she shouted. His eyes focused. He was bleeding out fast. She leaned in and whispered, "God has abandoned this world. So, I will raise a new one up. The man you poisoned shall rule this world. Think on that as you burn forever in Hell. Or do you think your faithless cries to God will move him?"

She watched for his eyes to widen, understanding her. At that exact moment of realization, she plunged her talons into his chest and ripped out his heart.

The great formation she had been drawing the entire duel sprang into life. Three, then seven, then fourteen, then thirty-three tiers; layers after layers of light rose, forming compounding holy geometries, mysterious even to the wise in the crowd.

The sand rose up, forming an altar beneath the limbless Alemu. The spark of his soul, that speck of the divine in every human, was condensed in the cavity where his heart once beat.

Etenesh closed her eyes for a moment, praying not with words but with her sincerity. God may have abandoned them. She could count on him for nothing. But that was okay. God had abandoned the world, but Etenesh had not abandoned God.

She just needed to find someone to fill that role. She was God's Wife, and her Husband would never leave her. She raised Alemu's still-beating heart in her clawed hand. And crushed it, letting the blood anoint her.

Inside the remains of Alemu, the spark of his soul became mired in twisting, corrupted black smoke. Grease fires and pollution, and burning down another cigarette because the cancer couldn't be treated anyhow.

The bright soul slowly sank toward the earth as the formation grew brighter and brighter. The structures of light grew more defined—flat-roofed palaces, colonnades, and processional paths. There were mysteries there, hidden in the forms and angles and shades of light. Enough to study for lifetimes.

As the formation became more defined, so too did the shimmering greatness around Etenesh. She grew even more perfect. Her skin smoothed. Her face and body were refined to absolute symmetry. A blazing light, ruddy with outrage, lit the altar under Alemu as temple bells rang.

Four great wings extended from Etenesh's back as Alemu's soul sank into the sands. Sank into Hell. Brilliant, glorious wings of black and gold. She raised her bloodied, clawed hands to the sun and lifted her voice in a wordless song of worship.

The seraphim dismissed the barrier around the pitch and joined its voice to hers. Theirs was a life of devotion. An often-painful life. But they would choose no other.

Watching from the stands, Truth thought she had never looked more beautiful.

CHAPTER 54

SHE CAN MANAGE

The stands were quiet. A young man, a flower of faded nobility, had been hacked into five parts, his heart crushed, and his soul condemned to Hell. Even then, those who supported Etenesh might have cheered.

The religious minorities, the civic-unity set, the conservatives who wished to preserve the life they knew, all should be cheering. Her family alone took up a big section of the stands. They were an ancient line and remarkably unified. They didn't make a peep. They looked awed. And proud.

Why wouldn't they be? A daughter of their house was graced with the faintest shadow of one of the aspects of God. For a clan of angelic summoners and mediums, it was a transcendent glory. None of them would dare raise a cheer when the hymns of the Watchers below the Chariot of God still rang in their ears.

Truth couldn't tear his eyes away from Etenesh. He couldn't believe what he had just seen. This wasn't the Etenesh he had sparred with for the last week. This was someone fierce and terrible and glorious. She raised her taloned hand to the sun, singing her praises to God as the heart's blood of his hated enemy dripped from her mouth and down her chest.

Truth had no idea what had happened, but he loved it. His mind skittered away from that thought and just watched her. Her family gloried in her nearness to God. Truth was just happy she had won and was coming back to him.

That, and he *really* liked the new look. He wasn't sure about the wings and the claws, but he would absolutely make them work.

Etenesh ended her song, lowering her hands. The seraphim had done its job and departed this backwater corner of existence with a few beats of its mighty wings. No less swiftly did Merkovah appear, blurring from the stands to stand by his student's side. He looked around at the crowd, smiling proudly.

The exorcist whispered something to Etenesh, who looked up at the stands. Her eyes met Truth. And she smiled.

The pitch slowly returned to normal as Etenesh was escorted away. Her wings faded back into nothingness. Thick talons returned to slim fingers. The perfection of her form faded too, though not entirely. From the other side of the pitch, Teacher Ferrenet descended with another anonymous-looking middle-aged man.

The other man was balding, bearded, dressed in elegant robes of turquoise and ivory. He was grieving, tears running down his face. Grieving but clinging to his dignity. Slowly he approached the bloody body and prayed over it. Servitor spirits appeared, collecting the parts and placing them in a plain wooden box.

Duke Red Valley would never again hug his third son. The body was unclean, the soul literally damned. The remains wouldn't even be dignified with a funeral. Instead, the corpse would be discarded at sea, no longer a part of blessed Siphios.

Truth studied his face, wondering if this would become a vendetta. If he needed to kill the man. It seemed that he would not. Duke Red Valley looked sad. Grieving. Hurting. But not angry. There was despair etched into those bones.

Truth wondered if that was what had driven his son into the arms of radicals and instigators. Kids study their parents and learn from them. If Dad thought the future was hopeless, how should his hot-blooded and loving son react?

Alemu would fight to bring hope home to his father. By any means necessary. And Etenesh had humiliated him, mutilated him, and directly cast his soul into Hell. Truth shook his head and left the stands. He wanted to go find her and tell her how proud he was. Not to mention he was eager to hand her her first loss of the day. Very, very eager.

His hopes were dashed when he found her climbing into a clay jar, carefully easing the long feathers of her belt and crown in around her. She caught another glimpse of Truth, gave him a devastating smile, and ducked under the rim.

Masked cultists quickly covered the pot with a wooden lid, sealing it with long paper talismans. They raised the clay pot up on a wooden stretcher and carried it, and her, onto the back of a glowing cloud streaked with ivory and gold. The cloud moved with deceptive speed out of the University and out of his sight.

"Her fellow cultists?"

"Indeed. The Cult of the Treasuries of Light is going to be absolutely insufferable after this. Not that I can blame them. But still. Insufferable." Merkovah was grinning widely, not looking bothered at all. "Heavens, did she bring them face!"

"On that subject . . ."

"Ah, not here. I know what you want to ask, but not here. Let's go to my office. Jember will be ages; he's going to be networking his ass off. He'll be twice as insufferable as the cult, and he's in a different cult!"

"Was that really Etenesh? I have trained with her all week. We were specifically working on her aggression and courage as well as her basic combat skills. Those were her spells, but the aggression, reactivity, tactics, all were beyond what she had been capable of." Truth cut straight to it.

"She was always fiercer than you gave her credit for. I deliberately sidelined Etenesh and Jember to give you more room to develop. It was no hardship for them. Neither are particularly bloodthirsty." Merkovah waved away his own quibble.

"Yes, that was Etenesh, but it wasn't *just* Etenesh. Remember our discussions about the nature of God?"

"Vividly."

"Good, because it's why the Cult, the Heaven-Beseeching Family, and the . . . let's call it moderate faction . . . are going to be completely out of hand." He rocked back in a comfortable, if scabrous-looking, office chair.

Truth had been condemned to the Student Chair. He wondered if Merkovah had personally ensured each leg was a different length or if it had just worn down that way. Making the wooden armrests a subtly different height was, however, clearly intentional.

"To be considered for membership in a mystery cult, one has to be *profoundly* devout. Truly, deeply, sincerely devout. The so-called 'Progressives' have their own 'Blessed Orders,' but do not be deceived. These are mere social clubs. If you ever want to raise money for a flowerbed in a roundabout, I can cheerfully recommend them." Merkovah's tone would have been more suitable for ordering a heretic's death by fire.

"Proper mystery cults worship God in additional ways, supplementing but subordinate to the Orthodoxy. They focus on a particular aspect of the Divine Self, expressed either in a saint or in some particular revelation. The particular nature of that worship, the aspects, and the tenets of their religious practice are, of course, mysteries known only to the adherents. And the Congregation on the Unity of the Faith, a supervisory organization within the Temple." Merkovah's professorial instincts had kicked in again. He shook his head and pressed on.

"I don't know the particular details of the worship of the Treasuries of Light, but clearly, Etenesh was channeling some divine aspect. Didn't you see the way reality shifted and bent around her? The shift in her mind? You ask about tactics and reactivity—is it so strange that an aspect of God would be fearless and ready to take every advantage?"

"God . . . has two sets of black and gold wings, bird claws, and is . . . well equipped for motherhood."

"Your literalism never fails to surprise me, Mr. Wells." Truth controlled a jerk and subtly gestured toward his ears. Merkovah microscopically shrugged, and Truth nodded. He respected that kind of caution.

"So?"

"So, this aspect of God does, yes. Remember what I said about contradictory information?"

"Ah. Right."

"It's also why the Orthodoxy not only tolerates the cults but quietly cooperates with them. We know they aren't being heretical, even if we don't agree that this is what should be focused on."

"Right. So, that was clearly extremely effective for her, and she's . . . technically not even an initiate. She's getting initiated now. So, why doesn't everyone just channel some aspect of God?" Merkovah almost collapsed out of his good chair, pounding his chest to stop coughing.

"Young man! Really, young man! Do you think this is easy? Even within a mystery cult, there aren't many that could do such a thing. Some years, it might only be the most senior or devout of their cult, just one or two people out of thousands. And those thousands are among the most pious of the very pious Kingdom of Siphios. Jember has been in his cult for three years now, and he couldn't manage a hint of what Etenesh did."

"Is . . . she going to stick that way? I saw the wings and claws vanish, but—"

"Like 'em top-heavy, do you?"

"Looked balanced to me."

"Honestly, after generations of students, I trained myself not to notice. Just better for everyone, really."

"How *is* your wife?"

"Oh, thriving, thriving." Merkovah beamed at Truth and refused to elaborate. Truth knew a losing battle when he saw it, and shifted back.

"So? Is she? Going to turn back?"

"I would expect so, mostly. Some aspects may stay, either mental or physical, though I wouldn't expect too much. It puts an immense strain on the body, mind, and soul. A bare initiate like Etenesh, well, it won't be much, if anything, that sticks." Merkovah shrugged.

"Think of it like this—you practice the Meditations to make you more real than the local reality. You spend hours on it, more or less daily. You are slowly accumulating local superreality, acclimatizing to it. It becomes your natural condition." Truth nodded.

"Etenesh just had that superreality imposed on her from on high. It's not her 'normal.' She can't tolerate it for long. You will note that for most of the battle, there were only minor . . . yes, yes, hohoho. *Minor* physical changes *compared to growing wings and claws!*"

Truth thought it over. It sort of explained why Alemu had barely touched her, and the spells that did hit weren't crippling or fatal.

She had pushed him to use his talismans and charms hard and fast, while conserving her own cosmic energy. She had controlled the battlefield. And when an opportunity came, she took it at once. Brutally so. Not exactly how he would have run the battle but . . . no complaints. It was good.

He thought about it a bit longer, then asked, "She has been planning this since the poisoning, hasn't she? That's why she was doing the ritual purification all week."

"Longer than that—her eyes started turning ocher weeks ago. She probably thought she would do the transformation at an initiatory ritual. I knew she had been quietly looking for a sacrifice."

"Speaking of—"

"Yes, Alemu is definitely in Hell, and his death is definitely a sacrifice. Allowable under Canon law as he can be said to have consented to be sacrificed when he agreed to the terms of the duel. The freely given life and soul of a pious man? Quite the sacrifice. The Cult will be *unbearable*."

"Wait, what? How is condemning his soul to Hell an act of piety?"

"The tortures of Hell are called 'eternal' because, from the perspective of the damned, they are. From God's perspective, however, that divine spark, their essential essence, remains within his command. God has not only lost nothing but the sacrifice volunteered for an eternity of suffering to glorify the Divine Chariot."

Truth just nodded. That sounded nuts to him, but he knew Merkovah would react poorly to his arguing the point. They grabbed a carpet back to Nag Hamadi, traveling in silence. Merkovah was gloating, and Truth was having a moment.

He didn't have to look after Etenesh. He wanted to. He really liked the idea of being her protector. The strong man in her life. But she didn't need him to be. She was entirely capable of looking after herself.

She was probably better at it than he was, all things considered. She was highly educated, with a large, supportive family, wealthy—by Truth's definition, if not Harban's—a very skilled ritualist, and apparently a more-than-competent solo combatant. She would have an astonishing career in academia or the Temple, assuming the world didn't end.

Etenesh didn't need looking after. In fact, she already was looking after herself. Truth didn't realize it, but he was smiling so much, tears formed in the corner of his eyes.

Etenesh didn't need to be saved. She could look after herself. She was someone he could trust his back to. Who would feed him even if he was crippled. Someone, at long last, who could look out for *him*.

Late that night, there was a knock on Truth's cell. Etenesh was there. Her body had slimmed, and her long straight hair kinked and started flying wild again. The fire in her eyes burned all the brighter. "I came back to you."

"You came back to me."

CHAPTER 55

TOO FOCUSED ON LIVING TO LIVE

Etenesh offered her slender hand, ripping talons now long gone, leaving neatly trimmed nails in their place. Truth gently took it and pulled her into the room. He looked deep into her burning eyes and deliberately closed the door. Her ocher eyes widened, breathing faster. Truth lightly pressed his hand to her chest and pushed her against the wall. Etenesh raised her hands, fingers splayed as though she were pushing back, but she didn't touch him. Her nose traveled along his neck, breathing him in but not touching. He could feel the heat of her kindling a fire in the always-cold core of him.

"Am I in danger again, Mr. Medic*i*?" she asked, her voice rasping as he caught her thin wrists and pressed her hands above her head.

Truth leaned in, letting his breath tickle her ear. "I'm going to bite you now, right on the elegant curve of your neck. I'm going to kiss it first, and then I will put my teeth to it and bite. I am trusting you to tell me when it's too much. Can I trust you with that, Etenesh?" She shivered.

"Yes."

Truth leaned in and gently pressed his lips to her skin, tasting salt and the faintest bitterness of oil. The sensation of her was overwhelming, and he gave in to his instincts. Teeth met yielding skin and strong muscle. Feather-light, just feeling his teeth press against her. Slowly, achingly slowly, he began to bite harder. He smiled as she wriggled and gasped. Letting himself have this moment. Trusting her to say—

"Ah, enough!"

He let go at once and looked at his handiwork. Two neat imprints of his teeth on the rushing sweep of her neck. It felt right.

"Too much?"

"It wasn't bad, but it got too much." She nodded.

"You lose." He grinned at her. She looked ready to argue the point, then grinned back.

"So, what are you going to do about it?"

He kissed her, and the world was a wonderful place for a few minutes.

Truth led Etenesh to the tiny bed and sat down on it. He patted the spot next to him, and she sat, not quite touching.

"I see what you are doing, you know. I get that physical contact is a big part of life in Siphios, and this must be hard on you. So. Thank you."

"It is hard. But worth it. It makes touching you so exciting. Every little touch becomes deliberate. Something to savor because it is so rare, and who knows when I will have it again?" She smiled up at him. "You know, I didn't *only* lose today."

"No, you did not." Truth smiled back. He carefully set her hands back on her lap. She looked confused. "This is your prize. You may hug me just how you like. While you are hugging me, you can kiss me just how you like. I will probably shake sometimes, flinch, or look scared. Please don't let go until I say when. I don't know how this works. But I've wanted it for a very long time."

Truth was in a funny sort of mood as he shook his body loose. The portal was almost open, but the thoughts kept crawling around in his head. The image of Etenesh's hand turning into a claw that could rip a man's heart out. The feeling of that same hand pressed to the back of his neck, his chest, his spine.

"You entirely sure you want to do this, Tommy?" Jember called.

"Yep. Cut 'em loose." It had been excruciating and one of the best, most exciting things he had ever done. Etenesh had booked a double room tonight. They agreed that they wouldn't get naked, but—

The portal burst open, bloody, skinless monkeys pouring out.

—he was pretty excited by the sound of "heavy petting" and the look in Etenesh's eyes when she said it . . . okay, demon time. GO!

The monkeys were small, about the size of a coconut, but there was an upsettingly large number of them, and they were *fast.* Truth rushed in and started slapping them away with a stick. This, of course, was about as effective as slapping away leaves with a stick during an autumn storm in a maple woods. The monkeys bounced back, clawing at each other to get to him.

Truth fell back before the horde, using the obstacles set up in the basement to break their rush. Of course, being monkeys, they saw no obstacles. Merely more opportunities to get vertical and launch themselves at his face.

Truth pushed himself harder. He focused on bodily positioning. His reflexes were vastly quicker than these demons'. It was his body that was failing to keep up. So, he pushed and pushed. He had been cultivating the Meditations carefully. The worms had started helping. No way was he slower than these scrubs!

Pushing, pushing. He knew he was a physical savant. He knew his body knew where to be. He just had to be there, and the way to do that was to make *full* use of his capabilities. A claw scraped past his calf, just missing. A skinless, screaming simian tore through the spot where his head had been a fraction of a second before. Two little bastards leaping for his crotch *certainly* got his attention, and he leapt back at speed.

"TIME!" Jember yelled. "SWITCH!" The skinless monkeys screamed in outrage as they were summoned back into the portal. Some tried to stay, reaching out to hang on to the newly summoned demon. There was nothing recognizably mammalian about this one. It casually demolished the impudent imps with flicks of its bony tentacle whips that sprang out all over its exterior. Always two or three in the right place at any time. And it was *fast*.

The inexplicable horror writhed along the floor with dreadful, hungry urgency. The very smoothness of its movement created a sort of terror—as though the universe itself was dragging it closer to you, ever closer, inescapably closer, its boiling mass of bone whips reaching for you, its maw filled with inexplicable things to hurt you with . . .

Truth ran. It was the smart choice. But the demon was very fast and very hungry. Truth ran as hard as he could, one hundred percent effort. He managed to keep ahead, but it was closing in slowly. He could feel the breeze as the bone whips almost grazed his back.

"TIME! SWITCH!"

The dreadful thing screamed, screamed in registers within and beyond merely human hearing, shaking the marrow of Truth's bones as it was hauled back into Hell. The skinless monkeys were back, somehow even madder than before. Truth sucked in a gulp of fresh air and got ready to dodge again.

Ten agonizing minutes later, Truth lay sprawled on the ground, gasping.

"That was one of the maddest things I have ever seen. And I have seen you charge demonic outbreaks," Jember said with forced casualness.

"I'm slower than I ought to be. My body is absurdly well cultivated, but I'm limited in what I can do with it by my own self-doubt. I *am* faster than I think I am. Now I just need to convince all the bits of me that that's true and do it. Be it. Whatever." Truth tried to grin up at dapper Jember, but it probably came out looking weird while he was lying on the floor.

"You already move like you are Level Four, maybe even Level Five. As a practical matter, you may be faster than them just because of your freaky reflexes. Which, damn. I am seriously rethinking learning Incisive for my next spell."

"It's a good 'un," Truth said, neglecting to mention that he hadn't cast Incisive and relied purely on his body and his senses.

"Maybe I should look into body cultivation for Level Four. Keep looking pretty for decades to come."

"Bet you a birr Merkovah has some good ones squirreled away."

"No bet; I know he does. Getting him to part with them, however, might take some doing." Jember grinned, seeming undaunted by the prospect.

"I have faith in you. Now if you will excuse me, I'm going to scrape together enough energy to crawl into the shower."

"Want any company?"

"'Fraid that ship has sailed." Truth smiled fondly at Jember.

"Oh, well." He paused. "You are that serious about Etenesh?"

"Different cultures, remember? Although . . . she gets me." Truth struggled to put into words what he was feeling, then just gave up.

"Damn. Good for you two. All right, I'll lay off."

"Good for my ego, though."

"Too bad. No more for you." Jember offered his hand. Truth grabbed it and pulled himself to his feet.

"No more?"

"None." Jember shook his head with mock firmness.

"This is terrible. Just terrible."

"Courage, Mr. Wells, courage. Etenesh isn't *that* bad. Though I must say I think, of the two of us, I'd be more fun." Jember grinned, then cracked up at the expression on Truth's face.

Truth was aware that he had virgin-itis, a disease he first observed in his hornier schoolmates, then again in the Army. Basically, the first lover—boyfriend, girlfriend, whatever, was THE ONE. The big forever love. Their connection was unique, special, and perfect. And, of course, it wasn't. Everyone else could see it but the poor bastards suffering the affliction. Having sex generally only intensified the symptoms.

Presumably, there were other girls out there. Women who would get him and could put up with his weird brain and his utterly violent life. But, to speak his truth, he didn't want to go looking for them. He might have virgin-itis, but he was determined to enjoy it. Safely.

He fixed the image of his rough patron in his mind. This guy didn't have virgin-itis. He had never had that disease. If he didn't have a harem, it was because he didn't want one.

Truth was sitting on the chair in his little cell, breathing and starting to meditate. Not trying to run the Meditations. Just meditate. It was time to reach out to the worms.

The first challenge was finding the little bastards. The rough patron had that nine-worm tattoo on his forehead, so he started by directing his consciousness there. No luck. Might have been a little ambitious to think he'd be exactly like that ancient. Truth let his consciousness systematically work its way through his body, starting at the very top of his head and moving down, muscle by muscle.

It was calming. Relaxing. And useless. He couldn't find the worms anywhere. *Hey, System, any idea where the worms are hiding?*

<<Kinda sorta? Keep in mind that while I interfaced with them for a while, I won't say I understand them. And yes, it is very weird to me that we have separate memories. I would say it's time to start researching the nature of the soul, but I get the impression that's a waste of time.>>

Truth waited patiently for the System to get back to the point. It seemed a little more scattered these days. Like it didn't quite know how to *be* anymore. Truth got to go on a journey of self-discovery when that happened to him. The System didn't have that luxury.

<<Your soul interacts with the universe on levels your body can't. I am usually hiding out in your apertures, so I can safely say they aren't hiding out in there. But keep in mind that's only half a step away from your body. And you just checked your body, and it isn't there. So . . . consider going a little higher through your soul. They hide out from me, too, by the way.>>

Huh. Well. That's unexpected. Higher up through the soul? He had no idea how to do that. Merkovah presumably did, but that did not seem like a safe or smart choice.

<<I do have an alternative suggestion—call them. They worked on your body. They might turn up.>>

Truth slapped himself on the forehead and tried to get in touch with his soul. Tried to call forth the worms. Was it working? He had no idea. But, ever so faintly, he could hear angelic chanting. And they sounded furious.

CHAPTER 56

GOD'S GIFTS

Truth allowed his inner vision to float up into his soul. Everyone knew that the body and soul were connected and that mind and apertures touched both. Being able to see your soul was just one of those side effects of cultivation. Do it enough, and it happens. Even old-timers stuck at Level One could do it.

A Level Three who had the benefit of a Stellar Dowsing ritual at a comparatively young age? He could *absolutely* do it. There just wasn't much to see. Not to sneer at the mysteries of the soul or anything, but if there were grand transformations happening there, he was too much of a rookie to spot it. Generally, he didn't bother poking around.

That may have been a mistake.

Following the sound of furious chanting, Truth's mind drifted up through his soul. There may have been a starry universe within, but it also had bounds. Pressing up against the edge of it, he could see them.

Nine glowing worms, yes, worms, but also dragons. World serpents. Void eaters. What name could bear to define such immensity? Serpent-like yet pliable, yet unyielding, soft cruelty made real, far, far too real. Some terrible creator had given them faces and mouths like the maws of entire prides of lions were pressed together into one circular mouth, their leonine features still present, still a reminder of their murderous origin. Most terrible of all, they were holy.

He kept tripping over that thought, again and again—they were holy. The worms were holy, the glow a divine light. They were the "realest" things he ever saw. The worms were holy, and they were *outraged*. They were absolutely *furious*. At him. At the sin of his existence. Something utterly fundamental about his existence was worthy of the most severe punishment.

His mind couldn't stand the pressure and crashed back into his body. He fell sideways out of the chair, landing harmlessly on the floor. It would have given a Level Zero a concussion, a fall like that. Raised a lump on a Level One. He hardly felt it, just a harmless sensation, not pain. Because of the endless body refinement. Refinement done by . . . the worms.

<<*While you were . . . dead . . . the worms turned up in your body and started making microscopic changes and repairs to you. I was able, with a lot of experimentation, to get them to make use of little chunks of the Meditations of Valentinian. In retrospect,*

they seemed kind of picky about what they would use. It sped things up a lot, but even by themselves, they would have rebuilt you. Whatever they are, they don't want you dead.>>

Why? Why would my rough patron create such a thing? Did he create such a thing? If he didn't create them, why send them out as part of his legacy?

The System was silent. Truth lay on the floor for a long time, trying to come to terms with what he had experienced. It didn't really go anywhere productive. Eventually, he uncurled, tidied himself, and went to the double room. The horny had been firmly banished from his mind, but grabbing hold of Etenesh and hanging on tight sounded very, very good.

Etenesh was there already, waiting in her pajamas. Her eyes were almost solid ocher. His plans would have to change.

It was a rather bemused-looking Truth that walked into Merkovah's little office/cell the next morning.

"There's the look of a man who rid himself of his virginity." Merkovah grinned.

"No, honestly, I'm not ready. It was an educational night in other ways. I have even more questions today than I did yesterday. I think Etenesh suspects."

"You say it like it's a crime. And so what if she does? Tell her. She's already having a ball with whatever you are doing together. I bet she'd enjoy training you up even more."

Truth considered that. The System had told him more or less the same thing, and clearly, nobody in Siphios gave a damn, but it was still embarrassing. He knew he had to just get over himself, but . . . he didn't want to look like a fool in front of Etenesh. Merkovah was grinning at him. Truth squinted.

"You are enjoying this, aren't you."

"Immensely." The grin emerged like a badger through the thickets of Merkovah's beard.

"Watching your students' love life."

"Mr. Wells, it might shock you to know that I was a terrible romantic in my youth."

"Women love a beard?"

"Some do! I wore it shorter in those days. Marriage changes a man." Merkovah's eyes had gone misty with nostalgia, but he managed to shake it off.

"Anyhow. I have a paying job for you. On top of the job I am already paying you for."

Truth perked up. *Paying job* was a phrase that had never lost its charm.

"The working group the University put together was more effective than expected. This was not the first time talismans of this type have been recovered, so there was a lot of information scattered around. Nobody had properly compiled it all until now, let alone under the supervision of the intelligence services and the police."

Truth waited somewhat patiently for the point to arrive. The humor evaporated from Merkovah.

"Have you ever heard of anti-theists?"

"I'm sorry. I don't think I understand the term."

"We aren't really sure what they call themselves, this generation. It's an ancient and particularly pernicious lie. Don't bother trying to understand their evil ideology. You will only contaminate your mind." Merkovah gathered himself. "The very short version is that there are really two universes, one material and one made purely of thought and spirit. We are trapped in the material universe, a universe that was never supposed to have existed. Our spiritual self, our divine spark, was always supposed to be part of that divine, spiritual universe."

"Okay, so . . . why are we in this universe?"

Merkovah snorted. "Because there are two gods, obviously. One, an evil, incompetent boob that made the material universe, the other the perfect divinity of the spiritual universe. Our divine sparks are trapped by the evil one and, therefore, 'it is every prisoner's duty to escape.' Which they do by committing the most depraved of atrocities. Trying to force their way through the bars of reality."

Shame. They sounded like they were on to something, but they lost him at the final step.

"They are periodically purged, of course, but like cancer, they keep coming back. The superficial details change and specific doctrinal conceits shift around, but it ultimately comes back to the same nonsense. God is evil. The universe is a trap. We must escape the physical and return to the purely spiritual."

Truth sat with that a moment, digesting it.

"The fact that we can see our soul?"

"We see it tied to our bodies, trapped in the prison of the 'real.'"

"Spirits?"

"Illusions, or some other creation of the material universe, that our degraded souls cannot differentiate from true spiritual existence. Incidentally, while the exact nature of angels and demons is in dispute among the apostates, it's much the same thing. They are all servants, one way or another, of the evil god."

Truth nodded slightly.

"What's this all have to do with me and getting paid?"

Merkovah winced and pressed his fingers to his temples. "Mr. Wells . . . Mr. Medici, do you fully understand the enormity of the crime these anti-theists represent? The sheer, calculated monstrosity, perversity, of their ideology? It is a mess of palatable half-truths and false dichotomies designed to lead astray the spiritually weak and theologically ignorant. It is, perhaps, the purist distillation of evil I know of."

Truth nodded. Then waited. The silence continued.

"Mr. Medici?"

"Oh, I thought it was one of those questions where you didn't actually want an answer. No, I really don't understand what's so terrible about their ideology, but if they're the bunch that killed all those people in the apartment building, and they sent the crow-headed smuggler that tried to kill me—"

"And called you a fuckboy, which seems a much more accurate description these days," said Merkovah, with the look of one who has completely given up.

"And called me a fuckboy, which is still outright slander,"

"Have to prove damages for it to be slander under the law. It was clearly a mere insult."

"Then they should probably be permanently dealt with. Which . . . you want me to do? Why? You can just call the cops. Hell, you can send literal armies of angels and demons after them."

Merkovah shrugged. "That was Plan A and Plan B respectively. Still is, sort of. Here's the thing, though. In addition to transmitting their ideology, these pricks pass down technology. In their insane quest to 'liberate' our souls from their physical prison, they have gotten very good at disrupting the material bodies of spiritual entities. They have also developed a particularly nasty form of anti-magic, which they tend to deploy liberally."

"Oh? What's that?"

"You are working on magic resistance—being so much more real than the things thrown at you that they only affect you to the degree you permit. Anti-theists view this approach as fundamentally wrong. Rather than becoming more real, you are becoming more like the false god and, therefore, more bound to the physical, false universe. Wards work by either forcibly resisting spellforms or by redirecting the cosmic energy generated by magic or a talisman."

Merkovah looked grim. "The anti-theists disperse cosmic rays. Essentially make the warded areas vacuums for the very stuff of magic."

Truth quickly connected this tidbit with Merkovah's plans for the System Astrologica. "Ah. You want it recovered, not destroyed."

"I want it destroyed, but I want the first look at it, and I want to see if there is something there we can use. I also want to know what that murderous apostate trash are doing in my damn country!"

Truth nodded again. This was the sort of logic he could understand. Another, more personal, thought intruded. "Apostate. Tefen?"

"Why, yes, Mr. Medici, that would be an appropriate use of the word. In fact, etymologically speaking, it's derived from a word referring to anti-theists generally." Merkovah managed a grim smile. "You can now understand a little better why Etenesh and Jember were so utterly furious, and for that matter, why I was too."

"They seemed calm enough."

"Don't kid yourself. They were holding it together to make sure *you* held it together. There is currently a massive debate among the faculty about restoring the ban on swords in the Well. You left quite an impression. 'Ready to wash away insult with blood,' one fella said. Nice turn of phrase, I thought."

Truth nodded. It was quite true, after all. "And you aren't walking in there and slapping everyone to death with the raw strength of your body because?"

"Because here in Xandre, where a cabal of these anti-theists has been discovered, I am surveilled by far too many eyes. You too, of course, but to an infinitely lesser extent. You would be much more able to acquire the technology and get away with it than I would."

Didn't entirely trust that but . . . okay for now.

"How much does the op pay?"

"We bill it as a recon/covert raid, undertaken by . . . certain agencies you don't need to know about. Use it as political leverage to get you access to those national treasures I mentioned; boost your level." Merkovah looked satisfied.

"Absolutely not. I decline." Truth stood and swiftly moved for the door.

"Pardon?!"

"My fee will be the operational supplies needed to do another job for you? No. Absolutely not. Cash is good, and elixirs are better, but I am *not* going to be scammed out of my fee." Truth was almost flashing back to some contract negotiations he was involved with at the PMC. Sergeant Murthey might not have been the most enlightened soul, but he represented a vast, cataloged, and indexed library of employer tricks and treachery. Truth had been a diligent student.

"Young man, are you somehow unclear on the phrase *national treasure*? These are not things I can simply gift on a whim, and the political consequences—"

"Are absolutely not my problem," Truth interrupted. "A bargain has been struck. If you want to renegotiate, we can talk about it, but I will tell you now—my fee will only be higher, with more to be paid in advance. If you want to hire me for a second job, you will have to pay for that separately."

Merkovah stared at him wonderingly. "Where has the young man gone who just said 'Okay' to everything?"

"He's still here. Along with the kid who learned you never, ever, not for any reason or for anyone, work for free."

CHAPTER 57

TOURIST TRAP

Truth was wearing what he thought of as his Desrin disguise, unwilling to acknowledge that he had gotten alarmingly comfortable wearing it over the last few weeks. The white zeph (no tassel; keep it low-key) was comfortably snug on his head, his sensible trousers and shirt were clean and looking sharp, and his sword rested on his hip. Although the latter still felt odd.

The Tongue of One Who Speaks for God, and wasn't that a mouthful, was a two-handed sword. It was on the narrower side, rigid for powerful, effective thrusting but beefy enough and balanced to be authoritative in the cut. It was also considerably lighter than Truth expected, though he knew that was actually normal. Swords were meant to be light. You would get tired fast if they weren't. And having one bouncing off his leg as he walked through a city felt damned odd.

He had looked into a back carry, of course. It looked sharp, and he suspected it dramatically improved mobility. Merkovah's laughter had been . . . unkind. It turns out, after some experimentation, that even with Truth's remarkable flexibility, it is almost physically impossible to draw a long sword from a sheath slung over your shoulder. You can pull it out a little way, but the range of motion just isn't there to lift it clear of the sheath. Merkovah grudgingly admitted there were scabbards, rare scabbards, designed to allow one to draw from a shoulder carry, but they were heavier and clunkier than the sword itself. Carrying the sword hanging from your waist really wasn't all that bad, comparatively.

Truth had been getting used to it, but it still caught him by surprise sometimes. For example, when walking into a crowded store. People gave the sword plenty of space, but bumps happened. Whacking into tables and shelves happened. Not often, but often enough to make him hyperconscious of his personal space. The prerogatives of the nobility, like private service and the masses not allowed to approach without permission, suddenly made a great deal more sense.

What was stranger was the number of swords in circulation seemed to be increasing. It wasn't just Desrin, either. He saw a cluster of middle-aged women proudly showing off their new machetes. It seemed a very odd fashion accessory, but given the way everything was headed, he saw the logic. Advertisements released by street teams would drift through the alleys, persuading people to visit a particular knife-fighting school or the such-and-such swordsmanship academy. Most shooed them away, of course, but there seemed to be some takers.

Truth worked through the winding, sandstone-colored streets, admiring murals and statues and the carts loaded with fat fruits or bright flowers that seemed to spring up everywhere. Prices were high on the fruit carts, and the vendors looked a bit grim. But the path of the foodie demanded sacrifice and eating a particularly spiky-looking pink thing with vivid magenta flesh. The vendor supplied a little wooden spoon to eat it with, which proved necessary and the only thing that saved his shirt from permanent purple ruin.

Having snacked well, he made his way to a little shop. It sold a great deal of things, all stacked in little clusters and clumps across shelves and window displays, even hung up the sides of the walls and hanging from the ceiling. A claustrophobic blizzard of modestly priced gewgaws, claptrap, and commemorative shirts. The Freedom of the Terraces had shifted colors. This was Birdie territory, apparently.

There were keychains hanging by the dozens, with little icons commemorating players on their ends. Truth found it morbidly fascinating—a mass-produced chain curtain of the martyrs of the pitch. He touched his scarf lightly. He couldn't do what Raffe and Gionne did. He could understand it, though. In his muted, simple way, he mourned them. He looked around at the hanging jerseys, cheap commemorative knockoffs the lot of them, and yes, right there at the front of the shop, in a carefully tasteful display, was the sole Brickies jersey in the shop. Raffe and Gionne, immortalized forever or for as long as the display moved units.

Beyond the commemorative pitz paraphernalia, there were little models of famous Xandre landmarks, some carved in wood or cast in brass or steel. Truth was seized with a sudden urge to buy. Some of them even had little charms on them, announcing *The Old Carriage House, Xandre*, or *Temple Bune*. A particularly grand one claimed to be the Royal Palace. He wanted to collect a few. He had the mad notion of showing them to the sibs.

"See—I went somewhere! I lived there for a while. I met people, did things, saw things, made friends, found a lover, or, really, she found me. I have grown. I'm not just a thug with a spell—I'm a thug with a spell and all these other things. These memories, these connections, and here I have proof of it that you can hold in your hand."

Shoved in a corner was a rather dull brass sculpture of Nag Hamadi. The artist had skipped all the inscriptions and carved only the most significant statuary. Truth grabbed it at once and marched to the front of the shop.

"Excuse me, how much is this sculpture?"

"Prices marked on the bottom. Small temple souvenirs are nine birr or three for twenty-five." The shopkeeper was a faded man, somewhere between fifty and the grave. Credit to him, he kept the shop clean and well dusted. He must have had plenty of time for it. A tourist shop in a locals-only side street? It was a wonder they were still in business. Truth might well have been the morning's only customer.

"That's too much. Look, it's missing the big statue of the eagle out front. Five birr, best I can do." Truth shook his head, pointing at the front of the sculpture.

"Prices are as marked. You want it cheaper? Buy three." The faded man somehow faded even more, his interest in Truth visibly evaporating.

"Come on, man. Five birr. I'm getting it for my sister. She's three. And sick."

The man snorted. "Save your money for the doctor, then. Buy something or scram." He bent over to pick something up from under the counter. Truth helped him get low—he smashed the brass sculpture of Nag Hamadi on the bony edge of the back of the faded man's skull, just above the spine. The shopkeeper collapsed like a stabbed waterbed.

Truth quickly hopped the counter, checked that the man was still breathing, and dribbled a potion in his ear. Having ensured no sudden wake-ups, he tapped the charm in his pocket twice. It faintly vibrated back twice. Apparently, a squad of heavily armored and specially trained police was on standby, ready to rush to the rescue at a moment's notice. For reasons of operational security, it was deemed best if he and they never met.

Truth quickly checked the storeroom behind the counter—box after box of cheap-jack inventory, a filing cabinet, a stool shoved under a shelf, no doubt used for taking a break while "checking in the back" for more stock. Next to it was an open, empty locker next to a jutting corner of the wall. No surprises there. Intelligence said that the cabal was entering from this shop, generally during the daytime to blend in with the occasional shoppers. There would, therefore, be a secret entrance there somewhere.

He ran through the usual search methods—blowing clouds of enchanted chalk to detect invisible or illusory doors, spell-hunting charms, looking for active enchant-ments, spirit tracers, all the usual stuff, and it was all coming up negative.

<<Because you are thinking like a mage. And the anti-theists aren't.>>

Eh? Everyone's a mage. Everyone who isn't a cripple.

<<Oh, my mistake. I guess there is a reason there is a meter-square corner of the wall sticking out just behind the man-sized locker, in a cartoonishly inefficient use of limited inventory space. Probably a magical reason.>>

Struggling with not being a dick, huh?

<<It's awful. I swear, I am doing my best. Don't get cute; this is a raid. Smash right through the wall.>>

Damn right.

Truth crouched slightly, then slammed shoulder-first through the thin boards. There was a deep hole behind it, but Truth's quick reflexes let him stop and brace against the far wall. He looked down. The hole was dark. How deep, he couldn't say, but there were metal staples driven into the wall, big enough for use as a ladder. He grabbed hold and quickly moved down. Speed and surprise were the twin gods of forcible entry, but they had a supervisory deity called *Scout before you breach*.

This op wasn't by the book in anybody's book. On the other hand, Merkovah had heard the good word, and now Truth was looking at a nice little Level Three elixir and fifteen thousand birr. He went faster. He only got paid five grand in advance. The thought of not collecting all of it was making him itchy.

The ladder wasn't all that long, maybe twenty meters. He quickly landed on a stone floor. So dark, even his gifted night vision from his rough patron struggled to see anything. He reached for a little summoning charm, ready to snap it and get a little light sprite in there.

<<NO! These are not mages! Their whole technology is anti-magic! You think maybe summoning something might set off an alarm?!>>

Ah. A valid point. But they had to have some way to see. So, presumably, either they brought something down with them or there was something right near the ladder. And he wasn't going to head upstairs and frisk the storekeeper unless he really had to.

Truth squinted around in the little puddle of light at the bottom of the ladder. There was nothing that would obviously be a source of light. There was mostly nothing at all, just bare stone and mortar walls. There was a little bucket hanging next to the ladder with a lid on it, and some thin, flat bits of wood in a basket next to it. There was a slot in the lid of the bucket. The sticks seemed to be the same dimension as the slot.

Seemed obvious if you were willing to accept that you had no idea what would happen. He picked up a stick and put it in the slot. Nothing happened. About half of the stick was jutting out of the bucket. Maybe you had to remove the stick afterward? He gingerly did so.

As the stick cleared the slot, the room started lighting up. A brilliant neon-green glow was now emanating from the stick. The stick looked a little damp, but the glow was coming from the wood, not whatever potion it had been dipped in. He had . . . no idea how that worked. But he could see now, no alarms had gone off, and maybe one of the anti-theists would think he was one of their own for long enough for him to put them down.

He gave the bottom of the shaft a quick looking over and found nothing but a door. The door wasn't even locked. Truth gingerly eased it open. There was a short hallway with three doors leading off of it. One on the left, one on the right, and one straight ahead. Generally, you would have a team breaching each room, one at a time, while a couple of the team members were covering the hall. But he didn't have that, so he just quietly walked over to the first door on the right and eased it open.

Some kind of closet. He didn't know why it was funny the evil anti-theists had a deck broom and mops, but it was. He had seen that brand of cleaner in stores around Siphios. He gave it a last quick look, but if there was anything nefarious in there, he didn't spot it. He went to the door opposite it. A workshop. He would definitely be doubling back to this—even the components would be very useful to study. There was a chance of finding notes and diagrams, too. Still, nothing immediately nefarious leapt out at him. He would come back once he had secured the area.

Truth eased up to the final door. There was a faint noise coming through it, a sort of moaning, but it kept on going when anything with lungs would have had to breathe. Air over a tube? There was something resonant about it, almost shaking his bones. He reached for Incisive. The anti-theists would know he was here in a second anyway. He made the spell form in his mind, and . . . it fizzled out. Anti-magic wards. Had to be. For a moment, he wondered what would happen if you lived in an environment like this. Your spell apertures would collapse, for sure.

Shit. He looked down at the Tongue. It wasn't visibly damaged, but he certainly wasn't going to try and use its magic. Worst-case scenario, it was still a sharp, pointy stick. He drew steel, tensed himself, and eased open the door.

CHAPTER 58

DESECRATION OF FALSE IDOLS

The anti-theists had converted a basement for their work. The roof was low, just a bit over two meters. Truth nearly scraped his head along it. All smooth, layered concrete laid by some ancient demon. Not a scrap of ventilation. It was hard to breathe. His only light was the glowing wooden stick in his hands, which threw everything into sharp reliefs of neon green and black.

Truth put his back flat to the wall next to the door and eased it open a crack with his left hand. His right hand had pulled back with his sword, ready to run through any bastard that saw the open door and chose to run through.

Credit where it was due—the anti-theists did a great job oiling the hinges. The door eased open, any sound covered by the endless droning noise. Truth steadied his breath. He instinctively reached for Incisive again and again; the spell just disintegrated. He felt acutely naked. It hadn't been long since he learned the foresight portion of Incisive, but it was habit-forming. There was a comfort in knowing that you couldn't be ambushed. This basement . . . was a place without comfort.

Truth crouched low and peered through the gap in the door. There were lights hung in there, more glowing green sticks stuck into the walls or sitting in cups on tables or shelves. There was a long, high table in the center of the room. A few people moved around the high table, shadows of black and green. He couldn't see what they were doing. Well. If he didn't have magic, then they didn't have magic. And he liked his odds hand-to-hand.

He eased open the door a little more, leaving his light stick behind the corner. Staying as low as he could, as silently as he could, Truth launched himself into the room. He tried to keep the shelves and large table blocking sight lines. He made it about three steps.

"UNCLEAN! UNCLEAN!" one of the shadows screamed. They all spun around to look at Truth, who was rising now, the Tongue sweeping up to collect the head of the nearest anti-theist. He could feel himself moving more slowly than he was used to, and there wasn't as much power in the cut. The shadowy figure got their hands up, blocking the blade with the outside of their forearms. He felt the bones break and saw the body tumbling back . . . but they held. The arms were bleeding, broken but still attached.

In retrospect, assuming that anti-theists had no magic of their own was . . . foolish.

"Get him!" one yelled, but the shadowy forms were already in motion. Four in total: one down with broken arms, two coming from the right, one coming over the table straight at him. The one on the floor yelled something—they exploded in a ball of . . . nothing, an expanding sphere of negation, shuddering and tearing the air as it passed. The other three popped off half a second behind. Too fast—no time to dodge. Truth brought up Tongue and braced!

The ripple passed over and through him. It didn't so much as stir a hair on his head but it still managed to drive him to one knee, gasping, clutching his chest. He couldn't breathe. He was sucking in lungfuls of air, but somehow, he couldn't breathe. The anti-cultists swarmed him, fists raining down, boots coming for his ribs, his head. He blocked as best he could, but he couldn't breathe. Something was wrong; something was very wrong in his chest. The Tongue was screaming, faintly, but screaming.

He had to get out. This wasn't about the mission anymore. He had to escape. Truth muscled the blade around, slicing legs. He caught one in the femoral artery, another across their ankles. He could feel the tendons snap under the blade. He lurched to his feet, catching a heavy right cross on his chin in the process. He got punched in the face. Nobody had done that since he was a kid!

Truth reeled back toward the door. The anti-theist ran after him, snatching a cleaver off a shelf. Ready to finish the job.

"Pasaele, NO!" the one with two broken arms yelled. Truth stopped his backward scramble, bracing himself and using the two-handed sword like a pike. The anti-cultist ran right onto it, skewering themselves. They . . . looked like anyone else from Siphios. Truth smashed him across the jaw, broke his nose, and kicked him off the blade. He wasn't dead yet, but a meter of steel through the gut would keep him out of mischief.

The pain in his chest was getting worse. The anti-cultists were injured but far from beaten. He could run, turning his back on them and their bizarre magics . . . or he could attack. He thought of the ladder, trapped in a narrow tunnel with mages out of stabbing range below. He almost cried with pain. Then rushed in again.

Whatever it was, it was getting worse. He smashed his pommel down on skulls, knocking them out when he could, sticking the blade into joints, fiddling around to sever the tendons binding arm to shoulder or knee to tibia.

"Too slow, Templar, too slow! You are already dead." The last of them, the one with two broken arms, laughed wetly. "Aah, if we had even a minute's warning, you would be dead already." They looked like one of the ladies shopping in the street outside.

The hell's a Templar? Truth wondered. Then took extra care giving her a traumatic brain injury. He believed them when they said they could have killed him.

Something was deeply, deeply wrong inside of him. He could feel himself starting to collapse. He had to get out. Something about this place. He had to get out. He made his way to the door, bouncing off the frame. Stumbled to the ladder. It looked kilometers long.

Truth wrapped his hands around the metal staple. His hands had been so strong this morning. Why did they feel so weak now? He pulled himself up. Foot on the rung. Climb. Try to breathe. Grab the next. Step up. Try to breathe. Grab the next. Step up. Try to breathe. Try to ignore the melting pain in your chest, the way your tendons feel brittle and your muscles are running away like a knocked-over bottle.

The ladder had to be cursed. It wasn't this long before. It would be impossible for it to have been this long before. Stars danced and spun in front of his eyes, brilliant colors fading to a gray that was the absence of color. A void more total than black.

Light. Normal talisman light. Shining down. Door. Door? Wall hole. No, door. Can't reach the hole.

<<*sealupsealupsealupDONTABSORBANYTHING TRUTH! You have to SEAL UP! DON'T ABSORB ANY COSMIC RAYS!*>>

Wha? Truth fell through the hidden door behind the locker. Just a friction lock on this side. Lay on his back, sucking in heavy lungfuls of air. He could finally breathe.

<<*Oh, no. NO! SNAP THE CHARM! CALL MERKOVAH NOW! NOW, YOU MISERABLE DUMBFUCK SLUMRAT!*>>

Oh, yeah, he had an emergency thingy. Everything hurt. He should get help. Mission scrubbed; come and get me. Clumsy fingers pawed at the pouch on his waist. Everything hurt now. He was breathing, feeling stronger, but everything hurt, and the pain was getting worse and worse. He found the right charm, the triangle clear under his fingers. His vision turned white, migraine pain, long iron nails being pounded into his skull to the rhythm of his heartbeat. His fingers convulsively crushed the charm. He didn't notice.

If the cosmic rays were leaking out of him before, they were flooding in now. More and more. More than his channels could handle. More than he could physically stand. More and more and more! Flooding in to fill the vacuum inside of him.

<<*Third part of Incisive, the scales. Use the scales. I know you haven't done it before. USE THE SCALES. DON'T ABSORB THE RAYS! KEEP OUT THE BAD STUFF!*>>

He tried. He really, really tried. But the migraine, the stabbing fire that covered each and every speck of his body, every droplet of that refined flesh that was sucking in more cosmic energy than his channels could handle, all of it was pain. He could no more cast a spell than walk to Heaven. There was a sudden rush, a cool sensation, and blackness.

He briefly came to again in a tub of some kind of liquid. He was totally submerged, with a mask covering his face. He had some vague notion that he should be afraid, but before the thought could really take hold, he faded out again.

Sometime later—

"And the mountains will shake, and the hills will be flattened, melting like wax before the flame. The land will be utterly torn apart, and all that exists upon the land shall die, and there will be a judgment upon everyone. But with those who live with his law, he shall make peace. He will protect the chosen, and mercy will be upon them. They will all be God's people."

Did he . . . This sounded kind of familiar? A woman's voice?

"And under his protection they shall prosper. They shall be blessed. He will help them and a light will appear before them, and there shall be peace between the people and their God."

Familiar, yeah, but the voice sounded . . . not right? But familiar?

"See, o people! He comes with ten thousand of his holy angels to execute judgement on all, to destroy the ungodly and the apostate. To convict all flesh of all the works of their ungodliness which, in their sinfulness, they have committed. To convict them of all the slanderous words sinners have spoken against him."

"Prophet?" Truth mumbled.

"An old patriarch. Welcome back, Truth."

He forced his eyes open. Etenesh was sitting on the hard wooden chair in his cell. She had brought a cushion, a stack of books, a jug of water, and salt-and-lime-flavored plantain chips. She was midway through a book thick enough to stop an axe blow. Her smile was sincere, and fragile, and as beautiful as anything he had ever seen.

"Truth. May I hug you, please? I really need to hug you right now. I think I'm going to explode otherwise."

Can't have that. "C'mere. Hug." He waved, struggling to move his hand. There was a needle in it, with a drip attached. Etenesh wasn't fussed, and launched herself bodily across him. The weight of her helped bring him back to his body. Slowly, he became aware of her shivering. She was sobbing but trying to keep the noise in.

"Shh. Shh. It's okay. It's okay." He patted her shoulder. His coordination was still off. "It's all okay. I'm here. You are here. Ah. I didn't get any souvenirs. That's a shame."

She hiccoughed. "Souvenirs?"

"There was this crummy little model of Nag Hamadi in bronze. Would have made a great souvenir of Xandre." He nodded. Faintly.

"Oh, you were out buying souvenirs, and you accidentally fell into a four-day coma."

"I am not usually that clumsy, I promise. And, if I am living up to my name, it was more going to be armed robbery."

The hiccoughs turned into outraged sputters. "Armed robbery?"

"I really wanted the souvenir, but the price was outrageous. I mean, nine birr for a not-very-good model? They didn't even get the big eagle statue out front."

"Oh, clearly, you were provoked. I understand entirely. Truth Medici, I have been sitting in that chair so long, my bum is flattening out and I am part tree now.

I've finally caught up with some of the reading I haven't been doing the last couple of weeks. On account of just sitting there, waiting for you to wake up. Confess at once, and you might be spared the death penalty."

Well, he didn't want that, but—

"Merkovah said you wouldn't, of course."

"Well, no. I think it would be an actual crime."

"He said that, too."

"Thoughtful of him."

"He also mentioned that it was shitty girlfriend behavior to put you on the spot and make you choose between me and the professional requirements of your job."

Thanks, Merkovah. I have thought many unkind things about you, but you still were looking out for me.

"I agreed, but I still plan to ruthlessly guilt you over this. I have not had a good few days, Truth."

He nodded. That was fair. "Nail polish."

"What?"

"That was the other thing that Desrin do, right? Men get their hair cut, and women get their nails polished. I thought, would you like it if I polished your nails? I was going to go to the shop after and see what stuff I would need."

He smiled up at her. "I don't know how. Teach me?"

CHAPTER 59

GETTING TO KNOW YOU

Etenesh was pushing Truth's wheelchair around a little park near Nag Hamadi. Truth had tried to decline, saying that he was getting around okay on crutches, but she was having none of it. As promised, the guilt trip came quickly and ruthlessly. Truth hobbled to the chair and obediently let himself be pushed around.

It was . . . more than irritating. Actually, it freaked him out. Letting someone control his movements like that. Not good. Not good at all. He focused on breathing through it. Just a few more days of this, and he would be able to walk freely. It was penance of a sort. And connection.

"You did fine for a first try. I guess the talisman-repair experience gives you a steady hand." Etenesh smiled, though her nails were free of polish. Supportive she may be, but she would be dead five times over before she went out with scuffed nails.

"It really helped that you were coaching me through it. It's a lot more involved than I thought. I genuinely just thought . . . get nail polish, paint on, job done."

"Hah! No way! There is a reason getting your nails done is a whole *thing*. Plus the hand massage." She gave a little shiver. "Which you are good at, by the way. Feel like trying a pedicure?"

"Sure." Truth shrugged. Same deal but with feet, right? He had a feeling he would learn otherwise. Then another thought occurred to him. "Does this mean giving you a foot massage, too?"

"Mmm-hmmm." Etenesh looked beatific. Which made sense to Truth. In another era, he suspected Etenesh might be a saint. Jember would certainly be a prophet. Jember had suddenly recalled a lot of studying he urgently needed to do in the temple library, so he couldn't accompany them. Good man, that.

"I guess you can teach me that, too."

"Gladly."

The park was nice. A little bland, as parks in Xandre went. The trees were a normal beige-and-green, the grass mowed short, the statues rather dull and silent. Still, it was nice enough, it was close enough, and you didn't need to prove your citizenship status to use it. You could just stroll right on in. No guards or anything.

He could feel Etenesh shift behind him. Her voice turned a little shy, a little pleading. "Actually, I really like massage. Really like it."

"Oh?"

"Would you . . . be willing to massage more of me than just my hands and feet?"

Truth thought about it for a moment. On the one hand, was this rushing too fast? By the standards of both Harban and Siphios, it was glacially slow. Okay, so, was it too fast for him? He would be the one doing the massaging, so . . . no. He was okay with it. Maybe it would mean seeing more of Etenesh. He smiled a little. He liked that thought.

"Okay."

She snorted, then started laughing. "Tommy Wells, did you just put covering your girlfriend in warm, glistening oil and running your strong hands all over her taut, bare skin on the same level as charging into a demonic horde?"

Truth thought fast, figured there was no right answer, and reflexively said, "I fell into the cerulean ponds of your eyes." Etenesh collapsed onto the handlebars of the wheelchair, shaking with laughter.

"How? How could you think that was relevant? You aren't even looking at me."

"It . . . might have been. It could be a saying," he said with wounded dignity.

"We have to get you some better romance novels. I don't read 'em myself, but we can ask around."

"Find a librarian. Guaranteed they have the good stuff."

"You think?"

"Librarian at Bule was a stone freak. You would not believe what was in her secret stash."

"No! Tell all."

Whew. Bomb defused.

"It might distract me from the demon-horde comparison."

Dammit.

Etenesh doesn't read romance novels. She's happy enough reading the prophetic writings of some ancient patriarch, but she doesn't read romances, or thrillers, or murder mysteries. She loves pitz, enjoys changing up her hair from time to time, and is a very tactile person. Loves to touch and be touched. She was a child of the Heaven-Beseeching Family, though he had never once heard her use a surname. Or Jember, actually. *Is there something there?* She seemed to be on good terms with her uncle, so it wasn't likely a rift.

They were rattling down an alley. Etenesh claimed that she still owed Truth a "real" dorowot and knew a good place. The city was a swirling mass of mysteries, where everything was significant and possessed of its own divinity. It was hard to believe that this was the city half-muted. The city was falling silent.

"Heaven-Beseeching Family?" Truth asked.

Etenesh took a moment to process that. "Yes?"

"You never mentioned it. I don't know anything about your family, beyond that your ancestral lands are adequate for your needs, and you used to be very close to the angels."

"You want to know more about my family?"

"I want to know more about you."

There was a long pause. "I may have underestimated romance novels." She slowed down a little. "So . . . you may have noticed some people use surnames, or family names or whatever, and some don't. The oldest families, or those trying to look like an old family, don't. The idea was that you didn't need a last name, because everyone knew who you were. Or if they didn't, they were nobody of significance. A surname was a sign of low status."

Truth thought that was a solid flex.

"Later immigrant groups had their own naming conventions. Nobody here discouraged it, because we are born snobs, and the foreigners tagging themselves as low-class was handy. This was thousands of years ago, you understand. These days, most people have a last name."

"And the Heaven-Beseeching Family?"

"We came to this world when it was first settled. Our ancestors walked the hills and mountains near Achi'ni. It was there they fell to their knees in worship. They saw messenger angels breaking the soil and making the land ready for farming." He could hear the smile in her voice, the warmth of her reaching him even at arm's length.

"They were the first angels we made pacts with. Our family has been beseeching the heavens ever since."

"And . . . do you all live together? Is there a big family mansion or something?"

"Hah. How could that be? There are thousands of us." Truth choked on that one. "Of course, some are so far removed from the direct line of descent, they are functionally unrelated. Still, the heritage is there, and the identity. Scattered all over Siphios. We never really emigrate out of the country. According to family lore, the longest a member of the Heaven-Beseeching Family spent outside of Siphios was one year, when we were at war with . . . well . . . the country that would become the country that would become the country that would eventually turn into the Ressilaud Free State. He hated it. Came home and never left his farm for the rest of his life."

Truth chuckled. He could imagine it, a sort of grumpy-looking Jember ditching his pack by a farmhouse gate and swearing to never step through it again.

"My part of the family is pretty close to the main line, for what little that's worth the last few centuries. Big on education, of course, and we are a famously devout family. Loads of us in the Temple. Loads. We had six high priests in the last thousand years. No one else comes close to that record."

"Priests!" Truth almost exploded. "THANK YOU! I wondered what to call the clergy in the temples, but nobody ever said. Priests. Good to know. Thank you."

Etenesh chuckled darkly. "You are welcome. Unfortunately, you have never met a Siphios Orthodox priest. They are all Teachers or Celebrants or Versifiers or some other job, but you have never actually met a priest."

Truth felt his brain lurch for a second. "I don't get it."

"There are currently twenty priests in Siphios. An all-time low, but the high was a hundred, so there has never been many of them."

"Priest is a high-up job in the Temple?"

"Very, but more than that, it's political. The position is a Crown appointment on the advice of the Congregation on the Regulation of the Faith. Which is a sixty-person committee made up of the most senior Teachers the Orthodoxy has. Basically, they send over a list of a hundred names, and the Crown can pick as many as they like."

"So, there was a king who picked them all?"

"Ugly story. He was twelve, his uncles were corrupt bastards, and his aunt was worse. Basically, they colluded with the Congregation to give very prestigious lifetime jobs to various family members. This was . . . nine hundred years ago? Still, we have a lot of regulations and rituals in place to make sure it doesn't happen again."

Her family could trace their line back to the founding of this world. More than that, there was a connection to those first people. She spoke of things centuries and millennia past as though it was last Tuesday. The private business of kings and priests was casual gossip. He suddenly imagined Etenesh as a particular spot on a long rope, stretching from past to future. Truth? A bit of frayed string. Perhaps the twist tie from a bag of cheap bread bought from a convenience store in the slums and left on the sidewalk when the trash can it was in was knocked over, and nobody picked it up. Ever.

"I can feel you when you do that, you know. When you go off somewhere in your memories." Her voice was calm, not judging. "Would you like to tell me about your family?"

"No."

They went on in silence for a bit.

"It's not me being paranoid this time. I mean, that too, but it's just . . ." He groped around for a way to explain it, not finding much.

"Look, imagine a canal, okay? Nice, big, long canal. Now, everyone dumps their shit in the canal, and it drifts along on the surface for a while before sinking and drifting along the bottom. Eventually, things just pile up on the bottom and stay there. Not moving anymore. Sludge stuff, with bigger, heavier things hidden in the gunk. The water over the bottom is kinda clear. Not clean, exactly, but clearer. Unless someone stirs up the sludge, trying to haul out those big pieces. Then it's a mess and stays a mess for a long while until the crud falls back to the bottom. This is a smelly, nasty time for everyone."

They rolled on a little farther. "Tommy . . . you can't leave them down there forever."

Truth half-choked and half-laughed. "I can try! I *emancipated* myself when I was seventeen and took the sibs with me." He frowned. He didn't know the word for *emancipated*. "*Emancipated* means *set free*. My parents are legally dead to me and my siblings."

Etenesh came to a dead stop. "You . . . can do that? Just . . . cut away family like that?"

"Took half an hour wait time and a single-page form. Magistrate couldn't stamp it fast enough, apparently."

"You cut the line of your family. With a single page."

"Yes. Weeping with joy as I did it."

"Tommy, you cut the line of your family! That's not—"

He twisted around and looked at her. She must have seen something in his expression, though he was trying to smile. "It's not only *okay*, it was necessary. Completely necessary. You have a wonderful family of wonderful people stretching back and forward through time. I have a bit of rotten string, with a tiny bit of good. I cut away the rot and protected the good. And that's that."

They kept walking silently for a while.

"My favorite after-dinner treat is tej, but *for some reason*, I haven't wanted any for a while. I also really like mandazi, when they aren't too sweet and have a nice bit of coconut chew to them. Coffee spiced with cardamom isn't an all-the-time favorite, but it is very comforting to me," Etenesh said.

"My favorite band is Nishaiar, but anything with that big, atmospheric energy is good for me. I love to dance, and as soon as you are feeling better, I'm hauling you out to a club and showing you off. I enjoy massage and am really looking forward to getting a massage from you."

She leaned over and whispered in his ear. "And the boy I like, my pretty man, is named Truth Medi*ci*."

CHAPTER 60

THICK SKIN

O ut of the chair?"

"That was Etenesh. I'm starting to think she has some kind of mothering, nurturing thing going." Truth had managed to gingerly walk into Merkovah's office/cell without crutches, but it was slow going.

"You think? *You think?* May the Lord Almighty preserve that poor girl. She's going to be ice-skating uphill with this one." Merkovah dramatically looked heavenward.

"Siphios is right on the equator. What do you know about ice skating?"

"Enough to know it's a madman's hobby. Ah, poor Etenesh. How she can look so happy, I don't know."

"She is teaching me how to give her massages."

"I bet she wants to massage you right back."

"I'm not ready for that."

"So, she gets to be lavished with your attention. Dim room, scented candles, you warm the oil between your strong hands before pressing them to the lovely curves of her back. How am I doing so far?"

Truth clapped his hands once, loudly. "So. We debrief the mission now?" he asked in a bright voice.

Merkovah nodded. "We debrief the mission now. Good news—it was a resounding success . . . for Siphios. Bad news, it was a so-so success for my personal goals. However, knowing you as I do . . ." Merkovah handed over an envelope and a box. "The rest of your fee and the elixir."

The tension visibly drained out of Truth. "Ah. Thank you." And then proceeded to count the fee immediately. It was all there. He examined the elixir, too. He couldn't judge just by sight and smell, but the pill was faintly haloed with golden light. Looked legit.

"You know, some people would consider that rude."

"Oh." Truth carefully put the money and elixir away. "All right, so, let's debrief. If you don't mind, could we start with why I got so messed up there and why I am still recovering?"

"We will get to that, but the order is important. From the top. You blended in with the street scene well. Infiltrated the shop. Brained the shopkeeper, then drugged him. Good job there, by the way. Completely clean from the street—our observers had no idea it had happened until you sent the signal."

"Thank you, Teacher."

"Though was it really necessary to use a model of Nag Hamadi to do it? I've been getting looks."

"He wanted nine birr for it. It's not even a good sculpture."

"WHAT! Nine birr for that crap? Nag Hamadi is one of the oldest, finest temples in the world! There are far, far better souvenir models available, and for a better price."

"I, too, was moved by outrage."

"He wouldn't lower the price?"

"He would not."

"Haaah. *Okay*. From that point, you searched the back room. Did you find anything?"

"Nope, just the passage down."

"Which you found by punching through the wall rather than locating the trigger to open the door."

"Yes, it's a common practice for breaching a building. Quite often, the doors will be trapped or armored, so where possible, go through the wall next to the door."

Merkovah considered that point, then nodded. "Rings a bell. All right, you went through and down. Then what?"

Truth described his brief exploration of the sub-basement, then walked through the fight. Merkovah nodded steadily, occasionally asking questions. He seemed particularly concerned by the descriptions of the anti-magic explosions that radiated from the anti-theists.

"About that, what should we call them?"

"The name of their organization?"

"That too, but . . . they definitionally aren't cultists, and *anti-theists* is just an annoying thing to say. Cabal? Coven?"

Merkovah shrugged. "*Cabal* sounds good. The names change, details change, the heresy remains the same. So, they were able to launch this . . . explosion without any tools, any sigils, or the like?"

"Not that I could see. Was there anything on their bodies?"

"An enormous number of tattoos and scarification. We are examining them now. Some even lived long enough to get treated." Merkovah grinned nastily. Truth didn't care to imagine the present condition of the Cabal members.

"Let's get to why you are feeling so wretched and how we can turn a negative into a positive. You feel like crap because they hit you with a double whammy. The basement was covered in one of their special wards that excludes cosmic rays. Any spells that were cast in there would fizzle out, and anyone not equipped to deal with the environment would quickly empty out their reserves of cosmic energy. Combined with that . . . explosion thing . . . which depleted even more of your cosmic energy, and you were hollowed out."

Merkovah sat back in his chair, steepling his fingers. "The pain in your chest that you reported was your apertures starting to collapse. No need to fret. You weren't down there long enough for there to be any permanent damage, but that's what was happening. A lightning-quick acceleration of the natural outcome of not cultivating steadily."

"But the rest of my body, my muscles . . ."

"Are seething with cosmic energy. That's what body cultivation is—making you more real. Closer to God. And crammed full of cosmic energy to power it all. I must say, they are an ingenious bunch. Sending body cultivators into their nests is how we used to clear them out. Looks like they worked out a counter."

Truth frowned at that. He had felt that, even by his jaded standards, the mission prep had been substandard. Had they really been relying on his body cultivation to carry the day?

"One did call me a Templar."

"Hah! That takes me back. Not in four hundred years, more's the pity. The Poor Brothers of the Temple of St. Ghertsip, also known as the 'Templars.' A militant fellowship, though they did raise a great deal of money for charities. The Temple used them as . . . well, as a private military company, to use a term you would be familiar with. Eventually, their duties were folded into the Office of Temple Security, and eventually, the order disbanded. Sad, but such is life."

"Sword-wielding body cultivators?"

"Body cultivators, yes, but they preferred heavy armor, heavy shields, and heavy maces."

"Nasty."

"They really were." Merkovah smiled with fond nostalgia, then shook it off.

"Obviously, a ward like that has enormous military applications. More pertinently, it could utterly screw Starbrite. It will take a little extra doing on my part, but I think I can still ensure the technology falls into my hands."

"Yes, Teacher."

"Likewise, a big weapon they can use against us. It would just *shred* summons and spiritual beings."

Truth nodded. Not his department, really, but that all sounded plausible.

"All right, there will be a lot more to pick through in the coming weeks, but none of that is your job. Let's talk about your current pain and how to turn it into gain."

"I'm slowly, passively recovering from cosmic-energy depletion."

"A remarkable bit of healing. Good job." Truth declined to mention that it was something his body was doing without his control. Seemed . . . unnecessary to draw attention to. "I notice that you are a truly diligent cultivator. Your progress through Level Three has been quite quick."

"Ah, it's my nightly habit. I had hoped to do it outside, but it didn't seem like there was a good place to cultivate."

"Oh, have Nag Hamadi show you where the roof garden is. It's not very popular, but a couple of people do cultivate up there."

Truth nodded. He would do that. He liked cultivating under the stars. Just felt better, somehow.

"But it does lead us to my point about how to turn this into a good thing. How has your progress on Incisive been?"

"Haven't succeeded in creating the scales yet, Teacher."

"Let's drill on that for a while. I'm upping your tutorial time to two hours a day. I am also arranging for you to have special herbal baths. This will help gently rebuild your internal systems—muscle, flesh, tendons, tissues. It will also be an opportunity for you to practice the scales. It's a good idea to look at actual snakes for inspiration, but do remember to be flexible in your thinking. Botis is a viper, yes, but also a highly intelligent being that considered Incisive for uncountable eons. There will be layers of subtleties to it."

Truth nodded. It made sense.

"Truth . . . hah. Still feels odd calling you that. Truth, I will be as candid with you as I can. Things are spinning out of control faster than even I anticipated." Truth sat up straighter at that.

"One of the oddities of becoming so old—we are quite used to things suddenly spinning out of our control, have many more tools available for managing things that spin out of our control . . . and we hate it far, far more than we did when we were younger. It almost feels like a personal insult."

Truth nodded slowly. He could believe that.

"So. Things are spinning out of control, spinning *badly* out of control. The Shattervoid, the weakening of the planet as a whole, spreading civil unrest, crop failures, increased military activity by several nations, and the ever more vicious desperation of the plutocrats. It all adds up to a grand collapse. It may well turn into an extinction-level event. Certainly for the more spiritual species, but quite possibly for us, too."

"I assume there is something you want to do about it."

"Collapse is inevitable. How we collapse is not. My determination to kill Starbrite, the C-suite, and the System Astrologica is unchanged. Our timeline *has* changed. I will need you combat-deployable in three months or less. And frankly, I am almost certain it will be less. I am cashing in old favors at an alarming rate, but your body and soul will be thoroughly improved in the next few weeks. You will be considerably harder to scry even if you don't advance with Incisive, but the benefits will be incalculably better if you do. Learning the Sword of Moshe . . . well, I will teach you, but I'm afraid you will have to self-study a lot of it. You will, however, be Level Four. Insanely fast. You have been Level Three for what? A year?"

Truth just shrugged. Merkovah shook his head.

"Yes, I don't really know what else I was expecting." He paused. "I know you strenuously avoid discussing your past, but . . . I can tell I overlap with someone in your memories, someone you distrust and despise. If I may ask, what is it that makes us so similar to you? I have a hard time imagining there were people like me in . . . the place you are clearly from."

"He made his victims feel special. Showed them, carefully and deliberately, how special he found them. He genuinely considered himself the 'good one.' And I don't think any of his victims lived more than two years after coming into his care." Truth smiled. "Etenesh said I understand the world as violence—either the act or preparing for the act. I think it might be more accurate to say . . . I am used to being both predator and prey."

He stood from the table. "Same time for the tutorial?"

"Same time. What's your plan for the day?"

"Stretching, light exercise, meditation. Then I'm being handed over to Jember before he sends me to Etenesh."

"Oh? Say more."

"I am to be dressed and styled. Jember is up on the latest fashions and apparently has a keen eye for what works. Once I am prettied up, Etenesh is hauling me out to a club. Etenesh says she has been very patient and giving, which is true, and quote: 'It is past time I put certain mooing missys in their place.' She also said, and again, I'm quoting here, 'I got a pretty, pretty man, and I'm going to show him off.'"

"Nice. Very nice! Good for you, Truth."

"Thank you. It . . . still feels unreal, somehow. Like I want to believe it, and maybe I can half-believe it, but it really doesn't quite reach all the way in, you know?"

"That you are neither predator nor prey but a desired partner for a dance between equals?"

"Yes."

Merkovah smiled a bit. "Have fun with that feeling. There is nothing quite like it. Ah, but allow me to help young love on a bit."

He ignored Truth sputtering his denials and fished a small box out of the bottom of the bottom drawer of his desk.

"Repeat after me—'Back sheaths are dumb.'"

"Back sheaths are dumb."

"'That's not how swords work, or arms.'"

"That's not how swords work, or arms."

"'You would leave yourself wide open to draw that way.'"

"You would leave yourself wide open to draw that way."

"'I am not dumb.'"

Truth looked Merkovah dead in the eye and said, "I am not dumb."

"Damn right, you're not. Here. From one predator to another." Merkovah passed over the box. "Play with it some. And enjoy!"

CHAPTER 61

THE WORLD I WANT TO LIVE IN

So . . . this nightclub," Truth asked Etenesh. "Can you . . . narrow down the description for me?" The carpet soared over the city traffic, a snarl of wagons and chariots and clubs riding herds of identical spirit beasts through intersections and slowing traffic for everyone.

Jember had him looking sharp. Truth could happily admit that. He had always been proud of his body, and Jember was not shy about slapping a tight-fitting robin's-egg-blue shirt on him that was practically painted over his biceps, tapered trousers, and, to Truth's immense surprise, the tasseled white zeph was declared mandatory. First, because it made a nice balance to the white casual shoes he was wearing, and second, "You will need it." And Jember wouldn't say more.

Jember did try to part Truth from the Tongue, but Truth showed off Merkovah's loan, and they both laughed. It was a set of rings that magically connected the sheath for the Tongue to his back and a ring for his finger. Run a bit of power through the talisman ring, and the sword would eject from the sheath and fly into his hand. It was ostentatious as hell, but it would mean he could go out and dance without leaving his sword behind.

"Ah. Now I feel suddenly bad. You . . . weren't a nightclub person, were you?"

"Personally? No. Professionally? Yes, a lot. That's why I wanted to know."

"Wait, you bodyguard people in nightclubs?"

"Yep. Lots of young masters and mistresses out for a fun night on the town. It was my job to make sure they could have their fun without having . . . consequences. That couldn't be solved with money, anyway."

"Huh. Now that you say it, I can imagine that did come up a lot. Well, the Garden Club is pretty chill. Dancing, some pretty good food, and plenty of drinks. But before you start worrying, there is a reason you're sporting the zeph. It's a Desrin club. Not very observant Desrin; they do serve meat and alcohol. They just charge triple the price for it compared to everywhere else. So, a lot of people drinking fancy teas, coffees, and iced drinks."

Truth thought back to the nightclubs he remembered. One of them, admittedly not one of the *nicer* ones, had a sign by the door reading MUST BE THIS HIGH TO

ENTER and a picture of an anthropomorphic rabbit about to ruin the chastity of a garbage truck. The truck was alarmingly into it. In fact, he couldn't remember a visit to a club where the protectee was sober. This would be a change.

Etenesh sharply waved her hand in front of him. "I want to turn your chin toward me with a finger. No, don't look over toward me. It will spoil the effect." She extended her index finger. Truth gave her a slight smile and nodded. She put her fingertip to his chiseled chin and turned his face to her.

"I want your attention tonight. Which means I want you to be here with me. Not in whatever unhappy place you drift to. We are here at my third-favorite club, and your job tonight is to be my date. My escort. My pretty, pretty man, who I *fully* intend to grind in the face of several notable young ladies, and several more young gentlemen, who in the past have made *comments*."

She smiled victoriously, then hesitated and raised her finger again. "I should stress that this is purely a social thing, and even if they are really shitty, which I honestly don't think they will be, I would be really upset if you were to, say, redecorate the club with their mangled remains before hunting down their families, friends, and anyone who owes them money."

Truth tried to look wounded. "I would never!"

"Uh-huh. Come on, pretty man. The music at the Garden is usually pretty chill. I bet you learn to dance fast, and I'm woman enough to admit I am looking forward to rubbing up against you."

Well, when she put it that way, he was pretty excited about it too. "Third-favorite club?"

"Number one is Lemmy's Stew, which is basically a booze- and drug-fueled riot supported by dangerously loud music. *Riot* in the sense of fun, but also in the sense that people are slamming around off each other." Truth could imagine it and directly refused to go in his head.

"I figured you would be four counties over and still accelerating by the time I finished describing it if I tried to drag you there," Etenesh continued, "Which also ruled out number two—Bloody Mace, which is Lemmy's but the drinks cost more and the lineup usually isn't as good. Better dancefloor, though, and some of the regulars are really fun."

Truth tried to think of something funny to say and struck out. He . . . probably didn't have a shitty personality. He could admit that to himself now. He was probably okay that way. But he still felt bad, like he didn't know what to say if he couldn't steal the line from a book. So, he just fumbled for a minute and said the only thing he could think of.

"Thank you for thinking of me. I feel like I make a scene whenever people take me places, so . . . thank you."

It sounded moronic. He needed to read more books, memorize more lines. That was dumb. He was dumb.

"Truth Medici, I want you to kiss me right now!" He stumbled but then happily did as she asked. The books could wait.

The bouncer waved them right in. There was a line down the block, and they didn't even have a chance to join the queue. The bouncer, a cone-shaped Desrin man with sausage fingers and cauliflower ears, saw them get off the carpet and immediately came and greeted them. His zeph had a tassel too. They were on the list. They would always be on the list. There was no cover for them. Ever. Etenesh looked as surprised as he did, but they went with it. A staggeringly attractive young lady in a sharply short skirt and abbreviated top led them to their luxurious booth. A VIP table in the cordoned-off VIP area, where they could see the stage well and be seen, but not bothered, by the masses.

Etenesh just shrugged at it all, which was more or less Truth's reaction, too. Their explanation came almost immediately as another cone-shaped Desrin, no tassel, rushed over to their table.

"Heaven-Beseeching Family's Etenesh, and the young Hero. They kept your name out of the news, so I won't pry. You both have done a lot for the Desrin community here in Siphios. I know you didn't do it for that reason, but you really did. Young man, you stood up for yourself but didn't get dragged into starting a riot. I—we all are so *damn* proud of you. And you, Etenesh. The only regular who reads theology in the booth between sets! A daughter of the honest-to-God *Heaven-Beseeching Family* coming out on the sands, staking her soul for the honor of a Desrin brother?"

The club owner was getting choked up, stumbling over his words. "You have no idea, no idea. You can see how bad the city has been getting. Things bad all over. But you two. Power, pride, grace. So much respect. Mutual respect. Stay. Eat, drink, free forever. Thank you both so much. I'm—" The owner was overcome with emotion and had to gather himself for a moment. "Have good night. May God bless you both."

Truth and Etenesh looked at each other with wondering eyes. The waitress, who had been waiting for the club owner to finish his piece, added, "I've got a brother. He's dating a Progressive girl, trying to keep it quiet, but that's impossible in this city. People threw stones at them. Or beer bottles. Spit in their food or wouldn't serve them at all. Smashed up their bikes. I saw a granny cross the street rather than speak to them. Not anymore. Now people say they set a good example. My name is Fatisame, and if you two need *anything*, you just wave."

Etenesh reached her hand out to Truth. He grabbed it. She squeezed hard, and he squeezed right back.

Truth thought he would be more uncomfortable dancing, but . . . it was okay, actually. Then it was more than just okay; it was fun. Etenesh was right—he did pick up the basic idea of dancing quickly. He wasn't good at it, particularly, but he could keep the rhythm and, between his incredible strength and flexibility, had no problem keeping up with Etenesh. Who, as promised, was having an immense amount of fun rubbing herself all over him.

When he started, tentatively, dancing back, she gave him a big smile. When he extended his arms toward her, she grabbed his hands and put them directly on her ass and snuggled into his chest for a slow number.

It was, Truth decided, one hell of a fun night. The food was outstanding, too, soft baked bits of flatbread with endless dips to try and fruits to eat. Apparently, you could mix drinks that had no alcohol but still tasted really fun and different. A balance of citrus and sweetness and bitterness and heady aroma after heady aroma. It was a whole new universe. He conferred with Etenesh, and they agreed they were part of the Path of the Foodie. They canoodled on the carpet home.

Drunk on the night, Truth decided to confess. "Etenesh, this is one of those things that's embarrassing for me, but you probably won't care. But still. Be nice to me."

She laughed softly. "All right, I think I can manage that."

"I really, really enjoyed tonight. And I really want to go to bed with you. But I'm also not ready for sex, and part of that is . . . I'm a virgin."

There was a strange pause. At the very edge of his hearing, Truth heard a faint *Squeeeeeeee*. Etenesh convulsed once, then gently detangled herself from Truth and got on her knees. She started murmuring something.

"Are you . . . praying?"

"Giving thanks. Don't interrupt."

Truth sat there, watching. Not how he expected this to go, but . . . The prayer took a whole minute. Etenesh looked *incredibly* sincere the whole time. She then returned to his side, grinning joyfully.

"You know, I had half-wondered about that"—she chuckled—"but at the same time, I absolutely couldn't believe it. Thank you for telling me. Thank you, thank you, thank you. I am going to make sure you have the very best time learning everything you need to know. Because that means I will have the very best time, and I know you will enjoy that too." Truth nodded, smiling.

"I read up on how body cultivation works. I'm guessing you weren't always so handsome?"

"No. But more to the point, my life kind of made real relationships impossible. What's more, I was . . . I don't have words for it. I was convinced that I was ugly to the point where I was unlovable. Literally unlovable. To be clear, it was something that was done *to* me. No unhappy memories. I want to be here with you, Etenesh."

She smiled and snuggled up against him. They shared the blessed moment. "This is what I want, you know. This moment, right here. A good, Godly man, and *yes, you are,* even if you don't think you are. A happy night. Good music, good food. Love, romance, the warm feeling of knowing sex is coming, and you are going to really enjoy it, but for now, you can just savor the anticipation. Peace over the land." She sighed happily.

"This is what I will fight for. My own holy path." Truth chuckled a bit at that. Then almost choked when she said, "And of course, we don't have to have sex, but I am damn well getting myself off tonight. Wanna watch and learn something?"

It was a rather thoughtful-looking Truth that sat down at breakfast the next morning. Jember demanded he tell all, and Truth just shook his head. Etenesh snorted at that and dove into a highly detailed retelling of the last night. It sounded like Jember strongly approved. He noticed Etenesh didn't mention to Jember that he was a virgin.

He really should get her a present or something. That was the kind of thing people did with their girlfriends, right? And she was his girlfriend. Which was . . . incredible. Though he had never said the words out loud. She had called him her man, so it would probably be okay if he called her his girlfriend, right?

"Etenesh?" he softly interrupted.

"Yes?"

"Can I tell people you are my girlfriend?"

She must have seen something in his eyes because hers suddenly filled with tears as she nodded and said, "Yes. I would like it very much if you did. The man I love should call me that."

CHAPTER 62

ROUGH SCALES

Truth was back in the reflection chamber. Naked again, but this time for a more practical than spiritual reason. Mastering the scales portion of Incisive was now an urgent necessity. He thought it was best to be comfortable in his own skin.

He looked around the tiny chamber. Still bare stone three meters square, still a bowl and a mat and nothing else. Only what he carried in with him. It had been . . . God, how long had it been? Not even a month, right? Or maybe a little over a month. Not long at all. But so much had changed. He had changed. The Truth who had been carried out of this chamber last time was quite different from the Truth who walked in today.

Truth looked into the little basin of water. Strong face. The "him" before the well didn't look much like this, but there were clues here and there. Something to the set of his eyes, particularly. That look that he had come to recognize as hardness. It . . . probably said something that he saw hardness in his eyes when he looked at his reflection. Though the look was less mistrustful. It was less . . . ready to lash out. Less afraid.

Had he learned to feel safe? To love himself and accept the love of others? The face in the water broke into a pained smile. No. Not really. He would probably spend the rest of his life learning to do that. However long that life wound up being. But he could believe that one day, he would love himself. That one day, he could sincerely accept the love and goodwill of others. That the words *I love you* wouldn't stick in his throat, and he would be able to tell Etenesh what she deserved to hear.

Maybe he would be able to tell her how scared those words made him feel. How vulnerable. Allowing her to become a weakness of his. Admitting to her that she had a hold on him. He was overthinking it. He knew that. But still, the words sealed up in his throat and choked him.

He was stronger, faster, more elusive, and deadly in combat. His knowledge of the world had expanded exponentially. He felt like he was coming out of the valleys of ignorance and starting to climb the mountains of wisdom. He could see so much further now. He could see he wasn't yet truly strong. He wasn't yet safe.

So, the scales, then. They weren't armor. Not on a real snake, not in the spell. Thinking the scales looked like armor was a human thing. For the snakes, scales were basically just skin. Useful skin. They retained water in dry places and acted as camouflage or warnings to predators. They could even help the snake climb and move along the earth.

All well and good, but the spell was called Incisive, not Useful Things for Snakes. Botis named it that for a reason. The rest of the spell all seemed to point directly to the name—the foresight, the cutting power, even the ability to debate or use rhetoric. But scales? How did scales tie in to the word Incisive?

Okay, he knew what scales did for vipers in the wild, but Botis was a stellar demon of ancient and terrible power, just a few short steps from God. He was far, far more than just a snake. What did the scales mean to him?

Snakeskin. Shedding? Not really incisive. Just the opposite, really. Identity? The camouflage or warning you show to the world? Again, not really incisive, and let's be real, Botis gives exactly zero fucks about anyone's opinion.

Oh, hang on. Wait . . . just a moment. There may actually be something there.

Identity . . . as a tool. Identity as something you grow into, then out of. Something you shed, an external layer that is part of you but not the core of you. You shed it when you grow, yes, but not only then. Vipers shed at least once a year. Removing all the dirt and grime they have accumulated before their new scales appear and harden.

Truth toyed with the concept for a moment. He wasn't really a deep thinker on the subject of identity, but when your face and body radically transform . . . well. He'd thought on it some. What did an identity do for someone? Hell of a question, really.

Identity is necessarily tied to one's sense of self, but it wasn't all that you were. He had two identities—Tommy Wells, a resident of Siphios, and Truth Medici, a Citizen of Jeon. But he never really considered those national parts of his identity unless they were immediately relevant to something. His identity as a brother to his siblings was always a core part of his identity. Soldier? Bodyguard? Mercenary? Those came and went, and he presented them like business cards to people . . . as and when it became necessary.

Identity, telling the world what you wanted them to know, taking in what you needed, keeping the crap off of you, and ultimately, something to be discarded and re-formed when all the crap burdening it got too much. Because while it was connected to you, and it was important, it wasn't all of you. And the core of Incisive, the first law of the First Gem of Botis, was "Love yourself." You didn't need to be carrying the world's shit.

The world didn't get to define your identity, no matter how much dirt they put on it. You did. You used it to get straight to the point of whatever interaction you wanted to have with the world. Camouflage to hide from predators, to ambush prey, to scare away the things that spot you. To attract mates or establish status. Your external identity, your scales, *was a tool to impose your reality on the world.*

The idea knocked him flat on his ass, ignoring the cold stone floor to stare blindly up at the ceiling. Incisive was a comprehensive tool for imposing your will, your *reality,* on the world and not letting the world impose its reality on you. It cut to the point, the point being whatever your goals were.

What brilliance. What arrogance. The First Gem of Botis—Love yourself and *fuck* everyone else. They will do as you wish or perish, and none of their shit will muddy your boots. Not for long. Botis truly was a supreme demon, a snake unwilling to bend its neck for any purpose but to strike.

Truth started laughing. He laughed so hard, he choked. He let his hands and feet drum on the ancient sandstone, applauding and cheering for the immortal arrogance of Botis. It all came together now. He had been doing things in a certain sequence because that was how Merkovah had lined them up for him, but that's not how it actually worked. It was all one spell. They all operated at the same time.

He could picture it perfectly. The scales—your identity in the world. How you defined yourself and how you wanted the world to define you. Changeable, as you grew and your needs changed. Foresight, the eyes, because you were always watching and wary. Opportunity and danger went hand in hand, after all. And to that end, the cutting portion, the fangs, retracted until the second it was needed to strike, then it vanished again. Always present, merely . . . reserved when not in use. Then there was the rhetoric. The debating, public speaking, and persuasive portion. The tongue, perhaps? Or the wisdom? Because one of the most potent ways to change the world was to make people change how they thought about it and themselves.

It was . . . almost perfect. He was sure there were endless details and layers of subtlety he was missing. But from the little corner of it that he could understand, the whole completed spell was sheer art. It was a whole operating system for living, as a spell. It was a statement about who you were and how you would live. More than merely a spell, it was a philosophy. The First Gem of wisdom bestowed by Botis. Love yourself. Then put that love into practice. Love may be in many forms, but it is never passive. The viper is coiled, waiting, but alert. Its mind and will were always in motion, ready for the exact moment when victory was to be seized.

He sat on the mat and cast Incisive. Foresight, then fang, then the scales. It collapsed, as he expected. Where did the spell start? From within. From his will. It started with *him*. So, his conception of himself was the place to build from. He cast the scales and felt it flicker around him. Not quite. Not quite stable yet. He could feel the air subtly change around him. It felt cleaner. The cosmic rays striking him were more . . . orderly, for lack of a better term. As though they were told to tidy themselves and behave properly before they approached too close.

He could feel himself alternately fading into the background as though the room were totally empty, then snapping into focus. Then an even-sharper focus, like he was the only thing truly real in the room. He couldn't hold on to it, let alone direct it how he wished. But it was a start. More than a start. It was the path forward.

Merkovah was delighted by the progress Truth had made when they sat for the tutorial.

"That is certainly one of the classic understandings of Incisive, though I will caution you that it is not the only one. Don't go looking for texts on it. They are rare and can only slow you down now. Concentrate on your own conception and your understanding of Botis. The revelation on the mountaintop has given you an extraordinary edge in learning this spell. It would be a shame to slow your growth by internalizing the thoughts of others. Become competent with it first, then once you have stalled in your growth, go and see what other people thought."

Truth thought that sounded sensible, however . . . "I want another crack at that demon, if that would be okay?"

"Which demon?"

"Child Eater. The one you made a specialized curse tablet for?"

Merkovah shot to his feet. "BY THUNDER, YES! Merciful heavens, it has been a stressful, miserable few decades, and the last month has been particularly trying. No offense, you, Etenesh, and Jember have been some of the rare high points, but it's hard to have a good time when the world is collapsing."

Merkovah rubbed his hands.

"Yes, indeed. Time to see what you can *really* do now that you have some grasp of Incisive. And relieve some stress by torturing a truly wretched demon."

"Should I pick up some snacks when I collect the cousins?"

"Yes. Get a variety, but avoid the 'cheese'-flavored plantain chips. I've investigated. The recipe is merely bad, not infernal, though the difference may be tiny."

"Is it really that bad?"

"I wouldn't even feed it to the Child Eater. Go!"

CHAPTER 63

A HOLE IN THE HEART, PART TWO

They had assembled once again in the basement of Nag Hamadi. The rough sandstone walls remained as sturdy as ever, the floors smoothed by centuries upon centuries of feet glistened in the talisman light. Even down there, the piney, warm smell of temple incense lingered. A place of reverence, though far from the altar and the clergy.

There's always someone who can't read the room. Today, there were four of them.

"All right, I'll set out the blanket and the snacks. Jember, Etenesh, same layout as before. I've added a *few* refinements to really up the suffering. Tommy, get loose. Shake it all out, limber up those limbs, and start working through Incisive. You are definitely not who you were when you first squared up against Child Eater, and you are going to really enjoy the changes." Merkovah opened the thick blanket with a snap of his wrists.

Truth took his advice, stretching out and getting limber. He didn't really need it, but it was nice to just feel his body. And to pretend he didn't notice Etenesh looking at him with hungry eyes. He was very happy to admit she was good for his ego. Jember was looking too, but Truth was firmly ignoring that fact. Merkovah was all eyes on the picnic. He had brought a thermos of spiced coffee and some kind of flaky, baked treat. Truth could smell the walnuts and honey from five meters away.

The cousins didn't take too long to set up the ritual, and the portal was up and running in just a few minutes. The colors of Hell remained heartbreaking, which Truth supposed was the point. How did he know that that green was the exact shade of gangrene as it set into bone? Or that one was radium burning the jaws of factory girls, next to the green phosphorous flames burning the bones of yet more factory girls, next to the emerald shine in a child's eye as he died in an illegal mine? He just did. It was the nature of the place.

Someday, he would find out what "radium" was, though he was pretty sure he'd heard of phosphorus. Alchemist stuff.

No, there was no ironic detachment in front of Hell. It was grief. It was despair. It was regret. It was the horrible knowledge that it was all your fault and nothing would ever be okay. And from that mess of despair, wriggling like a nightmare on a hook, was the Child Eater.

The demon hadn't changed. Three meters tall, roughly shaped like a man with the sickle blades of a mantis where their arms should be and no head on his shoulders. A bloody tear opened across its gut, showing a mouth with rows of circular teeth. And once again, Merkovah had shown his contempt for any words the horror might have. No matter. It managed to scream with outrage in body language.

"Teacher, before you cut it loose . . . I have a kind of random question for, well, everybody. When you think of a Spell-Blade, what does that bring to mind for you?"

Merkovah smiled. He knew how Incisive worked. "Well, Tommy, to me, they always seemed very disciplined. Self-control and restraint were a core part of their identity, and it showed. Even in the middle of a furious battle, their mind was strictly on the job. They were there to kill demons, fight Hell, and fight humans who would make this world a second Hell. Everything else was someone else's problem. Disciplined and pragmatic."

Truth nodded and looked over at Jember. "I only know them from books and scry, mind you. Ah, I'd say . . . romantic."

That got Jember some looks. He waved defensively.

"Not in the sense of sex but in the sense of pursuing an emotion over common sense. The Spell-Blades in the stories all love what they do, almost to the exclusion of everything else. It's why they obsessed over their swords, their worship, and their wives or husbands. They were the only things they had outside their vocation. And they loved that. They poured all of themselves into exactly four things. Disciplined, yes, but because they were doing what they absolutely loved."

Huh. Interesting wrinkle there.

"For me, and I know this is a . . . loaded word for you, Tommy, but the word is *hero.* Etenesh took a deep breath. "And even more unfortunately, the kinds of heroes you despise. Like Jember said, they seemed to be romantics. They didn't do it for applause or for money, or even for their families. They did it because the job needed doing and nobody else could. Or would. Against all odds, paying any price, all for the sake of people who didn't know them. And even if they were successful, they would be gone before the sun rose on the third day after victory. So. Sorry. *Selfless hero* is how I think of Spell-Blades."

Truth nodded at all that. Some of the ideas merged with what he thought of when he thought of spellblades, and some were new. He fixed his zeph on his head and carefully cast Incisive.

I am Tommy Wells. I am a Desrin spellblade from the Aussa Highlands of Siphios. I walk the wastes, the jungles, the streets, wherever the forces of Hell and hellish people gather. Accompanied only by my blade. Astride my trusty iron horse, I travel the land on errantry. My home is always with me, for I carry its memory in my heart. And one day, one glorious, beautiful day, I will put down my blade, kneel before my wife, and be showered by her blessings. Because the home I carried in my heart was her, and in her heart she carried no one but me.

The people of Siphios are behind me. A demon is before me. All that's left is doing the job. And I love my job. It makes my wife proud and delights God. What could be better than this?

With a smile on his face and in his heart, Truth charged at Child Eater. Truth couldn't tell if the demon recognized him or not, but it still gladly ran straight at him. Truth leveled the Tongue at the demon's breastbone, deliberately recreating the opening exchange from their first encounter. Child Eater swung the sickle blade of its left arm straight at Truth's head . . . and missed.

Truth's smile widened. No, *Tommy's* smile widened. He knew where that blade was headed and slipped aside with a tiny effort. All the power in his body suddenly seemed *properly* under his command. He parried the sickle arm with his sword. He was strong enough to push it to one side. Partially because he was strong but more so because he fully understood the sword now. Understood when and how to push. How to line up his body for maximum effect. More than pure instinct, it was now instinct married to experience.

And, of course, Incisive was doing its part. Tommy shoved the arm right, moving it across Child Eater's body while the tip of his blade stayed on target. He could feel the crucial moment—he lunged! The Child Eater retreated. The tip of the holy blade still caught it, tearing across the demon's chest. Flames, holy and sin-consuming, burst from the thin line.

Child Eater roared and summoned its infernal armor. The red script crawled over its body as it darted around the spelled arena the cousins had made. It took less than a second for the scythe arms to be reinforced, their edge visibly honed. Acid fetters lashed out, reaching for Tommy. Tommy snorted. Such magic was a nuisance, but it was only a nuisance.

The demon's skittering around might have fooled another spellblade, but Tommy's reflexes and awareness far exceeded his level. He fended off the acid fetters with the Tongue, ignoring the few spatters of weak acid that managed to splash on him. In a vague way, he was aware of the curse trying to infiltrate him. It was stopped by skin and flesh alike. Perhaps if the fetter caught him, it might work. As it was, it was too weak to stain this body consecrated to God.

He rushed in, faster now than he had been even a few weeks ago. He could anticipate where Child Eater would shift to. He was fast enough to get there before the demon. When the demon arrived, it found a holy blade hacking down on it. A cruel sickle was raised to block, crawling with infernal scripts. This time, things went a little differently. Tommy knew just where to cut. The blade flickered for just a fraction of a second as the spell coated the blade. The scythe arm was hacked away at the elbow.

Child Eater recoiled. The acid fetters swarmed at him, the spell tracery forming a net of pain and poison between him and the demon. But Tommy had been walking with God since he was a boy. Before he ever came down from the Aussa Highlands, he had hardened his body against pain. Hard as the mountains of home. Hard as God's demands of the Faithful. He held the Tongue firmly in both hands and ran at the . . . thing before him.

When he met the poison net, he *cut*. Cutting through the acid strings. Cutting through the spellwork itself. Cutting through any obstacle between him and his duty.

Whiplike strands of acid snapped and crackled against him, trying to weaken him, but they weren't even distractions. He pressed forward.

Breaking through the fetters, Tommy lined up for a lunge. The demon got there first, a sickle arm coming straight at Tommy's face. Tommy shifted, dropping down and right to hack at the creature's knee. The holy blade sank in behind what would be the kneecap in anything truly humanoid. Crippling. For the demon, it was more of an inconvenience. And pain. Holy fire burst from the cut joint. Mockery of the human form though it may be, that leg wasn't going to be holding weight.

The demon's remaining scythe-blade arm carved down at Tommy's back. Child Eater was willing to trade an injury for a life. It still hadn't understood. Tommy twisted like a snake, dodging the incoming hook. He recovered from the hack at the knee, standing upright, coming even closer to the roaring maw in Child Eater's stomach.

The monster kicked out, deliberately collapsing back to let its taloned claw rake at Tommy's balls. It should have worked. The collapse was total, sudden. An impulsive hero would have charged in for the kill and been killed instead. But Tommy was a spellblade through and through.

Such petty tricks. How many times had he seen them? He raised his own leg and stomped on the monster's thigh as it pulled back, pinning the leg, and the claw, harmlessly away from him. Then, seeing no reason not to, he stabbed straight down into the demon's groin. Pulled the sword out. Spun it in both hands and hacked off the legs.

The remaining scythe arm came whipping in. Tommy swayed back, then caught it under one arm. He stabbed the Tongue into the vile beast's chest, pinning it. Putting his whole weight on the horror's remaining arm, he drove the scythe into the beast's mouth and into the floor. He drew the Tongue out of Child Eater with a final twist and watched as the body lost cohesion, trying to run away to Hell. The enchantments, designed by Merkovah and arranged by the cousins, made even Hell an impossible hope.

He could feel the exhaustion hammering at him now, coming down like it always did after a hunt. His channels ached, muscles ached, and the ignorable stings and cuts were now demanding his attention. He slowly let Incisive go, and with it, he felt the identity of Tommy Wells fade away. It was . . . uncomfortable. Disorienting, almost to the point of nausea. Truth decided that he would offer one last thanks to the persona, a final grace note to his victory.

Truth flicked away what little gore remained on the blade, then sheathed it. He walked slowly back to the picnic blanket, where Etenesh and Jember sat cheering. Merkovah smiled at him but was focused on torturing Child Eater. No matter. Truth drew the scabbard from the frog hanging from his belt, holding the sacred blade in his hands. He stood in front of Etenesh and kneeled down. Set his blade to the side and reached for her hands. She smiled and offered them. He raised them and cupped them around his face.

"I'm home."

CHAPTER 64

A QUESTION OF IDENTITIES

Truth was feeling conflicted about the furious make-out session Etenesh demanded right then and there. On the one hand, it was really damn fun! On the other, it was awkward as hell. Merkovah was torturing a demon four meters away, and Jember was loudly cheering them on. Still, Etenesh was enthusiastic and, oddly, grounding. The transition from "Tommy Wells, Desrin spellblade" to "Truth Medici, Dead Man Walking" was unpleasant. It felt like reality itself had glitched.

Etenesh was happily wiggling underneath him, pretending that he had caught her rather than the other way around. Truth was starting to seriously doubt the whole "clothes on" part of their relationship. Etenesh had been very clear that hers, at least, were coming off in the very near future and strongly hinted that good things would happen if his came off with them. She playfully pretended to bite at him. He had the sudden urge to sink his teeth into her neck, tear her clothes off, and see if he couldn't finally be rid of his virginity. He went for the neck and was considering next steps when Merkovah clapped to get everyone's attention.

"Much as I hate to interrupt your fun, we need to do a little debrief before getting on to the next phase of things. I currently have Child Eater in the 'masticating juicer' part of the ritual, so now is a good time."

Truth didn't actually groan or pout, but Etenesh was pleased to see him look frustrated. Not least because she was pretty damn frustrated herself.

"All right, Tommy, let's start with the most obvious thing. How does it feel to absolutely dominate and humiliate a particularly deadly and sinister Level Four demon from a particularly nasty corner of Hell?"

Truth had a faint instinct to be self-deprecating but quickly banished it. "Absolutely incredible, Teacher. I felt like it couldn't touch me, physically or magically. Although . . ."

"We will get to that, but let's focus on the *untouchable* thing. Now, obviously, a big part of that is your incredible reflexes. Already great stuff, but there is more, isn't there?" Merkovah cocked an eyebrow.

"I feel like I can finally keep up with my reflexes. Like that fraction of a second head start from Incisive is enough time for my muscles to act on the signals my nerves are sending."

"Correct! Combined with your outstanding combat sense, you are now a certified nightmare in single combat against enemies that don't have wide-area attack spells. Depending on the enemy composition, you are a nightmare for groups, too. Now, speaking of multiple personalities, let's get to the main subject."

Truth nodded. "I tried to imagine that I really was the person they talk about on the scry—Tommy Wells, spellblade and demon hunter. My thinking was that if I could become that person, it could integrate all the other parts of Incisive and add another layer of spell resistance over what the Meditations provides. Spell resistance is just local superreality, right? And spells are slightly more 'real' than our corner of the universe. So, stacking a magically created identity over a magically enhanced body should produce good results."

"Always gratifying to see when someone has been paying attention during a tutorial. Correct, Mr. Wells; that is one of the correct ways to use Incisive. However, there are consequences. Aren't there?"

"I . . . really thought I was Tommy Wells, Desrin Spell-Blade from the Aussa Highlands for a minute there."

"Identity is not so simple a thing, is it?"

"I am learning that."

Merkovah chuckled lightly. "It's an appealing notion, isn't it? Just become the perfect person to do a job, then return unchanged to what you consider your real, or core, self. But it's not that simple."

Truth just shook his head.

"The thing you are missing, Tommy, is that your 'identity' is not something entirely within your control. There is how you identify yourself, of course, but there is also how other people identify you. Your identity can't help but be shaped by that conception. That collective weight. Particularly when you are casting a spell intended to manipulate how both you and the people who see you define you."

"So . . . because so many people believe I am the person they said I am on scry . . ."

"There was a lot of 'reality' attached to that identity. Not that mere belief or conjecture can reshape reality, but it can certainly reshape our understanding of it. The spell didn't have to work very hard to convince everyone that you really are 'Tommy Wells, Desrin Spell-Blade from the Aussa Highlands.' *Everyone* includes you, of course. Because while you are only changing your exterior, you are still, definitionally, changing yourself."

"I wondered about that!" Jember shouted. "I remember looking at him fight and practically hearing the theme music to 'One Sword for Heaven.' But it sounds like it would be more useful for ambush or escape. Why use it in a fight?"

"For exactly the reason Tommy said. It's an extra layer of protection against spells. Also, there is a more subtle reason. The way you approach a fight changes. Your morale changes. Hundreds of subtle, little changes as your mind conforms to the new identity. It also affects how people approach you. Violently or otherwise."

"Sounds like it would be easy to get lost in an identity." Truth frowned.

"Oh? Try it. Imagine you are Irridia Prem, an eighty-six-year-old woman, happily married to your husband of sixty years, and well loved by both your eighteen grandchildren and the kids at the elementary school where you teach. Visualize that, and cast Incisive."

Truth did his best, but the spell didn't so much as flicker over him. It just fizzled out.

"A much tougher reality to assert, compared to 'Tommy Wells, Desrin spellblade.' It wouldn't take much to make that real. Much harder to be someone totally different, who has led a totally different life than you. Try this—'Terry Bells, Talisman-Maintenance Specialist First Class, Xandie Department of Public Works.'"

Truth shrugged, cast the spell, and felt the identity settle lightly over him. He knew he was Truth Medici. No question about that whatsoever. But he could feel "Terry Bells" too. He moved a little slower, a little looser. There was a sudden feeling of wearing mittens and big boots—not crippled, just a lot less agile.

"So, this spell is unusual in a lot of ways. First, by its sheer premise. Rewriting your immediate reality by force of will is . . . a strong move, let us say." Merkovah slipped on his teacher hat once again. "Not something that you are going to be in a position to meaningfully do for a long, *long* while. But you can, oddity number two, align yourself with what people already believe, and hijack their beliefs into falling in line with what you want them to believe."

Merkovah gestured at himself and the cousins. "We know you aren't a maintenance tech. But we also know you tinker with your horrible two-wheeler, and you keep saying you trained as a talisman-maintenance tech, so we can *kind of* believe it. And if you went out in public without your sword and wearing a smock loaded with tools, everyone would believe it."

"Still not seeing the combat utility." Jember looked fascinated.

"Been too long since your last vision, I think." Merkovah wagged his finger reprovingly. "Tommy, do you think Botis would lose a fight?"

"No. Impossible."

"There are other beings as powerful, or more powerful, than he. Very few, but some."

"Still. Never going to happen."

"Why?"

"He wouldn't fight. He would either hide or change their mind or just run, but he would only fight if he was one hundred percent sure of winning and one hundred percent sure it was worth the effort."

"All right, but why?"

"It's just his nature."

"How do you know?"

"Pardon?"

"How do you know it's in his nature? I am quite certain you have never read a book that accurately discussed the details of his personality and the interpersonal relationships of beings of his extraordinary stature. And I certainly never told you any of that. So, why do you believe it?"

Truth puzzled that out. He wanted to say, *Because that's what Incisive does*, but that was just wrong. It wasn't what the spell was for. It was just one way to use it. Even then, his conception of the spell all came from . . .

"Because that's how I saw him during our vision on the mountain." Truth's voice came out slow. "I thought I got a very good sense of his personality, just watching him for a bit."

"So, put another way, you believe, based on seeing him, that Botis would be unbeatable in any fight he chose to engage in because he would never engage in it without overwhelming advantage?"

"Yes." Truth's voice was slower still.

"Get it now?"

"That's brilliant." Jember started slow-clapping. "He projects a reality that makes you destroy your own morale, weakens you, hell, makes you give up without a fight. That's absolutely genius."

"And he's powerful enough to make it *real*. If Botis fights, *he has an overwhelming advantage, and you will lose*," Merkovah emphasized carefully. "It is no mere illusion. Botis isn't being snobbish when he claims that no one has mastered Incisive. Its depths are almost limitless."

"So, wait, I'm confused. It's easier to make people believe what they already believed or wanted to believe. I get that. And it's a spell, so it ups my local degree of reality, making me more spell-resistant and stronger in combat. I get that. And since I am altering my local reality, I started to half-believe whatever identity I am projecting. I get that, too. But where you lose me is that this is a reality-altering spell, not a mind-altering one." Truth chopped his hand through the air.

"It can't possibly be. If my 'becoming' Tommy Wells, Desrin spellblade of the Aussa Highlands, is a change in reality, then there must be parents of Tommy. Teachers with sudden, vague memories of teaching Tommy. Grades written down in a book somewhere. Tax records. Grocery-store receipts. There should be a whole life that popped into existence with him."

Merkovah smiled and nodded approvingly. "Easy, easy. You are totally correct and simultaneously overthinking it. You aren't changing all of reality; you are changing your identity based on how you want reality to be, and everyone perceives the reality you are trying to project based on their own understanding of reality. Their conception of reality impacts your own identity via the spell, which makes it more or less 'real' for you and them."

Truth shook his head. "No, that doesn't work. Look, imagine if some unnamed company, through a combination of drugs, enchantment, and mental manipulation, convinced ten thousand employees that Gilbert Gilbert was an unkillable immortal, and Gilbert cast Incisive, does that make him an unkillable immortal? Does it only work if I know the legend of Gilbert the Great? What if I don't know him at all, and

I'm picking him off from three kilometers away using Graeme's Arrow on a heavy needler?"

"Gilbert might well believe he is immortal, but his belief, and their belief, even when combined with the spell, won't be enough to overrule God's belief that Gilbert's brain will be sprayed across the wall because that's how he ordered the working of the world. It's not omnipotent. Think of it like the Meditations. The belief provides the shape, the spell makes the change, but even in this little place, local reality can only be changed so far, so fast."

There was a horrible, lingering scream and a noise like a cross between a crunch and a squish. "Oh, splendid timing. It seems that the formation has finally killed Child Eater. Let's summon it again, and you can test out the Scales again. Play around with it. I booked the room for the whole afternoon, and we have barely opened the snacks." Merkovah smiled. "Let us learn by doing good."

CHAPTER 65

A TREE IN THE FOREST

Truth was in a thoughtful mood as he once again guarded a conference. This was a much smaller gathering, he was told, focused primarily on researching agricultural techniques without magical support. A few test fields had been trialed, and the results were disastrous. This, however, was not what had his attention.

Etenesh, as predicted by both Merkovah and the System, had been delighted to learn Truth was a virgin and was taking to his education with immense enthusiasm. The clothes had indeed come off and good things did, in fact, happen. To the point where he thought that he might finally lose the virgin tag, but Etenesh had persuaded him to wait just a little longer. She said she wanted to "make it special." Which was nice of her, but he was pretty sure it was going to be special regardless.

And he one hundred percent had virgin-itis. Soon to be first-girlfriend-itis. Falling this hard for literally the first woman to show serious interest in him was dumb. Classically dumb. But he still was, and he was rapidly coming to the conclusion that he wouldn't have it any other way. Which was a symptom of the disease, he knew, but . . . well, he wasn't going to make unnecessary drama.

His mouth quirked slightly as he stared at the engraved wall outside the conference room. Once upon a fairly recent time, he would have said he "wasn't that dumb." Now? He was content thinking that "he wasn't dumb." It didn't always stick. The intrusive thoughts came in. Even when Etenesh was demanding his attention, he couldn't escape them. But he could recognize them. Name them. Examine them and find the lies in them.

Truth was healing. Which was good because soon he would be returning to Jeon, and that was likely a one-way trip. Starbrite had been the king of this world for centuries, and if you take a shot at the king, you best not miss.

He had Incisive running almost all the time now but minimally. A steady, if tiny, drain on his energy and attention. It was worth it. Right now, Tommy Wells, Professional Bodyguard, anticipated the first guest to leave the conference room and opened the door just before they reached it.

"It's not a failure. Negative results are every bit as important as positive ones."

"That makes for great philosophy and a lousy dinner. Disease, pests, lousy yields, huge energy investment for the result, and, worst of all, the soil is depleted. The results will be even worse next time if we use the same fields."

"Right, but now we know what to work on."

"And no damn time to work on it in."

It seemed that the discussion hadn't stopped. It was merely being relocated from the conference room to the dining room. There hadn't been much meat on the menu recently. It looked like Merkovah was right about that. The price of beef or chicken was high and rising fast, from what he could tell.

Which sucked. He might pass as a Desrin, but involuntary vegetarianism wasn't appealing. The kitchen at Nag Hamadi did a roast chicken and lentil dish that blew his mind. It was that spicy red seasoning they used. Apparently, it was a blend of spices, adjusted as needed or desired for maximum effect. When the dish came out with a crispy drumstick sitting on a bed of lentils and diced carrots . . . damn. The visual alone made his mouth water. Then the smell, all roasted goodness and spicy intrigue, and he was ready to riot.

He had met the lay sister who ran the kitchen. She was very apologetic about making "cafeteria food."

He . . . didn't want to see Siphios collapse. He didn't want to see anywhere collapse, really, but especially Siphios. This country had been more than just good to him. Merkovah seemed firmly of the opinion that some degree of collapse was inevitable, and the conference attendees seemed to agree.

Nobody knew how to farm without magic. Why would you ever need to know that? Angels would be only too happy to bless your fields, renewing the soil, increasing your yields, and keeping disease or pests at bay. Weather magic would ensure your crops got the right amount of water or sun. Even the tilling and planting could be done with bound demons.

He checked inside the conference room just to make sure everyone was out. They were, but they had left up a picture. A farmer, weathered but upright, looking helplessly on as hail turned his vegetables from bounty to carnage. He looked so tiny, so helpless compared to the black clouds towering above him. He was a farmer, not an angel or demon. How could he hold back the sky?

What could he do but pray for God's mercy? Pray when God clearly wasn't hearing it?

Truth could imagine it. You only ate what you could grow. You busted your ass looking forward to the delicious veggies that would keep your family alive all year. And then God looked the other way. A storm came. Destroyed your harvest, destroyed your fields, destroyed your hope.

God didn't care about how hard you worked. He didn't care about how much you sacrificed. He didn't care about how much your family needed this. He didn't care that you would starve without it. That you would have to watch your kids go to bed hungry, getting weaker and weaker every day.

Next door, your brother is doing *great*. He keeps goats and sheep, and yeah, they have their own problems, but hail ain't one of them. God looks at your brother and smiles, blessing pouring down on him, his wives, and his fat children as yours get thinner and thinner. And your brother won't help you. He says he needs it all and what he doesn't need belongs to God. Your suffering is God's will and has nothing to do with him. He isn't your keeper.

So, you take him somewhere quiet. You pick up a rock and smash his fucking head in. You slaughter him like one of his damn goats. Which you then collect for yourself and your kids and your wives. Maybe you will take in his wives, adopt his kids. Maybe not. Looking at the ruins of your farm, it's hard to feel generous. Especially when everyone keeps calling you a sinner and a criminal.

You did your very best. It wasn't enough. God looked away, and now *you* were the sinner. Well. You would be the sinner with healthy kids. And if anyone didn't like it, they could come at you. Never any shortage of rocks.

Truth flipped off the light and locked up. Fuck farming. If the rough patron's legacy was one of violence, so be it. He would go to Jeon and be a killer. His family ate first. There might not be much of a future in violence, but there was none at all for the passive or meek.

Merkovah was leaning up against the wall when Truth turned around. Grinning.

"Let's get started," Merkovah said.

Step one of being a terrorist was, apparently, *don't look like one*. This was somewhat challenging for Truth, as almost any list of adjectives one might apply to him would also fit a . . . person of significant interest to the police. Merkovah had, therefore, prepared an identity for Truth. One which was much more boring.

"You want me to pretend to be a talisman-maintenance worker on vacation. To Jeon."

"It seems an easy fit."

"Vacation in Jeon."

"Many beautiful beaches, historical buildings, an extremely colorful nightlife, why not vacation in Jeon?"

"Because Harban is staggeringly expensive, and you can't even access most of it if you aren't a Citizen."

"Ah, you are wrong there. Tourists have wider permissions to visit places than Denizens do. Not as many places as the higher-tier Citizens, but more than Denizens."

Truth snorted at that but believed it.

"So, you will be trained on how to move and think like an operative—"

"I prefer the term—"

"—OPERATIVE and given a crash course in creating widespread unhappiness. Your goal will be to generate as much misery and unrest as you safely can while slowly chipping away at the underpinnings of the System. When the time is right, you will be given specific instructions on what to do. Others will be acting in concert, but it is best if you don't know them or what they are doing."

"Okay."

Merkovah twitched at that, started to talk, stopped, then forcefully moved on. "The idea is that the lower levels will be too busy putting out the fires you are setting to be useful in the main attack, while the disruptions will be too low-level to come to the attention of the C-suite. And even if it does, they won't care."

Truth just nodded. It made sense, he supposed.

"Will the System Astrologica?"

"Will it what?"

"Care? Its job is to be the management backbone of Starbrite, and I assume it's got some kind of self-preservation instinct."

"A surprising number of spirits don't, actually. But yes, we have been able to determine that it will act to preserve itself. It will certainly be issuing missions and instructions related to your activities."

"And my own . . . condition?"

Merkovah's expression was technically a smile, though without the slightest trace of warmth. A tiger's smile.

"Well, about that."

Merkovah's carriage wound its way through the mountain pass. The cousins had been left with a stack of homework back at Nag Hamadi. They didn't need to know about this.

"Is it just me, or is Jember glowing more these days?" Truth asked.

"It's not just you. I think Etenesh lit a fire under him to improve, and the ritual chastity has him bouncing off the walls. He's ready to be done with this."

"Is this another . . . I don't know what to call it. God-embodying rituals?" Truth stared at the trees, unwilling to even guess their species. *Dense* and *thick* are of marginal use for identification.

"More or less. More abstract and less specific than what Etenesh did. He is trying to embody the solar aspect of God. Plus a bunch of other stuff his cult believes in, but that's the bit I know about," Merkovah said. He was also staring at the trees, looking for something.

"Embodying the solar . . ." Truth trailed off. Merkovah probably wouldn't appreciate being told that sounded like grown people making up stories, then insisting everyone act like it was real.

"Personally, I think it sounds ridiculous, but I suppose everyone thinks that about the cults they aren't in." Merkovah frowned, not finding what he was looking for.

"Oh, are you in a cult?"

"Mmm-hmmm."

"Can't talk about it?"

"More like . . . it would take longer to explain what we are about than I intend to spend up in these mountains. The minimum prerequisite to join is to be one hundred years of age, married, and with a proven depth of theological study and rigor. The details of which would confuse and exhaust you, I'm afraid."

"Oh. Well. Thank you?"

"No problem. I tend to leave our little conversations on the nature of God feeling depressed, so this works for me, too. Oh, finally!" Merkovah jerked the carriage to the side of the road in a horrible squeal of metal on metal. Truth couldn't escape fast enough.

"Welcome, Mr. Wells, to the Silent Forest. Kindly get naked while I fish out the rope and other sacred gear."

"Ah . . . care to explain what, exactly, is going to go on here?"

"This is one of the national treasures I mentioned. Basically, we sacrifice you to the forest. You will hang by the neck from a tree branch from sunset to sunset. When the ritual is complete, you will be able to hide yourself from detection incredibly well. When combined with your existing spells and resistances, you will be almost imperceivable. Certainly, your 'intelligent spirit' will never be spotted. It's a genuine wonder and your supreme good fortune to benefit from it. Now."

Merkovah quickly made a noose in a rough hemp rope. "Let's get you strung up."

CHAPTER 66

HANGING AROUND

I am intensely uncomfortable with this."

"Oh, stop being a baby and put your hands behind your back."

"Standing naked in a forest, tied up, about to be hung from a tree by a strange old man, you can see why this might set off alarms?"

"Strange? Strange! How am I strange?"

"You are a six-hundred-year-old terrorist who lures young men out into the woods and gets them naked and tied up. Is this normal around here?"

"All right, I have had enough of this. We are *not* terrorists! *I* am not a terrorist! You haven't lived long enough to see it, but Starbrite has ruined, *ruined* this planet. I am a patriot and a champion for the world. You will cease to refer to yourself or me as terrorists."

"Sure, sure. Can't help but notice you're ignoring the rest of what I said, though."

"It is perfectly normal—don't wiggle; I need to line this up right—perfectly normal to get naked for a serious magical ritual. Especially one focused on transformation like this one. I can assure you, you have nothing I haven't seen many times before."

"That's reassuring. You have lots of experience—too tight, too tight!—lots of experience with tied-up naked young men in the woods."

There was a pause.

"Well. I do. Now that I think about it, I do actually have a lot of experience with that. It's a pretty common ritual thing. Not always woods, of course. Or always young men."

"Oh?"

"Mmm. Time was, hardly a solstice went by where I didn't have some youngster tied down over a stone altar on a mountainside or chained to the bottom of a pond or something. No, don't straighten up; I'm just grabbing my knife and a rag. This bit is always messy."

"Every solstice? Busy guy."

"Ah, nostalgia is both a curse and a refuge for the old. I look around and see the desolate remains of happier days."

"GOD! Did you dip that in ice water? What the hell is that?"

"The sacred oil needs to be kept in a cold box or it goes rancid. You don't want the cuts to get infected by rancid oil. *Believe me* on that."

"The voice of experience."

"You want a neophyte carving sacred geometries on your flesh?"

"Fair."

"But you do actually bring up a good point. I have spent a lot of my long life guiding youngsters, training them, and shaping them into the people Siphios needed them to be. 'Teacher' is never just a religious title. We are actually teachers."

"And part of that is guiding them through rituals?"

"Naturally." Merkovah looked sad as he looked around the forest. "What do you notice here, Truth? About this forest, I mean?"

"I'm not a trees guy, honestly. Big. Some saplings. Now that I'm looking at it, there are a lot of dead trees, too."

"Not to sound like the old-timer I am," the youthful-looking exorcist said, "but it didn't always look like this. The Silent Forest was mysterious. And terrifying. And heartbreakingly beautiful. The first time I fell in love, romantic love, was walking through the clouds of pink-blue lights that the toam trees scattered like pollen. She was my age, brilliant, and beautiful, and I wanted her more than light and air, and she was in love with another. Eventually, she left the woods. I didn't. They got married and had kids. I wound up teaching her great-great-grandkids at one point."

"The magic faded."

"The last toam tree died a century ago. We preserved some of the seeds and pollen, but unless the conditions change, it can't come back. The fairies vanished. Just vanished. Here one day, gone the next. The mystic, sacred waters became ponds. Wise beasts, more spirits than animals, became, simply, animals. Some were friends of mine. I hope you never see the light of understanding leave someone's eyes. Watch them forget you as they forget themselves."

Truth just shook his head. What could he possibly say?

"Same thing happened everywhere. Sacred mountains became just mountains. Sacred trees became ordinary. Holy places became just another place. A few tiny pockets remain, clinging to the last dregs of divinity. National treasures now, when once they were simply part of the commonwealth of the nation."

"This tree . . ."

The sun set. Merkovah didn't answer Truth. He just tossed the hemp rope up over a branch and hauled.

The noose tightened around Truth's neck, creaking as it yanked him up. So tight, it seemed to burn. Truth couldn't help panicking, thrashing. The hemp cords binding his hands were suddenly impossibly strong. They should have snapped like a thin string. They held. His arms could crush demons and shatter walls but couldn't stretch the rope. He tried to yell, to tell Merkovah to stop, but the rope had choked away his voice. He couldn't breathe. *He couldn't breathe!* The animal panic of feeling the air choking off made him jerk and heave and struggle wildly to get free.

Merkovah calmly tied off the rope around the trunk of the tree, then knelt in silent prayer. In a few minutes, Truth's legs stopped kicking. Merkovah didn't even glance over.

Truth knew that what he was seeing wasn't real. This was a hallucination, some part of the ritual he was undergoing. It still felt real. It still felt odd to be dressed in fancy clothes with an apron over it, serving what he could now discern were mediocre cups of coffee to seven warped-looking individuals.

Filling the entire width of the head of the table was a singular egg of a man, enormously fat, bald-headed, and conspicuously dressed in the finest suit a very great deal of money could buy. Then, working around the table were a series of visually distressing sorts, ranging from one fellow who would have looked healthier if he had been dead for a week, an opium fiend, at least one brutal edgelord, two who were desperately trying to act cool but weren't at all, and a handsome young man who looked like he had snorted all the cocaine and would agree with anyone who had more. And stab anyone who didn't have cocaine four hundred and forty-four times.

Egg Man had a dozen plates in front of him, but the rest just stuck to coffee and the free bread. A seven-top for brunch, and you just knew they were lousy tippers. Could be worse, he supposed. They could be church ladies.

"It must be poison. The most subtle and elegant of disposals, transitioning commoner and king alike into the primordial nothingness," Deadman said. "Death, the ultimate negation of meaning. The final humbling of any crown. Silent and invisible, a true comrade to the common man. An unmaking of structures most perfectly demonstrates the universal anarchy."

"Poison would defeat the entire purpose. Revolution is a BANG!" Try-Hard #1 slammed the table, making the spoons rattle on the saucers. "No need for complicated plots. I'll make the bomb, and we toss it through the carriage window when he parades through town. Anarchism is in the people but requires a spark to set the blaze in their hearts."

"No, this won't do at all, won't do at all. The emperor is the most wicked and cruel of his contemporaries. His serfs—serfs in this day and age, mind you!—still remain chained to their tenant farms and suffer under the knout." The edgelord snarled, jabbing with his butter knife. "We get in with blades. Blend into the hotel staff, knock on the door. 'Dinner time!' Then we *stab him*. Pigs deserve to be butchered."

"I could go for a pork trotter right now. It's been a long time since dinner, and even lobster mayonnaise can only carry one so far. Gentleman, let there be no quarrel between us—we can combine all these ideas. We put poison on the blades, strap the blades to the bomb, then throw the bomb through the hotel window. This will also give us the opportunity to paint slogans on the walls and pin up our manifesto.

Which . . . Does anyone have a copy I could look at? I've misplaced mine." The coke fiend was vibrating at the thought of carnage. He hadn't touched his bread but necked the coffee and was waving for a refill.

"The people are a sea, and we revolutionaries are fish in the sea. We are our manifesto, a living testimony to the truth and rightness of our cause. We must demonstrate by action what defies description. To do otherwise would cheapen our anarchic hearts." Egg Man casually demolished a plate of bacon and punctuated his pronouncement with a dainty sip of coffee. Then frowned, glaring at his cup. He set it down on its saucer firmly.

The opium fiend openly added a few drops of something to his coffee and drank deeply. "It's so wild to me. We are going to murder an emperor. We, sitting at this table, are going to kill a crowned head to make the point that no head should wear a crown. It's not like we are in hiding or anything. A conspiracy right out in the open. And nobody is even looking at us. No detectives peep from the bushes. No secret agents with hearing trumpets." He giggled.

"Our masters are too blind to set their dogs on the right trail." Try-Hard #2 sniffed. "They would rather smash up a dockside saloon than disturb the diners at restaurants of *quality.* This is why, incidentally, we need to kill the emperor at church. Smash the whole edifice of authority from the very top. I do like the bomb-knife-poison idea, though. Iconoclastic and innovative."

"The passion for destruction is also a creative passion," Egg Man agreed, wiping a bit of pastry cream from the corner of his wide mouth. "And the church idea likewise has merit. The existence of a boss in heaven is the best justification for a boss on Earth, after all, and where there is the state, there will be slaves. It thus follows that for humanity to be free, God must be abolished."

This was met with murmurs of approval. The Egg Man took the opportunity afforded by the brief applause to snag the coke fiend's bread roll and butter, directly merge the two, and swallow it in a single bite.

"Gentlemen! I thank you all for your input. You will receive your instructions privately, but rest assured that our great work is underway. We already control the newspapers, the telegraphs, the railroads, and the ocean liners. Our people are everywhere, invisible, and ready to act when they see the curtain rise. Go. I have things well in hand."

The table broke up, heading off singly or in pairs as the enormous man swept every remaining crumb into his mouth, including the sugar bowl and the little pitchers of cream. Truth felt that was his cue.

"Your bill, sir."

The gargantuan bulk jerked to a surprised halt, rotating in place to face Truth. "My bill? *My bill?* Young man, do you have the faintest idea who I am?"

"No, sir. Do you have an account with us?"

"*You* have an account with *me.* This is my place!"

"Very good, sir. I'll just need to verify that with my manager. I'm sure you understand. However, this was a six-person table, not including yourself, and that means a flat service fee of ten percent. Which must be paid."

The Egg Man was giving him an increasingly bewildered look. "Young man, do you grasp what was going on here?"

"Yes, sir. I think I was quite a good sport about your amateur theatrical group pretending to be anarchists."

The rich man burst out laughing. "Yes, you could call it that! As phony as could be. And I, the stage master behind it all. Each actor lost in their role. But the play's the thing, isn't it?"

"I'm sure you are right, sir. And yet, you can hardly expect the audience to pay for the ticket if they were never asked if they wanted to see the show. Far less if they were used as ushers and stagehands."

This got him a hard look from the Egg Man.

"You aren't big on metaphor or symbolism, are you?"

"Cash on the nail works for me, sir. Literal as you like."

"Your accent seems familiar. What's your name? Where are you from?"

"Truth Medici, recently from Siphios."

"Honest in your fashion, I suppose. I vaguely recall Siphios. Better coffee than here."

"True."

The Egg Man was looking distinctly less eggy. His face was extending into a muzzle as long horns sprung from his bald head. A mane silently grew out, and a terrible blend of dragon and lion slowly rose out of the enormous body. The skin slowly rolled down, revealing the serpentine coils within the bulk.

"Well, I think you have learned something today, Truth Medici. Who should not be here past the end of our little play."

"Couldn't say, sir. Above my pay grade. Speaking of pay . . ."

"You even carry an echo of that youngster's curse. You would think he could take my hint. Goodbye, Mr. Medici. In some tiny way, I might possibly remember you." The figure grew and grew, the cafe fading away, the city, the whole world fading away until there was only Truth and the impossible enormity in front of him. The being became so vast, Truth lost sight of where the being began and the universe ended. From somewhere, there came a terrible light. A terrible, blinding light! And he couldn't breathe!

CHAPTER 67

BANG BANG

Truth fell on his ass on the forest floor. The noose loosened. He took great hacking gasps of air, snapping the ropes around his wrist with a thoughtless flex.

"Here, have some water. You are probably dehydrated." Merkovah crouched next to him and handed him a bottle. Truth grabbed it and chugged it down. The cool of the water eased the pain in his throat. Though, now that he was paying attention to it, that pain was fading fast.

"Basically an illusion." Merkovah correctly interpreted Truth's expression having seen it many times before. "You firmly believed you were being strangled, that the ropes could really keep you bound. It wasn't true, of course. Your neck is never going to be throttled by just your body weight at this point in your development. You could hang up there for a month, and you might be bored and uncomfortable, but you wouldn't choke."

Truth nodded.

"It would be pretty strange if the ritual killed the person it was supposed to empower. No, it's a ritual suffering, the lived illusion of sacrifice, fueling the tiny echoes of divinity still held in the tree. That's where the magic comes in. We will play with it some before we head home."

"Stiffed me," Truth rasped, then coughed and drank some more water.

"Pardon?"

"The fucker ran out on the bill!"

Truth ran Incisive, trying to carefully remove all traces of his identity. Identity would be what he wished to present, and right now, he didn't want to present anything. He wasn't even a hole in the air. He sat with his back to a tree and tried to concentrate on being an absence of meaning.

"Good heavens. You are picking that up very fast. I sort of thought you would, what with everything, but that is still *remarkably* fast. Possibly a new record." Merkovah cocked his head as he looked in Truth's direction.

Truth slowly breathed in and out. "Actually, it's something I learned back in the slums. Get low and pretend you don't exist. That way, the predators are less likely to see you. Funny how I have a spell for that now."

"*Funny* . . . is one way to think of it." Merkovah looked sadly into the woods. He looked lonely, Truth thought.

"Thinking about the one that got away?"

"Thinking about all the ones that didn't. It's all context. That's why you need to study history. You need the context."

Truth sat with that thought, breathing in and out slowly. Trying to find the rhythm of the forest, blend that little bit more.

"You aren't the first kid from the slums I've taken here, you know. She said the same thing you did."

"That fat bastard skipped out on her, too?"

"What? No, not . . . whatever you saw in the vision. No, about holding still and hoping the predators don't see you."

"Didn't know Siphios had slums. Well, slums like I know."

"Our slums have never been as bad as they are in Jeon, but, hell, we are a monarchy with a hereditary aristocracy. Of course we have slums. We have predators that hunt their fellow humans. Brutalize and exploit them."

"I sort of wondered, with the way Siphios uses demons so much."

"Oh, Truth. You are so young, but not so young you don't know the answer to that."

Truth just nodded sadly. "The point is that they are other humans."

"The cruelty is the point. Establishing dominance. Hierarchy. Binding their fellow humans like they were demons and driving them with the same lash."

"Remind me again why we want to save the world?"

Merkovah laughed. "Force of habit, in my case. My main goal is to kill Starbrite, the C-suite, and the System. Saving the world is a nice bonus."

Truth could respect that. He understood it a lot better than altruism.

"You are trying to rescue your siblings, right?"

"*Rescue* seems like the wrong word. *Rescue* is step one. Step two through infinity is trying to arrange things so they don't need rescuing in the future."

"Delightful. Saving the world is an incidental benefit for me and an unfortunate prerequisite for you. Neither of us has it as our actual goal." Merkovah went quiet for a while. "What about Etenesh? Or Jember?"

"Oh, I want them safe and sound, too. It's just that they can look after themselves. They don't need me to rescue them. My siblings . . . probably do." Truth thought a moment longer. "Maybe not Vig. Boy's got that demon in him."

There was a pause. "When you say *demon* . . ."

"Not literally. At least the last time I saw him."

"Just checking."

A bird landed on Truth. It apparently thought he was a part of the tree.

"What ever happened to that drop?"

"What drop?"

"The drop of extradimensional water we found at Station Six?"

"Ah. That one is need-to-know, I'm afraid."

Truth just nodded.

"Got a feel for it?"

"Think so. Let's go for a walk, then head back. I want to test it out some."

Merkovah nodded and got to his feet. The two wandered off, Merkovah lost in thought and Truth trying to perfect his grip on his new abilities. Neither noticed that among the dead trees, thin green shoots were emerging.

Merkovah had an . . . interesting idea for the return journey. He would drive his doubtlessly structurally sound carriage. Truth would run alongside. Truth objected but was stumped by Merkovah's brilliant reply—

"Why?"

Truth was flummoxed for a moment. On the one hand, the answer seemed obvious. On the other hand, he probably could run as fast as the carriage moved normally, at least for short bursts. So, for at least part of the journey back to Xandre, he could be comparatively safe from vehicular homicide.

He ran. The air up in the mountains was cool for Siphios, which made it a steam oven for a Jeon boy like Truth. His clothes quickly glued to him. He stripped off his shirt almost immediately, throwing it through a window into the carriage. He then flagged down Merkovah and did the same with his shoes and socks. He knew from running through the desert that pebbles and the like were no threat to him, so really, there was no need beyond habit and comfort. And he was sweating so much that the shoes were miserable little braising dishes.

As naked as public decency would permit, he set off running again. And it was effortless. He ran down the road, keeping pace with a carriage doing mountain-high-way speeds, and it was effortless. It really hit him then, in a way that it had just never connected before. He was utterly beyond the overwhelming majority of humanity. And he was just Level Three.

Just . . . Level Three. Most people in Jeon got to Level One and stuck there. Level Two, you were a god in the slums, though nothing particularly special in the nice part of Harban. Level Three? Now you had some status. Maybe not head-turning status, but you were no one to casually cross. Level Four—Captain Clavegaugh, who ran the Starbrite PMC branch in goddam Harban, was Level Four. That was a position of serious power and authority. She might not name-check outside her industry, but there probably weren't more than a couple thousand people at her level in the city. And it was a big damn city. Richest city in the world, with all the best elixirs poured into its elites.

Truth wasn't certain he could take Clavegaugh. She had decades of experience, her own body cultivation, and the System was insanely powerful in skilled hands. But it wouldn't be impossible. Not with the right arrangements.

The accumulation was showing. The deep study of Incisive, the steady grinding away at the Meditations, the consistent effort he put into proving to his mind that his body could, in fact, handle whatever he threw at it. It was all adding up. When he climbed out of the well, he had a body he couldn't make the best use of. Now? Now he knew he was strong. Not invincible, but strong.

It was a heady feeling. Racing alongside a carriage and comfortably keeping up. Truth saw a pond just off the side of the road. With a mad gleam in his eye, he sprinted. Hard as he could, fast as he could. Little, quick steps. *Taktaktaktaktaktak*, swerving off the road toward the pond. Faster now, fast as a sporting chariot on a highway. Fast as he could go. He stepped off the grassy verge and onto the pond. *Taktaktaktaktaktak*, the water shot up behind him, but he didn't fall. He was too fast. Fast enough to run on water.

Truth crossed the pond and got back on the road, now just jogging along, damn near laughing himself sick. He was so fast, he could run on water. That was a thing he could do. And he didn't even feel winded. Merkovah pulled up next to him and rolled down the window. "Try concealing yourself and running at the same time."

Truth shrugged and did so. He still couldn't quite wrap words around whatever the forest gave him. It wasn't invisibility; it was just . . . unimportance. He just faded from attention to the point where it was almost impossible to consciously be aware of him. He wondered how it would work in, say, a crowded hallway.

A cloud of ghosts started forming around Merkovah's carriage. Seekers, it looked like. They started sweeping up and down the road, clearly looking for something. Truth grinned. He wouldn't be bored, running back to the city.

When they did finally hit the exurbs around Xandre, Truth had reached a couple of interesting conclusions. One, the drain on his energy for using the passive concealment provided by the forest was negligible. About equal to his normal replenishment rate or less. He could effectively keep it going indefinitely. *National treasure* was a pretty damn reasonable description.

The second, arguably stranger, thing was that he wasn't dehydrated or overheating. Which . . . he absolutely should be, right? He was sticky and sweating from the humidity and heat, so clearly, his body was reacting to the temperatures. But was it? Was this another situation where his brain hadn't caught up with where his body was at? It really should have already. He ran through the desert like it was nothing, and that was when he was still Level Two. But *Sweat when you are hot* isn't a conscious reaction. It's something instinctive. It would be tricky to learn to ignore the weather that way.

Truth had also learned that drivers would unconsciously avoid him while he was concealed. It was a little freaky. From what he could tell, looking in their windows as he did it, both people directly operating their carriages or the bound demon compelled to drive, would move to avoid him, without seeming to be aware that they were doing so. They wouldn't get into an accident doing it—they would slow down or swerve as needed, but they wouldn't go off the road, for example.

That seemed . . . exploitable. Actually, it seemed bloody terrifying. There must be some counter to it, or Merkovah would have already walked into Starbrite's corporate offices and murdered everyone there. He would ask later.

In a moment of mischief, he hopped onto the roof of a passing carriage and sat like a gargoyle, leering at the passing traffic.

He had a sudden thrill of mild danger, and he dove off the roof of the carriage, landing on his hands and flipping up into a sprint. A flying dagger had whipped through the hole in the air he had just been filling. It twisted in the air, a little silvery fish dodging about, then dove for him again. There was a cheerful toot from Merkovah's horn. It seemed he was right about there being a counter. The last leg of the journey was a lot more . . . intense.

CHAPTER 68

CRUEL EMPATHY

Truth was feeling a bit sorry for himself when he finally jogged into Nag Hamadi. By the time they had reached the city center, a comfortable run had turned into a three-dimensional, high-stakes obstacle course as he bounced over carriages, across chariots, off buildings, and between pedestrians. All while Merkovah's dagger hunted him. It was fun and doubtless a learning experience but exhausting.

"How did you keep spotting me? I thought I was pretty thoroughly hidden most of the time?" he complained. Nag Hamadi kept the temple comfortably cool. Truth sprawled flat on the ground, trying to shed his accumulated heat. He still wasn't sure how much of it was in his head, but the cool stones sure felt good!

"The answer is distressingly simple—the higher one's cultivation, the more in tune they are with the stars and, by extension, those grand excellencies who emanate them. In other words, the higher one's cultivation, the more in tune with 'reality' one is. Given how thoroughly concealed you are, anyone under Level Four can directly forget finding you, and almost all Level Fours can too. Weaker Level Fives would have to be actively looking for you to find you. I would say your odds of detection from anyone below the middle of Level Five, or specialized tools or spells of that level, are negligible."

"So, you can just see me."

"I kind of have to squint, but yes. Also, there is another point you aren't considering. Incisive is letting you overwrite your immediate local reality, asserting a slightly different reality. Between the Blessing of the Silent Forest and Incisive, you are projecting an identity of 'not something to pay real attention to.' Well, how much harder is it to ignore someone running through traffic and jumping around like a frog?"

"I wasn't . . . helping them fill in the blanks, as it were?"

"More or less. Incisive and the Blessing both need to work harder, the more you deviate from the expected reality, and both are operating off the cosmic energy within you, so . . ." Merkovah shrugged. "Same thing is true with detection spells, by the way. The more you pass for a permitted person, the more they will ignore you. It sounds bizarre, but with low-level guards and basic spells, you can break into an army base wearing a green cap and a blank piece of paper the size of a pass. Secured facilities, not so much. But just onto the base? Very doable."

"Fun." Truth grinned.

"Yep. Although, and I assume there is *no reason* I would need to mention this, but you know that Nag Hamadi can see right through you, right?"

"Right. Yes."

"Uh-huh. All right, that's it for the day. Wash up, rest up, and get ready for a crash course in life as a revolutionary."

Truth jerked at that.

"Revolutionary?"

"Oh, yes. A revolutionary. And all methods must be considered."

Truth decided that Etenesh was doing a real number on his head. And he liked it. She simultaneously made it clear that he was in control every step of the way . . . while guiding him every step of the way. Having a *very* attractive girl lead you into pressing her up against a wall, making out with you, then whispering in your ear exactly how you are going to press her down in bed that night and take charge of her . . . Well. It did things to him.

He had his own ideas, naturally, which tended to get enthusiastic approval. Which also *really* worked for him. And Etenesh knew it. It was . . . incredible. She put him firmly in control by making sure there were no surprises of an unpleasant sort. Everything that was going to happen was planned and approved in advance. They were teased. They were seductive. They fascinated him. Far from making things restrictive or predictable, they made them safe, which gave him room to be daring. She encouraged his daring.

Several days had passed since Truth returned from the Silent Forest, and while he might still be a virgin, he sure wasn't feeling like one.

"Want to try something?" he asked.

"Sure. What did you have in mind?"

"Well, you liked the blindfold. Would you like to play around with me being imperceptible?"

She frowned a little at that. "This and that aren't quite the same. Mmm. I'll try it, but if I say stop, I do mean stop, okay?"

"Always. Close your eyes and count to three."

She did, and he put Incisive into action. She opened her eyes, the ocher in them dimming. He reached out and stroked the lovely curve of her face. Etenesh's eyes opened wide with shock, and she almost screamed, "STOP!"

Truth snapped back into view. "I am so sorry!"

"God! That was horrible. Hold me!" Truth grabbed her and held her while she shivered.

"We aren't doing that again," he said.

"Too right, we aren't!" She took a deep breath and settled down. A few minutes passed that way. Truth wished she would say something, but didn't want to ask. He felt like he had already fucked up enough for one night.

"Oh, stop that."

Truth jerked.

"You spend so much time focusing on projecting your reality around you that when you aren't focused on hiding, I can read you pretty easily."

"I didn't realize."

"I pay a lot of attention to you. Believe me when I say I can feel when the world shifts around you. I can always tell when you are slipping into a depressive spiral. And you need to stop that. I'm the one freaking out here, not you."

"Um. Okay?"

She gave Truth a micro-glare, then leaned her head on his chest. "Look. I liked the blindfold because it made me that little bit helpless and really focused my attention on my ears and sense of touch. I could feel safe because I knew you were there while feeling a little scared and excited because I couldn't see what you were doing. It was a lot of fun. But this . . . this was . . . gross."

Truth felt like scum.

"I SAID KNOCK IT OFF!"

"I can't help feeling bad about making you feel bad, Etenesh!"

"Yes, but you are making me feel bad about making you feel bad about making me feel bad! Just settle down, and let's talk it out."

He took a deep breath and tried his best to push aside his feelings. Just . . . be present. Listen. He didn't know how long he could hold it for, so he nodded encouragingly at Etenesh.

"Look, the way you explained it is that Incisive projects an identity you want, and the Blessing helps erase your presence even more, right?"

"Something like that."

She sighed. "A reminder that it's both partners' responsibility to think things through. Dad was right again."

"Huh?"

"You managed to eradicate the presence of the person named 'Truth Medici,' or any other name I might know you by and replaced them with 'Someone else. Someone you can't see and don't know.' And then I felt you touching my face, an invisible stranger touching my face and twisting my perception. I felt . . ."

He heard the word *violated*, even though she eventually chose *extremely uncomfortable*. And he didn't know what to say. He struggled to stay in that empty place of just listening.

She sighed. "I think part of the reason I've been so weird about you—"

"You have been weird about me?"

"Compared to what I'm usually like? Yes. But I really enjoy doing this with you. Don't get that wrong. But I'm being weird because, for the first time in my life, I get to be really possessive with someone I want to be possessive with."

Truth almost choked on that. He could feel Etenesh grinning at his sudden burst of humor.

"You are in Siphios, pretty man. Possessiveness before marriage, and even argu-ably after marriage, is a sin. To be clear, and you had best be clear on this, *monogamy* is not *possessiveness*. You and I are an exclusive deal, or there is no deal."

"I don't think you have much to worry about on that front," Truth said dryly.

"Oh, I don't? Mr. tall, handsome, mysterious, dangerous, brooding man. Riding around on his iron horse, sword by his side? Practically screaming his loneliness but with a fierce look that would chase away the weak-willed or insufficiently thirsty? I have nothing to be worried about there, do I?"

"No. You don't."

She convulsed a little, grabbing him harder. He felt her shake a bit. His chest got a bit wet. "Etenesh?"

"You have first-girlfriend-itis. Or whatever you call it. You have no experience with healthy relationships, so I seem amazing. And it's not fair to you at all. Because I am doing my absolute best to be amazing for you. To completely dye you in my colors. To make whoever you meet next seem bland and boring and ugly. So that you have no choice but to come back to me."

Truth had no idea what to say. He wanted to deny that he was going anywhere, but . . .

"Oh, I know. Merkovah needs a bodyguard like the sun needs a torch. You are another one of his students for the job everyone knows he does for the Crown, but nobody can come out and say it. If the job even has a name. You aren't sticking around, Truth. You are going to leave me. And you don't know if you are coming back."

"Yeah."

"Is it worth it? Worth leaving me? Leaving Siphios? I assume you are going back to that hell you escaped."

"It is. I am." Truth tried to sort out his words. "My siblings are still trapped there. And if I don't do the job he needs me to do . . . Etenesh, I'm not sure there is going to be a future where you and I could be together anywhere. I'm not sure there is going to be a future for this planet at all. At least, not one that involves humans."

Etenesh was openly crying now. "You are going back to Hell to save your broth-ers and sisters and the whole damn world."

"I only have one sister. Her name is Sophia. She is the smart one in the family. I hope you will like her. Harmony is the steady one, always ready to help out. He tries to sound tough, but he's the most thoughtful of us all. Vigor is the youngest and the best-looking, damn him, before my self-improvement. Him you can stay away from."

Etenesh snorted through the tears.

"I have been looking out for them since . . . I don't know when. Since around when Harmony was born, or a little after. I knew nobody else would, and somehow, I just knew that's what an older brother should do. So, I did it. I don't think I ever put it in words, but I looked at that fucked-up situation, shrugged, and said, 'Okay,' then went and tried to do something about it."

"I swear you are going to give me a condition. I'm never going to be able to hear the word *Okay* the same way ever again."

"I'm okay with that."

She calmed down a little, then pulled him over on top of her. Which was a . . . dangerous choice, given her insistence on not having sex just yet. Especially when she had him pin her hands above her head the way they both liked.

"I want you to know." She looked up at him, ocher eyes blazing in the dark, with the sound of rustling feathers around them. "I *want* you to know. I am enjoying this so much. I am getting off on this so much. Being your first everything. Guiding you through everything. Convincing you that what I am showing you *is* everything, even though it isn't. I am dragging it out as long as I can because I want you, *you*, Truth Med*ici*, completely focused on me. The way I focus on you. I want you as possessive of me as I am of you."

She started rocking her hips slowly. Side to side. Up and down.

"I really am planning something special for your first time. It's going to literally be a religious experience. I am doing everything I can think of to make it the most memorable sex possible. And I'm going to lie to you, Truth," she whispered, drawing his face closer to hers.

"I'm going to look right into your beautiful eyes and lie. I'm going to promise that if you stay with me, it's going to be like that every time. That the world is big enough and ugly enough to look after itself, and the two of us can just vanish into the mountains and live together forever. Loving each other forever."

She arched her back, pressing herself against him, eyes fever-bright. "I'm going to do my very best to ruin you with love. Because I am greedy. I am selfish. I am walking without God's guidance anymore, and some part of me hopes you aren't strong enough to tell me no."

Truth groaned and bit down on her. Pressing her down into the mattress. Needing her.

"Because if you do tell me no, Truth, then I am truly lost. Because that means you are the man I think you are. You will have dyed me in your colors, and I will never escape you. So, you must come back to me."

She gasped as his teeth tightened on her neck. "You must come back to me. My hero."

CHAPTER 69

NURTURING AN EMBER

have another contract job for you. Purely infiltration. I would usually frame this as a training mission and a test of your development, but I know you won't move an uncompensated centimeter." Merkovah looked torn between laughter and frustration.

"By the way, you do understand that the things you have been benefiting from since coming to Siphios are truly profound and incredibly rare treasures, right? Even at our peak, the Blessing of the Silent Forest would only be bestowed on young elites of the very best families. People who had sworn their life to the service of Temple and Throne."

He flipped his thumb at the Tongue. "A genuine holy blade has always been a literally priceless treasure. A guided vision of the heavens by a Level Seven teacher. Daily tuition on the true and correct Incisive. Free room and board. And yet you want me to pay you in cash for anything beyond basic bodyguard duty."

Truth just stood there waiting. Merkovah sat there waiting. They both remained, waiting, each clearly expecting the other to say something. Merkovah finally groaned and buried his face in his hands.

"Mr. Wells, do you have any comment on all that?"

"Yes. I didn't ask for any of it. You simply decided I needed it for a job I had yet to accept. They are not gifts, nor are they part of my fee. They are the necessary equipment and training needed to do the job."

Truth was hard as a coffin nail on this point. He had long since decided that he would never again work for free or for less than his true worth. Never again a slave.

"Although I do wonder why you are trusting me with all of this employee development."

"Divination. And I have gotten to know you on a level that you simply do not have context for. As much as I am still capable of trust, I trust you to behave in the ways I want you to behave. Given the correct motivation and conditions."

"Divination. You tossed some coins in a tortoise shell—"

"Young man! Really, young man! You take me for some conjurer of cheap tricks? Divination and necromancy, along with a few . . . other things . . . have been banned in Siphios since the founding *because we were too good at them.*"

"God forbade divination and necromancy because you were too good at it."

"Well, it was dressed up by the Teachers of the time as 'going against God's plan' or 'blasphemously interfering with the souls of the honorable dead,' but basically yes."

Merkovah's eyes were hard as he stroked his furious beard. "The spells and rituals were buried, of course. The location was deliberately forgotten for thousands of years."

"You have them on your bookshelf as we speak, loaded with notes in the margins and plenty of bookmarks."

"Correct. Though not here, obviously."

"Starting to wonder if your wife is actually a book of necromancy."

"She is a lovely young lady, and we have been happily married for longer than you have been alive!" Merkovah bellowed.

"I can see books. Haven't seen the wife."

Merkovah raised his hands, fingertips twitching and clenching. "Infiltration mission. Kill no one. Harm no one. Be seen by no one. Cause as little disturbance or destruction of property as possible. Obtain the relic from the safe. Details in the folder on the table. Fee is ten thousand birr. Take the folder and go before I pop your head off your neck like a pimple."

Truth collected the folder and got. Ten grand was good money.

Truth read the documents. A high-end home, a duplex penthouse in what was apparently a *very* exclusive apartment building. The homeowner's name was listed, but details about them were not. Still, it was emphasized, repeatedly, that under no circumstances whatsoever were the residents of the home to be harmed.

Which was a change from his usual *I'll take it from your cold, dead body* asset-recovery missions. Hah. Usual. Been a minute since he had done one of those, even if you didn't count Well Time. Maybe it would be a nice change. No mantra of *That's not right; that's fucked-up.*

He figured out his route in, committed the plans to memory, and decided to scout the place this afternoon, with the burglary tentatively scheduled for tonight.

Before that, however, he was going to spend a bit of his accumulated pay and take Etenesh out for lunch. It was scary how much he was coming to think of her as someone he needed. It had always just been him and the sibs. Now it was him, the sibs, and Etenesh.

She said she wanted him utterly fixated on her. He didn't know about *fixated*, but he had to confess she had already left a toothbrush and a change of clothes in the messy apartment of his mind. He was considering getting her a copy of the key.

"You want me to get you a delivery-man uniform," Jember said slowly.

"Well, clothes that kind of look like a delivery guy. Or maintenance or whatever."

"Why?"

"Can't tell you."

Jember was faintly glowing now. All the time. He was almost impossible to look away from. The handsome, sporty man was now devastatingly beautiful and untouchable. To be admired, not acquired.

"Are you . . . going to do sex things with it?" Jember asked hopefully.

"Sadly, no. Wait, is Etenesh into role-playing?"

"Not that I ever heard. And actually not something I want to know about my cousin. Sorry, I'm really doing my best to stay focused, you know? You get into a kind of zone where it stops being as pressing. But now that we are in the end stage, the ritual is testing me. Pushing on me."

"Wants to see if you are firm in your *muq*."

Jember barked a laugh. "Right idea, wrong religion. It's about embodying an aspect, yeah, but it's also about what you are willing to give up to *be* that aspect. Can I be a nurturing, purifying light for everyone I meet, not just those I love? Can I give up the physical gratification of sex to embody a higher form of love?"

"And? Can you?"

"I don't know. I'm trying. It's hard to accept the idea that you need to nurture those who hate you as much as those who love you. All right, I know some shops around here. Let's get you kitted out."

Truth walked into the Residences at Juniper and Olive dressed in a gray hat, trousers that looked like they had only scraped a win against years of dirt, and a clean checked shirt. Secondhand, total cost of wardrobe, twenty birr. Which Jember looked scandalized by, and the shopkeeper looked helpless. Not many people selling but a lot of people buying these days.

The shoes were extra. Comfortable workman's boots, new, if carefully scuffed and dusted with stone powder. You only really appreciated good shoes when you have been without them for a long time.

He walked up to the security desk, putting down his bucket loaded with a dizzying collection of pipes, hoses, and plumbing supplies.

"Got a work order here. Apartment 75001."

"Angelkin family?"

Truth looked at the blank sheet of paper. "Yeah. Fish-tank repair."

The security guard nodded. "That thing has problems all the time."

"Leaking, apparently. Should be quick. I'm in the book. Name of Dagnaw, Cerulean Dreams Aquarium Solutions."

The security guard checked his log, his eyes going vague as he looked where Truth's finger was tapping.

"Yeah, we didn't have your name, just *aquarium guy*. Got a business card?"

Faintly impressed by the level of professionalism displayed by what should be an F-Tier drone, he reached into his pocket and pulled out a coin.

"We use these fancy-schmancy calling tokens. It's got my name on it, company info on the back."

"Oh, God, they are still using these? I thought they went out of fashion years ago."

"I dunno. Boss handed me a stack of 'em, told me to give them to clients."

"Tell your boss it's cards now. Nice little glowing illusions running over them. Maybe something with fish?" The guard's eyes were pretty glassy at this point, drifting back to whatever he had hidden behind the counter. Truth figured it was either food or a book.

"Sounds good to me. So . . . do I get a temporary pass or what?"

"No pass; I just buzz you in. You want the third elevator bank on the right, and if you need to shift big stuff in or out, the freight elevator is all the way back on the left." He buzzed him through the gate, the demons bowing and making way.

"Got it, thanks. Have a good night."

"Night." The guard wasn't even looking in his direction anymore.

Truth started to walk away, then stopped. "Uh . . . not to be a dick, but . . . could you please make sure to get the time down next to my name? My boss is probably going to call later and check."

"Already logged; don't worry about it," the guard lied. He was already visibly forgetting the brief flash of color in his boring shift, going back to watching the scry discreetly hidden behind his counter.

"Thanks."

"Mmm."

Truth got on the elevator, bucket in hand. There were innumerable little tricks to Incisive, but the strangest of them was just how little cosmic energy it required . . . most of the time.

You could very faintly have the foresight running, just enough to give you a fraction of a second's warning or a vague sense of danger. You could keep the scales up and running almost constantly, provided you were changing very, very little about your identity.

It was things like the Fangs, or using foresight a second or more into the future, or completely erasing your presence; those things ate power like crazy.

Tommy Wells, certified talisman technician, was not a big step away from Tommy Wells, licensed journeyman plumber and Siphios Fish Fanciers Federation–approved fish tank installation and repair technician (salt water, tropical). Not when he turned up looking like a plumber and going to an apartment with notoriously unreliable custom fish tanks.

Not that Truth gave a damn about the fish. Not even in the top hundred list of dumb/creepy/scary/morally wrong things Truth had seen in wealthy apartments.

He reached the top floor. The family was home tonight, but it was two in the morning. Besides, he was more than just quiet.

The door was comparatively well defended. Very well defended for a private residence. Steel door, enchanted, and before you could even activate the unlocking enchantments, you had to get past the imp over the door. The imp wasn't very smart, but it was more than smart enough to keep out anyone not on the approved list.

Oh, for the happy days when he would just blast through the wall next to the door or run down the side of the building and cut through a window. Now he had to work to break into a home.

Tool, he murmured in his mind. The spell activated the talisman around his neck, temporarily stunning the imp. It would wake in about an hour, hopefully none the wiser. Hopefully.

The door was fairly trivial to bypass as well—while the spell work was sophisticated, it was still a very standard lock. Which meant that a very standard lock bypass could get through it.

Truth examined the door closely, looking for hidden traps and alarms, but . . . no. Just a very nice version of the same kinds of locks you would find on homes almost everywhere.

Truth eased open the door and slipped in. The home was decorated with pictures, mostly. A lot of the same people, shaking hands and looking at the talisman. The owner of the apartment was in most of them, smiling fixedly. In one, he was getting a sash hung on him. In another, he was signing a paper with someone.

It didn't exactly look like a businessman's wall of vanity. He didn't know exactly what this was. The Scales clad him, disguising him as an invited worker. He entered the house like a demon. Silent. And cruel.

CHAPTER 70

WHAT IT MEANS TO BE RUTHLESS

The front entryway had a spot for people to take off their shoes and admire the professional pictures on the wall. Truth ignored both. He made his way to the living room, a vast space connecting the first and second floors of the duplex penthouse. There was glass covering the entire wall, giving a breathtaking view of Xandre at night. There were comfortable sofas, enormous potted trees, and here and there a toy or ball shoved under a sofa. None of which detracted from the simply vast fish tanks that dominated the room.

Step by step, he walked through the quiet house. The fish tanks were bewilderingly enormous, breaking up the living room and lining the walls. Even in the dark, the fish shimmered and glowed. These were not any ordinary guppies—they were electric-blue, buttercup-yellow, the green of a peacock's feather and the orange of a tiger's stripes. Some looked like they were made of gold; others sparkled in the dark. Those ones, Truth noticed, got their own tanks.

That which shone was by no means safe.

Truth kept his eyes moving. The item to be acquired would be in a sealed container, fireproof, and roughly the size of his bucket.

His first thought was a safe. A wealthy house like this, it would be strange if there wasn't at least one safe. He had the horrible feeling that the walk-in closet attached to the master bedroom would have a safe. Fingers crossed the owners were already asleep. Maybe they took something to help them sleep. Understandable in these dark times.

Cracking a safe while the owners slept barely one room over was possible but difficult and dangerous. He was under the strictest orders to abort and run rather than harm the residents of the house.

In the middle of the living room was a giant, two-story fish tank, utterly dominating the space. A living coral formation grew in it, and he could see an entire miniature ecosystem swirling around it. Even small water spirits darted through the sea grass and kelp.

Truth kept exploring. There was an office marked on the floor plans he had studied. Truth tested the door to the office—unlocked. He eased the door open. It was utterly standard-looking. More pictures on the wall, showing family rather than career triumphs. There was a medal with a plaque above it, and a flag folded into a triangle below.

There was a young man in uniform in a lot of the pictures. Maybe sixteen or seventeen, a beaming older couple wrapping their arms around his shoulders.

The desk was kept neat, the drawers locked. The bookshelves were stuffed with binders, reference books, books on politics or history. Horizontal meters of reading material Truth wouldn't touch on a bet. A surprising number of guides on things like survival medicine or foraging. Making shelters from scraps or woodland material.

He made a swift, silent check for a safe. There was one concealed under a bit of carpet under the desk, more or less where he expected it would be. Truth frowned. It looked too small to hold the item. At a guess, it was for holding confidential files.

It wasn't a cheap safe. He could see the alarm spells built right into it. It was buried in the floor, so he couldn't just grab the safe and run with it. Or bounce it. Shocking, how many safes just popped open when you dropped them from a modest height.

Truth had some safecracking tools with him, but it took time, and there was a significant risk of setting off the alarm. He covered up the safe. He would try to open it later if he couldn't find a more likely option.

He went back to the living room and looked again at the biggest fish tank. It ran nearly floor to ceiling. The weight of the water must be unreal. Some good spell work, he assumed. Which would explain the coral reef and the fish inside it, with little ghostly shapes swirling among the fishes. Those water spirits must be keeping things clean and the environment healthy.

Ha-ha, could you imagine if they just dumped the sealed container in there and told the water spirits to hide it inside the coral reef? Ha-ha-ha. Oh, how silly that would be, trusting the multiple physical barriers and their bound spirits to guard the treasure. No way they would ever do that. How would they get it out again? Just order the spirits to hand it to them?

Truth quietly and vehemently swore. He would tear this whole damn house apart before he tried to get things out of the fish tank.

He moved upstairs. If the downstairs was the public area, this was the private, family area.

"You know someone is going to kill us for it, right? They are going to kick in the door and kill us in our sleep."

Truth froze, his breath seizing. There was a door ahead, cracked open. No light coming out.

"Nobody's coming to kill us, Liya. I'm trying to make sure they don't in the future, either."

The man's voice was tired. There was a warmth and depth to the baritone. And a terrible weariness. The man wasn't physically tired, or wasn't just; he was emotionally exhausted, too.

"It's a national treasure, Abiy. Worse, it's a treasure of the Temple. You know they will do anything and call it God's will." Liya paused. "Hypocrites."

"There should have been five of them in the treasury. There were three. It's happening all over. Treasures, elixirs, land, businesses, permits, you name it. It's all going to the highest bidder. And it's a buyer's market. If anything, I'm late to the game." Abiy laughed bitterly.

Truth looked at the pictures on the wall, his night vision showing the faces perfectly. Abiy was strong-faced, not handsome but charismatic. You would believe him if he told you he would fight for you in parliament.

He was smiling, or confidently serious, in all the pictures. Now his voice sounded like a man about to break.

Like a man who kept doing his best, and it kept not mattering.

"So, what's the plan? You sell it to some billionaire or aristocrat or something and then what? Book tickets off-world?"

"You know I can't, Liya. I swear on my soul I would if I could."

"They just say that, you know, to keep people on the planet. Obviously, they make exceptions for families, or how would anyone emigrate?"

"They don't make exceptions. Every emigration costs a terrifying amount, and the Shattervoid bitch for centuries about it. Millennia, even."

The room went silent again. Truth gently stretched out his right foot, slowly touching his heel to the floor and letting his weight roll forward up the sole to the ball of the foot. Ready to take the next step, when—

"She's six."

"I know."

"Six."

"I know."

"And she's brilliant. Whip-smart. She's so funny. Better-looking than I was at six."

"I know."

"She loves all kinds of birds. She laughed and laughed when she saw the special ducks in the park. She begged me to paint ducks on her walls."

"I know." Abiy sounded muffled, choked.

"Why? Why can't they take her? She's smart and funny, and beautiful and . . . perfect. I can stay if they take her. I would stay."

"Me too."

"So, why? Why can't they take my baby?" He could hear the tears in Liya's voice. The pain and the frustration and the bone-deep despair under it all.

"I don't know. I don't know. But I won't leave this planet without her or you. So, we have to be ready. For . . . whatever."

Truth couldn't stand it anymore and slowly moved down the hall. Silently padding through the dark home.

Closets filled with long dresses and robes, a little library. A doorway cracked open, with thin, warm light trickling out. Truth carefully eased up to the door and peeked in.

It was a small room, a single bed against one wall, two dressers, a window with a million-birr view. The floor was a war zone of toys, stuffed animals, clothes scattered where they fell. Books too, stacked up by the bedside table, under the bed, scattered like steppingstones across the floor. The light came from a nightlight that was projecting the night sky on the ceiling, each major star accompanied by a sigil noting what eminence it was.

Two ducks flew across the wall from the bed. Cheerful, energetic, and magnetic. Whoever painted them was a good artist.

On the bed, blankets pulled up to her chin, was a little girl. She had a serious look on her face as she slept. Her hair was wild and free. It reminded Truth of Etenesh's hair when she humored him and let it fly as it willed.

She was a beautiful child. In a comfortable room. Safe. Warm. Fed. Loved. He didn't hate her for having all those things. He didn't even envy her. He just felt sad.

Truth kept moving. The container wouldn't be in her room.

There was a little family chapel. Truth kind of stubbed his eyes on it because he had never seen or heard of the like before. About the size of a walk-in closet. There was a tiny almadel, an icon of a chest on the wall, a few prayer books, a small bowl.

Truth carefully checked every inch of it, but it seemed that sacrilege was not one of the family's sins. It was just an entire, if very small, room whose only function was to be a place of prayer, worship, and contemplation. In this penthouse worth ten million birr.

Siphios, land of saints and scholars. But what do the scholars and saints do when God is gone, and the books fuel the cookfires? What do they do when there is no Siphios?

He walked over the wide boards of the hardwood floor, letting the soft rubber of the boot heel absorb the noise as he searched through the home. Silent spectral fingers tracing through the minutiae of daily life, peering behind pictures for hidden safes. Seeing without being seen.

At the end of the hallway, there was a picture of an angel treading on the neck of a vicious serpent demon. It was rather tall, at a bit over two meters, and painted in that old style that made everything feel rather flat.

The angel was one of the scrubs, the humanoid ones with just one pair of wings. It must have done something to piss of the higher-up angels, too, because its spear looked more like a thin dowel with a metal point bolted on. Not that the demon looked much better. In his increasingly expert opinion, it hardly looked like a snake at all.

For all that Truth didn't think much of the subject matter, the painting had a quiet charm to it. You could see, quickly, that every portion of it was made with a fixed intention. The spear had a meaning, the bare feet, the way the serpent coiled around a very distinct-looking flower. As though the serpent was unwilling to crush the flower, no matter how vile it was.

This was something the artist really cared about. Something this family really cared about. And it was mounted flush with the wall. No signs of a picture hook.

Could they be that dumb? Could he really be that lucky? He had already concluded he would be taking a swim, but just maybe . . .

Truth carefully ran his fingers around the edge of the painting. It was firmly attached to the wall. Unmoving. He ran his fingers around the frame, feeling for a switch. Nothing. Which was normal. Who would install a switch for a secret safe?

Truth reached into his bucket of "plumbing equipment" and produced a ninety-degree pipe joint. He cast Tool, and the thing started floating, letting its invisible rays trace over the picture. A simple glyph slowly emerged in shuddering orange light on the right-hand side of the frame.

Nothing too unusual there, basically intended to be triggered by some kind of amulet or ring or other token, then open the door. A latch for a door, not the lock of a safe. Truth pulled a prepared lead tablet out, made the necessary alterations for the trigger, and unlocked the latch.

The painting swung open, revealing the safe inside. This was almost man-sized. The container would definitely fit in there. It was also absolutely crawling with spell wards, alarms, and other, nastier defenses. It was crackable, anything was, eventually, but it would take a long, long time.

Or you could bypass the whole damn thing. Truth grinned. He had a whole bucket of sophisticated safecracking widgets, and he wasn't going to bother with any of them. Because while he might not know much about safes, he knew quite a bit about talismans, and particularly Starbrite talismans.

And the control pad for this safe was a Weppler Rin Co. Lcc, (Part of the Starbrite Family of Companies) Authentication and Control System Model SM-1-33-980(c). A device widely appreciated for its low price, versatility, ease of use, ease of installation, and, best of all, ease of repair. A device that appeared with appalling regularity on the SAT.

As a qualified talisman-maintenance technician with the ability to sense danger, it would be embarrassing if he couldn't bypass it. He pulled out a new tablet and got to work. This one was a bit more complicated than most, but he hadn't forgotten how it was put together. Almost all Weppler components used the same structure. Hadn't changed in thirty years . . .

The door of the safe popped open. No alarms sounded; no traps went off. Seemed Weppler hadn't updated while he was in the well.

The container took up a big chunk of the safe. Round, stamped with the chest symbol he associated with the Temple. Truth pressed the amulet Merkovah had provided him to the symbol. The amulet vibrated and glowed violet. Contents confirmed.

He was going to steal this . . . whatever it was. This thing that an apparently good, successful man was relying on to provide some measure of safety for his family. Not to get off-world himself. Not to harm another in some mad quest for vengeance. Just doing absolutely everything he could to be the best dad he could, for his wonderful daughter.

And he was going to steal it. He wasn't going to touch anything else in the safe, not the stacks of birr or other currencies, not the bundles of files, not the glowing weapons. Just the one thing a good man was truly counting on. Because it was the job.

No. He couldn't hide in that excuse anymore. It wasn't just "the job." He was doing it because this was *his* best shot at protecting *his* family. And maybe, incidentally, possibly, the family that lived there. But probably not.

Truth gave the canister a thorough check for any unwanted spells, disabled what he found, and stowed it in his bucket. His family ate first. He could manage the weight.

CHAPTER 71

THE SEA OF BRASS

Truth accepted that he wasn't going to feel good, emotionally, for a while. It wasn't fun. Well, definitionally, right? It wasn't a nice feeling to sit with. But he did sit with it. He gave himself time to fully experience the sensation. He knew he had come a long way, emotionally and educationally, since coming to Siphios. And yet he kept coming back to the same phrase he thought of on the banks of the canal in Harban.

That's not okay. That's fucked-up. But I'm okay with it. Which is fucked-up.

The op could not have gone better. Basically, he walked in and walked out. The combination of advantages on him was simply too much for the static defenses of even a wealthy home to resist. The guardian spirits and devils were no match either. He didn't touch a hair on anyone's head. And terrified them. His burglary would leave them unable to sleep. Paralyzed by the horror of someone simply walking into their home, bypassing all their defenses, stealing their greatest hope, and leaving without a trace. Leaving everything as tidy as he found it.

That little girl would grow up pretty as Etenesh one day. If she got the chance. As long as she was still able to eat well. Still had soap, and medicine, and a life free of manual labor. As long as the pimps and gangsters didn't get her when the whole world turned into a slum. When she became another shiny bit of the beautiful past for a warlord to display.

He shook his head free of the unwanted thoughts. Merkovah had set something up. Time to go see what it was.

"It's a tub."

"It's a ritual device. Ancient and holy." Merkovah was determined this time.

"It's a broken tub. Look, the top's wobbly. I don't trust something made of metal that's wobbly."

"It's a ritual basin used almost exclusively by priests. The water overflows the *divinely significant* rim, and you wash your hands and feet in it."

"Can't be that significant. It's wobbly. It looks all wrong."

"That, Mr. Wells, is proof of its divinity." Merkovah was growling at this point. "The ratio of its circumference to the diameter is superimposed—existing in this layer of reality and a higher one simultaneously. It's a more than minor miracle it still functions."

Truth had to stop and process that one.

"Sorry, I think there may be a glitch, well, another glitch in my education here. The *what* is *what now?*"

"The ratio of the circumference to the diameter—you know what that is?"

"Of a circle? It's three point one four one five nine . . . something. Goes on a long while, right?"

"Infinitely, young man, infinitely. Proof of the shoddy nature of our existence. Well, not here. Not at the Sea of Brass. The ratio of circumference to diameter of the lip of the Sea is *simultaneously* your three-and-a-bit number and the far more divinely perfect number of, simply, three."

Truth felt certain hitherto-unknown gears in his head grind to a halt.

"The ratio of circumference to diameter, the thing that kind of defines a circle, and this is clearly intended to be a circle, is simultaneously three and not-three."

"Correct. A miracle."

Truth wanted to argue that nothing worked that way, and it was flatly impossible, but the Sea of Brass was huge and right in front of him, so it apparently *was* possible. Merkovah looked at the expression on Truth's face and smiled beatifically.

"Why does it have snake legs?" Truth was unwilling to be defeated and attacked on another line.

"The vast sea of God's infinite grace suppresses all demons and protects the faithful. The brass lavar is a metaphor for the mutable strength of the Law, the Sea, the weight of God's power and capacity for infinite blessings."

Truth had to think that one through for a moment. "Wait . . . isn't *mutable* a word for something that can change?"

"Exactly. Brass is comparatively easy to rework, but only comparatively. It still requires immense care and effort. The Orthodoxy does change and evolve, but only if there is a very, very good reason. And, of course, the *obviously divine* nature of the Sea of Brass adds to the legitimacy of the Orthodoxy's rulings."

"Snake legs, though." Truth hung on feebly. Strictly speaking, he couldn't call this thing *cursed*, but it just looked too profoundly wrong to be blindly accepted.

"It does, in fact, have snake legs." Merkovah nodded with a victor's generosity. "It is also a source of ritual purification, though, before you ask, not baptism."

"Wait, an enormous bowl full of water that could easily have a half dozen people use it for a hot tub and is allegedly divine *isn't* for baptism?"

"It is not. The *obviously and unquestionably divine* Sea of Brass is for purification. Water overflows the lip and falls down onto the platform, allowing the priests to ritually cleanse their hands and feet before entering the throne room of God."

Truth perked up.

"Which is obviously just a name for a room that God visits, not his actual throne room."

Truth deflated again.

"It is, however, one of the most unspeakably holy sites in all of Siphios, so as you can imagine, the Sea of Brass has significant importance to the entire faith."

Truth couldn't understand that. God surely didn't care if you washed your hands before saying "Hi!"

Merkovah was looking at him with almost-exhausted bewilderment. "You . . . really have no reverence for God, do you? You aren't opposed to the idea; you just don't see a need for it. You put it on the same level as toothbrushes for chickens."

"You don't have to clean their beaks?"

"I have no idea."

"Funny. It seems like the kind of thing someone should know."

"Presumably, someone does. *God*, for example, would know."

"Makes sense, sure."

"The reverence bit?"

"I mean, he doesn't give a damn, so why should I?"

"Because he's God? Because reverence, devotion, and worship have proven bene-fits for one's character and morality? And assuming that God does not care about your indifference is a *bold* assumption."

"Oh. And it's not an assumption. We know he's not paying attention to this world, or not paying it any more attention than he does the entire universe, so he clearly doesn't care about our opinions on anything, least of all him. He'd have to be pretty insecure to care about that, and he's, y'know, God."

"I have entire shelves of books that demonstrate exactly the fallacy of that logic."

Truth nodded. He believed it.

There was a pause.

"I'm not going to persuade you that this holy relic is worthy of your respect, am I?"

"I mean, I respect it. Someone worked really hard to make it a great washbasin. A lot of skilled work went into that bowl. Lotta detail on those snakes. I respect that a lot. And I see it means a lot to you, so I won't screw around with it, obviously."

"And with that, I'm done. Stand under the lip of the bowl, yes, great, like that. Normally, I would explain what's happening, but suddenly I don't want to. Make sure you put your toes on that join in the masonry representing thousands of years of numerological study, with your hand held straight over them, so as to maintain the sacred geometry of one of the very few directly God-touched places on this planet."

Truth did as instructed. Directly God touched?

Merkovah reached into the container that Truth had stolen and, with consider-ably less ritual pomp than he had intended, pulled out a burning spark. It looked like a coal from a blazing fire. And it was holy.

If anything was holy, it was this ember. This burning coal. If anything in the world was pure, it was this. If anything was true, it was this. Truth could see it dis-torting reality around it, furiously raging at the impure world it had been thrust into. Determined to exhaust itself to right the sins of this existence.

Merkovah said a brief prayer, even as his hand started to char. He swiftly threw it up and into the Sea of Brass while his fingers could still move.

The water in the Sea exploded, boiling furiously and coming down like rain over the lip of the basin. Truth's hands and feet were quickly drenched in the boiling water, the pain seeming to drill in from every direction. The steam rose too, soaking him, scalding him. It became terribly hard to breathe. He couldn't breathe!

Truth was unsure of where he was or what was going on. He stank. The man in front of him stank. The whole room stank. Windowless bare stone walls, a foul-smelling candle the only light, and sodden straw covering the floor. A rough desk, a rougher stool. He and the man in front of him were wearing matching robes, which also stank. The man in front of him, an old man, was sitting on the stool and carefully penning the last few words in a letter.

"There. That should fix them!" The old man grunted and put down his quill.

"Going after the Gnostics again?" Truth heard himself asking.

"No, this time, it's that bunch back in the old country. They try to insist that only one gospel is *the* gospel, rather than all four."

"Well, you say all *four* . . ."

"Oh, shut it! You want to argue it out, you can read my book on it."

"I did read it. I understood it, too."

"So, why are you here bothering me?"

"Because I understood it. The phrase *self-serving* seems . . . inadequate."

The old bishop furiously sputtered.

"It's circular logic—our church is the right church because our traditions go back to the founding of the faith, not theirs, which goes back to the founding of the faith."

"It is *slightly* more complicated than that!"

"True. Though your description of their cosmology is clearly pure fiction."

"AHA! No, you are wrong there. Every word, every insane bit of nonsense comes straight, *straight* from those Valentinian clowns. I think I even have some of their books around somewhere. Believe me, I considered innumerable ways to demonstrate their idiocy and found nothing better than quoting them extensively."

"God, God's wife who is also God, beings that might as well be gods created by God's wife, who then try to create their own life, but it goes wrong, and he becomes the God of Abraham and Isaac and creates the world."

"And is evil and the source of evil. Oh, yes. All of it was carefully and faithfully reported. Writing that part of the book was easy. It was the rest that required serious prayer and thought."

"All right, I would love to see those books, but let's just assume you fairly and accurately represented their views—"

"Which I did because everyone around here knows them. Blast it all."

"They are just another set of views. Other schools of thought, as you branded them. Don't think I had ever heard someone called a 'heretic' before as a slur. Nor 'Gnostic.' Took me a minute to figure out who you were talking about."

"Followers of Simon the Magician, not the Son of God." The old man sneered, slapping the table. "There are no other 'schools of thought.' There is the orthodoxy, transmitted by apostolic succession, and there is spiritual error, devolving swiftly into sin, corruption, and death eternal."

"And God is eternal."

"And God is eternal, and he plans for the span of all time. We are put in this world to suffer, yes, and in our sufferings grow. Generation by generation, we suffer, learn, grow, and grow closer to the divine bodies, the eternal life as perfected beings that God intends. All have been saved who can be saved, from the very day of creation until the end of time itself."

"The world isn't evil, and God isn't evil; the world is intentionally shit."

The old man grinned, reached into his robe, and pulled out a pack of cigarettes. "Got it. Light me?"

Truth frowned but found a plastic lighter in his pocket and used it.

"Pretty sure this isn't in the script."

"It's not. This vision went off the rails from the start. It's not *me* being the asshole here."

"It was getting pretty good. We were getting into some deep theological weeds."

"Oh, please, that's some baby-level stuff. Go to a seminary with that, see how fast they run your ass out. Look, this vision is intended for the faithful of Siphios, okay? It's a purification ritual, juiced by an ember taken from the very literal braziers in the throne room of God. Actual seraphim have to use tongs to pick this stuff up. I mean, the ember has degraded to almost nothing now, sure, but still." The old man took a long drag on the cigarette, exhaling a six-winged angel.

"Water boils over, falls over the anointed one, purifies your hands so that you can smite evil, and washes your feet so that their evil won't taint you. Evil often comes in through the feet, you see."

"Really?"

"Sure, why not."

"Still not seeing the problem here."

"The problem, pal, is that this is *supposed* to be a vision about the inherent correctness of the Siphios Orthodoxy and the vital importance of stamping out evil, especially including heretics. And I don't know if you noticed, but this ain't that."

"Yeah, I wondered. It smells like shit here."

"It literally does. These idiots think being dirty is somehow proof of godliness."

"Delightful."

"Yeah, also, where are we?" The old man looked curious.

"Wait, you are supposed to be telling me stuff, revealing the secrets of the world and all that."

"I am a teensy-tiny trace of divinity left in the Sea of Brass, empowered by the ember. Usually, I have people act as an attendant for Saint Ephirimdot as he combats the Six Devils and Seven Liars of Moyle."

"MOYLE!?"

"Miserable place; never go there."

"It's fine, I have been there, and it's *fine*."

"*Point is*, this is nowhere I know, I have no idea who these so-called Gnostics are, or . . . any of this, really. All this comes from your soul."

Truth stared blankly at the old man, who was sucking down his butt like he was angry at it.

"No idea."

"You haven't had weird visions or anything? Strange dreams? Your soul randomly changing?"

"Err . . . it seems to improve now and then for no good reason?"

"Yeah, it's tied in to this. Not my department, so I can't explain it. But I'd bet you anything you like your soul is having visions without you."

CHAPTER 72

THE RUSTY IRON POLE OF DEEP LOVE

Truth stared at the old man. The rancid geriatric was indifferent to the hard look and lit another cigarette off the burning cherry of the first.

"My soul is having visions without me."

"Best guess? Yeah." The old man nodded. He held up the cigarette and examined it. Truth was momentarily glad it wasn't Red Bats or something. He didn't recognize the brand.

"That's not a thing."

"Buddy. Who're you talking to right now?"

"I have no idea?"

"I already told you. I am *literally* a tiny piece of divinity attached to the Sea of Brass, whose whole job is giving people visions. Now. Tell me again, what, in your expert opinion, cannot be a real thing?"

"No, look, the mind, body, and spirit are all connected. You can't have them just go off on their own. I had a vision of the heavens. Mind and soul went together. Some people get bodily snatched up into Heaven on a vision journey. You can't have just one bit going off and doing its own thing."

"You can't, huh? Look, I'm not saying it's *common*. First time I've ever seen it, actually. But that doesn't make it not real. Your soul clearly has a weird relationship with the rest of you. Not my department. I'm here for the orthodoxy and the demon-smiting. As we 'speak,' your body is getting a tune-up, and you are going to be a lean, mean, spiritual-error-destroying machine. So, look forward to that."

The old man shrugged and sat on his desk. "I have no idea what this thing is, but I'm *loving* it, by the way." He took a long drag on his second cigarette.

"Cigarettes?"

"Is that what these things are called? I mean, I know about tobacco, obviously, just not this kind of packaging. No, I'm talking about that semi-detached bit of soul you have running around in there. It's kind of great, you know? I like the way it's been tempering your psyche."

"Wha?"

"Yeah, from what I can see, you have some kind of *incredible* curse refining your body, you got a mini-bit of soul tempering your mind, and you have your soul itself, which goes off and has adventures, nudging it up the reality hierarchy. It's an impressively complete system."

"What do you mean, *tempering my psyche?*"

"Felt any strong compulsions to do anything recently?"

"No! Other than a random dislike of farmers, but that's the curse."

"Weird, but okay. No, I mean, your psyche, your . . . brain? Thoughts? The part of you that is the intellect. It's been repeatedly tempered. I'd bet cash you are a pain in the ass to mentally whammy now."

All traces of saintliness had fled from the old man. He now gave the impression of a bum sharing his "wisdom" with gullible kids in exchange for them getting him schnapps from the convenience store he has been banned from due to a "complete misunderstanding, and the owner's an asshole."

"First of all, you don't have any cash."

"Of course not. Gambling is a sin and money an evil illusion." The old man frowned at Truth.

"*Second,* that thing was literally torturing me. It tried to get me to commit suicide."

"Meh. You lived. The point is that your brain is a lot stronger now. You might not be any smarter, but you are a lot more aware of who you are and what you really think about things. Compulsions and illusions are going to have fits dealing with you. Air demons must hate you."

The old man leered.

"I'd say someone built you this way on purpose, but I'm honestly not sure how that could be done. I'd look into the soul-vision thing if I were you. On your own, though; our time here is up. Go, young seeker! Crush demons, destroy devils, and cleanse the world of heresy!"

"What's heresy?" Truth yelled as everything started fading out.

"Whatever the boss says it is." The old man grinned as the vision faded away.

"That's no answer!" Truth shouted, stumbling through the steam. "Define your terms, you son of a bitch, and fucking pay me if you want me to work!"

"He's fine," a voice came through the fog. It sounded muffled for some reason. "I assume. I don't know him. Maybe we should call the police."

Truth was a bit confused, but he was an old Harban street kid. Someone was calling the cops? He turned on his heel and ran. There was a loud, pointed sigh, a brief chant, and a giant silver hand grabbed him. Truth tried to struggle, but the hand just ignored him and hauled him back in front of . . . Merkovah? And some other not-priests. Teachers, maybe.

"Did he just demand wages from Saint Ephirimdot?"

"Let's not be hasty. There is a decent chance he was negotiating a contract with the Liars." Merkovah sounded so done.

"Twice! I've been stiffed on my fee twice!" Truth was furious. "I'm going to hunt that fucker down and take it out of his hide!"

"Oh, dear, he's still confused by the vision. What a pity. We are going now. Actually, we were never here. Bye."

Merkovah was a beardy blur toward the door, dragging a swearing Truth through the air behind him.

Merkovah, for reasons that had nothing to do with his mental and emotional exhaustion and everything to do with his commitment to training Truth, chucked Truth into a deep pit in an abandoned building site. He then filled the pit with demons. Then he sat down, leaned back on a pile of half-rotten framing lumber, put his feet up on a rock, and tried to rest his eyes. A moment later, Merkovah shifted a little, got more comfortable, and covered his face with a handkerchief.

There were noises coming from the pit. *Swoosh*es and *ZONG*s and crackles of lightning. Screams, mostly demonic. Chanting. A lot of chanting. Some rhythmic thuds. Probably the earth demons getting in the mix. At the very edge of his hearing, demonic whispers attempted to nibble at his mind. He ignored it.

There was a long *rippling* noise. In Merkovah's expert opinion, it was the sound of a flaming sword moving at *very* high speed through the air. Then a rapid succession of meaty *chunk* noises. A sort of bubbling *hiss*, and that kind of sharp, acidic, chemical smell that burrows directly up through your nostril and starts stabbing into your brain.

Must be a lot of acid if he could smell it all the way up there, Merkovah thought.

Was that a black-headed oriole singing? Merkovah listened happily. *What's it doing here? Really lovely little birds.*

There was another series of *chunk* noises, followed by incredible snapping sounds as bones were shattered and spines torn apart.

"I didn't forget you, fuckface. Eat it. Eat it! YOU HUNGRY? I GOT DINNER FOR YA!"

There was a sort of throttled gurgling noise accompanied by hammering. It eventually went still.

"Don't forget to leave a review and a five-star rating. IN HELL!" There was a final *crack-splat* sound like a melon hitting concrete at speed.

"I hate air demons. I don't care who knows; I hate 'em. They got me talking in the middle of a fight. Who does that shit?"

Merkovah sighed and stirred himself. No dust clung to his clothes as he stood. He walked over to the edge of the pit. Truth was standing in a pond full of demonic gore, the blood and bile bubbling from the intense heat and acid as slowly dissolving bits of demons faded back to Hell. All of Truth's clothes appeared to have melted or burned away, though he seemed only a bit scratched up. One of the demons had its various limbs forcefully jammed into its slavering maw beyond its normal, enormous capacity.

"Okay, the spell resistance and demon-smiting work," Truth yelled up. "Also, you need to replace my clothes."

Merkovah nodded thoughtfully at that. "Certainly. A reasonable expense that should be covered by the employer, as I failed to provide you with the appropriate protective clothing. I will certainly pay for a new set. After you finish the next few waves."

Merkovah filled the pit again and went back to the timber pile. Everything was so tiring these days.

System, how close are we to Level Four? Truth had eventually made it back to Nag Hamadi, dressed in a poncho with the words *attractive clothing* hastily written on it. He was both impressed and annoyed that everyone seemed to believe it. One girl wolf whistled him. The constant buildup of spells was really showing.

<<Given how insanely fast you cultivate and all the "national treasures" you have . . . ingested? Not literally ingested, but . . . You know what, who cares? About fifty percent of the way. Which should leave you a gibbering monstrosity, but no, you are better than ever.>>

Still struggling to not be an asshole?

<<It's getting better. I've got to admit, I am kind of fascinated by the idea that I am somehow tempering your brain against mind control. Seems counterintuitive.>>

Why? Remember what Merkovah said about those . . . prenuptial spells?

<<They . . . Oh. Yeah. They overwrite any existing mind-control spells.>>

Right. Starbrite went for the soul, then used the soul to literally, permanently change my mind. Ultimately, there would be no magical compulsion. I'd be doing what they wanted of my own "free will." At least until the System Astrologica moved in and took up residence.

<<So, the last thing Starbrite would want is for you to be easily enchanted. It would be a serious security risk. But if they had me temper your mind so that you listened to me and only me . . .>>

No security risk. Now that I think about it, air demons haven't managed shit against me with their mental attacks.

<<The low-level trash hasn't. Let's not assume you are unenchantable.>>

Probably for the best.

He was lying on his bed, staring at the tiles on the ceiling. They stubbornly continued not to have any secret wisdom, hidden messages from earlier occupants, or anything of dramatic interest. And the latest novel was shit.

Great, you seduced seven women, but you lied to each of them, and now you are in trouble. Am I supposed to feel sorry for you? I feel sorry for the girls. Some of them clearly have some kind of brain damage or psychiatric problem, and you went and took advantage of that. You are trash. The other girls need personality transfusion urgently, as they are either boring or awful. One of the girls is outright abusive. They are all some manner of unwell.

Takes one to know one and all that.

He smiled. Well. Maybe he wasn't quite that bad. Etenesh liked him. She liked him a lot. She . . . sounded a little . . . fixated these days. But he hadn't had much in his life that he could rely on. People least of all. Having her obsession felt safe. Safer than ordinary affection would. He knew it wasn't healthy for her and potentially for him. But like a carriage ride to the pastry shop, he would take comfort over health.

He still didn't fancy his chances of seeing thirty. Hitting twenty-five was an achievement already. He was determined to live well, if only for a little while.

He picked another book off his short pile. "*Ludmilla is bored with her humdrum office life, so she leaps at the chance to work for the hunky, demanding Mr. Gertwig. But what should she do when it turns out Mr. Gertwig is actually an incubus in disguise?!*" he read aloud. His smile turned into a grin. Sounded promising.

He flipped to a random page.

I stepped into his office, the air heavy with anticipation. The room was a den of opulence, lined with dark mahogany bookshelves that whispered of secret, terrible, forbidden desires. Desires so scarlet, so fevered, the books were sealed with brass and iron. My eyes were drawn to the large, deeply carved stone desk, a symbol of his power and dominance. He stood there, impeccably dressed, exuding an aura that both frightened and captivated me. His eyes, piercing and enigmatic, seemed to see right through my façade. As I approached, my heart raced, my palms clammy with nervousness. The scent of attar, the corruption of roses, wafted through the room, mingling with the forbidden desires that danced between us. At that moment, I knew I was in his thrall, unable to resist the allure of this handsome, cruel man.

All right, he was in. Before he could turn to page one, there was an urgent hammering at the door.

"Tommy, TOMMY! Get your ass up; you need to see this!" It was Jember. Truth was up, sword in hand, and running to the door.

"What?"

"The Black Ships are back. And they aren't here to trade."

CHAPTER 73

THE ARRIVAL OF THE BLACK SHIPS

They all clustered around the scry together—Etenesh, Jember, Truth, and Merkovah, joined by what seemed like the entire staff of the Temple Nag Hamadi. The newscaster was stuttering, trying to explain what was going on as their brain was desperately trying to keep up with events.

Dozens of the legendary Black Ships of the Shattervoid Clan hung above their planet. Each so vast, it was impossible to get a sense of their scale. Each so vast, yet they were still lost in the void between stars. The camera couldn't cleanly capture their exact shape—long, a sort of flattened cylinder, hollow in the middle. Their exteriors were a sleek, matte black, emitting not a hint of light.

Truth remembered Merkovah saying that the Shattervoid merged with their ships somehow. Was he seeing the outraged extended family of a little girl?

"We still don't know what they want or what the problem is. They haven't answered any messages, and any spiritual or physical messenger is destroyed when it comes within a thousand kilometers of the ships."

The newscaster was speaking fast, papers flying across the desk. "They have forced the orbital stations to evacuate back to the planetary surface. The lunar colony has been, likewise, forcibly evacuated. Even the private cultivation retreats have been cleared out. Those not leaving at once . . . appear to have been killed. Without explanation."

The newscaster's head glowed gold for a moment. "It . . . We are now learning that a manned mission is being launched from Jeon. Jeon, as you probably know, is the country with the closest business ties to the Shattervoid Clan. We have footage from Rhakeem Balion, a tourist near the off-planet launch site outside of Harban."

There was a cutover to a crudely captured video taken on some cheap recording talisman. The orbital lifter was sleek, white with red accents, and big windows so the VVIPs could enjoy the view. The seven-pointed star of Starbrite was painted clearly on the side, just slightly smaller than the proud Tiger of Jeon next to it.

In a flare of blue light, the shuttle lifted from the ground in a flare of blue light. It accelerated deceptively quickly, reaching orbit in bare minutes. The newscasters nattered away, desperate to seem knowledgeable without actually knowing anything.

Everybody knew things were bad, and the strangeness of the Shattervoid was part of it. The truth of just how bad things were hadn't trickled all the way down. The newscasters, at least, seemed to hope for a return to "normalcy."

The shuttle was picked up by an orbital camera, presumably from some imp tasked with the purpose. It carefully came to a stop just outside the atmosphere, far from the thousand-kilometer red line drawn by the Black Ships.

"We are hearing that the shuttle is carrying Minister for Trade Mun Gaebolin and Special Envoy Plenipotentiary Harnken, a close confidant of the—"

The shuttle seemed to twist in space, or rather, space twisted it, writhing and knotting on itself, separating into thin filaments that quickly spiraled around each other, then knotting again. Truth felt a sudden, sharp nausea as his brain tried to process what it was never evolved to comprehend.

Space returned to normal. There wasn't even dust left of the shuttle.

"I . . . It seems . . . Ladies and gentlemen, we are trying to confirm what happened on the shuttle. Nothing has been confirmed at this time—"

"It was the Shattervoid," Merkovah said with grim certainty. "This is their way of fighting."

"We are hearing from several sources that this appears to be an attack. An attack by the Shattervoid. We cannot rule out deliberate terrorism or accident at this time, nor do we know what possible motives they may have—"

The newscaster was sweating, his makeup melting over his face. His head suddenly glowed with a golden halo. "They are broadcasting a message!"

The camera cut back over to the ships. There was no visible change, but a voice, alien, detached, neither male nor female, still reached the planet.

"Your world is dying. You foolish, greedy people are dying. There is no saving you. At best, only some of you will survive. Living like animals in a world you no longer recognize. Groveling in your own filth. As you deserve."

The room was silent.

"We can save some of you. Not all of you. Not even a nation's worth. But many. Tens of thousands, from your billions."

The Black Ships started spreading out, forming a globe around the world.

"The price of passage shall be equal for all. Return her. Punish those responsible. There will be no further communication. Any attempt to leave the atmosphere will be intercepted and destroyed. None shall enter, none shall leave."

The ships assumed their new station.

"You have until your world collapses."

The camera was destroyed; the scry turned to black.

The room was silent for a minute. Then— "She? Who the fuck is 'She'?!"

The room exploded into noise, everyone trying to talk at the same time. Merkovah, furious, swept out of the room without a backward glance. Truth trailed behind him.

"It's Starbrite. I know, *know* that shitheel is responsible somehow. He's the only one who would, or could, dream of daring to touch a child of the Shattervoid Clan."

"Yep."

"And now he has finally, officially killed off what tiny hope this planet had for a future. This will be a dead world for millennia, tens of millennia, until its spirituality can finally regrow."

"Yep."

"I take some small pleasure in knowing that he will die with the planet, of course, but since I don't for one minute believe he hasn't some kind of escape route planned, it is a very small pleasure."

"Mmm-hm."

"I should inform you, Mr. Medici, that if you try to up your fee right now, I may throw you directly into orbit."

"No, this is actually me volunteering something."

Merkovah snarled out half a laugh. "Well, it is the day they announced the end of the world. What is it?"

"In your office and under the wards, Teacher. Also, remember that you have invested irreplaceable national treasures in me, so if you hit me, it's your loss."

Truth had never really seen Merkovah in action. He could more or less judge the bounds of a Level Seven based on his own stats, but he had learned, painfully, that the stats were not to be trusted. At the very least, they didn't tell the whole story.

For example, Truth did not believe there was a stat that covered *Nigh-instantaneously summon a Level Four demon, and quicker still smash it into the wall so hard it pulps on impact, then do that six more times until you finally feel calm enough to talk.*

Hard to imagine what the Average Starbrite Employee's demon-pulping rating would be. Truth was now doing his best to remain unnoticeable. Standing still and playing make-believe seemed like a very good idea.

"You aren't going to convince anyone you are a potted plant, Mr. Medici."

"I thought it was better than just pretending I wasn't here at all."

"Oh, no chance of fading into the background, I'm afraid."

That, Truth reckoned, was a damned lie. *He* was the one with good reason to fear for his life. The demon goo on the wall was sort of bubbling as the lower layers dissolved back into Hell, making the higher layers or bigger chunks shift around.

"Let's quickly recap. You led the security detail of a natural science team transporting a box. You were ambushed, came under heavy assault by forces unknown, retreated to an abandoned farmhouse, were told by the enemy, an enemy that knew you were Starbrite deathsworn, that the box contained a child of the Shattervoid clan. You then proceeded to knock down several spell birds and covered the evacuation of the natural-science team with the box."

"And then I was killed and spent five years or so in a well, yes, Teacher."

"You shot down multiple spell birds, with a standard-issue needler. A sidearm."

"Yes. I think you underestimate how effective I am with the support of the System."

Merkovah took some deep breaths, calming and centering himself. "Now that you say it, you really were a match made in Hell when you joined Starbrite, weren't you?"

"Loyal as a dog. Trained like one, too, I have come to understand."

"I may have done a bigger good deed than I thought, training you," Merkovah growled. "And you didn't think to mention any of this before . . . why?"

"Because I was worried about this exact scenario? And if word reached Starbrite that I was alive and talking, they would vanish my sibs before turning them into school lunches in the slums?"

The growling from Merkovah reached subterranean levels. "We are going to go over every tiny detail, from when you got the mission brief to when you died. Everything you saw, heard, smelled, inferred, every. Single. Detail."

Truth feebly waved goodbye to the next few hours. "Yes, Teacher."

"A few hours" proved to be an overly optimistic timeline. Merkovah hadn't been exaggerating when he asked about every single detail, from the construction of the witchcrafted puppets to the summoned ghosts to the make and model of the attacking spell birds.

Merkovah didn't come out and say it, but it seemed clear to Truth that he hadn't an inkling this operation had occurred. That offended the exorcist's professional pride.

"Somebody screwed up. Badly. Because it means that someone outside of Starbrite knows that a child of the Shattervoid Clan is imprisoned or dead somewhere on this world. And we didn't hear a peep of it."

Merkovah had calmed down, now merely volcanic in his fury.

"All right, this . . ." Merkovah clearly wanted to say something like *doesn't change anything*, but that was far too enormous a lie.

"This changes a lot. Not just what you told me, but the . . . accelerating chaos that will come from the arrival of the Black Ships. I don't know how long it will take for open war to break out. It probably already has broken out in some places. Jeon will hold together longer than most, on the surface, because Starbrite won't want his nest disturbed."

He breathed out explosively. "I'm going to rewrite your mission plan, start shifting pieces around. You are still going to be tasked with causing chaos and weakening the System Astrologica, but your . . . co-equal task will be discovering what happened to the Shattervoid girl."

"Do you think she's still alive?"

"I haven't the faintest damn idea. The Shattervoid Clan is only debatably human at this point. I mean that literally; it is a question of philosophy about the definition of *human*."

Truth stared blankly at Merkovah. "Me? Things that look like me?"

"Oh, really? So, is Nag Hamadi a 'human'? It's walking around in a human-shaped statue."

"Obviously not."

"Why obvious? It looks like you." Merkovah sighed. "This is a very old, very long discussion that I don't care to have right now, even if I had the time, which I don't. Let me set you a 'small' project. Say a man gets a prosthetic leg. Still human? Two prosthetic legs. Still human? Balls get blown off, rendering him unable to reproduce normally. Still human?"

Truth thought about it and nodded. "Still human."

"I agree. Now, how much of that body would have to be replaced with prosthetics for him to no longer be human? And if there is no upper limit, then I think you really have to answer the question—what is a human, exactly?" Merkovah smiled, radiating a rare, genuine happiness.

"I tell you what. Let's table all discussion on theology until you can answer that question."

Truth had only reached the door of his cell when he was intercepted by Etenesh. "Leaving your girlfriend to process a world-ending calamity on her own is *bad* boyfriend behavior, Mr. Medici." She didn't add the little lilt to the end of "Medici." Truth figured that put her on the high end of pissed but below furious.

"I had information directly on this that I had to tell Merkovah. He then interrogated me thoroughly."

"Wait, really?"

Truth nodded. "I don't mind telling you about it now, though Merkovah probably doesn't want it to spread around."

Etenesh sighed and looked torn. Then she extended her arms toward him and gave him a look. He stepped over and hugged her hard.

"I don't care about whatever top-secret bullshit. I just want you hugging me." Keeping an arm around her, he guided them into his cell. He held her like he did the day after she learned of God's contempt. Shaking, weeping. Like she would fly away. The storm passed with time, leaving behind exhaustion.

"I thought I would have more time," she said.

"Me too."

"Do you know when you are shipping out?"

"No. Sooner than planned by months, I expect."

"Yeah. Sounds right." Etenesh sighed. Silence pooled in the room, slowly rising around them.

"Do you feel obsessed with me yet, Mr. Medici?" The lilt was back, though only just.

"Sorry. I am pretty sure I . . ." The words caught in his throat. He tried to get them out. Now, of all times, surely *now* he could tell her! But he couldn't stand it. Couldn't stand making it real. Being that vulnerable.

"It's okay. I can feel you, you know? The storm of you, when you stop locking yourself down. All those emotions under that cool exterior."

"I'm cool?"

"You sure act it."

"Really? You know you are the first person to ever call me cool, right?"

"Hah. Another first for me."

"Mmm-hmm. Another first for you."

There was a long pause. Then a soft little sob. "I'll take it. All the firsts. And all the words you can't bear to say. Tomorrow night, Mr. Medici. Even if the sky falls and the seas burn, and the land gives up its dead. Tomorrow night, I'm going to show you what you've been missing."

CHAPTER 74

DIVINE CONSORT

Truth had never let anyone ride with him on his iron horse. Another first for Etenesh. She snuggled behind him, pressing against his back as her arms wrapped around his waist. She was so warm.

He took them through the streets of Xandre at a speed most Level Threes would consider unwise and most Level Ones would consider suicidal. Splitting the gap between lanes, darting between heavy wagons, and even going through notionally pedestrian-only alleys. He never once had to slow down. His reflexes and Incisive were more than enough to see them safely through.

Just one more casual display of superhuman ability, Etenesh thought. She had just pointed at a mountain southwest of the city and asked if he would take her there. He nodded and pulled around his iron horse, missing the pun entirely. And now they were moving as fast as a flying carpet through the streets and alleys into the suburbs.

The glories of Xandre, the towering trees and mushrooms and spiraling palaces and temples all faded into sprawl. Not too bad in Xandre. They built dense neighborhoods. But suburbs are suburbs almost everywhere and always boring.

Truth saw a gathering outside some kind of building. Fifty Desrin, kneeling and facing a man with a stringed instrument in his lap. He was sawing away at it, singing. The crowd was singing with him, repeating the same few words over and over again. Their arms crossed over their chests as they rocked back and forth, endlessly repeating the words.

Then on, and there was a sudden increase of angry young men on the street, not angry at anyone in particular just yet but working up to it. He saw bottles. A lot of bottles. The set of shoulders and the squinting eyes of young men looking for a fight. He nipped quickly through the crowd. He wasn't wearing the zeph tonight, but he figured, why chance it? Maybe people just didn't want to see that kind of PDA during the end of the world.

Past some kind of technical school now, pointlessly big lawns surrounding boxy white buildings with students pouring out of them like furious ants. It took one day to get from confusion to panic, anger, then despair, then right back to anger. Anger was a wonderful thing, Truth thought. Despair was paralyzing. Angry gets things done. If only there were things worth doing.

There was some kind of meeting going on outside a temple. It didn't look like Nag Hamadi hardly at all, but some of the iconography was similar. Progressive, maybe? People were dressed a lot more casually. A cleric of some kind was in front of the crowd, yelling, waving his hands in the air. A woman stood next to him and would jump in with words of support. With calls to praise God, praise the angels, bless your brothers and sisters.

Not a hint of a cop. Must be needed somewhere else. Not his problem. He sped up.

Now the city was flashing by—office parks and industrial zones, gravel parking lots filled with spellwagons or carriage dealers, or mattress-liquidation stores. Whatever the hell they were. Faster and faster, watching the city blur and then fall away. They were in the green now, and rising.

The road up the mountain was busy, traffic jammed stuck, all headed up. Truth ignored the queue and zipped right past. Iron-horse privilege. There were carpets coming in too and flying spirits carrying the rich and powerful. Something big was going on up there.

He was quite certain it wasn't him.

"You know, you never hesitated even once, the whole way." They had slowed enough for Etenesh to talk normally. "Right into a wall of traffic or a busy intersection, or what looked like a mob forming up. You just went for it, and a way appeared. Totally in control the whole time."

Truth nodded. It was easier than explaining that, for him, the way had always been there. Etenesh just couldn't see it.

"I *was* leaning into the control-and-danger play because it's what you needed to feel safe. I really, really get off on knowing I can give that to you. But it wasn't something I was into by itself, you know?"

Truth shook his head. He didn't know.

"I'm into them now." He could hear the grin as she whispered in his ear. "That was hot as hell. Pretty man."

Truth was still trying to get his words in order as they pulled into the packed-full parking lot of what looked like a monastery perched most of the way up the mountain. Etenesh flashed an amulet, and the guard directed them around back to what appeared to be staff parking.

"I don't think I have seen a Siphios Orthodox monastery before."

"Ah, we don't have monasteries, at least in the sense you mean the word. This is a temple, yes, but also a spiritual retreat and a ritual site. A popular one, too, being on a mountain just outside the city."

"I can see that. Um." He searched for the right words. "I know what we are doing here, but what are we doing here?"

Etenesh giggled a little, a surprisingly happy little sound that suddenly, shockingly lifted his spirits. For a second, she was the sunny woman he first met, hair flying wild and free.

"Our particular faith, Siphios Orthodox, believes that in the beginning, God created a perfect person. Everything else was less perfect, so there were two or more of them, but this human was perfect because they were made in the image of God. And there is only one God."

Truth nodded at that.

"But the human saw how all other living things reproduced and grew and filled the world. Not this world, you understand. *The* world, the first one."

"Oh. I don't think I know where that is."

"It's not there anymore." Etenesh waved off the disappearance of the ancestral planet and plunged on. "The perfect person was lonely. They were made in God's image, but they were made of matter. Limited. So, they begged God for a mate. God was wroth because the perfect person was *perfect,* and now they were asking him to make a less-perfect version."

Truth nodded along.

"God tore the perfect person in half, returned them to the mud, and rolled each half into a little ball. One ball he shaped into a man, the other into a woman. Both with the memories of having been the perfect, holy androgyne."

"I think I am seeing where this is going."

"And, of course, the only way they can even slightly return to that divine state of grace is in acts of reunification."

"Called it."

"*Reunification* being a term defined a lot more broadly than just sex, and it's why the marriage sacrament is arguably our most holy."

"Ah. Killjoys get in everywhere."

Etenesh snorted at that but gladly grabbed his elbow and snuggled up when he offered it.

"Ironically, it was that duality that finally made humanity part of the world, not somewhat above it. Now, it was part of the eternal cycle of duality—man and woman, day and night, life and death. Everything existing in opposition and only becoming divine when it transcends that opposition. And, of course, since they were no longer perfect and were now bound up in that cycle of duality, they were condemned to suffer death after life. Had man and woman not separated, they would be eternal."

"Huh. So . . . what about the things that aren't really one thing or the other?"

"There are endless quantities of teachers and scholars standing by to find a place for everything and things to put in opposition to said everything."

"No, but . . . there are things that are kind of alive and kind of dead. There are solar eclipses, and when it's night in Siphios, it is day on the other side of the planet. People who aren't really one gender or the other. Seahorses. Just . . . seahorses generally. They aren't anyone one anything. There is way too much gray for a black-and-white world."

Etenesh looked like she wanted to argue the point, paused, then laughed softly.

"You know that I am a subject-matter expert on this point, right? I study the origin of God and those powerful enough to be deemed subordinate 'gods,' aka the stellar eminences, at a postgraduate level. My department is likely the best in the world on that subject."

"I did not actually know that. Honestly, you told me what you were studying, and I didn't understand a word of it."

"Fair. Most don't. It's not a big department. I'm laughing because I can see why you give Merkovah a headache. You are applying analogies and logic to an incredibly simplified description of a vastly complicated topic. It's not 'wrong'; you are just working with less than the total information necessary. And to get the total information necessary, you would need to study these questions of philosophy and theology to at least a university level. If not postgraduate."

"Ah."

"You aren't dumb, Truth. You are damn smart, in fact. But the universe is so, so big. There is so much to learn. Even ancient mages only understand a tiny part of the whole."

She looked up at him, her dark eyes now a brilliant ocher in the fading light. "For tonight, in this place, at this time, can you accept that we are two parts of a whole? Not identical but equal. Complete by ourselves, but perfected together?"

He smiled at her. When she looked at him like that, he would agree to a lot of things. "I can."

"Good. Because I have wanted this for what feels like a lifetime. Now, my cult sent over some ritualists—"

"Wait, what?!"

"I promised you a religious experience for your first time, Mr. Medici. And you know I take my faith very seriously."

"I'm just not used to making an appointment for sex. As a concept," Truth tried to explain. The cultist just shrugged.

"This is sex in only the most technical sense. Basically, it's going to be you and her symbolically reversing the creation of humanity and restoring perfection to the self and the faith." The cultist was masked and robed, their voice muffled. Truth had not the faintest clue as to their identity.

"Not . . . exactly reassuring."

"You will be fine. She knows what to do, and believe me, you *will* be up for it." Truth was led up the side of the mountain to a small clearing. It was surprisingly private—the dense grasses and shrubs blending with the ancient trees to wall out the light and sound of the rest of the world. There was just the moon above and the earth below. Five cultists had surrounded the edge of the clearing, patiently waiting. When Truth entered, the sixth left his side and took up their station.

The cultists raised their arms and started to pray. From out of the night sky came a sound like sighing. Feathers drifted down, and among them was Etenesh. Not fully clad in her God-raiment but still falling on his senses with a warm fire. He wanted her. Burned for her.

He strode toward her, his obsession growing. The cultists were forgotten as their prayers transformed the grove into a blessed garden. He had eyes only for Etenesh. He discarded his ritual robes. He had nothing to be ashamed of. Nothing to hide. Not there. Not from her. She was as naked as he—wearing the glory of the heavenly night around her.

The cold in Truth, the empty place where love should have lived, screamed at him, told him to go to her, hold her. To warm himself, at long last, in another. He strode toward Etenesh, more than just "hungry."

He didn't see how he shimmered, bending the world as he bathed in the moonlight. He didn't see what the cultists saw—a god claiming his bride.

CHAPTER 75

THE VIEW FROM THE MOUNTAINTOP

His name was Truth Medici, and he was not alone. He didn't have to work alone, think alone, fight alone. Truth Medici shared his life with another—Etenesh. And Etenesh loved him. Truly, wholly, passionately. He could feel her obsession, her need for something real and tangible she could devote herself to, and it was Truth.

It was at this moment that Truth truly believed that he was loved. That he was worthy of love and capable of loving in return. He knew that he was more than a slumrat, a violent beast, a thug with a spell, or any of the other belittling names he put on himself. He was Truth Medici, who loved Etenesh and was loved in turn.

The chanting of the cultists formed a background drone that worked with the enchantments in this place. Connecting the two of them to both the mountain below and the heavens above. The flesh outside and the soul within. Truth could see it now, could finally understand what cultivation was.

It was the unification of mage and the universe. It was to continuously perfect oneself and approach God, as Truth and Etenesh perfected each other. The opening of the nine apertures wasn't the end of cultivation. How could it be? Truth groaned and bit Etenesh on the shoulder. When you reached the peak of this world's cultivation, what was the next step? What wonder would be born from that union?

He was in a state of divine ecstasy, lost in the joys of the flesh as his mind and soul were lifted heavenward. He felt Etenesh's nous with him. They didn't plunge into the heavens, merely looked up. To cultivate, to grow as a mage, to approach the heavens? To one day become a stellar eminence? Did it matter so long as they did it together?

They fell back down into their bodies. Two became one. One became none. And from nothing was born everything. A timeless, selfless moment of divine joy. It lasted for a moment, or an eternity, or just long enough.

When the moment passed, the two lay cuddled up on the grass. Covered in sweat, smiling like fools. Happy. Just happy to be in the moment, together. It was Etenesh who stirred first, rolling onto her belly to look Truth in the eyes.

"You know I love you."

"You know I love you, too." Truth smiled.

"You do. I could feel how much you wanted this to be real. That desperate ache in you. I'm real. This is real. You are loved. You are not alone."

"Neither are you, Etenesh." This time, it was Truth's turn to lovingly caress the syllables and let them trip lightly from his mouth.

"How was your first time?"

"Magical." Truth grinned. It was a wonder to Etenesh—his smile was so loving, mischievous . . . young. For the first time she could remember, Truth had put down all his pain and was simply happy. Not healing, not content. Happy.

She prayed she never forgot this one singular moment. The one fragile second when her beloved put down the blade.

She could feel it slipping away. They were no longer in that perfect eternity, and soon the blade would be fused back into him. This was her chance. Her only chance.

"It doesn't have to be just this once, you know. What was done with ritual magic can be done with practice and skill. Two people who love and trust each other totally. They can find that perfect union, that peace, all on their own."

"Oh, really?" Truth's smile deepened. "I like the sound of that. A lot. I don't think I would enjoy normal sex much after that." Her heart sang, but she knew her man and replied—

"Don't knock it until you've tried it, Mr. Med*ici*."

Truth admired her, the curves of her, the way her eyes burned with ocher, and her voice thrilled with heavenly harmonies. Her god was upon her, and he found he loved her and desired her in every form. She leaned her forehead against his, gently running her nails along his arm.

"All kinds of things become wonderful when you have the time," she murmured. "And we can make the time."

"The one thing I seem to always be short on." Truth smiled. The pain was coming back. She could see it, and it hurt her, too. But she had to try.

"We don't have to be. You don't have to be. The end of this world is ordained by God. He turned his back on us, let us ruin ourselves, and now we reap the consequences. But we won't all die. You and I won't die. This world will one day be reborn, holy and new. A blessed garden for those who lived. Let's retreat up into the mountains. You are a mighty warrior. Finding food will be easy. I'm a ritualist, which won't be much use, but it means I can teach and I can learn. I will garden, and keep the house, and teach the generations of our line."

Her eyes were fever-bright, staring into his.

"We will be that first couple of the new world, and our children will be strong and wise."

"Children already?" Truth murmured, lost in her. "I can't imagine it. I can't imagine what a good father looks like, let alone being one."

"I can teach. You can learn. This is Siphios, beloved. You think we are sexual libertines because we seem casual about sex before marriage. Not so. We just make sure that we know ourselves so that when we get married, we can give our everything to it. Both partners, equally, though not identically, committing totally to their ideal of marriage in the faith."

"The 'prenuptial' spells."

"Yes, literally cast immediately before the sacrament of marriage." She rolled Truth on top of her, guiding him to pin her hands above her head as her expression turned fanatic.

"Anything. I will promise you anything. Everything you need to feel safe. To feel desired. To feel at peace. Anything that is in my power to give, or that one day will be, I will give it to you. Just so long as you promise me that you will always be mine and mine alone. That you will stay with me. That you will not return to Hell, blade in hand, but live in peace with me in the mountains."

She writhed underneath him, pressing against him. Her body as sincere as her words.

"I will give you everything, and the world itself will be ours. The evil ones turn on each other and consume one another already. I will give you everything, so long as you stay with me, always."

"My family—"

"You owe them nothing. *Nothing.* Your parents are monsters, unworthy of the name. You have no kin beyond your siblings, who you raised at the cost of your very life and soul. You sacrificed far more than any demand of blood. Far more. The world *tortured you.* I wondered why you could fearlessly charge into hordes of demons. How could they be any worse than the hell of your life? You. Owe. The world. *Nothing.*"

Her voice trembled, grief and rage twisting around each other, feeding on each other.

"Why keep fighting? Fighting against the will of God? Fighting against the mighty and their armies? Against the entire world and even your own desires? Why not win, by refusing the battle? Why not win, by leaving and being happy. With me. Forever."

He kissed her hard on the mouth. Not even sure what he was feeling, just that it was overwhelming him, and she was there and so willing. He could see it. He could see it! How often did he want to just throw up his hands and walk away?

It could be his new dream. Not some dreary C-Tier apartment in an anonymous block of apartments. A little house in the mountains. A hut they made, or better still, an existing home whose owner decided to be somewhere else. He could learn to hunt. He would bet he was good at it. He wouldn't farm; that could be Etenesh's job. Maybe they would keep goats. Have a dozen fat kids running around.

Kids he would never hit. Kids who would never, ever miss a single meal. Who knew that their parents supported them and encouraged them. Kids who wouldn't have to wait a lifetime to know they were loved.

It had taken Truth a heavenly vision, meditation on the nature of a snake god, friends, counseling, and ultimately the love of a good woman to finally, barely believe he was loved. That he was worthy of love and deserving of it. It shouldn't take that much. Not for his kids.

He could see it in his mind's eye—the little house, timber-clad, metal-roofed, on the side of a mountain stream. Goats and chickens in a pen, a kitchen garden just outside the door. Etenesh, pregnant again, joyfully laughed and scolded the children to do a better job getting the eggs. Not to fear the pecks and scratches. He was there too. His son ran up and hugged him around the waist. Not afraid of him. The boy just loved his father and couldn't wait to show him.

"No tears, beloved. No tears. It can be yours. It can all be yours. We can pick out names on our way up. We won't even go back to the city—just jump on your iron horse and ride to our heaven. Just say you give up on this world. Just admit to yourself that you are done with this *horror*. That you are ready for love, happiness, and acceptance."

"The magic will fade. We will be too unreal to cultivate. Our forever will be short."

"No, it will be forever. Our bodies may grow old and die, but each moment will be an eternity of bliss. Together forever, in life and death. See the house, beloved. See our children, our livestock, our love. Can't you see it? Can't you hear their laughter? Our laughter? Do you still smell of sex? I bet I do. Our kids will laugh at us and make faces at their embarrassing parents. And we will shake our heads and scold them, and our hearts will be singing, singing, singing with joy."

He could see it. He could hear it. He could smell it and feel the echoes of joy reverberating back in time toward him. He could be this happy. It could all be his. He just had to choose. Give up on everything. On everyone. A final, grand act of selfishness after a lifetime of service to others.

Hadn't he earned it? Hadn't he done enough? By any measure, he had, surely. He deserved his happy ending. What could be more perfect than front-row seats to watching the world burn?

So, why was there that little discordant clatter, like an empty beer can down a stairwell? Like the giggle of someone who finally got their fix? He would be getting away from all that. He would watch the world rupture, then be *clean*.

What exactly did he want to do, going back to Jeon? Kill Starbrite? He wanted revenge on the System, certainly, and he wouldn't mind seeing Starbrite get a kick in the nuts . . . but that was really Merkovah's dream. The System and Starbrite would eat shit anyway when the magic faded from the world.

Rescue the sibs? He did want that. That little bit of familial love was all he had for most of his life. That sense of duty to them was all that had gotten him through the bad years. Which, even if you counted the dead time, was most of his years. That could have been his tombstone—*Here lies Truth Medici, loyal as a dog, and like a dog, his life was nasty, brutal, and short.*

But he did love them and wanted them safe and well. Which might happen if he did nothing, but given the desolation that would be Jeon as the world ended . . . probably not. They were tough kids. Slum kids, with a good education. But a bomb or a falling building didn't care about any of that. If he wanted them safe, he would have to go do it himself.

The girl? Did he want to save the little Shattervoid girl? Honestly, he didn't care. He didn't kidnap her, and he died protecting her. Likewise, he didn't much care about getting off-world.

Hey, he would need to renegotiate his fee. If he saved the girl, and they killed Starbrite, he would need tickets for the sibs.

And for himself? For Etenesh? Would they want to start a new life on a new world, or would they join hands and watch their magic fade away? Happy to live simple lives in the healing garden. With big floppy dogs, and playful otters in the river. His happily ever after—being exactly where he would have been if he didn't go to Jeon. Didn't return to Hell.

So, why was there that damn rattle in the pipes, that damn corpse stink from the dumpster?

CHAPTER 76

A HEART FULL OF BROKEN BOTTLES

Truth teetered on the edge of what should have been an obvious decision and started to laugh. Deep, honest laughter, coming from the gut and bubbling through the pain and anger and joy and lust until it reached the open air as mirth tough enough to go the distance.

"Why go back to Hell? Because *fuck 'em*, that's why! I do want to save my siblings, but it's not that, either. Do you . . . Yes, actually, you do. You do know exactly how badly they fucked me up. But you haven't lived it. You haven't been there. For which I am so, so thankful."

Truth leaned in and kissed her again. Slowly, possessively this time.

"My entire life, before you, could be defined in one phrase—'*That's not okay. That's fucked-up.*' And I told myself that I was okay with it. I could accept the fucked-up-ness because I had to. It was a necessary thing to get through the day. But it wasn't okay. Even if I was okay with it, it wasn't okay."

Truth smiled. It was sincere, but Etenesh could see the pain there, too.

"My earliest memories. The first thing I really remember thinking was that what I was seeing was *wrong*. That it shouldn't be this way. It *was* this way, but it shouldn't be. A mother shouldn't burn her baby's hands because he cried and she's tired and hurting. Dads shouldn't break their son's ribs when he asks if he can have food today."

Etenesh shuddered.

"Though there will be a lot more of that when the collapse comes. A lot of starving people and a lot of dads and moms not able to do anything about the hungry bellies. Not that my going to Jeon will prevent that from happening, even if I succeed."

Truth sat back and pulled Etenesh up with him.

"I've known my whole life the slums were wrong. Poison. Everything in them is poison. Not just for me, for all the slumrats living in there. They make cruelty a necessity. You can't care about people. You *can't*. You are too sick and tired and scared to care. You barely care about yourself, and then only enough to numb the pain. Drugs, booze, sex, scry. Maybe a bag of something cheap from the convenience store if your hunger fights through the schnapps and base and cigarettes."

She caressed his face, crying silently, letting him get the words out.

"The slums are wrong. The slumrats are wrong. All the people who support that whole . . . arrangement. I don't even have words for it. The people who live in the nice part of the city in houses built by the people living in the slums, eating food prepared by people who can't afford a bite of it, driving chariots assembled by people they could run down legally. All those people are wrong too."

He started talking faster. "They are wrong. Starbrite is wrong. All of Starbrite, every little twist and corner of it, all the good things it does for cruel reasons. It's wrong. The way the whole world, yes, even Siphios, leans in to it. Supports it. They are all wrong too. I'm not fighting the world, love; I'm the logical result!"

She smiled through the tears at that.

"Think about it—I'm the product of all the shitty, evil, wrong decisions made by *billions* of people. Doesn't make me special. There are billions more, just like me, all over. But it's the roots of me. I'm someone who's the product of all the wrong things, who got through the day by saying, 'That's not okay. That's fucked-up.' And now I've got a sword. Now I've got everything I needs to be an A-Tier pain in the ass. And I've got motivation."

He was waving his hands now. "I don't owe the world shit. You are right. I don't. I did my best for the sibs. I *died* for the sibs. I don't owe them. Never did. But you know what? I'm okay with it all. Because looking out for them *wasn't fucked up*. Looking out for them was, actually, okay. So, now I'm going to go back to Jeon. Back to Harban. And for a brief, glorious time, I'm going to be part of the problem. I'm going to make life hell for as many people as I can so that I can rescue the sibs, get some revenge, and at the end of it all?"

He breathed, looking Etenesh dead in the eye. "At the end of it all, I'm doing it because, against all logic, I refuse to think I can't make a difference. That nothing I do matters a damn. I'm going to pick up my blade and cut away those things that hurt me, and if it doesn't matter in the grand scheme of things? Fuck it. Fuck it. I'm just another slumrat, and you know what slumrats do? They climb. They go right up your trouser leg and climb until they find somewhere fatal to bite. And if they can't manage fatal, so painful you want to die."

"And cultivation?" Etenesh asked. "Are you trying to save that, too?"

Truth felt his rant derail for a moment, then grinned. "It was the first thing I felt like I could really control. It would be nice if I could save cultivation. Of course, that would mean reversing centuries of damage. So. Unlikely."

"Ha-ha. No. No, that's not right. You aren't saving *cultivating*. You are saving the idea of cultivation. That by their sole effort, a mage can transcend the limits of reality and become something greater. I can see it in you. The path of the mortal feels like running away. Only cultivation offers a path to a long life. I see it. I see it in you. Part of you is convinced that you will die young, but part of you is swearing and wiping the blood off your lip and daring the world to stand in your path to the heavens."

Truth watched the black wings unfolding behind her, the gold flashing in the moonlight. Her feet turned into talons, but her hands stayed soft and warm as they cupped his face. "You won't accept a mortal life. You will kill your way to godhood."

"That's too high for a slumrat to look up. I'm just gonna climb. One day I'll run out of 'up.'"

"But I am not a slumrat. I am a beloved child of the Heaven Beseeching Clan, and in this place, at this time"—she leaned in to whisper—"I'm not just the first woman; I am the first *idea* of a woman. I am God's consort, made by him to shape all that should be. You have made your choice, pretty man. You are exactly who I feared you would be. I am lost." She breathed out. Truth was confused, more confused.

"You're lost?"

"Yes. How could I bear to watch you rise alone?"

She reached toward him. "Give me something of you—make a hole for me. Give me . . . a piece of that fury. That cold flame that freezes you. I will give you some of my warmth. Let us perfect each other so we know we are never truly alone. Or truly parted."

He could feel it then, that they were still in the ritual. That he could reach in and give her some of himself. He hesitated. He was willing to lose the pain, but did he want Etenesh to have it? But she had reached into her chest and pulled out a drop of burning blood. So, Truth did the same, the ritual guiding him to pluck some of the pain out. They pressed their hands into each other's chest. A little bit of themselves in the other. Never to be parted.

Something in Truth snapped into place. What . . . he still wasn't sure. But he would find out. The chanting slowed. There were a few ritual claps, then those stopped.

Etenesh wiped away her tears. "I knew that would be your choice. I hoped I was wrong. But I knew. You were never going to run away."

"It's just not who I am . . . these days, anyway. Ran away a whole hell of a lot when I was a kid. Underrated survival tactic, I'd say."

"These days, of course, you are merely tactically repositioning to the rear."

"Precisely."

"So you can jump the fuckers when they aren't looking."

"You really do get me."

The wings vanished, and so did the claws. The long, straight hair kinked up and started flying wild again. She looked like the idea of sex made flesh when she was God-touched, but hand on his heart, this was the Etenesh he thought of. The Etenesh he had fallen in love with. "I love you."

She smiled brilliantly at him. "And I . . ." She stopped, horror creeping over her face. "And I . . . I—!"

"Etenesh?"

"I can't say it! I want to say it! You know it, but I can't say it!"

"Etenesh, what's wrong?"

"I can't say it! I can't! They'll get me if I say it. They will use you against me!"

"Who, who will?"

"THEM! ALL OF THEM!" She was screaming now. "Every single dog-fucking shitbird on this cursed rock! I hate them. I hate them! I HATE THEM!"

Truth looked at the cultists. "If you aren't Level Four or over, run for your life. Get help, someone who knows how to deal with this." They froze, their masked faces looking confused. "RUN!" he barked. Of the seven, five ran down the mountain.

"Oh, fucking pussies! Weak little cowards. I should have known I couldn't count on you. Things go even slightly bad, and you fold like a paper fan in a toilet." Etenesh sneered. Truth had kept his eyes on her hands, though, and he could see her fingers twitching, tiny spell forms starting to drift from her fingertips.

"You are feeling it, a bit of it. I am so sorry, love. I feel the warmth of you. It's a poor trade. I never wanted you to understand me. Not really."

"It's not fair."

"No. You deserved some better part of me."

"Not that! It's not fair that you feel like this. This is you all the time? How does anyone live around you? How? *How?* All I can think of is that everyone is out to get me. That those cowards ran off to get someone who could take me in a fight, and they will because they want something from me. Or just want to hurt me."

"You learn to deal. Calculate the risks. Learn to protect yourself. Remember that I did accept when you reached out."

"But they will hurt me! You—!" She stopped. Forcing herself away from that cliff. "No, you won't. Not intentionally. You wouldn't have before, and now, with my fire burning in you, it's even more impossible."

"Yes. I knew since our first kiss that I could never cut you. Maybe even before that. I will be as dangerous to you as you need me to be."

She smiled, a fragile, little lost thing. "I will endure being in danger. As much as you need me to be. A harder thing now."

"Yes. Hard." He reached out to her. "But now I will worry less."

"You will?"

"Yes. You haven't stopped casting this whole time." Truth smiled a lost little smile of his own. "You are finding the blade in your heart. That blade you can never quite put down. It takes a while to learn how to use it, but really, there's nothing quite like it."

"For cutting my pain off?"

"For getting to the heart of things." He grinned a little more sincerely. "I made a stupid joke. Maybe I am ready for kids."

"You really think we can bring children into this world? Now?"

"No. But don't you love the dream?"

Etenesh nodded.

"So, what are you willing to cut to make it happen?" Truth asked.

Etenesh looked up as a flying carpet raced into the clearing, more cultists coming in, looking worried. "I would kill every demon and wicked soul and make for you an offering of their lives. I would weave from their flesh a robe and from their bones forge a crown. I would dress you in them and anoint you with my own heart's blood."

She smiled brilliantly, the madness in her eyes clear. "I would kill the world for you. I would make you a seat upon the Chariot of God."

CHAPTER 77

MAN MAKES PLANS . . .

Truth was sitting in the little chapel in Nag Hamadi, the same one he had found Etenesh praying in before the duel. He wasn't sure why he was sitting there. He hoped some sliver of explanation would come to him. Some divine revelation.

He had finally found love. Loved. Been loved. And his very existence was poison to the person who loved him best. To know him was to be unable to love him.

The thought kept going around and around. He poisoned Etenesh. It was the slums. It was all the things he ranted about on the mountaintop. Slumrats were poison, and even the smallest taste of their flesh would fuck you up. And he fed himself to her with his own hand.

He could feel Etenesh inside of him. Warm, confident, loving. Devoted to a "him" he was certain did not exist. He had proof that the "Truth" Etenesh loved existed only in her imagination. What was she even talking about at the end there?

Did she think he wanted to replace God? Did she *want* him to replace God? Was that what she understood cultivation as? He knew it was all about moving up the material hierarchy, becoming more in tune with the heavens. He knew, now, that opening the nine apertures wasn't the end of cultivation. It was the end of the initiation.

He really didn't imagine his first time would be like that. How could he have imagined that? He had had fantasies, of course, but he figured that fucking someone over the trash cans out back of a bar would be more his style. Maybe a quick fumble and a tumble on the plastic-coated mattress in a short-time hotel with someone whose interest was measured by the quarter hour.

Not "making love," having a powerful spiritual experience, or feeling that the union of two people could be more than just mutual masturbation. Just fucking, quick, dirty, and meaningless. Purely for his own pride and gratification. Using someone already poisoned by the world. Can't infect the infected, right?

Given his current success rate, you probably could, actually.

"Psst! Buddy. Are you praying? Because I'm not allowed to talk to you if you are praying, but it doesn't look like you are praying, so . . ."

Truth jumped so hard, he nearly hit the ceiling. Which was a neat trick, given how high the ceiling was.

"Oh, so close! Next time."

"Not a great time, Nag Hamadi!"

"Aw, don't be like that. You know I love a good gossip sesh. Word around the temples is that on your very first time having sex together, you gave it to her so good, she called you God, and then when you traded heartstrings, she had the fury to make it happen. High five!"

Truth left the stone statue hanging as his vision slowly went red.

"She went insane. She took a piece of me into herself, and she went insane. And you come in here, talking this trash . . ." Truth didn't realize that he was starting to draw until he felt the blade stick in the sheath.

"Makes you furious, huh? Of course, anger is a secondary emotion. Do you know what the primary emotions are in this case?"

The sudden change in attitude gave Truth whiplash. He tried to breathe and figure out what the hell this heretical temple was on about.

"Primary emotions?"

"Yes. Anger is a response to other emotions. When you are hurt, you feel pain. You don't want to feel pain. It's painful. So, you react to that pain. A common way is with anger. Same thing with fear. You see something that scares you, and you want it gone. You want it to not scare you anymore. So, you get angry. Angry, as the old saying goes, gets things done. It feels good, too. Your brain pumps you up on all kinds of fight chemicals. Anger is a free, natural high. Self-medicate the pain away."

"So, you are saying that my sudden need to find out if a temple can be stabbed to death is a result of my fear and pain."

"Yep. You don't have an obvious *productive* answer to the source of your pain, so you lash out. Super common; see it all the time. I expect I'll be seeing it a lot more in the near future. Gonna be a lot of that going around."

"Is there a *reason* you are here, Nag Hamadi?"

"I'm everywhere in my temple. But talking to you specifically? I really am here for the gossip. The counseling is just a, y'know, freebie."

The giant stone statue leaned in, its painted face grinning. "You know your little lover will recover, right?"

Truth stopped with a jolt. "She will?"

"You dumped a ton, one might even say a *load,* into her. She's processing it. It's all pretty alien to her right now. She was already in a delicate emotional state, obsessed with you, and had been channeling her aspect of God as the Divine Consort. Not to mention she had just been taken up to heaven by the man she loved."

"She was emotionally vulnerable, and dealing with even a fragment of my shitty emotional health was enough to drive her into temporary psychosis."

"*Psychosis* is a strong word, and honestly, I'd not medicalize it. Leave it for the professionals, like the ones who are with her right now."

"So, she'll go back to being how she was before?"

"Ha-ha! How could that be possible? She just integrated a piece of your apparently horrible life into her nous. Just like you integrated a bit of hers into you. You just haven't really been feeling it yet. Believe me. It's going to throw you when it hits."

"But you said she will get better!"

"Yeah, from the, let us say, unsettled emotional state that she is in right now. Given some time and support, she will be more conventionally rational. She will come to understand what emotions are really hers and what she's getting from you. But how could she possibly be unchanged from the experience?" Nag Hamadi *tsk*ed. "She's going to be a lot better equipped for the collapse, I will say that."

"When the whole world turns into a slum."

"Yep."

Truth buried his face in his hands.

"Sex was fun."

"That's what I hear. Tell all."

"It was my first time, you know."

"Bullshit. I can believe a lot of crazy things, but *you* were a virgin into your twenties? Get fucked. Again."

"Really. Wait, I know you heard me talking about this with Etenesh and Merkovah."

"I'm not allowed to listen in on Merkovah, and I figured you were just seducing Etenesh!"

"Why? Why would I even want to do that?"

"Humans are into some weird shit. How am I supposed to know how a committed pervert like you gets his jollies?"

Totally against his will, Truth started to laugh.

"None of the other temples will believe me when I tell them. None of them." Nag Hamadi sighed.

Merkovah had commiserated with Truth but was clearly distracted. After a scant few minutes, he shoved the conversation onto his preferred track.

"Look, the plan was to get you up to Level Four, give you some basic proficiency with the Sword of Moshe . . . very basic . . . and then insert you as a tourist. Obviously, that's not possible anymore."

"Right. No tourists around, if nothing else."

"And our time manages to be even shorter. I don't know when the world is going to collapse, but the Black Ships don't tend to hang around long. If they are here now, we can assume the collapse is likely *very* soon. A year or less."

"Well. That's not great. I don't suppose there is anything we can do to slow it down?"

"Oh, we are. The embargo is going to be the biggest help there. As we speak, there is a frantic global effort to set up cosmic-ray-attracting arrays in the hopes of permeating the planet with more energy. It might have done something noticeable in ten or twenty years. Maybe even reversed some of the damage in half a millennium."

"Got it."

"This situation is centuries in the making. It *cannot* be repaired in a matter of months."

"Got it."

"So, we will do the best we can."

"To go down with our teeth in each other's throats."

"Yes, exactly." Merkovah nodded approvingly. Then violently shook his head.

"Mr. Wells—Truth, did you know you have the damnedest way of pulling people into your pace?"

"Blame Incisive?"

"I blame your natural talent and the inherent sadism of the world."

"Hell of a take from a teacher."

"It's canon!" Merkovah bellowed.

"'The world is sadistic, and by extension so is God is canon?"

"No, obviously—" Merkovah cut himself off, his hands clenching. "My end-of-the-world gift to me is going to be never discussing philosophy or theology with you. In fact, I think I set you a little assignment on that front."

"Yes, not much progress there, I'm afraid."

"I am shocked. Shocked. Well, keep at it."

"Yes, Teacher."

"And while you are doing that, how close are you to Level Four?"

"I'm about halfway. I've been cultivating hard every day."

Merkovah nodded lightly, then frowned and took a hard look at Truth.

"Check again."

Truth did. *System?*

<<*For once, I didn't want to say anything. It's been a hell of a day for me, too. And Merkovah's right—you are sitting at closer to eighty percent, and even with the . . . new guest . . . your soul is looking damn fit. A big notch up the reality hierarchy.*>>

"Huh. I guess the ritual did something there."

"Yes. It looks like you absorbed a great deal of cosmic rays and were able to process them safely."

"From Etenesh?" Truth asked, the horror in his voice rising.

"What? No. Don't be silly. You were in a ritual that temporarily created a holy land, and you were in a state of religious communion. By all accounts, you were displaying aspects of some powerful figure yourself. It's not too surprising you absorbed and processed a great deal of cosmic rays."

Truth opened his mouth, but Merkovah cut him off again.

"If you ask, 'Then why doesn't everyone cultivate that way?' I will drop you back in the well. How many people do you think are like Etenesh? For that matter, how many people do you think there are like you? You absorb cosmic rays like they were nothing. It's uncanny."

"Might not have asked that. Might have been asking something completely different."

"This situation is centuries in the making. It *cannot* be repaired in a matter of months."

"Got it."

"So, we will do the best we can."

"To go down with our teeth in each other's throats."

"Yes, exactly." Merkovah nodded approvingly. Then violently shook his head.

"Mr. Wells—Truth, did you know you have the damnedest way of pulling people into your pace?"

"Blame Incisive?"

"I blame your natural talent and the inherent sadism of the world."

"Hell of a take from a teacher."

"It's canon!" Merkovah bellowed.

"The world is sadistic, and by extension so is God is canon?"

"No, obviously—" Merkovah cut himself off, his hands clenching. "My end-of-the-world gift to me is going to be never discussing philosophy or theology with you. In fact, I think I set you a little assignment on that front."

"Yes, not much progress there, I'm afraid."

"I am shocked. Shocked. Well, keep at it."

"Yes, Teacher."

"And while you are doing that, how close are you to Level Four?"

"I'm about halfway. I've been cultivating hard every day."

Merkovah nodded lightly, then frowned and took a hard look at Truth.

"Check again."

Truth did. *System?*

<<*For once, I didn't want to say anything. It's been a hell of a day for me, too. And Merkovah's right—you are sitting at closer to eighty percent, and even with the . . . new guest . . . your soul is looking damn fit. A big notch up the reality hierarchy.*>>

"Huh. I guess the ritual did something there."

"Yes. It looks like you absorbed a great deal of cosmic rays and were able to process them safely."

"From Etenesh?" Truth asked, the horror in his voice rising.

"What? No. Don't be silly. You were in a ritual that temporarily created a holy land, and you were in a state of religious communion. By all accounts, you were displaying aspects of some powerful figure yourself. It's not too surprising you absorbed and processed a great deal of cosmic rays."

Truth opened his mouth, but Merkovah cut him off again.

"If you ask, 'Then why doesn't everyone cultivate that way?' I will drop you back in the well. How many people do you think are like Etenesh? For that matter, how many people do you think there are like you? You absorb cosmic rays like they were nothing. It's uncanny."

"Might not have asked that. Might have been asking something completely different."

"Alternatives. One that happens to gel nicely with Incisive, actually, and the nature of your mission." Merkovah looked uncomfortable, then slightly ill.

"I'm suggesting this because it's a fantastic fit for the mission profile and because we both believe you are very likely going on a one-way trip. If you don't want to do it, I'll throw open my library to you. No need to be precious at this point. You can have your pick of Level Four spells, and I will do my best to teach you them in the little time available."

"And after that hard sell . . ."

Merkovah reached into a pocket and pulled out a palm-sized shard of crystal. Clearly brand-new, the etched words and symbols still perfectly crisp. Truth tried to read it and quickly got a headache. It didn't seem to make the least bit of sense.

"It's been a quiet project of the Temple's Office of Temple Security for a few hundred years now, and I think they finally cracked it. A way for a mage to replicate the magic-destroying power of the anti-theists. It is called Obliteration, and I think it suits your needs alarmingly well."

CHAPTER 78

AND GOD LAUGHS

Truth looked at the shard of glass. Then Merkovah. Then back at the glass. Then at Merkovah.

"I think I finally snapped. This is the what now?"

"Only just now? Sorry. I hate that thing with every fiber of my being. Not your fault." Merkovah waved his apology. "Obliteration. The functional components lead you into some fairly tall technical weeds, but simply put, you use magic to simulate, then ultimately generate the anti-magic magic used by the anti-theists. You can understand why it took a hellishly long time to work out."

Truth took a moment to process the words because he was sure he hadn't understood them properly.

"I . . . use magic, which is definitionally the cosmic energy inside of me interacting with the cosmic rays *outside* of me, to cast spells that do basically the same things as that cabal of anti-theists. Which is to destroy cosmic energy, letting me unmake spells and cripple mages by emptying the cosmic energy inside them. Do I have that right?"

"Yes."

"That . . ."

"Sounds insane?"

"Yes. Very much yes."

"As I said, we have been working on this for a long, long time. The short version is that at the most basic level, you create a field that excludes cosmic rays. They just bounce right off. At the more advanced level, you force the rays away, channeling your own magic to disrupt incoming magic. At the highest level is true obliteration, except unlike what the Cabal did, this would result in a very energetic reaction. The spell is somewhat brain-melting to learn, but in practice, it should be a great deal simpler to master than Incisive.

Merkovah caught Truth's eye. "It will also get you killed if you get caught using it . . . basically anywhere if you manage to get off-world. It will certainly get you killed if you get caught using it on this world. It's a spell that, when mastered, accelerates the diminishment of magic in this world. Which is to say, the end of technological development. The end of clean water and plentiful food."

"And warmth in the winter and coolness in the summer. Not to mention the number of buildings that will just collapse when the magic stops holding them up. I get it."

"On the other hand, at even a basic level of mastery, you will be a one-man killing machine. Starbrite and Jeon share a combat doctrine. They rely almost entirely on range-based weaponry layered with spells. You could negate most of its effectiveness and power through the rest with your over-refined body."

"I just couldn't leave any witnesses."

"No. You could not."

Truth shut his eyes and imagined it. He infiltrates Jeon. He looks and sounds like a local boy because he is a local boy, so ninety-nine percent of the population would ignore him in the first place. They would be encouraged not to notice him by the Scales portion of Incisive. He needs to break into a building. Alarm spells, flying curses, spellhounds, the whole bit. Most just ignore him because he is wearing military-style clothes and has a bit of paper saying *Pass*. For the higher-tier stuff, they just . . . vanish. Wink out of existence. A local district manager would be found dead in their office with their throat slit and painted on the walls *No Salvation for Starbrite. FREE JEON!*

He could blow up a lot of shit that way. And that was just him thinking casually. For example, he could murder the spirit controlling the bus network. That would cause more than a little chaos. Truth would be a top-notch murderer and saboteur, even more so than he already was. But it would mean that, at least until he was Level Five, it was all that he could be.

Wait. Wait just a goddamn moment.

Truth started laughing.

System, memorize this shit!

<<*ON IT!*>> Truth could hear the system cackling.

"Teacher, why don't you just pass along the Sword of Moshe and, let's say, a good healing spell?"

"Young man, it's a dangerous weapon, but—"

Truth shook his head.

"Teacher . . . I still have the internal System. I may not be a Starbrite Man anymore, but who says a man from Nag Hamadi is any less prepared?"

Later that same day, Truth found himself up on the roof, ready to ingest the elixir. It was a pitch-black pill that looked too big to safely swallow. Nevertheless, he was to swallow it. He looked up. The stars were hard to see in the city glow. Shame. He would have liked to do it in the sun again. Seemed fitting. Merkovah was already grumpy as hell over "feeding the demon spawn within" and flat-out rejected him.

Truth figured it was wisest not to press.

He examined the elixir. Black, spherical, with faint dashes of green and orange scattered over its glassy surface. There was a faint smell to it, just the faintest hint of cedar and musk. He tapped gently with his nail. It made a faint *tok* sound like a monk striking a wooden fish.

A long way from Old Feng's. A long way from something brown and homemade in an unlabeled glass jar stolen from a trash heap. Of course, he was wrong about it being homemade.

Actually, no, he wasn't. Huh.

The elixir had an austere beauty. High-end Level Three elixirs would always have been something precious and absurdly costly, even before . . . Well. Before the end of days was announced. An ordinary family couldn't afford a sniff of it in Harban. But if you were breaking into Level Four, you weren't an ordinary person, were you?

Truth had only known one Level Four person, Captain Clavegaugh. A Level Four ran the *Harban* branch of the Starbrite PMC. At least in Jeon, you were really somebody if you were Level Four.

"We're ready!" a voice yelled. He had seen that guy around the Temple. Never got his name. Truth nodded, opened his mouth as wide as he could, and put the elixir in. It was exactly like trying to swallow an egg-sized rock. The results were predictable.

"Start cultivating!" somebody yelled. Truth tried to control his choking enough to start circulating the Nine Worm Path. The cosmic rays flowed into him at a furious rate, and as they circulated, they eroded the elixir, melting it. The elixir poured down his throat as the rays hammered into him.

Execution method? He believed it. It was like every millionth of a square centimeter of his skin had a needle jabbed into it thousands of times a second. He could feel himself teetering on the edge of burnout as the energy overloaded him. Then, twisting through him and lining the tiny channels, came the elixir. The scent of cedar and musk flooded the rooftop garden as his body made frantic use of the medicine.

Truth desperately wished he could run the Meditations as he cultivated. There was so much energy hitting his body. It was a shame to waste it.

<<Forget it. If you screw up, you'll explode. Focus on the job at hand.>>

He did just that. He leaned into it, driving his cultivation as fast and hard as he could. He could feel the cosmic energy filling him. The apertures widening and spilling from the first, to second, to third, then washing away the seal to the fourth. The cosmic energy pooled in each aperture in turn, then spilled like warm honey to the next.

The weight gathered in them and pressed in on him. Making him that little bit more like the stars. Growing and shifting up the color scale, brighter now, having shifted from red to orange to ruddy gold. Larger too, now, as the masses of cosmic rays flooded him, swelling, those points where body, soul, and the universe mingled.

There was some tingle, some outside nudge on his awareness. He let the energy flow along the Nine Worm Path, as mindlessly instinctive as breathing now. He could safely divert a little attention. A song, and an offer?

He focused a little more. It was the Tongue of One Who Speaks for God. The angelic blade had accompanied him almost every waking and sleeping moment since he arrived in Siphios. He could imagine living without it. He didn't much like the thought.

The blade just felt so *right* to him. The way it danced in his hands and worked with his body like the very best sort of partner. Content to let him lead but always ready to do her part.

Merkovah be damned, the Tongue was a woman and a very fine one. His heart may belong to Etenesh, but his platonic life partner was the meter and a half of angelic steel that lived on his hip. Apparently, the feeling was mutual.

There was a tentative offer, an invitation to greater closeness. Not a merger, exactly, but a closer joining. Truth smiled. He would like that very much. He extended the path of his energy cycle slightly, reaching out to the sword.

There was an unpleasant moment, like being caught between the bells of two cathedrals each ringing out their call to prayer. The shard of demon-punishing steel at the heart of the Tongue seemed to find something it recognized in the Nine Worms, and they in it. His perception suddenly lurched as some seemingly solid piece of the world *shifted*.

The Tongue changed—not its shape but its nature. The angelic blade shed much of its physicality and became spiritual. That spiritual sword then swam with the cosmic energy within him and took up residence in his first aperture. The bells tolled a joyful clarion, as though the sword had at long last found its home. The Worms cheered too, though their cries had a darker tint to them.

It was all much too much. The furious flood of the array-driven cosmic energy. The cooling, strengthening elixir. The Tongue joining with him. It was all far too much.

Within his fourth aperture, a new star was born. Rapidly shifting into luminescence, then into blazing light. The stars within him seemed so vast now, so furiously bright compared to that dim light of Level One.

Truth smiled, letting the array pour more and more power into him. He couldn't wait to see how much he had changed.

"Saints and angels preserve us, how much power can he absorb?"

"Dunno, but if he's still at it by dawn, I'm calling it. This is absurd."

"Was the elixir *that* good?"

"Nothing is that good. This is freaky."

Truth could hear the people running the array muttering. He decided to ignore them for now. He could feel the elixir wearing off, and he wanted to pour as much into his newly widened apertures as he could. When he finally stood, he took the time to really feel his body. He stretched, reached for the sun, and did a final round of moving cultivation. Glorying in the power of his body and the star-stuff within him. With a subtle flex of his magic, he declared his presence. His strength. He knew himself, and for today, he was enough. Tomorrow he would learn something new.

He felt a spell go off to his side. Jember was there, taking pictures. "Etenesh is going to love these pictures. Actually, I know a lot of people who will."

Truth laughed quietly. "It's fine if Etenesh sees, but please don't let my face get around too much."

"Still worried about bad guys in the old country?"

"For a little while longer, yes."

"Fine, fine." Jember smiled, glorying in the sunlight. "And this, too, is God," he murmured.

"What do you say we give the Desrin community one last gift, a thank-you for all the moral support?"

"What do you have in mind?"

A week after Truth left Siphios, news stations across Siphios carried the picture. A Desrin man photographed from behind. He was proportioned like a hero, tall and imposing as the Aussa Highlands of his birth. He stood on a rooftop and watched the sunrise. His zeph was proudly tasseled, his sheathed sword hung comfortably by his side. Around his neck was a scarf, proudly declaring him a regular in the terraces at High Chirchin. Even from behind, you could tell he greeted the day joyfully. Unafraid.

"The Hero released this statement, and nothing more—'One day, I will rest. One day, I will come home to my mountains, lay down my blade, kneel before my wife, and let her blessings shower upon me. Until that day, I fight. But I am not the last sword in Siphios, and I do not fight alone. Brothers and sisters and every soul that loves our land, put down your fear and draw the blade in your heart. The time of heroes is upon us. Time for the swords to rise up. And bring low the armies of Hell.'"

CHAPTER 79

NO PRODIGAL SON

Truth smirked vindictively as he walked to Merkovah's office. He had a fair idea of what would happen when that picture was published, and he *really* looked forward to the headache it would cause the "Hooray for heroes!" crowd.

"You look cheerful. I'm suddenly worried. *Ah!* Where is your sword?!"

Truth's smile got a lot warmer as he stretched out his hand. The Tongue of One Who Speaks for God appeared as beautiful as ever.

"God be praised. It accepted you fully. I was afraid it might not." Merkovah breathed out, almost whispering. He looked a little torn.

"She just needed a good opportunity. I was too weak before, and she needed the extra power from the array to join me."

"Yes, the last wielder was Level Seven. A truly wonderful woman. Pious, and wise, and funny, and furiously unwilling to retreat."

"She sounds like a great person."

"She truly was. The last prophet of Siphios, God rest her."

Truth nodded.

"Killed by Starbrite. And the idiocy of people who should have known better than to put her in harm's way, but really, Starbrite."

Truth nodded again, more slowly this time.

"I find it hard not to hate the deathsworn. It's because you enslaved yourselves willingly. Every one of you a volunteer. You might not have known exactly what you were volunteering for, but . . . volunteers. And you have killed so many people I have loved. So many of my students. My family."

Truth had nothing to say to that. It was true, after all.

"Talking with you, teaching you, has been one of the strangest experiences in my long life. I now have a better appreciation for what the deathsworn are—your 'PMC.' You are spirits taught to suffer so that you might make others suffer."

Truth didn't quite see it that way but figured there was nothing good to add, so kept quiet.

"Nothing to say, Mr. Medici?

Damn.

"I'm not in the PMC anymore. I died on the job."

"Are you furious about that fact?"

"Well, I'm pretty damn mad about the betrayal, but *furious* is a strong word. I did get paid, after all, and the death benefits are very generous."

Truth flexed his will, and the sword returned to his first spell aperture. It felt . . . right, in there. Like it complemented the Meditations.

"No *Sorry for your loss?* or perhaps *That's why we have to kill Starbrite?*"

"Is that what I should say? I thought that was strictly for comforting the heroine by the grave of her late husband."

Merkovah searched Truth's face and came to a terrifying realization. "You are serious. You genuinely have no idea how to comfort the grieving or even pretend to be sorry for your previous actions."

"Only as a tactic to avoid being beaten by my parents. Other than that? Never came up, so I never learned."

"Not on the SAT, I suppose."

"Exactly. Or bodyguard training."

"I would have assumed soothing the client was a big piece of that."

"It was, but these are rich weirdos. Sincerity is not a major factor in their life, and they all, *all*, love yelling, 'I DON'T PAY YOU FOR EXCUSES! I PAY YOU FOR RESULTS!' I think they have some kind of manual they all follow."

"So, you never bothered to learn."

"Yep."

Merkovah started rubbing his temples. "How odd. I keep feeling more and more empathy for people in your PMC."

"Some of 'em were pretty okay, actually. Not the protectees. They were all scum. Well, the succubus was okay."

"You guarded a succubus."

"Yes. We got takeout and watched a movie." Truth grinned. "On that basis, I am qualified to open a school of demonology in Siphios. At least in Moyle."

"I'm not sure the country is ready for a demonology school taught by a heretic." Merkovah looked on the verge of laughter and tears. "You understand what's about to happen, right? You are going to be dropped into Jeon with nothing but what you can carry. No contraband, no secret artifacts except for the Tongue. Just a head full of spells and a list of objectives."

"And the benefit of several national treasures."

"Yes, you should be almost impossible to find, a thought that would be much more reassuring if I didn't know that Starbrite has been perfecting its anti-infiltration systems for centuries. You will be operating functionally alone, launching a campaign of sabotage and, yes, you little prick, terror across an already tense, desperate nation. And you have all the motivation of a retail clerk starting their eighth shift in a week. The fire of a shallow pond. The furious need for vengeance of someone who got less than the expected portion of potatoes in their lunchtime stew."

Truth shrugged. "They have my family, and the only shot of any of us living through this is recovering that girl and getting on the ships out of here. Anything else, and we need to prepare for the end." Truth let the bland ease fall away. Dropped the laconic face he had presented since his rebirth.

Underneath was the man who skipped meals so his siblings could eat. Caught beatings their tiny bodies couldn't stand. Who waded through blood and fire and unspeakable cruelty, because it was necessary. Because that was what survival meant for his true family. A family Starbrite stole from him.

Starbrite was his God. Etenesh thought he didn't understand a world where God despised you. Not true. He knew about it before he fell down the well.

"You know, I say I got paid, but it did occur to me that *credits* is another word for *We aren't actually paying you.* And you know how I feel about that."

Merkovah slowly nodded. "We are running you through a six-week intensive course on being a massive pain in the ass. We are condensing it into one week on the basis that you can directly skip the combat and weapons training, already have some talisman-formation skills, and there is obviously no need to do more than catch you up on the local language and culture."

"Makes sense."

"By the time you get on the bird, I should have *some* information on your siblings. As you might imagine, things are a little tense in Jeon right now, but that also means the smaller things slip more easily through the cracks."

"Good. Thank you."

"Part of your fee." Merkovah couldn't bring himself to smile. Truth just nodded.

"Your goal is to weaken the System Astrologica to the point where I, and forces you do not need to know about, can launch the killing blow against it. Your goal is also to try and locate the missing Shattervoid child. *Not* to rescue her, just *locate* her. You will be provided multiple redundant dead drops to use to communicate with me. Use them very sparingly."

"Okay."

Merkovah twitched. "I'm starting to get a complex about that word."

"I hear there's a lot of that going around."

"We can no longer plausibly insert you as a tourist. You will be dropped off on the coast and will have to infiltrate. We will provide you with an initial identity, but you will have to secure something that will hold up better on your own."

Truth nodded. He wasn't going to use any identity they provided him. His faith in others was limited as it was.

"Anything else you want to ask?"

"Can I take the iron horse with me?"

"No. As a special favor, I will have Etenesh store it for you. Should you successfully complete your mission and elect to stay on this planet, you will find it in the attached garage for the small but very modern home that will be waiting for you."

"Good. Can't be bothered to clean or upkeep a big house."

"Somehow, I knew you would say that. Did you spend *any* of the money I paid you?"

"I did. I took Etenesh out a couple of times, got some supplies for the two-wheeler, and raided some thrift shops for novels. Oh, I also got some grilled skewers with Jember. Yeah, they were crazy pricy. Like, seven birr for two."

"What? What sort of damn skewers cost— No, no, I'm not doing that again. I'm shipping you off at once and then returning to the normal level of insanity."

"Not quite at once."

"Oh?"

"I want to see Etenesh before I go."

"Truth . . . in all sincerity, that's not necessarily in either of your best interests."

"How so?"

"She is dangerously obsessed with you. I hadn't appreciated just how devastated she was by learning the truth of God's indifference. She doesn't worship you, exactly, but she sees herself as becoming your wife or consort or queen when you assume your godhood and rule over this world. And naturally, she understands that you are a long way from that, so she is looking to . . . pave your way while making you as deliriously happy as possible. So long as you remain fixated on her romantically. She decided you would be the new object of her devotion."

Merkovah paused. "I shouldn't have to explain to you why this is a bad thing. Especially now that you have given her a strand of your rage and paranoia."

Truth nodded. "What comes after opening the nine apertures?"

"Pardon?"

"I got a little feel of it up on the mountain. Something comes after the nine apertures open, some kind of transformation or rebirth. One might describe it as stepping toward godhood."

"*One* might. *I* would not," Merkovah growled. "I don't know. Something, for sure, but I don't know. No one on this backwater planet has made it that high, and we haven't been able to import the information. Even the higher-dimensional spirits we contract just say variations on *You'll know when you get there.*"

"Unhelpful."

"That was when I developed the 'macerating juicer' enchantment for demon-punishing."

"Nice. Never miss an opportunity to learn and improve."

"Quite right. HOW?! HOW DO YOU DO THAT?"

"I think people get confused by me being sincerely interested in things."

Merkovah groaned. "Knowing what I just told you, do you still want to go see Etenesh?"

"Yes, of course."

"Mr. Medici—"

"I'm likely to die, and even if I don't, the world is likely to end, and even if it doesn't, I will definitely need someone I can trust my life to. That ain't you. As much as I like the guy, it isn't Jember, either. But Etenesh will not betray me."

Truth smiled, a hint of maddened slumrat gleaming from behind the iris. "In the Army and the PMC, they always said, 'Never stick your dick in crazy.' So far, it's been one of the best things that ever happened to me."

Truth slipped back into his amiable persona. Then his smile took on a more playful tilt. "Besides, it's only fair that she thinks I'm a god. She's the only person I go to my knees for. God and King will have to make do with a polite nod."

It wasn't a mental hospital, exactly. Or a temple or one of their not-monasteries. It was some combination of all of the above. Etenesh wasn't drugged or restrained. She was merely counseled in a safe environment. One with heavy wards against spells. It was rather pretty, with a big, attached garden and lots of glazing to let in the natural light.

Truth found Etenesh sitting on a bench, watching little birds dip in and out of the flowers. She looked kind of bored but also a little interested. "It occurred to me that I don't know how to call you. 'Ms. Heaven-Beseeching' seems much too formal and awkward. It doesn't roll off the tongue as nicely as 'Etenesh.'"

Truth took care to enunciate each syllable, showing just how much he enjoyed saying her name. "Should I call you Ms. Et-en-esh?"

She smiled back. "That is the correct, formal way to address me, Mr. Me-di-*ci*. Though I think I like it best when I am just Etenesh."

"Not going to lie, the way you say my name does things for me. Please, don't stop."

She giggled. "Knew it."

Truth nodded. He let the silence gather a moment, then said, "My Etenesh?"

"You know I am. Too much. I didn't consciously realize how much until very recently. I think the God-embodying exaggerated my already-big crush on you to something more extreme."

"You have gotten that far in therapy?"

"I can put words to it. Doesn't make me any less obsessed. And I am. I know it. You know it. I am. I want to put you on God's Chariot and chain you to me so that we will never part. Turn you into that fixed point in my life that was once filled by God."

Truth nodded. "Okay."

Etenesh had to catch the armrest to keep from falling off the bench. "Okay? Okay?! How is that okay? Is that something you can just 'Okay'?"

"Yes, it is."

"*No*, Mr. Medi*ci*, it is not. It isn't remotely okay. I know damn well it's unhealthy."

"Oh, yeah, super unhealthy. Under other circumstances, I'd be fucking terrified and running for the hills. But things are what they are, so it's okay."

She gave him a *look*. "All right, keep digging. How is it 'okay'?

"The world is ending, and I am also crazy. I am, if not clinically paranoid, close enough. I have serious trust issues. I have intrusive thoughts, chronic low self-esteem, and a willingness to embrace violence that most people would find frightening."

Truth faced Etenesh calmly. "And I have a bad case of first-girlfriend-itis. It was virgin-itis, but someone cured that."

Etenesh snorted.

"So, I'm a bit obsessed myself. And knowing that my sexy, brilliant, capable girlfriend can look out for her damn self while the world goes to shit is very reassuring.

Second only to knowing that my sexy, brilliant, capable girlfriend is going to stay loyal." He held eye contact. "You aren't the first or only person looking for that fixed point. And you know damn well I will be true."

"Do I? Know that?" She smiled. It was supposed to look playful but wasn't.

"Yes."

"My pretty, pretty man, who won't even take a blank prenup, is going to stay faithful in the home of cosmetic glamours and custom lovers, will he?"

"Yes."

She searched his face and found only honesty. "You really mean that. I don't suppose you would be up for a quickie marriage before you go, would you?"

"No. Very, very tempting, but no." He smiled at her a bit. "I will do you one better, though." He reached into his pocket and handed Etenesh his cash roll and his keys.

"There—all my money in the world and the keys to my iron horse. Machete and spear included, in case you need them. I'm taking the scarf and sword with me."

He laughed at her bewilderment. "You didn't grow up poor. Money, and . . . stuff, it all matters so much more. It's what you need to feel safe. The only measure of success you can trust. I have been obsessed with earning money for most of my life. And now I'm giving all my money to you. Magic won't tie me down, Love. But you can be certain I'd crawl back from Hell for you."

Truth was riding in the back of a cargo bird, feet up on the cargo net that was holding down the boxes and packages in the hold. They were very well wrapped packages with several layers of plastic over deep packing foam. It was the fourth short-haul bird he had taken after the long-haul flight from Siphios put him two countries over from Jeon. He was supposed to be met at General Visk International Airport by Comrade Sobol, who would arrange further transportation. The good comrade also apparently had news of his siblings.

Deciding that sounded like a *superb* way to get stabbed in the back by someone who, in the best case, already knew too much, Truth elected to skip the meeting. Instead, he found a bird headed in roughly the right direction and walked up the loading ramp into the cargo hold. The Level One cargo handler didn't even notice him.

He repeated the operation a few more times, consistently making his way closer to Harban. Finding food was a bit of a bastard, but he was Level Four. He was fine. They were over the ocean now, a few hundred kilometers from shore.

Bit of turbulence. To be expected. The bird shook harder. Then it rotated forty-five degrees on its longest axis and shot down and to the left. Then it snapped its wings out flat and turned hard right. Then up, then left again.

Truth had a quick look around for the exit hatch. He had a bad feeling. There was a sudden spike of alarm from Incisive. A brutal jolt, a shaking, screaming tearing of metal. Enormous claws, black and stinking, ripped apart the bird. Paper talismans exploded into fire or dissolved into corruption.

The whole side of the bird ripped away as it fell into a fast death spiral toward the sea. Truth caught a faint glimpse of a three-headed demon laughing and flying away. Not important right now. Parachute? Forget it. Jump out of the hole? In a death spiral? Forget that, too. The water was coming up fast. Too fast for anything smart. Truth decided the answer was to get dumb. He jumped straight up as hard as he could, punching through the thin shell of the bird. As a result, he found himself a hundred meters above the ocean, with no land in sight, and still falling *fast*.

He formed himself into a tight pillar, desperately hoping that what he remembered about falling into the water was actually true. It was the surface tension that killed you. It turned hard as steel when you fell at speed. The bird smashed into the water, shattering and scattering talismans and bits of luggage over the surface. Truth cast Incisive by his feet, hoping that the cut would break the tension and let him land safely.

Truth, alas, was wrong about how water impacts worked. The surface-tension thing was a myth, which he figured out as he started feeling his organs tear apart. His mission in Jeon hadn't even begun, and he already felt right at home.

ABOUT THE AUTHOR

Warby Picus is a lifelong fan of science fiction and fantasy. One day, he figured he would see if writing books was as much fun as it appeared to be. He hasn't looked back since.

DISCOVER
STORIES UNBOUND

PodiumAudio.com